The Counterfeit Princess

Melinda Young

Book One of
The *Royal Double* Trilogy

Fiction For Real
MADISON, WISCONSIN

Melinda Young/Fiction For Real
Post Office Box 46025
Madison, Wisconsin 53744-6025 U.S.A.

Publisher's Note: This is a work of fiction. Names, characters, places, and incidents are a product of the author's imagination. Locales and public names are sometimes used for atmospheric purposes, and references to historical events, real people, or real locales are used fictitiously. Any resemblance to actual people, living or dead, or to businesses, companies, events, institutions, or locales is completely coincidental.

Book Layout ©2013 BookDesignTemplates.com
Text font: Crimson by Sebastian Kosch.
Place stamp font: Theano Modern by Alexey Kryukov.
Title and Header Font: Bonning by Greater Albion Typefounders.
Signature font: Texas Hero by Three Islands Press.

Ordering Information:
Quantity sales. Special discounts are available on quantity purchases by corporations, associations, and others. For details, contact the "Special Sales Department" at the address above.

The Counterfeit Princess / Melinda Young. -- 1st ed.
ISBN 978-1-68023-000-0

Acknowledgments:

My sincere gratitude goes out to my editor Vicki Hessel Werkley, who made me accept responsibility for every single word and punctuation mark (a list of her objections to my final draft is available upon request).

Thanks also to the cover team of Jean Staral for the concept fine-tuning, Raechelle Cline for the technical assistance, and Sandra Ragan for the expertise and finishing touches; Sarah Stegall; my readers and proofers Debra Duerst, Janice Lipsey, Kris Nielsen, Loretta Slauson, and Karen Torvell; Jean Laidig for being a pre-print maven; and to Sherri Steffel for having multiple swords lying around the house and for organizing the Swords & Tiaras Board of Directors. I'm grateful to Michael Maue for the loan of the sword used in the cover illustration. I especially wish to thank author Rachel VerHeest-Berens, who gave me the hook that turned an interesting idea into a novel.

This book is dedicated to my college advisor, Dr. Ben R. Schneider, Jr., who taught me that not only is being both an English major and a computer geek perfectly normal, but it's also a darned useful combination.

Men are easily dealt with—but when you get the women started, you are in for it, you know.

—MARK TWAIN

THE CAST OF CHARACTERS

THE UNITED STATES OF AMERICA

Abigail Smithfield, a student at Amos College in Connecticut

Daisy MacMillan, Abigail's friend

The MacMillan sisters, who are Daisy's aunts:

    Mrs. Deborah Caruthers, owner of the Escorted Tour for Young Ladies of Quality

    Miss Ruth MacMillan

    Mrs. Esther Weatherwax

Mr. Ignatius Porter of the Connecticut Premier Bank and Life Assurance Corporation

Mr. J.D. Briscoe of the Binterman Detection and Investigation Agency

Dardanel Penwright, the president of Amos College

Yael Amos, the granddaughter of the founder of Amos College

THE KINGDOM OF SWAVICZA (schwah-VEET-zah)

THE LOYALISTS

Princess Rosamunde

Zaaf, Rosamunde's senior adviser

Lutz, the head of Rosamunde's household cavalry

Lady Zaaf

Franz Antonius, Count of Heigenlizt, cousin of the princess

Josef, Count of Ramsl and Tuharen, cousin of Franz Antonius

Baron Mleist, the major domo of Chetova Castle

Baron Austerlanden, the major domo of Schoenberg Palace

THE SUSPECTED CONSPIRATORS

Michael Gregorski

Vasily Medyev

Wolfgang Guttmann

Julius Živo, Gregorski's right-hand man

Baron von Redki

AT THE PALACE

Varni, Princess Rosamunde's secretary

Kaspar, Rosamunde's valet

Frau Meyer, Rosamunde's dressmaker

Maria, a woman who oversees Abigail

Beĺza, a maid assigned to Abigail

Frau Witj (*VEECH*), supervisor of the maids

JOSEF'S MEN

Biedric Halle

Jowan Halle

Phillip Zujaken

Mikal Schwarze

IN TOWN

The mayor of Tirigovina

Jovacź Chešqu (*JO-vash CHESH-que*), a leader of the Sálacene ethnic minority

The Royal Ultimatum

The Royal Palace of Schoenberg
Capital City of Tirigovina, Kingdom of Swavicza
Late May 1878

"We refuse to sign this document!"

Her Most Serene Highness Princess Mary Rosamunde Isabella Francesza Elisabeth rose from her chair and glowered at the paper on the desk before her. It was an outrage to her ancient and God-given privileges as a monarch. The men clustered at a faux-respectable distance in her drawing room, who were wearing their finest dress uniforms of her own army, were an abomination. This was treason, and they would pay.

"Your Highness," urged the suave, dark Baron von Redki, "you must sign."

"That is not true," she countered. "We are not *required* to do this. You *wish* it."

"No, Your Highness," he said with a bow not quite low enough to be sincere. "The people need the security of knowing you have chosen an heir. Without this, if something should—God forbid—happen to Your Highness, the people will have the comfort of a secure succession."

"And you have the comfort of a hand-picked puppet," the young woman said, then regretted it.

Von Redki said, "He is of the Marespi blood."

The child was from a lowly cadet branch of her family, but she had already said too much.

Rosamunde knew this wouldn't be happening if she were a man. She was nineteen and old enough to rule when her father died, but the council balked and gave the crown to her uncle. She had to wait five long years for what was rightfully hers. When the wastrel died last year with no heirs of his own, the council conceded defeat and accepted her ascent to the Falcon Throne. She'd suspected the resentful ones would try something, but she didn't expect the humiliation of being forced to name someone else's choice as her successor.

But Rosamunde knew she had no choice, at least for the moment. She sat again at the desk, then pulled her reading glasses from a small drawer. She was vain enough to wear them only when necessary, and she wanted to see every detail of this travesty.

With suitable hesitation, she picked up her pen, looked over the document one last time, and then dipped her pen's nib in the ink and affixed her official signature.

The men bowed as her young valet Kaspar stepped forward. His straight blond hair fell into his eyes as he leaned forward to sprinkle drying powder on the wet ink. For a loyal servant, she thought, he seemed a little too eager to complete his task. As she watched him work, Rosamunde wondered if he had been bribed by the conspirators. She would have to relegate him to public matters and find someone else to serve her in her other plans.

After the young man finished drying her signature and poured the powder back into the dish, one of von Redki's officers poured wax for the official seal on the bottom of the paper. He waited for the princess to give her permission; she gave a slow nod. From the side of the room, her ancient, loyal secretary stepped forward. The stooped, gray-haired Varni brought her official seal out of its velvet pouch and, showing some reluctance, pressed it into the wax. Varni returned the seal to its pouch and moved back to the table at the side of the room and locked the seal in a small metal chest. He stood between the chest and the others in a pose demonstrating he would die to protect it. Ah, yes, Rosamunde knew she could trust old Varni. He would be useful.

The princess removed her glasses and returned them to the drawer. "There, Redki, you have your victory. May it give you as much joy as it gives us."

Von Redki picked up the document and admired it. "Your people thank you, Your Highness."

"Some of them," she said. She dismissed them with a wave. "Go and gloat elsewhere."

Taking their precious document, they backed out of the room, heads bowed.

The princess fumed. She glared at her too-eager valet. "Get out!" The young man bowed and retreated. In her defeat she had no sympathy even for old Varni. "Take that away," she ordered with an impatient gesture towards the seal. The old man took it out of the room.

She drummed her fingers on the mahogany desk. For generations the men of her family had used this desk to sign clever treaties and arrange brilliant dynastic alliances that had kept little Swavicza independent and sovereign in central Europe's ever-changing sea of conquest, re-conquest, and suzerainty. Now she had the shame of signing away her right to choose her successor. Didn't these fools understand while they were trying to take the country away from her, others were trying to take it away from all of them? Shortsighted, vainglorious idiots! They would pay for their cupidity and arrogance. She called: "Zaaf!"

The door to the library opened, and in came the Margrave Rudolph Von Meitz-Sunderlin Zaaf, the elder statesman of Swavicza's loyalist faction. Lean and proud, the silver-haired Zaaf carried on his straight shoulders the weight of many years in service to her family and her country. He gave her a low bow. "Your Highness."

"You heard it all?"

"Yes. Your Highness's restraint was most admirable."

Rosamunde stood and paced the room. "Who's behind them, Zaaf?"

He shook his head. "I wish I knew."

"Redki has ambition, but he's not smart enough to come up with this plan."

Zaaf agreed. "As Your Highness surmised, by presenting this to you in private, they have revealed they don't represent a majority in the council of advisers."

She asked, "And have you heard yet from your sources inside Austria? Do they still intend to use the revision of the Treaty of San Stefano as an excuse to make themselves our masters?"

"I'm afraid so. Unless Your Highness can provide sufficient motivation. . . ."

"Money."

He nodded. "Without an offering of substantial value, I'm afraid we will be a pawn in the game to which we have not been invited."

She growled with discontent. She had diplomats standing by in Berlin, ready to represent her nation in the congress that would determine the fate of every country in the region. And yet, all the attempts she and her representatives made to participate were being thwarted. The bullies of Europe would brook no interference from the little countries they wished to realign and absorb. Surrounded by the empire and its satellites, Swavicza was one small bite ready to be swallowed whole.

A knock on the door stopped her pacing. Zaaf called, "Who is it?"

A welcome voice replied: "Lutz."

After a nod of approval from Her Highness, Zaaf said, "Enter."

The young colonel of the household cavalry entered with a bow to Rosamunde before joining Zaaf. His sandy hair and resplendent muttonchop sideburns, freshly combed for the meeting, made him look older than thirty, but she thought they suited the dignity of his position in her service. With fervor he said, "I hope Your Highness is well."

She did not reply. How well she felt depended on his news. "What have you learned?"

He lowered his head. "It is as you feared." Her expression turned grim. "The reports continue to indicate there is a conspiracy against the life of Your Highness."

"Who?" she asked, almost pleading.

"No one knows. It is all very quiet, but forces are at work . . . to harm Your Highness."

She went to the window and looked out. Beyond the palace grounds lay her small country's capital, nestled in wooded mountains and old valleys. She once took comfort in the smallness of her homeland and the closeness of the dark forests and wild places. Now it was all alien, a place filled with faceless conspirators. People who wanted to take her country away from her. People who wanted to kill her.

"Could it be merely a rumor, to frighten us?"

Lutz hesitated. "No, Your Highness."

The afternoon light warmed her face, but it could not dispel the chill in her heart. Her homeland had turned against her. "We must assume it's the same people behind von Redki. They have their puppet in place, and now all they need to do is clear his way to the throne." The men gave their murmurs of assent. But knowing that did not get her closer to a solution. "What say you, gentlemen? What shall we do?"

Lutz urged, "Your Highness's safety is of the upmost importance. You should leave the country. Go to Vienna. You have friends there, allies who will rise to your aid. Your godmother the empress will certainly lend you her support. You will be safe there until your enemies reveal themselves."

She turned away from the window and faced them. "If we leave during a time of unrest, the moment we cross the frontier we will be accused of abandoning our country. Besides, even if the empress offered more than sympathy, what would the people think if she and the emperor sent troops in our aid? Foreign soldiers on our soil! And from a country that's plotting our subjugation! That's exactly what we do *not* want." She eyed her senior counselor. "Zaaf, what say you?"

He drew himself up straight and proud. "Marry, Your Highness. You cannot be crowned queen until you are married, and until you have a husband and heirs of your own body, you are vulnerable."

Rosamunde had heard this a hundred times before, and the advice was as tiring and loathsome now as it was the first time. "And whom would you have us marry? A foreigner, and split our country's factions into civil war? Or marry a native son, who might be behind the conspiracy to eliminate us?"

He shook his silver mane. "Marry young Heigenlizt or Ramsl. I am certain neither is part of the plot."

She resumed her pacing. The two cousins were at the top of her list of prospective husbands. They were close to her in age, and their families were nearly as lofty as her own.

Between them, her first choice was the older cousin, Lord Franz Antonius, Count of Heigenlizt. His father was related to her mother, and until she was forced to sign that abominable succession document Franz Antonius's father had been her heir presumptive. Not only did Franz have excellent connections through his military training in Berlin, but he was also popular with her army, and he cut a dashing figure with the people. However, his ambition worried her, and if she elevated him he would soon grow discontented with being merely her consort. She could use him, but only if she could channel his ambition outward.

Lord Josef, Count of Ramsl and Tuharen, who was a year her junior, had recently returned from his military training in Vienna, and he too filled out his uniform to great advantage. His father's family was not part of the Marespi lineage, and he had shown no desire for power. Smart, both with books and people, he had the flaw of being too kind-hearted. Josef thought too much about the populace as people instead of as an asset to be used. She knew if she elevated Josef, he would balk at some of the terrible decisions she would be willing to make for the country.

There were other candidates, both at home and abroad, but even though she had already started secret negotiations with several families, she had to sort through all the various advantages before she made a final decision.

And how like her stolid, old Zaaf, to want to marry her off and relegate her to the role of brood mare for future kings while he and her husband took from her what was rightfully hers. Even after she married, she had no intention of letting go the reins of power.

But this wasn't solving the problem of the moment. She stopped by the edge of the desk. "Dear Zaaf, the role of our consort is too valuable a card to be played in haste. And children are years in the future. Our concern now is the people who want to take our life. How can we make them reveal themselves?"

Lutz said, "I'm afraid they're too cunning to be easily drawn out."

Zaaf added, "They'll let their underlings do their work until the deed is done."

She turned and paced towards the library door. "Yes, when I am dead. Your spies can tell you nothing?"

Lutz shook his head. "No, Your Highness. I'm afraid the only way the masterminds will come out is when they think they've succeeded."

An idea began to brew, and she turned a steely gaze on her advisers. ". . . What if we announce I'm dead? I'll go into hiding, and you can say I have died—you'll say illness but hint at foul murder. Then they'll seize control and we will have them."

Lutz shook his head. "They'll know it's a trick because it won't be of their doing. And then they'll know you've discovered their intentions. That will drive them further underground, and we'll never find them until it's too late."

Zaaf agreed. "It is a noble suggestion, but doomed, Your Highness."

The idea didn't go away in Rosamunde's mind. It merely turned into something more cunning. "Then we shall kill the princess."

The two men started with horror. "Your Highness!" Zaaf growled.

Lutz exclaimed, "You cannot even think of putting yourself in danger!"

"Oh, not me," she assured them. "They shall kill someone they think is me."

The men exchanged baffled glances. Then Lutz the soldier understood. "A decoy."

She nodded. "And, as you said, once they think it is safe, they'll rise up 'in defense of Swavicza,' and when they reveal themselves we will have them."

Lutz countered, "But, Your Highness, how will we find someone willing to take your place? No one in Swavicza would have the audacity to impersonate you."

Zaaf added, "And certainly no one—no *woman*—will volunteer to be in harm's way. A peasant would not be able to fool anyone into thinking she is royalty, and we cannot ask someone from a family of rank to take on such a dreadful role. If the girl does die, the family would never forgive Your Highness, even though that sacrifice would be the highest honor someone could bestow. And even if someone with all the courage in the world does volunteer, she will break under the pressure of the constant danger and reveal the scheme."

The princess gave a royal shrug. "Don't tell her."

The men stood speechless.

She smiled. "Surely somewhere out there in the world is a young woman of passing resemblance to me who is silly enough to want to play at being a princess for a week or two—and who won't be missed if the worst befalls her."

CHAPTER ONE

Casting the Net

City of Graz
Austro-Hungarian Empire
June 1878

Miss Abigail Harriet Astrid Smithfield, late of Cincinnati, Ohio, and now of Hartford, Connecticut, sighed as she sat in the safety of the sidewalk café and looked out at the bustling university city. She and her fifteen compatriots from Mrs. Caruthers' Escorted Tour for Young Ladies of Quality spent every moment under the watchful eyes of Mrs. Deborah Caruthers and her two sisters, Miss Ruth MacMillan and Mrs. Esther Weatherwax. Between their cautious chaperones and the strict local guides, the Hartford and New Haven girls would see only the educational—and safe—highlights of Europe.

At first glance, Abigail appeared to be just another young lady from America. Polite, poised, and intelligent, she enjoyed music, gardening, and literature. She preferred sensible clothing, she worked hard to tame her curly light brown hair, and most days a genial smile lit her dark blue eyes.

However, her true nature was hidden from the casual observer. She was every inch a child of the Midwest, from her self-reliance and her love of the out-of-doors to her no-nonsense distrust of vanity. She was not tall, but she was lithe and quick, and when she was a child she loved to ride horses astride "like zuch a vild Indian," as her

Oma Siebold used to lament. Until she started wearing a corset, she easily shinnied up trees after her older brothers Samuel and John, and she was as comfortable handling a rifle as she was quoting Shakespeare.

She had another inner fire not shared by the other Young Ladies of Quality. Her devoted parents, who were pro-suffrage intellectuals and abolitionists, raised her to be more than a docile wife or pretty ornament. Abigail's mother had been mentored by Harriet Beecher Stowe, and even though the Stowes left Cincinnati before Abigail's birth, she was the famous writer's goddaughter. She lived in the Stowes' home in Hartford during breaks in the school year at nearby Amos College, where she had just completed her junior year. In the Stowes' exalted neighborhood of Nook Farm, Abigail mixed with the great woman's friends and neighbors, including another expatriate Midwesterner, Mr. Samuel Clemens, known to the world as the great storyteller Mark Twain.

Although he was nearly the same age as her parents, he and Abigail had become friends. They reveled in their Midwestern roots, their longing for the rivers and wild places of their childhoods, and their skepticism of all things self-important. When she regretted being treated as an outsider by the Connecticut natives, he cheered her with tales of his own outsider history, having been away from Hannibal since the age of eighteen. He reassured her that "being from somewhere else was superior to any native status" because having that additional knowledge of the world gave her "a triangulation perspective unknown to the locals," and it was only her vast wisdom that triggered in some of those around her "an occasional childish jealousy otherwise uncommon in this corner of New England."

A week earlier, she had visited him when the Escorted Tour passed through Heidelberg, where he was working on a new manuscript. In Nuremberg, she also enjoyed a pleasant rendezvous with cousins from her Bavarian-born mother's family.

The two meetings were bright spots on a trip otherwise overshadowed by the problem awaiting her when she returned home.

Abigail glanced up from her untouched Linzer torte as Mrs. Esther Weatherwax sat down at the café table Abigail shared with Daisy MacMillan, the silly and sweet-natured niece of the three sisters running the tour and Abigail's only real friend in the group. Mrs. Weatherwax, a plump and fussy Civil War widow, looked older than her forty years, and her earnest intensity of late added another five years to her face. Ever since Abigail had explained the reason for her preoccupation to the tour leader, the woman had been fretting over her. With no children of her own over whom to hover, Mrs. Weatherwax took it upon herself to solve other peoples' problems, even if she didn't know how.

After acknowledging her niece, Mrs. Weatherwax spoke to Abigail in low, confidential tones. "My dear, I've been thinking about your problem. You can't blame your professor for being angry. When you're older, you'll understand that men are so sensitive about that kind of humiliation."

Abigail flinched at the memory. When the granddaughter of Amos College's founder perpetrated her surprise, Abigail was as much a victim as the intended target. Two years before Abigail applied for admission to the prestigious school, Miss Yael Amos, as the chairwoman of the trustees, had forced the school to accept female students. The college's president, Professor Dardanel Penwright, retaliated by restricting them to a curriculum that was little more than finishing school material because "women were physically incapable of higher education."

Miss Amos had fought back without success—until she read Abigail's application. Seeing her chance to make an inroad, the wily sphinx changed the name on Abigail's paperwork to "A.H. Smithfield" and sent it to the male curriculum admissions committee.

Mrs. Weatherwax continued her unhelpful observations. "Imagine his embarrassment when you turned out to be a girl. You can't blame him for how he feels about you."

The café's strolling violinist came by and offered a melancholy tune that matched Abigail's mood. Her college application essay on the Roman Republic ranked her as the top entering freshman. Unaware of the admissions subterfuge, at the matriculation convocation Abigail answered President Penwright's call for "A.H. Smithfield" to come up and accept the award. She politely ignored his dumbfounded stare when she joined him at the podium, and when she saw her award—an engraved pocket watch—she committed the unforgivable sin of smiling. Peals of laughter from Miss Amos and the student body destroyed any chance for her to make amends. Only the intervention of Miss Amos's lawyer kept Abigail from being removed from the curriculum to which she had been duly, if inaccurately, admitted. President Penwright made clear his disappointment. He wanted her expelled.

Mrs. Weatherwax continued, "Since you must take your senior classes with him, and he promised to flunk you no matter how well you did, I'm afraid you cannot win. You must either complete your degree in the women's curriculum, or you must transfer to another school."

Abigail looked at Daisy, who was the picture of sympathy. Her frothy blond hair and large baby blue eyes make her look younger than her twenty years. Abigail hadn't consulted with her meek new friend about her school troubles as the girl had no inclination for schoolwork. Abigail returned her gaze to the world passing by the café. She did not want to give up. She had won over her other professors and achieved honors in her classes. Only President Penwright's grudge stood in the way of her diploma.

Miss Amos had turned out to be no ally. After she got Abigail into the school, the founder's granddaughter offered no assistance. The woman only saw her as a way to fight Penwright. If Abigail didn't succeed, Miss Amos would find someone else. Abigail's parents supported her desire to stay in school and fight for her degree, but they had no influence with the school's administration. She was on her own.

And just as this school year was ending, and she savored notions of earning President Penwright's admiration after three years of stellar scholarship, she herself had driven the last nail into her hope's coffin. As she chatted with her literature professor in the hall after her final exam, his glowing compliments about her classwork evoked a snide remark from a passing male student about how "Dr. Ross must have used grammar school guidelines" to grade her work. The lout, a senior days away from graduating, had often bragged about his poor grades. Abigail rankled at his insult and retorted with common knowledge among the student body: "Mr. Harrison, you have only your father's bequests to this school to thank for the undeserved diploma you're about to receive." A familiar harrumph behind her sent a shudder down her spine. President Penwright appeared, condemned her with his searing gaze, and marched down the hall. As Mr. Harrison walked away, his laugh echoing off the walls, she could take no comfort in knowing she'd spoken the truth. She had ruined everything.

How could she convince President Penwright to judge her by her merits and not her sex? When she returned to school in September, she needed a solution. At the moment, she had nothing.

At an eruption of raucous laughter from another table of Young Ladies of Quality, Mrs. Weatherwax turned and glared the girls into silence. "My word," she fumed in a low grumble, "you'd think that Harabeth Pritchard would have learned some manners at that expensive finishing school. And if I hear one more time about her cousins the high-and-mighty Boston Pritchards. . . ." She eyed her giggling niece. "You may not repeat that." She gathered herself and said to Abigail, "My dear, isn't it better to avoid the conflict and humiliation of what awaits you at school? That is the role of the modern woman—to rise above the pettiness of life's sordid details and lead by noble example."

Something caught Abigail's attention outside. She saw two men in the doorway of the bakery across the street. Aloof, straight as ramrods in their dark jackets, they didn't fit in with the everyday bustle of students, vendors, and shoppers. Even though their civilian clothes were nondescript, the men had an unmistakable intensity that seemed almost military. She observed them as they looked at her and turned away, but they didn't go inside the bakeshop. She realized they had been watching the group of American girls. Abigail turned her gaze back to Daisy, but out of the corner of her eye she kept her attention on the two men. They turned back to face the street . . . and the café.

Oblivious, Mrs. Weatherwax said, "As you know, I did spend two years at the Connecticut Seminary for Women. I could write a recommendation for you. I'm sure they would give you credit for most of your schoolwork."

Under the cover of pretending to examine the cleanliness of her spoon, Abigail held up the piece of silverware towards the street. She looked towards the men. They noticed her attention and went into the shop.

She put down the spoon. The men had been watching them. What could it mean?

"Abigail, my dear, are you listening?" Mrs. Weatherwax asked. "Do you want me to help you when we get home?"

Abigail looked across the street. She couldn't see through the light reflecting off the bakeshop's window, but she was sure the two men were inside, looking at them. She asked her table companions, "Did either of you notice the men who were across the street by the bakery?"

The two looked, but the men were not visible. Daisy asked, "Do you mean the soldiers in the nice blue uniforms?"

Abigail had seen the soldiers standing at the corner earlier. They were admiring the passing women and, unlike the two mysterious men in the doorway, they were intent on drawing attention to themselves.

"No. The ones who went inside the bakeshop."

Mrs. Weatherwax patted Abigail's hand. "There are so many soldiers and policemen in all these foreign countries, it can be unsettling. I'm sure it's fine. But I want you to think about what I said. I'll be happy to write a letter on your behalf." She gave Abigail a reassuring smile and went back to her table.

Daisy looked again across the street. "I'm sorry, I didn't see them."

Abigail gave her a nod of thanks and returned to her dessert. In her preoccupied state, perhaps she had created something out of nothing. But she couldn't dismiss her suspicions.

The next scheduled stop for the Escorted Tour for Young Ladies of Quality was an art museum in the old town. The three sisters bustled to and fro, keeping the girls together and making sure they concentrated on the works of art and not on the soldiers and young male students. As usual, the most troublesome coterie belong to Miss Harabeth Pritchard. Despite the fact that she would marry the second most boring man in Newport, she was very keen to let everyone know she was the most eligible girl on the tour. When she caught the eye of a junior officer, it was all Mrs. Weatherwax could do to keep the two apart.

Abigail was amused by the commotion, but she had heard Harabeth's bragging about her matrimonial plans and recognized this as a mere flirtation of the moment. Besides, as attractive as some of these European men might be, the Young Ladies of Quality would soon be returning home across the ocean, so how could they hope to find a meaningful, lasting romance on this trip?

As she concentrated on the artwork at the end of the gallery, she had the feeling of being watched. She turned to catch a glimpse of a figure disappearing through the archway into the next gallery. She thought he looked like one of the men from in front of the bakeshop. She started for the archway when Mrs. Caruthers corralled her and expressed her disappointment that Abigail, sensible Abigail, could even think of wandering off. Abigail gave in and rejoined the group, still looking back towards where the man had disappeared.

The rest of the day passed without incident, and the girls returned to their hotel for the evening. After dinner, they were escorted through the lobby to the grand staircase on their way up to their rooms. Just for a moment Abigail caught a glimpse of a man intentionally hiding behind a newspaper when they passed.

As they changed into their nightclothes in their shared room, Abigail asked Daisy if she ever had the feeling they were being spied upon.

The dear and simple girl regarded her friend. "Do you know anyone in Austria?"

"No."

"Have you broken some sort of law?"

"Daisy!"

The girl giggled. "I had to ask."

Abigail relented and sat before the small room's dressing table and unfurled her hair from its simple arrangement of being combed to the back and falling into long, tightly-wound curls.

Daisy pondered the situation. "Well, there must be some reason you feel that way. I mean, there are so many countries so close together here. Perhaps there's some trouble we don't know about. Maybe someone heard you speaking German and got worried. It makes sense to keep an eye on foreigners if there's something going on."

Her friend's logic was somewhat sound. "Even a group of touring young women?"

Daisy finished buttoning her nightgown and wrapped the tie of her dressing gown. "We could be spies. Or couriers used by malevolent beaux to carry state secrets across international borders." Her delicious smile gave away her joke.

The two laughed. As Abigail brushed out her stubborn hair, she said, "I feel embarrassed about being suspicious. But I just *know* someone is watching us."

"I'm sure we make quite a sight. Sometimes I feel like we're a flock of geese and my aunts are children with sticks driving us to market."

Abigail laughed at the apt image. She wanted an explanation of who those men were and what they were doing, but she would not find it that night.

CHAPTER TWO

The Ruse Begins

The next morning, Abigail had the first answer to her mystery. As the group ate breakfast in the hotel dining room, the three sisters were approached by the hotel manager, Herr Schulz, who seemed quite eager to have them speak with a pair of serious-looking men standing in the dining room doorway. The men were wrapped in so much dignity that the sisters became flustered at the prospect of talking with men of such quality. They quickly consulted amongst themselves as to which two would talk with the strangers and which one would stay with the girls. As usual, the unmarried sister lost. The two widows, giddy as the girls they were supposed to be chaperoning, left with Herr Schulz to be introduced to the men. The girls couldn't believe their eyes when they saw Mrs. Caruthers curtsy to them before they were all escorted out.

Rumors buzzed from table to table until the hotel manager returned with Mrs. Weatherwax. The stout woman moved with an unexpected energy and her face was flushed as she approached the table Abigail shared with Daisy and four other girls. "Abigail, my dear, would you please join us? Some very important men have some very important questions that only you can answer."

Surprised, Abigail agreed. Amused whispers rose around her as she stood. Mrs. Weatherwax hissed the girls into silence.

Abigail followed Mrs. Weatherwax and the hotel manager to his splendid office. The two men were in guest chairs to the side of the manager's desk. Abigail didn't recognize them, but she knew they weren't the men she had seen in front of the bakeshop. If they were connected somehow, she guessed these were the superiors of the men on the street. Opposite the two dignified gentlemen in another guest chair sat the bubbling Mrs. Caruthers. Abigail had never seen her so full of unfocused energy. Her sister joined her, and they shared an excited whisper.

The men rose as Abigail entered the room and gave her solemn, but not deep, bows. Despite her suspicion of the entire matter, she found herself rather charmed by their courtesy. However, at their introduction, she did what Mrs. Caruthers had forgotten and resisted the urge to curtsy; that might be proper etiquette at a dance, but as an American she agreed with Thomas Paine that showing such deference was unjustified by "the equal rights of nature." She hoped the men would consider her merely unschooled and not take offense.

The older man, the Margrave Rudolph Von Meitz-Sunderlin Zaaf of Castennenia, had a fine head of silver hair and a tailored suit of the highest quality. The younger man, Colonel Heinriczh Von Auren Lutz, had elaborate muttonchop whiskers and wore a military officer's uniform. They were introduced as being from the Kingdom of Swavicza. Abigail had never heard of it.

The hotel manager said in English, "Miss Smithfield, these two most distinguished men are grateful you have chosen to come here. They wish to ask you several questions. Are you agreeable to speak with them?"

As formalities went, Abigail found this especially, even exceedingly, formal. Either Swavicza was an especially formal place, or these men were especially intimidating to Herr Schulz. She looked at Mrs. Caruthers, who nodded eagerly for Abigail to cooperate. "Yes, I will be happy to talk with the gentlemen."

They nodded their thanks, and the hotel manager directed Abigail to sit in a chair between the men and Mrs. Caruthers. After they were all seated, the older woman spoke to Abigail in a much more familiar manner than she had ever used with her before. "My dear, I know you have connections with Baden, and these gentlemen have a question about that."

"No, I don't," she corrected Mrs. Caruthers.

The two men frowned with consternation.

"My mother was born in Bavaria, not Baden."

The men exchanged a quick glance, then Colonel Lutz smiled. "Bavaria! This is even so much better! The King of Bavaria is a strong ally of ours. And you are related!"

She blinked at them. To say she had a connection to Bavaria was true, but to say she was related to the king—or anyone else of political significance, for that matter—was ridiculous. She had as much of a connection to the Bavarian royal family as she did to President Hayes.

"Miss Smithfield," the margrave said in sonorous tones and well-spoken English, "if I may be so bold, may I inquire as to your mother's maiden name?"

"Siebold."

The two exchanged a thoughtful look and spoke in a language Abigail didn't recognize. She concluded it must be the language of Swavicza.

The margrave said to her, "Is it possible you are part of the ancient and most honorable Bavarian family of Siedboldsdorf?"

Her mother's family was made up of doctors, scientists, and professors. All noble professions, to be sure, but hardly the stuff of hereditary nobility. "I do not believe I am, sir."

The men consulted again.

Her puzzlement grew. Her family was not significant. "Sirs, may I ask what this is regarding?"

The two glared at her effrontery. The hotel manager held his hands up to her in dismay. "It is not for you to ask questions of someone of the margrave's importance."

Abigail felt no embarrassment at having ruffled their feathers. She wondered how Mr. Clemens would speak to these men of infinite self-importance.

The men eased their indignation, and the younger one spoke in their language to the older one, who nodded. The margrave said,

"Miss Smithfield, you show the spirit of nobility. Perhaps there is more to your family than you think."

She agreed, but in ways that would not please these *very* important men.

The margrave asked, "May I inquire, Miss Smithfield, were you born before 1854?"

"No. I was born in 1857."

The men exchanged a glance. Her answer seemed to settle something for them, but they gave no indication of what it was.

The margrave continued, "We are the subjects of Her Most Serene Highness, Princess Rosamunde of Swavicza. You bear an uncanny resemblance to her. We are inclined to believe you are a distant relative."

If they intended for their speech to flatter her, it was not succeeding.

Colonel Lutz said, "If we may say so, Her Highness—your cousin—is in need of assistance, and you have the peculiar opportunity to help out someone of great importance."

Peculiar indeed, she thought. Oh, if only Mr. Clemens were here! He'd set these fossils—yes, that's what he'd call them—back on their self-important heels. She would endeavor to do her sly Midwestern cohort proud, if in a more polite way. "And what assistance does your employer require?"

The men seemed disconcerted by her choice of words, and they exchanged a few words in their language. The margrave corrected her: "You misunderstand. She is not our employer. She is our liege lord."

She had been too subtle, she realized. "Thank you."

Colonel Lutz said, "I do not wish to go into too many details, because even here the walls, as they say, have ears."

Herr Schulz flashed a frown of polite indignation.

The colonel continued, "But you could help with a matter of political importance—and help maintain the safety of the realm—if you would leave your tour for a week or two and come to our capital, Tirigovina."

Mrs. Weatherwax gasped and Mrs. Caruthers started. The older sister intoned, "Leave? And go with you? Complete strangers?" The sisters stood and fluffed up to their full heights, which weren't much. "Gentlemen, you do not seem to understand how proper young American ladies should behave. I'm afraid we have severely overestimated you. Good day."

Before the startled men could apologize, Mrs. Caruthers caught Abigail by the arm and pulled her to her feet. With an indignant flounce, the sisters escorted the girl from the room.

Once they were safely out into the hall, Mrs. Caruthers pronounced, "Well, I never, in all my days! Thinking you were the type of girl who would gallivant off with strangers! Nonsense!"

Mrs. Weatherwax was not of so firm an opinion, and as her older sister led the way down the hall, she said, "Deborah, we shouldn't judge them so harshly. After all, they are foreigners."

Mrs. Caruthers harrumphed. They passed two young men who stood in the hall, their backs turned as they studied a small, unnoteworthy framed print on the wall. "Those 'noblemen' are grown men—supposedly gentlemen—and they should know that good young women do not do such things."

Mrs. Weatherwax tried again. "Well, perhaps we can forgive them because they were trying to help their ruler—who is a woman, after all."

"Stuff and nonsense," Mrs. Caruthers dismissed. "Chivalry doesn't take such outrageous forms." She stopped to make the matter clear to her little sister. "Men who would compromise the honor or one women to help another—well, they are no gentlemen." She took a long breath. "We mustn't discuss this with the others. You know how girls are. They'll fill their heads with all kinds of romantic notions. And that can lead to unwanted, spontaneous behavior." She nodded to Abigail. "Dear, you understand. As much as you might want to talk about this ordeal, it's for the best that you don't." She added in a quiet voice, "Especially don't tell Daisy. She's so impressionable."

Abigail hadn't been as affronted as the sisters, but she respected their feelings. "I promise."

As they continued on towards the dining room, Mrs. Caruthers said, "We'll tell the others this was a case of mistaken identity and leave it at that. They were looking for someone, and when they realized they had mistaken Abigail for that someone, we ended the interview, and the entire matter is over."

As the sisters led the way down the hall, Abigail realized these noblemen must have had people out searching for a girl who looked like their princess, such as those men outside the bakeshop. She had been justified in thinking people were watching her.

For a moment she had that sensation again. She glanced over her shoulder. The two men they'd passed in the hall had been watching them but turned to look the other way. Feeling unsettled, Abigail returned to the dining room.

The Young Ladies of Quality spent the afternoon at the outdoor market in the old town, but so bored was Harabeth Pritchard that she hardly noticed the wares for sale. Under other circumstances, she would be finding a way to get out of wasting the night at the opera. But more pressing—and intriguing—was her burning need to find out the truth behind all the secrecy this morning. Harabeth saw through the ridiculous story the sisters told about "mistaken identity." They were much too agitated for that. She knew the source of all this had to be that irritating Abigail, who had gotten into some sort of trouble, although Miss Self-Sufficient was so very calm about the matter. What a troublemaker she was! The entire tour would've been so much better if that hick from Ohio hadn't come along.

The vendor at this booth tried to offer Harabeth something, but since she didn't know any foreign languages—especially one of the many little tongues people spoke around here—she just nodded and looked bored until the vendor gave up.

Her usual companion, Emily Lockett, had wandered off somewhere. Harabeth thought to look for her, but her spine tingled at the sound of a soft-spoken male voice near her: "You are an American lady, are you not?"

She turned to see a handsome fellow next to her. Dark, tall, and in a smart black coat that reminded her of a uniform, the striking young man smiled coyly at her. She was startled that a stranger—a strange man in particular—would speak to her when they had not been introduced. But perhaps this was a local custom, and she would insult him if she didn't reply. She managed to say, "Why, yes."

He nodded, apparently smitten. In an intriguing accent, he said, "I thought so. I have so often admired you Americans."

A little knot settled in Harabeth's throat. ". . .Truthfully?"

"Yes, he cooed as he took a small, smooth step closer to her. "You are so independent, and so simple."

It did not occur to her that "simple" might not be a compliment. "Why, thank you."

He looked at the wares, but his attention was on her. "You are traveling with your servants?"

Dazzled by his interest, she needed a moment to understand what he meant. "Oh, ah, no. Tour guides." She thought better of that. "More like instructors." Somehow that sounded better.

He reached across to touch one of the trinkets for sale, and his hand slowly brushed hers. She shivered and caught her breath. Oh, these European men! How forward! How . . . refreshing!

"And yet," he said, "you seem unhappy. Unfulfilled."

How did he know? "Well, one can't always choose one's companions."

The man turned away to look at something as Emily Lockett bounded up to her friend. "Harabeth! Oh, you just have to come see the most beautiful silk shawls! They're over in the next aisle!"

Harabeth gathered herself and said, "Go on back. I'll join you shortly." Emily returned to her discovered treasures.

The man didn't look at Harabeth, but she noticed he had inched even closer. "I saw you yesterday at the museum," he said, turning to give her a long, deep gaze.

His rich hazel eyes were quite unlike anything Harabeth had ever seen before. She was beginning to feel rather warm. "You did?"

"I said to my friend, 'Now there is a fine lady.'"

Suddenly, a second man stepped up to the market booth on the other side of Harabeth. He had the same swarthy coloring of her welcome companion, but his face was filled with anger as he glared at her. "You are another American," he growled in an accent similar to the other man's.

His harsh tone caught her by surprise. "I beg your pardon?"

"You should be ashamed."

The stranger lectured her: "An American woman was asked to help a troubled nation—she barely had to lift a finger to save them— but she refused." He glowered at her. "You Americans have no honor, no compassion!"

With a soldier's resolve, the first young man moved around Harabeth in a flash and gave the stranger a forceful push. "Go away. You are rude. You have no right to talk to this lady."

The second man grumbled and stalked away.

Harabeth's rescuer turned to her. "Are you all right?"

Only after the angry man stalked off did Harabeth's astonishment turn into pangs of fear. But, oh, how chivalrous *this* man was! "I'm fine. Thank you. But what was he talking about?"

"I have heard—the rumors are everywhere—there is a small country in need of help. A young princess stands alone in a valiant struggle. An American woman could help—and yet she does nothing. I'm afraid her refusal has damaged how people feel about your country. I hope all of you do not suffer because of it. . . . He may not be the only one who is angry."

Harabeth shuddered. "Who is this woman?"

"I believe she is part of your group."

Mortified, Harabeth knew the culprit could only be that agonizing Miss Smithfield. How dare she put all of them in danger with her selfishness!

The man lowered his head in a respectful gesture. "I apologize. I have already said too much. But I must ask you . . . if I may see you again. Will you still be in Graz tomorrow?"

The tremor returned to Harabeth's heart. "Why I believe so. I, ah, I believe we are leaving tomorrow night."

"By chance, to Vienna?" he asked with a brightened tone.

"I, I believe so."

He smiled, and her heart puddled between her lungs. "I am traveling on that train as well. . . . I hope you are not delayed by the deeds of this woman." He took her hand in his. She nearly gasped at this breach of etiquette. "I should very much . . . enjoy seeing you again." He bowed over her hand. Thank goodness he didn't kiss it because Harabeth certainly would have swooned then and there.

"I . . . do wish that myself."

He looked up, deep into her eyes. "At the station . . . tomorrow."

"Tomorrow. . . ," she breathed as he bowed and backed away several steps, then turned and departed.

She was still frozen in that spot when Emily came to retrieve her. "Harabeth, what have you been doing all this time? Come on!"

Her reverie broken, Harabeth knew what she had to do. She had to find Mrs. Weatherwax. They were all in danger!

Mrs. Weatherwax proved no match for the iron will of Harabeth of the Connecticut Pritchards. In a quiet corner of the market, after ten minutes of Harabeth's verbal bombardment, she gave up the ship.

Harabeth mulled over the implications, and with Mrs. Weatherwax in tow she tracked down and cornered Mrs. Caruthers. In a small café, she told the widowed sisters what she'd experienced—omitting the tender ministrations of the mysterious stranger—and how they were all in jeopardy because of Abigail's refusal to help the princess.

Unaware that she was accusing the very people responsible for Abigail's refusal, Harabeth succeeded in convincing them they had created an international incident and they would be blamed when the Austro-Hungarian Empire declared war on the United States.

The sisters canceled a planned excursion to the famous Schlossberg above the center of town. Instead, the confused and disappointed girls spent the sunny afternoon in the hotel so the sisters could discuss the crisis. Since this had moved beyond a simple misunderstanding to an affair on the world stage, they needed the guidance of men who would have calmer heads than theirs and who had the experience to handle foreign intrigue. They wanted to talk with representatives of the United States government. Alas, there was no consulate in Graz. The closest equivalent they could find was the small office of an American business.

The clerk of the Connecticut Premier Bank and Life Assurance Corporation listened to Mrs. Caruthers and Mrs. Weatherwax explain the looming calamity in alternating verbal cascades, then had them wait while he spoke with the branch manager. The august executive, Mr. Ignatius Porter, came out to greet them, saying he always had time to talk with people from Connecticut, being a New Haven man himself. He ushered them into his office, leaving the clerk outside.

Mr. Porter listened with great interest to their entire emotional and confused tale. When they were finished, he said he knew Harabeth's father, and he expressed his distress at her unpleasant encounter. He soothed the sisters with reassurances that he knew all about Swavicza. He would send a telegram to the American embassy in Vienna for guidance, and then he personally would make inquiries with the margrave. He sent the women on their way with a promise that he would send for them as soon as he had resolved the situation.

Late in the afternoon, Mr. Porter's assistant fetched the two sisters—as well as a surprised Abigail—to his office. Mr. Porter shooed the assistant away after ushering the three into his office. Leaning in a friendly pose on the edge of his desk, the grand man started with his hopes that the sisters had had a better afternoon than they did morning. He continued, "I have had two most insightful conversations. One was with the margrave and Colonel Lutz. Ladies, you cannot imagine how mortified they are that you misinterpreted their intentions."

"Sir," Mrs. Caruthers spoke up, "if you had heard what they said, you would agree there would be little room for misinterpretation. They made quite clear their intentions to abduct her."

Mr. Porter gave them a placating gesture. "I'm sure this entire misunderstanding was produced by their faulty knowledge of English's subtleties."

Mrs. Caruthers countered in arch tones, "For foreigners, they seemed quite fluent to me."

Mr. Porter offered an apologetic smile. "No, I assure you, after speaking with these gentlemen in person, I am quite certain their intentions are completely honorable." He gave Abigail a sincere gaze. "They don't want to 'abduct' you. They merely wish, if you will, to 'borrow' you for a few days. A week or two at the most."

Abigail had been giving the proposal a great deal of thought since her meeting with the Swaviczens, and she didn't share the sisters' rumor-fueled anxiety. She asked him, "To do what?"

"They wish for you, if you will, to help their princess in a few public events."

Abigail couldn't see a logical way she could help. "I still don't understand."

He crossed his hands and nodded in a genial fashion. "It seems the Princess Rosamunde is, if you will, somewhat indisposed. A slight illness, nothing serious. But she has important public functions she must attend in the next few days. We Americans don't put much value on ceremony. But in the Kingdom of Swavicza, ceremony is vitally important. If she misses even one of these events, it would be a blow to her prestige. It would also be an insult to the ethnic group whose festival she won't be able to attend. And there are certain unscrupulous nobles who would like nothing more than to cast doubt on her abilities." He gestured towards the sisters. "Surely you ladies understand the extra burdens society places on the women who, through no fault on their part, must lead their own lives and chart their own course."

After a moment, the widowed sisters agreed.

Mr. Porter continued, "So you ladies are sympathetic to an honorable woman beset by forces beyond her control."

The two nodded.

Mr. Porter's explanations may have been sufficient for the sisters, but they weren't for Abigail. "So, what exactly do they want me to do?"

"They wish for you to 'stand in' for Her Highness."

She stared at the businessman. "I'm supposed to make people believe I'm a princess? And not just any princess, but their ruler?"

"You would not impersonate her. You would, if you will, be there in her stead."

Abigail wasn't convinced. This sounded like bunkum. Even his odd, repeated use of "if you will" felt like a prod with a stick.

"I assure you, Miss Smithfield," Mr. Porter continued, "these gentlemen say you resemble the princess enough that in large, public venues and dressed in her clothing and with your hair styled her way, your mere presence will be enough to accomplish their goals." When she didn't respond, he added, "Of course, your time is valuable, and the margrave said the government will compensate you for the time you'll lose on your excursion. He said you won't find them ungrateful."

Abigail wasn't moved by the financial bait dangled before her, but Mrs. Weatherwax had become lost in the romance of the scenario. With a playful smile she gushed, "Think of it, Abigail—princess for a day! What girl doesn't dream of dressing up like a princess?"

"Esther!" Mrs. Caruthers exclaimed with embarrassment. "This is hardly play!"

Abigail regarded Mr. Porter. "Surely there has to be some rather questionable legality with this."

She caught a glimpse of a frown on his face, but he smoothed it over. With only a hint of stammer he told her, "Well, certainly it wouldn't be illegal there, because it is, if you will, sanctioned by the princess."

"But as an American," she countered, "am I allowed to impersonate an official from another country?"

Mr. Porter flinched at her question, but he gathered himself. "My other conversation today, that I mentioned earlier, was on that very topic. By telegraph I communicated with the assistant U.S. ambassador in Vienna. He instructed me to work with our good allies in the Kingdom of Swavicza and to help them in their hour of need. He assured me he will contact your parents and inform them of the situation and confirm that you will be the recipient of all good and thorough ministrations provided by the margrave and his associates. Not a moment will go by that you are not watched, chaperoned, and protected. And your actions will have the complete backing and support of the United States government."

Abigail wished she had the valuable insights of her sensible and forthright mother. "I would like to send a telegram to my parents to discuss this."

Mr. Porter seemed surprised by her request, and not a little alarmed. "Um, well, I'm not sure that's possible. Uh, the assistant ambassador said he would have liked to have instructions from Washington, but, apparently, there's a problem with the telegraph lines between the continent and England, so messages can't get through to the United States. He said messages have been delayed for several days. We are, if you will, on our own."

Abigail frowned. "Then how was the ambassador planning to inform my parents?"

Color rose in Mr. Porter's face. With vigor he countered, "His message will be a top priority and go through with all urgency when the problem is resolved."

Abigail's dislike of Mr. Porter deepened. But her contentiousness ebbed at Mrs. Weatherwax's gentle words. "Surely, my dear, in your heart you know what your parents would say."

Abigail nodded. She did know: Approach the situation with caution, but her duty was to help others when she was able.

Once again gathered and calm, Mr. Porter said, "To reassure you ladies of their good intentions, the margrave and the colonel wish to meet with all of you—and me—in my office, tomorrow at two in the afternoon. You would have the opportunity to reassess them and the situation. Is that agreeable to you?"

The sisters wished to discuss the matter, and they agreed to return the following afternoon at the appointed time. Abigail, too, wanted time to think things over and sort through all the odd details.

CHAPTER THREE

The Trap is Sprung

The Escorted Tour for Young Ladies of Quality still had tickets to go to the opera that evening, but the ladies would go only after the three sisters had a long and private discussion. Before they disappeared into their caucus, they promised to share the results with Abigail at an appropriate time.

While they waited for the outcome, the Young Ladies of Quality were stuck in the hotel's lounge listening to an afternoon serenade given by the establishment's trio of musicians. Abigail wanted to escape. She couldn't see the point in their being cooped up again. Besides, there as a mystery surrounding her, and she wanted to learn whatever she could. She knew if she figured out a way to leave the hotel she should have someone go with her, but she didn't want to get any of the others in trouble. Besides, even if society demanded women not travel by themselves, it would be better to make that misstep here where gossip wouldn't reach home.

Abigail left Daisy sitting with another friend near the front of the gathered chairs and migrated to an open chair by the door, where she sat next to one of the local chaperones. Frau Steiner, a fine old woman with a good heart and bad hearing, had been listening to the music with her hand held up to her ear.

In a soft voice, Abigail said in her fluent, Bavarian-accented German, "I see you're enjoying the performance, Frau Steiner."

The old woman nodded. "It reminds me of my younger days."

As Abigail looked at Frau Steiner's faraway smile, an idea slipped into her head. The previous afternoon's performance ran for nearly two hours. At the rate the MacMillan sisters were handling the recent developments, they would need at least that long to reach a decision. She would have time to go out.

She whispered, "Frau Steiner, I have to return to my room for a while."

The old woman shook her head. "No, my dear, you must stay in the lounge."

Abigail offered an apologetic glance. "I'm afraid this can't wait."

Frau Steiner gave her a sympathetic smile. "I understand. Their fried sausage does that to me, too."

Abigail gestured towards the front of the gathered chairs. "Why don't you sit in my chair? You'll be able to hear so much better." When the old woman seemed tempted and yet reluctant, Abigail added, "I'll find my way back with no trouble."

Frau Steiner nodded with a smile. The musicians finished the scherzo to warm applause, and the old woman took the break in the performance to leave her seat and move forward. Abigail watched her settle in next to Daisy, and then she slipped out of the room.

In a hurry, Abigail didn't bother to go to her room and put on a hat and jacket before leaving the hotel. She hoped if anyone gave her a second thought about being underdressed they'd decide she was a shop girl on an errand.

With a quick step she moved down the sunny street, looking for a library or some other place that would have information about the region. She located a bookshop that had both books and newspapers in languages other than German. She asked the owner if he had any information on Swavicza, and to her delight he knew the country. His ethnic group, the Sálacene, had been living peacefully side-by-side with the Swaviczens for centuries. "Trouble started two generations ago," he said, "when the king at the time make the Sálacene scapegoats for all of his own failures." She asked about the politics, and while he didn't follow their current events, he did have a new book about the country. It was written in Swaviczen, which the store owner couldn't read, but at least she had the opportunity to look at the illustrations.

After the title page she found what she sought—an engraved official portrait of Princess Rosamunde. Abigail could see a superficial resemblance between her and the princess. Perhaps this wasn't bunkum after all.

She asked the book seller a few questions about the kingdom and the princess. He did know the princess had been reigning for somewhat less than a year, but by law she couldn't be crowned queen until she married. Normally, that would make her a most sought-after bride. "But," he lamented, "there's such a glut of eligible German-speaking princesses on the market right now, and Swavicza has little strategic value or material wealth, so from what I understand suitors aren't pouring into the country."

Abigail needed to return to the hotel, and she thanked him. In return, he thanked her in German, and then with an impish grin he thanked her in his own mellifluous Sálacene tongue. She tried it out, and he worked with her to get the correct inflection. As she departed, he said with delight something she didn't understand but that sounded like well wishes. When she thanked him in Sálacene, he gave her a rousing "Bravo!"

She hurried back to the hotel, but as she approached the lounge to her dismay she discovered the performance had ended. The girls were milling around while Frau Hessen, the no-nonsense other chaperone, was questioning them in harsh, anxious tones. Abigail tried to slip into the room, but Frau Hessen spotted her. "There you are! You know you're not supposed to leave the group!" Without waiting for an explanation as to her whereabouts, Frau Hessen hustled the girls out of the lounge and up to their rooms to wait for dinner and the evening at the opera—if they were going.

Back in her hotel room with Daisy, Abigail felt restive. She was embarrassed about being caught, even if the only punishment had been disapproving glances from some of the other girls. She didn't want to answer Daisy's many questions about what had happened and where she'd been, especially while the hotel maid was helping them dress for dinner. Giddy about the mystery of it all, Daisy could barely wait for the maid to finish and excuse herself before begging her friend to tell all.

Despite promising the sisters she wouldn't discuss the matter, she knew she would have no rest if she kept the truth from Daisy. She shared the basic details of the interview with the margrave and the colonel, leaving out the aunts' reaction and some of her own doubts.

Daisy bubbled with excitement. "Oh, to be a princess for a week! What a joy! What excitement! The clothes! The palaces! I bet the princess dines on gold plate and nothing less. Oh, how I wish I could go. I'd gladly trade places with you."

"Your aunts would never allow it." Besides, Abigail thought, silly, trusting Daisy would probably spoil the plot on the first day.

"But I can dream, can't I?" She held out her hand as if it were being kissed by a handsome soldier. "My dear count, how wonderful to see you again." She laughed and spun around.

Daisy's delight brightened Abigail's mood. She wondered if she was being too suspicious. Surely, if the assistant ambassador in Vienna wanted her to do this for an ally, it must be safe. The Swaviczen authorities would protect her, and it was her duty to help others. Even if, from what she'd seen so far, the Swaviczens were the most stolid and thankless people she had ever met. She would consider participating in this masquerade.

Before the scheduled dinner hour, Abigail was summoned by Miss Ruth MacMillan for a private meeting with the sisters. Abigail liked Ruth. Unlike her sisters, she was tall and lanky and had no silver in her dark brown hair. Ruth seemed to be the level-headed one in the family, and Abigail sympathized with the woman's frustration when she, as the unmarried sibling, was always being outvoted by the others. If Ruth weren't the only sister who spoke some French and German, Abigail wondered if the other two would have decided she should stay at home. As they walked down the hall to the meeting, Miss MacMillan gave nothing away about the sisters' decision and conducted herself with an air of deep seriousness.

In the room the three women shared, even before Abigail could sit in a guest chair Mrs. Caruthers began her pronouncement: "My dear, we've given this entire matter a great deal of thought, and in light of what Mr. Porter and the ambassadors said, we've come to the conclusion that you and Esther and I should meet with the margrave and his associate tomorrow."

Mrs. Weatherwax couldn't contain herself and announced: "And if you're willing to go to their country, one of us will go with you."

Mrs. Caruthers gave her little sister a frown. "Esther, please." She returned her attention to Abigail. "Are you willing to meet with them? Please think it over and we'll send a message to Mr. Porter in the morning."

"I've already thought it over, and I'll meet with them."

The sisters were delighted, and Mrs. Weatherwax went to tell the other girls that they would be resuming their schedule as planned this evening. Mrs. Caruthers talked with anticipation of the adventure to come. Miss MacMillan listened, apparently resigned to knowing that once again she would be excluded from the proceedings.

Abigail listened in silence to Mrs. Caruthers's plans for the meeting. The tour leader seemed to think her agreeing to the meeting equaled her acceptance of the mission. Far from it. Abigail was going to scrutinize these people, and she fully intended to ask more questions and ruffle some feathers.

That evening's fine performance of Verdi's *Un Ballo in Maschera*—with its plot involving intrigue, disguise, and murder—gave Abigail a restless night and disturbing dreams. She was grateful for a bright morning to dispel the cobwebs.

After breakfast, the girls packed their belongings for their evening departure to Vienna. The hotel porters gathered the bags to transfer them to the train station. Daisy wondered aloud if Abigail would be traveling with them or if she would be traveling incognito to Swavicza in the dark of night. Even as Abigail hushed her, she wondered that herself.

To Abigail's surprise, all three MacMillan sisters went with her to Mr. Porter's office while the other girls were left in the care of the local chaperones. When they arrived, they found as grim a welcoming committee as one would hope not to meet: the Margrave Rudolph Von Meitz-Sunderlin Zaaf, Colonel Heinriczh Von Auren Lutz, and an unexpected new member of the party, the margrave's wife. Lady Zaaf, a dour, gray woman of sixty in a heavy black dress twenty years past its fashion, had a face that seemed etched into a permanent scowl. Abigail did not say it, but she allowed herself to think this woman was the very epitome of "a tough old bird." Abigail hoped she wouldn't be left alone with her. She had the feeling Lady Zaaf didn't want to be there and didn't like her. Abigail suspected Lady Zaaf didn't like anything or anyone.

After Mr. Porter make the introductions, the margrave gave an awkward apology for the previous day's misunderstanding. He seemed unfamiliar with apologizing to his social inferiors. He assured the women from America he never intended to impugn Abigail's honor in any way. He made multiple promises, which were eagerly echoed by the more congenial Colonel Lutz, that every effort would be made to preserve Abigail's dignity and comfort, and that the princess had expressed her deep, personal gratitude that Miss

Smithfield had considered coming to the aid of a total stranger. The margrave explained that Lady Zaaf—who had been here the entire time, waiting to meet the Americans—would act as a chaperone to ensure that nothing that could be construed as improper would happen at any point during Abigail's sojourn.

The margrave once again spelled out that all Abigail had to do was appear at one or two functions as the princess. The most important was a public presentation. Happily, at the event no one who knew the princess would be close enough to know she wasn't Rosamunde.

Abigail asked if she could ask a question.

The margrave nodded his solemn head.

"I don't understand why the princess needs someone to stand in for her. Why doesn't she just delay the events until she feels better?"

The colonel gestured to the margrave for permission to speak, and the nobleman consented. The younger man said, "At the moment, all is not peaceful in Swavicza. There are persons who wish to portray Her Highness as weak and unfit to rule. They believe if they can loosen the peoples' loyalty to their sovereign, they can carve up the country for themselves."

The margrave added, "In Swavicza, form, ceremony, and consistency are very important. Of course, you cannot understand this, with your commoner leaders changing all the time."

Abigail gritted her teeth at his offhand insult but did not reply.

The solemn man continued, "We crave stability. This handful of men wishes to create instability for their personal gain. Her Highness loves her people, but these men only see them as cattle to be herded to and fro. At this dangerous time, if Her Highness is perceived as vulnerable in any way, it might lead to a situation that we fear these men will use to their advantage."

She frowned. This seemed like a very big rigmarole for something relatively simple . . . unless their problem was bigger than they were letting on. "Is it possible Her Highness is not going to get over her indisposition?"

"No," the margrave protested. "She is fine. Well, she is not fine, but she is going to be fine."

Abigail fought a smile. She'd hit a sore spot. She would keep at this until she got her answers. With a sweet smile to cover her true intent, she said, "There seems to be more to this that I should know."

The margrave stammered with anger, unable to form a response.

"Enough!" Lady Zaaf growled in crusty English.

The room fell into a stunned silence.

The woman glared at Abigail. "Is it true that you have a Bavarian mother?"

"Yes," she answered with a sudden meekness in the face of an overwhelming force.

"Did she not raise you to be a dutiful and obedient daughter?"

"She did." However, she also raised her to be a thinker and fighter for—

"And has not your own government told you to obey us?"

Abigail wouldn't use those exact words.

As she hesitated, the stern old woman barked out an exclamation of disgust. "*Pah!* Let us leave! She is useless and unworthy. She could never for a moment make anyone believe she is a woman of any strength or intelligence." Lady Zaaf stood with an angry rustle of her heavy dress and faced the door, waiting for someone to open it for her.

Abigail frowned, knowing she had more than enough strength of character to pull off the silly masquerade they had described. Pushed by the insult, she forgot her apprehensions. "How long would my services be required?"

All three men reacted with surprise at her sudden turnaround. The margrave sputtered, "A week . . . ten days, fourteen days."

Mrs. Caruthers chimed in, "And we insist she be escorted properly at all times and delivered back to our group. Personally."

The men agreed.

After a nod from Colonel Lutz, Mr. Porter spoke up. "Ladies, I'm sure you understand the seriousness of this situation. The ambassador himself sent me a telegram this morning, reaffirming the previous instructions and informing me that even if you chose not to help our allies in Swavicza, you must keep this matter in complete confidence. You can't tell a soul."

One by one, the faces of the sisters registered their disappointment. How could they not brag about this amazing undertaking? But if the ambassador insisted, they had no choice but to comply.

Mrs. Caruthers stood, and her sisters followed. "We must make arrangements, and very quickly. What time shall you expect us?"

They settled the arrangements to meet at the station before the dinnertime train departed for Tirigovina. The Swaviczens said Abigail would not need to pack clothing or personal items, because everything she needed would be provided.

The women began the trek back to the hotel with suitable dignity, but by the time they reached Abigail's room the sisters were in a planning tizzy. Foremost on their minds was which one of them would accompany Abigail. All three expressed a wish to go, but each tried to couch it in selfless terms.

Abigail herself wasn't sure how her feelings about the matter had changed so quickly, but her own anticipation was growing at the prospect of the adventure. After her bags were returned by the hotel porters, she packed a satchel so she could bring a few personal items and her passport while sending the rest of her belongings with the group.

The sisters tried to exclude Daisy from the room while Abigail packed, but when she told her aunts that she knew about the proposition, they reluctantly let her stay—with the threat that if she whispered even a word about this she'd be sent home after a good spanking.

The niece watched the preparation with dismay, listening glumly to their chatter about the latest meeting and what they expected to happen and what clothes Abigail would wear and a dozen other speculations. When her aunts were about to draw straws for which of them would accompany Abigail to Swavicza, she had to speak up.

"I can't believe any of you would even think of abandoning the rest of the girls."

The three women were stunned into guilty silence.

"Those girls need your guidance. And you know what a handful everyone has been—just two of you can't possibly keep control over Harabeth and Emily and all those harebrained diddies. I mean, Aunt Deborah, for the last five years this has been your life's work *and* your income. What will happen if one of you picks up and leaves the group at a moment's notice? It'll be the end of your fine reputation, and you'll be ruined."

Mrs. Weatherwax replied to her niece, "Well, Abigail certainly can't go alone!"

"Of course not," Daisy said. "I'll go with her."

The prospect of the flighty young woman being involved in international intrigue caught all of them short, but no one said so.

Hands on hips, Daisy declared, "Abigail needs a companion. Who *else* are you going to send with her?"

There was no response from the sisters.

Daisy frowned. "If it's safe enough for Abigail to go, why isn't it safe enough for me to go?"

She'd cornered them with logic, which none of them had expected.

Miss Ruth MacMillan tried one last argument. "How do you expect us to explain this to your father and mother?"

"You said the ambassador wanted Abigail to go. So you can tell my parents I'm doing my patriotic duty. Just like any other American would."

The sisters stewed on her words, but no one had a rebuttal. With shared glances of disappointment, each now had to face the sad reality. After a heavy sigh, Mrs. Caruthers looked at Abigail. "My dear, are you content to have Daisy travel with you?"

Abigail had mixed feelings about being given the final decision. She could see the bubbling excitement in her friend's eyes. How could she say no? "I think it's a fine idea."

Daisy squealed and clapped her hands, hopping with joy. Abigail wondered what Lady Zaaf would have to say about their enthusiastic travel companion.

Abigail, Daisy, Mrs. Caruthers, and Miss MacMillan reached at the train station well before the appointed time. Abigail's mixed feelings over being responsible for Daisy had dampened her excitement. In turn, the sisters voiced their growing trepidation. They'd committed their brother's youngest child to this irregular scheme, and none of them would be there to oversee the affair and ensure every propriety was maintained.

Their ruminations were cut short when the Swaviczen contingent arrived. The group consisted of the margrave and Lady Zaaf, Colonel Lutz, and a number of servants and staff, including two young men in dark green military uniforms. Abigail thought one of the soldiers looked familiar, but she couldn't be sure.

When Mrs. Caruthers announced that Daisy had been selected as Abigail's traveling companion, the nobles were roundly against it. They argued there was no reason to bring another woman along, and having an additional foreigner involved would complicate secrecy.

Given a way to back out of the arrangement, Mrs. Caruthers announced, "You promised Miss Smithfield would be escorted properly at all times. How could it be 'proper' for her to go alone to a foreign land without someone from her own country to escort her? It's clear you don't intend to keep your word. I insist we call this off. Ladies, we're leaving."

As Mrs. Caruthers picked up Abigail's satchel, she turned and discovered to her surprise that the uniformed soldiers were standing behind the Americans. Their poses seemed casual, but to Abigail's eyes they were well positioned to block any attempt to leave. The margrave's face turned an undignified purple as he sputtered in his country's language. He finally found some English. "My good ladies!

Please! Wait for just a moment." He and Colonel Lutz had a brief consultation in their language, and he gathered himself into a stillness that mimicked calm. "We understand your concern. Yes, this young woman may travel with us, but only if she demonstrates the utmost discretion."

The delighted Daisy giggled her assent, which earned looks of dismay from the men and a searing scowl from Lady Zaaf. Embarrassed, Abigail gave her friend's hand a squeeze.

"But sir," Mrs. Caruthers countered, "we have the most severe misgivings about this entire scheme. We really must discuss this further with our government."

The Swaviczens glared at the sisters' reversal, and the air hummed with anger.

Sensing the meeting's dark turn, Abigail raised a placating hand to Mrs. Caruthers. With a mix of trepidation and resolve, she said, "I promised I would go. That doesn't mean Daisy has to. But I gave my word. I can't go back on that."

Daisy locked her arm through Abigail's in a gesture of support. "And if she's going, I'm going. And that's that."

The disappointed sisters saw their last escape route close as the conductor approached the group and requested the passengers to take their seats on the train. With tearful goodbyes between the aunts and niece, the party for Swavicza boarded the first class coach of the southbound train. The three women settled into a compartment, which wasn't large enough to accommodate the entire group. The men went to find a conductor and made other arrangements in the coach. Lady Zaaf was displeased to be alone with the girls and refused to speak with them.

As sunset clouds gathered, the American sisters watched with tears and waving handkerchiefs as the expedition set forth.

After the train had gone, Mrs. Caruthers began to speak of having been tricked into this whole misadventure. Miss MacMillan wondered if they should contact the embassy in Vienna for advice on getting the girls back. Then, remembering Mr. Ignatius Porter's firm instructions for secrecy, they turned over the matter to Providence and hoped for the best as they returned to the hotel to gather up the remainder of the tour for their evening train north to Vienna.

As the other Young Ladies of Quality boarded the second class car bound for Vienna, Harabeth Pritchard lingered on the platform. That handsome soldier had said he'd be on this train. She'd kept a sharp eye and even risked telling Emily about him and positioning her at the other end of the group as a lookout. But he never appeared. Harabeth tarried as long as she could, but moments before the train pulled away Miss MacMillan fetched her with a none-too-gentle yank of her arm.

Harabeth stayed on the car's steps as the train began to move, looking not at all ladylike as she craned her neck to catch a last glimpse of the platform. Why wasn't he there? She just knew it had to have something to do with that too-good-for-her-own-good Abigail and that silly-brained Daisy and why they had left the tour. That story Mrs. Caruthers had told them was as thin as Presbyterian charity. Were they supposed to believe Abigail had been called away to tend to a sick relative, and Daisy had to go as her companion? Ridiculous!

As the platform disappeared and the train chugged out of the station, Harabeth gave up and climbed the last steps up into the coach. Whatever might befall those awful girls was better than they deserved.

CHAPTER FOUR

Into the Gilded Cage

The Royal Castle of Chetova
Chetova Mountains, Swavicza

The train heading to Tirigovina made an unscheduled pre-dawn stop in the small mountain town of Mytiwa. In the pale light, the noble party—including two women draped in heavy cloaks despite the warm summer air—bustled through the dark train depot into closed coaches. The carriages departed with all due speed and disappeared from the town on the road up to the small royal castle of Chetova.

In the first coach, Abigail and Daisy sat across from Lord and Lady Zaaf and the major domo of Chetova Castle, who had been waiting for them in the closed train depot. Baron Mleist was about forty, and he wore an elegant dark linen suit instead of a uniform. His graying hair wanted to curl under the heavy hair tonic he favored, and deep furrows crossed his forehead. From his manner, Abigail judged him to be officious and someone who resented the task of turning her from a sow's ear into the most royal of silk purses. He didn't seem to know what to make of Daisy's presence, and after he gave her a nod during their introduction he didn't look at her.

As the carriage bounced along the bad road, Abigail tried to suppress a yawn. Unlike the other women in her train compartment, she had been awake for the entire rail journey, wondering about a great many things. What exactly would she be doing? What illness did the princess have that would prevent her from appearing in public? Perhaps English measles or the mumps. Abigail and her younger brother Fred went through both of those childhood rituals before she turned ten. She understood the illnesses were tougher on adults. Certainly for someone in the public eye, those spots or the swollen neck would be embarrassing and unsightly.

Another bump in the road aggravated the kink in her neck. She hoped when they arrived at the castle she'd be able to sleep a little. Another yawn escaped. If she wouldn't have time to sleep, perhaps someone would have coffee waiting for her. . . . Were women even allowed to drink coffee in Swavicza?

In perfect English, the baron gave an apology for the condition of the road and how it wouldn't provide a last chance for rest. He then began introducing Abigail to her duties as a temporary princess. First, she must not speak to the staff in the castle without the presence of Lady Zaaf, the margrave, himself, or two designated individuals whom she would meet later. Everyone at the castle had been handpicked for their loyalty, and they would do their best to help her in her role. But it would be hard for her to communicate with them because the staff only spoke German and Swaviczen, so in order to avoid misunderstandings Abigail would need someone to translate for her. Fortunately, they had found one maid in the main palace who spoke some English. Even though she was hardly the stuff of a lady's maid, she would have to do, and he hoped Abigail would be understanding of the inconvenience.

Daisy interrupted him. "Abigail speaks German."

Baron Mleist frowned at the news, and Abigail saw the three Swaviczens exchange a glance.

Daisy didn't notice and continued, "Yes, she speaks it just like a native. Why, the other day—"

The margrave ignored Daisy and asked Abigail, "How is this?"

"My mother grew up speaking it, so she taught all of us. There's a significant German population in my hometown." Continuing frowns met her reply. "Besides, it's useful to speak more than one language . . . *nicht wahr?*"

To her surprise, they shared troubled looks, and a brief and urgent conversation in Swaviczen followed. They came to some understanding and regarded her with set faces. The margrave said, "That is most interesting. We did not anticipate that an American father would allow his wife to train his children in a language from other shores."

Abigail rankled at the disrespect underlying his words.

He continued, "I'm afraid you will still have to tolerate the maid we chose for you. As the English say, she is 'downstairs.' Common and coarse."

Lady Zaaf asked her husband in German, "What is her name?"

In German he replied, "You would never have had the occasion to meet her. I believe her name is Bełza."

The woman made a face and said something in Swaviczen that couldn't have been a compliment.

The margrave continued in English to Abigail, "We cannot send her back to the main palace because she's been told about the situation, and we can't have her talking about it. I hope you'll be able to tolerate such a creature for a little while."

"I'll do my best, sir," Abigail said.

He nodded, apparently grateful for her condescension in tolerating an inferior.

Baron Mleist again took charge of the conversation. "When we arrive, you will be taken to the guest chambers where you will be met by Her Highness's official dressmaker, Frau Meyer. She will make adjustments to the clothing you will be wearing from Her Highness's wardrobe."

Daisy put an eager hand on Abigail's arm. "How exciting! You'll be wearing clothes from the princess's own closet!"

Abigail had to admit to a little excitement at the prospect. After the discomforts and irritations of the adventure so far, that might be enjoyable.

"Horrible!" Frau Meyer snorted in German when Abigail was presented to the royal dressmaker. "Why do women think they can wear plaid? In France it is the height of fashion, but it makes them look like cushions!"

Abigail stood before the triple mirror in the guest chambers at the back of the castle. True, her dress was tired and wrinkled after the overnight trip. But it was new and from the best dress shop in Hartford. Thank goodness this poor woman wouldn't see the rest of her wardrobe. She'd probably have an apoplectic fit.

The petite but strong-looking woman shook her head of wavy auburn hair as she fussed with the dress's simple cuffs. She eyed Abigail's traveling hat with utter disapproval and removed it without asking first. She tossed the brown cotton and silk hat onto a chair. It bounced off the seat and landed on the floor, snapping off two of the pheasant feathers. "Rubbish." She glared at the girl. "You should never wear such ridiculous clothing. You look like a rustic, a clown. You are much too pretty to dress like a buffoon."

It took Abigail a moment to realize her severe taskmistress might have just given her a compliment.

The woman turned to the two maids Elsa and Ada standing by. "Take her dress off and have it burned."

Abigail objected. "No, I'll need it to wear when I leave."

Frau Meyer squinted, and the maids waited for her decision. "If you insist. But take these things out of here. I do not want to see them again."

Daisy was watching the proceedings from the corner of the room, not following the words but apparently understanding Frau Meyer's disapproval. As Abigail was being unbuttoned and disrobed by the efficient maids, Daisy said in a meek voice, "Can I help?"

Abigail said, "Just don't let them burn my clothes."

Daisy was shocked. "They're lovely!"

The maids had Abigail down to her corset and petticoats. "Not by Frau Meyer's standards."

As the maid Elsa put the outfit over her arm and picked up the hat to leave, Daisy intercepted her by the door. In clear, precise English and with firm gestures, she said, "Do not burn these."

Elsa turned to Frau Meyer, having no idea what Daisy had said. Frau Meyer dismissed her with a wave. The maid left the room.

As Abigail turned back to the mirror, Frau Meyer stepped up behind her, scrutinizing the reflection and putting a firm grasp on Abigail's waist. "You are about the same height as Her Highness, but you are too thin through your middle and bust. Her clothes will not be a good fit."

Abigail's mother used to say she didn't take after the Bavarian side of the family in that regard. She asked, "Can you take them in a little?"

Frau Meyer's eyes flashed. "I do not take in the clothes of Her Highness for you!"

Daisy asked about the cause of Frau Meyer's unhappiness, and Abigail explained as she wondered if she'd misunderstood the baron. Hadn't he promised Frau Meyer would adjust the clothing for her? Daisy thought for a moment, then said, "Maybe you can let out your corset a bit. And you can put a little padding in the top. A handkerchief or two can make a big difference." She winked at her friend, who was impressed with her ingenuity.

Abigail asked the maid Ada to loosen her corset, and as the maid uncinched her she asked Frau Meyer for handkerchiefs. Some were found, and Abigail tucked them under her breasts before the maid redid the corset in a looser configuration.

Frau Meyer assessed the difference. She nodded. "Good. It's good. Your friend suggested this?" Abigail nodded. Frau Meyer asked Abigail the English word for *pfiffig*, and Abigail told her. The royal dressmaker gave Daisy a nod of approval. "Clever." The girl beamed. Frau Meyer added, "Perhaps I can help her with her clothing, too." She shook her head. "Why do you wear such awful hats?"

At the end of an hour, Abigail had tried on several of Princess Rosamunde's outfits. By then the sun was reaching over the dark mountains and both girls were famished. After Abigail was put in a dressing gown finer than any dress she'd ever owned, more servants brought in breakfast. The intimidating feast filled the table—eggs in heavy white sauce, ham, sausage, bread, butter—but the girls fell on the food without hesitation.

After they'd eaten their fill, Baron Mleist returned and began Abigail's instructions in how she would conduct herself in public. He spoke in English, for which Abigail was grateful on behalf of her friend. During breakfast Daisy had admitted to feeling overwhelmed. And why not? Abigail was beginning to feel a little overwhelmed herself in this strange sojourn in a strange land.

The baron concentrated on the basics: She should always stand erect, with complete dignity, and she must never bow or curtsy to anyone. In public, she was not to speak, except to her attendants at the event, and while she could look pleased or happy, she must not smile.

"Not smile?" Abigail knew at some point she would smile and not even realize it.

"No. You may look pleased. But under no circumstances may you show your teeth."

Abigail blinked. "Does the princess have bad teeth?"

"Of course not! Her teeth are excellent." He glowered at the insult to his monarch's dental health. "But smiling so broadly as to show teeth is most common and undignified. That is not how royalty behaves."

Abigail thought of the story her godmother Mrs. Stowe had told about her jolly meeting when she was introduced to President Lincoln. The two, who at the time were the most famous people in America, laughed and carried on like old friends. At the risk of being a lowly commoner, Abigail liked the American way better than the royal protocol.

She said, "I will do my best."

The baron didn't seem mollified by her lukewarm statement.

Perhaps he needed a little buttering-up. "I will rely on your good instructions in all matters."

He nodded and appeared pleased.

At a knock on the door, the baron bid entry, and in came maids with a splendid ensemble in royal blue. At the lead was a somber and forbidding woman clothed in severe black and gray. She gave Abigail the slightest of nods and then ordered the two maids to bring the dress forward. Carrying the bodice and jacket was a bouncy young woman with curly black hair and sparkling dark eyes. Unlike the other castle maids Abigail had seen, all of whom dressed in subdued tones, this young woman wore a bright costume with red and pink trimmings. She announced to the baron in accented English, "Frau Meyer has finished a gown and wishes us to dress the miss."

The baron gave his acknowledgment to the somber lead maid. In German he said, "Maria, I would like to introduce you to 'the *fräulein.*'" He turned to the two Americans and said in English, "Maria will be in charge of your care during your stay in Swavicza." Maria gave Abigail another slight nod, and Abigail returned a nod of thanks. With noticeably less respect, the baron added, "And this is Belza. She will be your personal maid."

Abigail smiled at the eager, dark-eyed maid, but then she thought better of it and decided to practice "pleased but not smiling" right away, especially in front of the baron. "I'm happy to meet you, Belza."

The young maid flashed another charming smile, then told the baron with a short curtsy, "Sir, we will send for you when the miss is dressed."

As he went through the door, Baron Mleist said, "I look forward to seeing the result."

With the man gone, the three maids went to work on the task of dressing Abigail. More accurately, Maria supervised and the others did the work. The maids Elsa and Ada came in. Elsa carried a large wash basin and a pitcher with steaming water, while Ada held flannel cloths, a slop bucket, and a bar of soap. Maria supervised as the two new maids removed Abigail's dressing gown and undressed her down to just her chemise. Holding her dressing gown around her to form a curtain of privacy, they gestured her to remove her chemise and then presented her with a clean one. Once she was covered again, the dressing gown was handed to Beĺza. Elsa and Ada lathered up the flannels and gave Abigail's neck and arms a good scrub. Abigail shivered as they efficiently moved on from one limb to the next, respecting her modesty as they scrubbed with one flannel and rinsed with the next. Of course Abigail washed herself this way every morning at her washstand, but she'd never had it done *to* her. She felt embarrassed at having others do for her what she could do herself. Was this really how "important" people lived? There was something wrong with a world where people could become so lofty that they expected others to bathe them.

The quick scrub and rinse done, the maids positioned Abigail before the mirrors and assembled the dress's underpinnings. Daisy reminded them to use the handkerchiefs and to keep the corset loose. When they finished putting the exquisite gown on her, Abigail could only stare at her reflection. The lustrous blue silk nearly matched the color of her eyes. A brocade trim of bold orange and red Jacobean roses around the waist looked so startling and modern that Abigail marveled. In her thrifty family, her practical wardrobe never knew the splendor of fashion. This was truly magnificent. Tears began to fill her eyes, and she had to ask Beĺza for a handkerchief, which the maid quickly produced. Dabbing the tears away with a laughing apology, Abigail said in English, "I will not ruin this dress with my silliness."

"Not silly, miss," Beĺza said. "You are lovely."

Daisy seconded that. "Beautiful!"

As Abigail looked in the mirror, for the first time in her life she wanted to see herself bedecked with jewelry. She looked at the modest pearl drop earrings *Oma* Siebold had given her when she graduated from high school. She wondered how she would look in diamond earrings and a magnificent necklace. Would she have the chance to wear a tiara? She hoped so. She blamed this moment of madness on the dress, but what a wonderful madness!

The servants made quick work of undoing her hair. Before Abigail could say a word, Maria produced a pair of scissors and took hold of her forelocks, lopping them off into short, curly bangs. Stunned, Abigail stared at her discarded tresses in Maria's hand as the other maids parted her hair down the middle and brushed it into a simple bun at the nape of her neck. The maids admired their handiwork, then one went to fetch the nobles.

Daisy stepped up next to her friend, and they both looked at the reflection in the mirror. "Abigail," she said with awe, "I can hardly believe my eyes. You've become a princess!"

In this dress, she felt like one. "I wish someone could make a photographic portrait of me like this. I don't think anyone would believe it."

The door opened, and in the reflection Abigail could see Baron Mleist and Lord Zaaf enter. She made certain of her regal posture, then turned to face them. The men hesitated at the sight of her, then gathered themselves and continued into the room. A moment later, Colonel Lutz, Lady Zaaf, and Frau Meyer entered. Lady Zaaf only harrumphed when she saw Abigail, while the royal dressmaker admired the gown and the young woman in it. "*Schön,*" she murmured. "Beautiful."

Daisy stepped into the background as the Swaviczens gathered around Abigail. The men sized her up and down. "Good," was all the margrave had to say.

The baron added in English, "Her Highness is more sanguine. We will need to find a way to make her face rosier."

Daisy perked up. "Abigail can do makeup. She played Beatrice in *Much Ado About Nothing.* And a few other things I can't remember."

She turned to her friend. "I'm sure you can come up with something that'll work."

The ones who understood English glowered at her. Daisy shrank back in dismay, her attempt to help having backfired somehow.

Their venomous gazes settled on Abigail. The margrave growled, "You are—an *actress?*"

For a moment Abigail was embarrassed. Her theatre experience had been in high school. That was no source of shame in America, but apparently here any connection to the stage must carry a stigma.

She replied in a calm voice, "It was a school production of Shakespeare. I am not an actress." Although, she thought, isn't that exactly what they were looking for?

After a brief discussion in Swaviczen, their horror subsided, slowly. Frau Meyer, now understanding the situation, nodded with the others' assessment and then added in German, "Makeup will help. Also with the shape of the cheeks. Her cheekbones are not so high as the princess. We can fix this. I will send for what we need."

The group conferred another few moments, and all but Frau Meyer exited the room. The royal dressmaker called for a maid to fetch a simpler outfit she had left in another room, and then she supervised Abigail's wardrobe change. Maria took the sumptuous blue gown away for another day.

For the rest of the afternoon, Baron Mleist taught Abigail how to stand, how to walk, and otherwise how to move like Princess Rosamunde. Abigail had the most trouble remembering to keep her chin up at all times, but eventually she mastered the art of looking down without moving her head. Daisy watched from a chair in the corner of the room, and she wisely offered no further observations.

By dinnertime Abigail's exhaustion caught up with her. Between all the lessons and no sleep the night before, she was having trouble keeping her eyes open.

Belza and Ada brought a supper of meats, bread, and boiled root vegetables. As the baron headed for the door, he assured Abigail she was doing well and would be ready for her first public appearance in three days.

She perked out of her fog. "Three days?" The baron nodded. "That's all the time I have to get ready?"

He said, "There is nothing for you to do at this event. Representatives will come to pay homage to the princess, and they will give you a few gifts, which others will accept on your behalf, and then you will withdraw. You don't even say a word. All you have to do is stand and move like Her Highness. Which you already know how to do."

She found some comfort in that. "Where will this take place?"

The baron had reached the door, and with a sigh he stopped. "In Tirigovina. You will be taken there the evening before. Tomorrow important people will be arriving in the morning. You will meet with them for additional instructions." He put his hand on the knob, then paused. "It is better for you not to wander the castle. I know you are curious, but it will be disruptive to the staff to have you outside this room unescorted. The door will be locked and a guard posted outside to make sure you are safe."

Daisy sat up from her half-nap in the corner chair. She looked around the room, which contained one master bed and a narrow cot along the side wall. "Where am I supposed to sleep?"

He nodded towards the cot. "That should suffice. The maids will stay in here as well. Bedding will be provided for them. If you have any needs, tell the maid Maria to ask the guard. Good night." Before the girls could respond, he was gone.

The friends looked at each other. The room was pleasant enough, and it even had a small chamber in the back for their toilette. But no matter how gilded, a cage is still a cage.

Daisy's pout turned to tears. "Oh, Abigail, I'm so sorry. I feel like I talked you into this."

Abigail put a comforting arm around her friend's shoulders. "Nonsense. And you're doing me a great favor by being here."

"I am?"

"Yes, of course! You're my only friend in this whole country. And just by being here, you always remind me that we'll get through all of this and go home."

Her words cheered Daisy, who tried to chuckle through her tears. "What a story we'll have to tell, too. Not that anyone will believe us."

"We'll make them believe us."

The two flinched with surprise when the door opened. In came the maids, followed by men carrying great armfuls of bedding. Maria directed them to arrange the featherbeds and pillows around on the floor. She then gave the order to place a comforter and pillow on the cot. From the way she spoke to the others, Abigail surmised Maria had claimed the cot for herself. Abigail asked her in German where Daisy's bed was, and with a dismissive gesture Maria indicated the other bedding on the floor. Abigail bristled. She was no princess, but she didn't like having her friend ordered around by someone who was supposed to be a servant.

Abigail didn't want Daisy to know about the disrespect Maria had shown her. She said to her friend, "You know, my bed is a terrible waste of space for just one person. And it'll certainly be more comfortable than that little cot. Why don't you share the guest bed with me?"

Daisy watched the maids claim their sleeping spots. "It'll be like a little house party."

Abigail gave her a smiling nod and joked, "But we mustn't stay up all night telling ghost stories." As she looked at all the maids and the locked door, she muttered, "This place is scary enough already."

CHAPTER FIVE

The Real Lessons Begin

Despite her concerns, Abigail fell asleep moments after she crawled into bed and slept hard through the night. She awoke with the dawn, which promised a bright and clear day. Everyone else was asleep, so rather than disturb the others she stayed in bed. As she listened to the cheerful morning serenade of unfamiliar birds, she thought about the days to come. She wondered if she would actually meet the princess and what her "indisposition" might be. So many little troubling details that meant nothing on their own were beginning to stack up into a worrisome pile. Why were they so concerned that she spoke German? Why was she being kept away from everyone in the castle? Secrecy mattered, but didn't someone say everyone here had been chosen for their loyalty? And why had no one mentioned her name? She had been introduced to Maria as "the *fräulein*." But no one called her *Fräulein* Smithfield. She wished she could discuss her disquiet with Daisy, but there was no point in getting her tenderhearted companion more worried than she already was.

When Maria awoke, she roused the maids with a sharp clap of her hands, and the little army sprang into action. Daisy sat up and rubbed her eyes as the maids gathered their bedding and shuffled it into the closet. Maria knocked on the door and exchanged quiet words with the guard, who listened to her instructions. Abigail pretended to be still sleepy, and through half-closed eyes she watched the exchange with great interest. It was clear Maria was not just a maid. She gave orders and expected them to be obeyed.

Her accent was from the north—Prussia, perhaps—and not the local German dialect that resembled Austrian. She wasn't from the area, and she seemed to be someone important who was pretending to be a servant. Abigail decided it would be wise not to confide in Maria.

The soldier closed the door, leaving the women alone. Maria greeted the two Americans with a cheerful *"Guten morgen!"* and announced breakfast would be served in the room when everyone was dressed. After a knock, the door opened again and the soldier brought in fresh clothing for the maids.

After the soldier withdrew again, the maids dressed, and three went to fetch breakfast. They returned with another full meal, this one with pastries and jams in addition to meats and breads. The novelty of the heavy food was wearing thin, but the two Americans did the best they could.

After they finished, Abigail and Daisy were dressed in simple, pale-colored summer frocks by the maids, but instead of being subjected to another lesson, they were left to wait. Maria went on an undisclosed errand, so, as the maids chatted among themselves, Abigail and Daisy discussed the day to come. They would be meeting the new people Baron Mleist had mentioned, and they might actually be able to leave the room.

Even as she listened to Daisy speculate about the day, Abigail watched the maids interact. Belza was eager to be included in their conversations, but the others weren't inviting her to join in. Perhaps these maids worked in the castle and that would mean Belza was an outsider from the main palace. Perhaps, as Lord Zaaf had said, she was "downstairs" while all the others were "upstairs." Or maybe there was some other division that Abigail didn't understand. But she felt a little sorry when she saw the dark, bright-eyed girl being ignored by the others.

After a half-hour wait, their patience was rewarded by Baron Mleist's return. He dismissed the maids from the room so he could have a private conversation with the visitors. In English, he began with an apology. "We were expecting important personages from Tirigovina, but they seem to have been delayed. You will have to wait in this room until they arrive."

Fed up with being a prisoner, Abigail countered, "It's unhealthy for us to be stuck in here. At least let us go outside for a walk."

Clearly the baron didn't like her idea, and neither did he like Abigail attempting to tell him what to do. "For your own safety, you must remain in here."

"Safety? We're in a castle surrounded by hand-picked people. Or are you saying you don't trust their loyalty?"

He frowned, but she could tell she'd given him pause.

She continued, "Besides, if I'm going to represent Her Highness well, I need to keep up my strength. I can't do that by sitting here all day in this stuffy room. And it's not as if we can go anywhere. Send Maria and Belza with us. They'll make sure we don't get into trouble."

Annoyed by her logic, he conceded. "But do everything Maria tells you," he ordered, confirming Abigail's suspicion that Maria was more than simply a maid.

Saying what he wanted to hear, Abigail replied, "We will be very obedient."

Not completely convinced, he departed, leaving the two girls alone.

Daisy said with a sigh, "Thank you! I couldn't stand being cooped—"

Abigail cut her off with an apology. "We have to arrange a plan before the maids return."

"What? I don't understand—"

"Just listen: I'll keep Maria distracted while you talk with Belza. Speak quietly so Maria can't hear you. Ask Belza everything you can about the princess, about the country, about what's going on. Everyone else here is in on the plan, but I don't think Belza is. They chose her because she speaks English. But I think she's as much an outsider as we are."

Daisy's eyes brightened. "Oh, I see. Pump her for the details."

Bless Daisy and her fondness for dime novels! "Yes, but don't let her know what you're up to. She may tell someone what we're doing."

Daisy's brightness faded. "But how do I—"

The door opened and Abigail put her fingers on her friend's lips to hush her. As the maids entered the room, she turned her gesture into straightening Daisy's hair. "We must always look our best here."

Daisy frowned at the sudden turn of the conversation, then with a quiet "oh" she figured it out. "Yes," she said in stilted tones, "I sure miss . . . having someone do my hair."

Abigail feared Daisy lacked the makings of a good spy, but she hoped for the best.

Most of Chetova Castle's interior dated from the seventeenth and eighteenth centuries, a time after sieges were the rule, and the castle contained a surprising amount of open space within its fortifications. The main living quarters had a cramped garden in front, but it led out to a long and open courtyard surrounded by clusters of smaller buildings. A smithy, a smokehouse, an outdoor kitchen, and places for other useful trades made the castle a small, self-contained mountaintop village.

As they walked on their morning constitutional, Abigail arranged it so she and Maria were in front—which was only fitting, as Maria thought they were the more important people—and Daisy and Belza followed. Abigail chatted with Maria in German and kept her occupied with innocuous questions even as she strained to hear Daisy's chat in English with their talkative maid.

Abigail did ask Maria a few useful questions about the upcoming event she would attend in the princess's stead. Maria explained the traditional midsummer festival had been turned into an annual exercise in obeisance by Rosamunde's grandfather, King Ernst VIII. During the ceremony, in the place of the princess Abigail would receive an oath of loyalty from a representative of the local Sálacene popula-tion, followed by a performance of several of their folk dances and a few gifts of Sálacene food.

When Maria's ears pricked up at Beĺza's laughter, Abigail quickly asked Maria about the Sálacene: "Who are they? Are they im-portant?" Distracted from the conversation behind them, Maria ex-plained the Sálacene were the country's other major ethnic group after the Swaviczens, and they were dreadful troublemakers who needed to be reminded that they were ruled by others.

Remembering the pleasant bookseller in Graz, Abigail asked, "What are they like?"

With a dismissive gesture, Maria frowned and pointed her thumb over her shoulder at Beĺza.

Abigail understood her observation of the others excluding the bright-eyed maid had been accurate. "Does the princess speak Sála-cene? Will I be expected to know it?"

Maria spat out a sharp laugh. "Her Highness, speak that dog-like language? Nonsense! She won't even speak Swaviczen. She knows it, but she only speaks German. Or French or Italian or English, when the need arises." She laughed again at the absurdity. "Speak Sálacene!"

Abigail caught a bit of the conversation between Daisy and Beĺza. The lively maid was saying that the army's loyalty was uncertain with a woman in charge.

Maria stopped at the hushed tones behind her. She whirled around to face the two. "What are you talking about?" she demanded in German.

Daisy blanched, and Beĺza's mouth fell open in dismay.

"What?" Maria demanded again. Abigail translated the question for her friend.

Before Beĺza could speak, Daisy blurted out, "Men!"

Abigail translated the word for Maria.

In the face of Maria's withering glare, Daisy said with a fright-ened pout, "I was saying men who play baseball are so handsome and athletic when they . . . run."

Maria continued to glare at the doe-eyed girl as Abigail conveyed her reply. After a long moment, Maria shook her head and turned away, continuing on the walk. Abigail let out a tense sigh and fell in next to her. Maria shot her a sour glance and said in German, "Your 'friend' is not very intelligent, is she?"

Abigail smiled. "She has her moments."

As their walk took them past the castle's closed gate, suddenly the guards on the low parapets called out something in Swaviczen. The gate began to open, and Maria backed the three away and stood in front of them to block their view. She exclaimed with dismay, "They're here—we are not ready!" Before Abigail could wonder who "they" were, the heavy wooden gate opened to reveal a drawbridge being lowered over a gap that surely held a moat. In awe at this moment out of a fairy tale, and despite Maria's attempts to keep the visitors hidden, Abigail watched as the drawbridge landed on the road outside, and a brace of mounted soldiers in forest green uniforms trotted through the gate. Two young men, also looking quite military, followed on dark bay horses, and then a resplendent carriage rumbled through. Another small detachment of soldiers in dark blue uniforms brought up the rear. At a shouted command, the drawbridge began its rattling climb back up, and the gate swung closed.

Peering out from behind Maria, Abigail fixed her gaze on the two handsome, dark-haired men on the tall bay horses. They wore shining helmets that reminded Abigail of the gleaming helms with long-flowing plumes worn by the English Household Cavalry. The first man in a crisp white uniform was taller, broader through the shoulders and sported a tidy moustache. He carried himself with a coolness that spoke of privilege and self-assurance. His companion, wearing a uniform of the same dark blue as the second cadre of soldiers, was clean-shaven and not quite as tall. His bearing was both poised and relaxed. Even though he seemed important, in small gestures he showed deference to the man in white.

As the two dismounted, servants appeared, some to take care of the horses and others with small brushes to remove the dust of the journey from the men's uniforms. The man in blue caught sight of the cluster of women and nodded to them with a small smile.

Horrified at being seen out in the open, Maria herded the group back to the living quarters. She scolded them: "These men are very important! I am ashamed for them to see you like this!" Abigail didn't bother to translate for Daisy as Maria hurried the others back up to the guest chamber. Maria gave Belza strict instructions to clean them up before they were to be presented to the visitors. Then she dashed out. Abigail noticed the door locked behind her.

Belza got the two friends tidied up as Abigail peppered her with questions about the new arrivals and why they were here.

The maid said she knew all the gossip. "The tall one is Franz Antonius of Heigenlizt. He's a distant cousin of Her Highness. All the palace staff thinks Her Highness will marry him. He's the only son of an archduke, and his family is second only to that of the princess. The other is his cousin, Josef of Ramsl and Tuharen. He's second on the marriage list. His father is only a duke—although a very important one. But Josef is either the second or third son, I can't remember, so he won't be as important. They were abroad for military training, but a few months ago they were summoned home. The palace maids think it's so Her Highness can choose one to marry, but the manservants think it's because she needs them to keep the other nobles in line." Belza gave them a confidential wink. "And they are both in love with Rosamunde, and it's all terribly chivalrous and romantic!"

As Daisy rattled on about how fine-looking they were, Abigail thought several things at once: Josef, the one who smiled at them, was just about the handsomest man she'd ever seen; he might be spending time with her over the course of her masquerade; and yet he might be marrying the princess.

Abigail told Belza to go find Maria and learn what was going on and when they would be expected to meet the gentlemen. Belza went to the door and, after a knock and a little negotiation, the guard let her out. The door locked behind her, leaving the Americans alone.

Abigail urged her friend, "Tell me everything Belza said."

"Well, first of all," Daisy began, "I don't think we can trust her. I mean, she's sweet, but she's a gossip—you probably noticed—and I don't think she could keep a secret to save her life."

Seeing a whole new side to Daisy, including a shrewd judge of character, Abigail was favorably impressed.

"She's also a bit of a mooch. She's heard all Americans are rich, and she's angled a few times for a gift or a job."

Abigail knew they didn't have much time. "What about the country? Or the princess? Or any information she had?"

"Belza only works in the pantry, so she doesn't know much. But she said there are rumors in the main town—whatever it's called— that some nobles and rich people don't like the princess." Daisy shrugged. "But what can they do about it? Aren't royalty in charge for life?"

Abigail pressed her, "Anything else?"

"Yes. She said—"

The door opened, and Maria strode in with Belza close behind. "Good," said the stern woman who wasn't a maid. "I see you are both ready. The baron would like to present you to the two special visitors."

Abigail wanted to hear what Daisy had to say, but now that they were on their way to meet the young noblemen, she could only think about the butterflies in her stomach.

CHAPTER SIX

Soothing Salve on a Burr

Maria led Abigail and Daisy to their destination of Baron Mleist's office, which was up a floor and all the way across the castle's main building. Judging from their room's position on a low floor at the back, Abigail wondered if their guest quarters were really a glorified dungeon. Following them came Belza and two soldiers. Were the men an escort of honor, or just guards? Abigail wanted to believe the former but was inclined to think the latter.

The upper corridor walls held displays of swords, lances, and other weapons. Suits of armor from several centuries stood like sentinels along the way. Abigail wondered if people could be hidden in them to stage a surprise attack on unsuspecting guests. She shook her head at her fanciful thoughts, which were the stuff of dime novels. At the same time, she wondered if her dramatic fears could be justified. As Daisy looked at the forbidding display with growing concern, Abigail offered her a smile to give her comfort she herself didn't feel.

At the end of the long hallway, two more guards flanked double doors, which they opened to let the entourage enter.

Tapestries and bookcases lined the small yet overwhelming room. Comfortable chairs were gathered around an ample desk, and another seating area surrounded a cold fireplace on the far wall. From above the bookcases, trophy heads of animals Abigail didn't recognize looked down at her, and a rug made from the skin of a large black bear—complete with snarling head—lay before the hearth. The room felt both cozy and intimidating. Was this the princess's study or office? Abigail wondered if royalty had offices.

Maria stepped aside, indicating her charges should continue into the room. Before Abigail could register all the people present, a squawk of surprise behind her made her glance back to see the soldiers preventing Belza from coming in. Maria moved out into the hall and closed the doors behind her.

In passing, Abigail saw the baron rise from the chair behind the desk. But the Americans had their attention on the new arrivals. Franz Antonius lounged across a loveseat, one booted leg draped across the armrest in an insouciant pose. He held a riding crop in his hand and every so often tapped it against his boot. Josef stood in front of a chair next to the loveseat. Franz Antonius's smile was half a smirk; Josef's was genuine. Abigail directed a disapproving gaze at the senior cousin. She understood there was a powerful class system here, but couldn't the man at least pretend to be respectful of ladies in the room?

In turn, Franz Antonius eyed Abigail up and down, making her feel a bit like a filly at the county fair. "So," he said in smooth English, "this is our temporary Rosamunde." He squinted at Daisy but said nothing.

Josef stepped forward and took Abigail's hand. In English he said, "Miss Smithfield, I am very pleased and honored to meet you. I am Josef of Ramsl." He nodded above her hand, and then he stepped over to Daisy and repeated the gesture. Daisy couldn't help herself and giggled, dipping into a quick curtsy.

The baron frowned at the eager count's breach of etiquette. "You will please remember, My Lord, that when anyone else is present we are to address our honored guest only as '*Fräulein.*'"

"Of course, Baron," he apologized. "I shall not forget again." Josef returned to his place before the chair but did not sit.

The baron straightened his shoulders as if shaking off the social misstep. He said to the young women, "Miss Abigail Smithfield, Miss Daisy MacMillan, I present you to Lord Franz Antonius, Count of

Heigenlizt, senior cousin to Her Highness, and his cousin, Lord Josef, Count of Ramsl and Tuharen. They are here to assist in your mission. As far as the world is concerned, the counts are here visiting Her Highness—who has been recuperating in Chetova from a slight cough—and then they will escort her back to Tirigovina for the ceremony."

Franz Antonius added, "As you aren't really my cousin, you won't see us very much. But since we can't go anywhere while we're pretending to wait on Rosamunde, we're almost as much prisoners as you are."

Abigail didn't care for his attitude, but at least he admitted to her situation. She also knew now it was intentional that no one used her name. She acknowledged Franz Antonius's honesty with a small tilt of her head.

The baron, however, was irked at his statement. "My Lord, please don't say they're prisoners. They are guests of Her Highness. And highly regarded as such."

Franz Antonius tapped his riding crop against his boot, then stood. "Yes, thank you, baron, you are correct. My mistake." He glanced at his cousin. "Josef, on the other hand, has expressed an interest in helping our foreign guests with this masquerade. He will be a much better guide for you than I would anyway, so you two are in luck." He chuckled, then tapped his boot with his crop to punctuate his statement as if it were a joke. He used the crop to give the two women a jaunty salute. "I will see you . . . whenever our host arranges it." He offered Baron Mleist a sly look, then headed out of the room.

After he had left, a chagrined Josef said to them, "You'll please forgive Franz. He only returned from military life in Germany a month ago, and he is not used to having so much freedom and so little responsibility."

Abigail wasn't sure how accurate his assessment was of his cousin's bad manners, but at least his statement seemed to be genuine and not an insult. As she smiled at the Count of Ramsl and Tuharen, she had the feeling she would enjoy the next two days.

The first lesson from the young count began with a surprise. As she and Daisy were leaving the study, Josef asked Abigail what she wanted to do most. "Go outdoors and go somewhere, anywhere! I feel like I've been trapped indoors for weeks." Half an hour after they were locked up again in their room, Maria arrived with a sour announcement that they had been invited by the Count of Ramsl and Tuharen to partake in a horseback ride outside the castle.

Baron Mleist objected to the excursion, saying the American guests should be kept from public view so there could be no questions about them. Josef assured him they would ride through a remote section of the forest with his soldiers in escort, and even if they were seen, the two would be viewed only as guests or ladies in waiting. With great reluctance, the baron acquiesced.

Abigail was pleased by Josef's thoughtfulness and generosity. Daisy, on the other hand, was no horsewoman and confessed to her friend that she dreaded the outing. However, after they were suited up in borrowed riding habits and the disgruntled Maria brought them to the courtyard, Daisy saw the splendid sight of Josef and four of his soldiers waiting for them, and she announced she had the courage to try. With the assistance of Josef's adjutant, a fine young man by the name of Biedric Halle, Daisy managed to get up the steps of the mounting block and to slide sideways into the sidesaddle of her tame black palfrey. She giggled at Biedric's chivalry and gushed out her thanks several times more than necessary. He seemed equally smitten with her. He didn't speak English, but they both had a working knowledge of French, and soon they were lost in their own world.

Abigail greeted her own gentle mount, who was the same unfamiliar breed as Daisy's. She asked the animal his name as she presented him with an apple she'd had Belza fetch from the castle's pantry. The compact horses reminded Abigail of her Uncle Gustav's prized Morgans, except these were solid black and had a sturdier build. The eager gelding made quick work of the apple and nuzzled her in thanks.

As she patted her horse's neck an apologized for not having another apple, Abigail caught a glimpse of Josef smiling at her while he stood at the side of his stately bay. She tried not to blush. "I'm sorry. I know you shouldn't give a horse a treat when it's bridled, but I wanted to make a good first impression."

With a small smile, he said, "You have."

With his continuing smile at her, she felt her cheeks grow warm. He laughed lightly, and she tried to hide her embarrassment by returning her attention to her horse. But even as she wanted to deny it, she had to admit to herself that this count was a most likeable fellow. "What are these horses?"

"They are a local breed. We call them Luckovskara."

Abigail repeated the name, not confident she said it well. "They are an admirable animal." Without thinking, Abigail patted Josef's patient bay and gave him a soft greeting. She asked the horse, "And what's your name?"

Josef said, "If he spoke English, he'd tell you it's Hercules."

She patted the horse's neck. "You are a big, strong fellow indeed."

Josef nodded, pleased. "You know horses?"

In her mind, Abigail could hear Granny Smithfield and *Oma* Siebold calling after her to be a good girl and quit playing tag on horseback with her brothers and come into the house to mend socks. She said, "They're a favorite distraction."

Josef led her horse to the mounting block. She needed no assistance to get onto the compact horse, and in her heart she would have preferred to discard that sidesaddle and ride the animal astride. But when Josef offered her his hand to help her up the mounting block's steps, she understood that sometimes conforming to society's demands had its compensations.

When everyone was ready, Josef and Abigail rode at the lead of the group out through the gate and over the drawbridge. As she passed above the grassy trench that surrounded the castle and that surely had held water in a previous era, she smiled to herself that her fairy-tale expectations of a moat had been accurate. They made a turn to the right and headed into an airy, light-filled forest. Daisy and Biedric followed, and the other three soldiers of Josef's household cavalry took up positions at the rear.

Once the horses settled into a sedate walk in the woods, Josef said to Abigail, "I'm so grateful you're willing to help Her Highness. It's very brave and generous of you."

She hadn't thought of herself in those terms, but it was nice that he did.

With some embarrassment he continued, "And I must apologize for Franz's ill manners. He thinks. . . ." He paused, searching for a polite turn of phrase, then gave up. "Please forgive how I say this, but he thinks you're an adventuress."

Abigail tried her hide her shock at being thought of as a woman of intrigue on the fringe of society. "Why would he think such a thing?"

"He said a good woman would never show your level of courage."

She concluded Franz Antonius hadn't met many good women.

Josef added with a shy smile, "He also doesn't understand that honor and gallantry are not solely a product of noble birth."

Abigail had no reply. If she were back home, she'd know how to respond to a polite flirtation. But she wasn't home and, with this of all men, she wanted to avoid a misstep.

He inquired, "How long are you visiting Swavicza?"

"Only as long as I'm needed."

She saw a touch of disappointment on his face. "Are you residing in another country for the summer?"

"No, Daisy and I are part of a tour. The rest of the group is in Vienna for a few days, and then Berlin." She was glad she had memorized the itinerary so she would know where to contact the tour when this masquerade ended.

As he nodded in thought, a slight swirl of wind came through the trees. She caught a whiff of something that smelled of dark, sweet spices, like a cured, fragrant wood. Could it be the forest or a native herb? She liked it and took in a deep breath.

He said, "It's wonderful that you have a chance to visit other countries when your country is so far away. I studied in Vienna, but I've traveled throughout Europe. There's knowledge that can be gained only by going and experiencing it yourself. It helps you see home more clearly."

Abigail blinked with surprise. If he'd said "triangulation perspective," she would have fallen off her horse.

He continued, "I have only met a few Americans, but I've read many of your books. In English," he added with a touch of pride. "I wish I could visit your country."

"Why? We're rustic and unsophisticated."

He chuckled. "I think not. In Vienna I befriended an American medical student. I was astonished at how easily he moved through all levels of society. He was as comfortable with a landgrave as with a butcher. He treated all as if they were his equals. I didn't know people could be like that. We are so structured here and tied to our class. We must do what we are told, even if we do not wish it."

"Like marry the princess?" Abigail shuddered at her forward question.

He didn't seem to take offense. "Have you heard that? I know she prefers a foreign match, both for the prestige and to make the country safer through a good alliance. But that is complicated, and Swavicza is not . . . valuable. There are many people who want her to choose from one of the local families. She has to choose soon, however."

Abigail wondered why the princess had to hurry, but she decided it was rude to ask about such intimate affairs of state. As they rode on, she thought about the rest of what he'd said. He was cheerful and friendly, and yet he appeared resigned to the life that fate had chosen for him. She guessed that came from living in an authoritarian society. She had one more observation: Beĺza's gossip that both cousins were deeply in love with the princess didn't seem to be correct in his case. Abigail admitted to a certain satisfaction with that.

They rode through the dappled sunshine, and Josef soon called back in German to one of his officers: "Phillip, will you sing for us?" The man responded with a lighthearted song in a language Abigail didn't understand.

It was so peaceful here. She thought this could be Arcadia. Daisy's laugh made both Abigail and Josef turn to see her sharing a joke with Biedric.

"You see?" Josef said with happiness for his friend. "They can find their own match. This is not the way with people of my rank."

Abigail marveled at her riding companion. Perhaps she had misjudged Swavicza through her dour escorts. That thought raised a question. "I was told Lady Zaaf would be my escort the entire time I was here. But I haven't seen her since we arrived. Do you know why?"

She watched him take care choosing his words. "She's not a favorite of the castle residents. With the permission of Her Highness, Lady Zaaf has been sent back to Tirigovina. I'm sure you'll see her there."

Abigail wondered how many other promises made to the MacMillan sisters would be broken.

Josef scrutinized her. "Do you . . . miss her?"

Resisting a chuckle, Abigail chose her own words carefully. "Given the choice between the correct escort and the current one, the situation at present is not a disappointment."

He pondered her well-twisted response, and when he realized what she'd said he beamed with a hint of a blush. "Well, it is true you have a correct escort, with Maria. She doesn't like horses, so she'll resume her attendance to you when we return."

She wanted to ask him Maria's true identity, but she'd already been forward enough for one conversation. She saw wisdom in changing the subject. "You were in Vienna, but you said your cousin was in Germany. Why weren't you together?"

He didn't seem disappointed by the change in topic. "Our kings choose where the young men of noble families go for military training so there will always be someone with friends in a useful country. Prussia, Bavaria, Austria-Hungary, France, Italy, England."

"Perhaps you'll be able to go to America someday." She hoped she didn't sound eager.

"That would be wonderful! You are so different from us. In my favorite American book, the author is making fun of Americans even as he says nice things about them. I can't imagine such freedom. I wish I could meet the author. So extraordinary!"

"What book is that?"

"*Innocents Abroad*."

She couldn't keep her laugh to herself.

His brow furrowed. "Is that funny?"

"No. I'm sorry. You don't have to travel to America to find him. He's in Heidelberg."

Josef's gaze turned skeptical.

"Samuel Clemens—Mark Twain—is a friend of mine. His family lives next door to where I'm living with my godmother and her family."

His skepticism deepened. "You live in Hannibal?"

"No, Hartford, Connecticut."

He considered. "Is that near Hannibal?"

Before she'd left America, she would have said they were worlds apart. "No. It's more than a thousand miles."

He thought for a moment. "Heidelberg certainly is much closer." He chuckled as he thought, but then he shook his head. "I couldn't even get to Heidelberg now, with . . . this going on."

"What *is* going on?" she asked.

He shrugged. "All I know is Rosamunde is doing something in secret. I think she's negotiating with the Austrian emperor or arranging for money. But she doesn't confide in me."

His ideas were logical. She asked, "How long do you think this masquerade will last?"

He shook his head. "I am to help you for a week. That is all I know."

The group rounded a bend in the path. A long straight stretch of a quarter mile lay ahead leading to a small rise near a boulder. It was a perfect place for a race. She felt her willing horse tense as if it expected her to give the command for a dash.

"You are smiling," he said.

"If Daisy weren't with us, I'd race you to that rock."

He marveled. "You ride a horse that well?"

She nodded.

"You are amazing."

"No," she said, but she congratulated herself that he thought so.

"I will accept your challenge," he said with a smile.

"No. It would be too much for my friend. I'm afraid it would spook her horse."

She gazed back at Daisy, who was lost in conversation with the smitten Biedric as they rode stirrup-to-stirrup.

Josef nodded with understanding, then looked at the couple. "Your friend is staying on well."

Abigail agreed. "But it seems Biedric has fallen."

Josef frowned, studying his lieutenant, and then he understood her wordplay. His resounding laugh echoed through the forest.

Biedric glanced at his superior with some embarrassment and asked in German, "Is something wrong, My Lord?"

Josef said, "No, Biedric, everything is just right."

He gave a smile of approval to his lieutenant, then gazed at Abigail in a way that made her catch her breath. Could he be falling, too? . . . And was she? How sad that they only had a week together.

They continued their ride through the idyllic forest, talking about history, opera, travel, literature, and about nothing at all.

Washing up after the ride, Daisy could not stop talking about Biedric. He was so handsome, and so charming, and so friendly, and she just knew he liked her as much as she liked him.

Abigail listened as she ran her washcloth over her neck. Yes, she understood. She kept thinking about Josef. They were from such different worlds, and yet they had so many interests in common, from history to language to music. She smiled in spite of herself, wondering what someone born and reared in a monarchy would think of women's suffrage. But Josef had to do the bidding of his monarch, and she had to return to Connecticut. While she could enjoy knowing him for the short time they'd be together, she knew he would soon be no more than a pleasant memory.

Maria led the way into the room as Elsa and Beĺza carried in fresh clothes for the two guests. "You are both requested to dine with the counts and the baron this evening." Abigail couldn't tell if this annoyed Maria, or if she merely disapproved of their invitation.

As the maids held up the dresses for them to admire, Daisy grew ecstatic about the magnificent creations. Hers was a billowing creation of soft yellow satin with ruffles that cascaded down the back, while Abigail's was a slim-profiled bodice and gown of creamy silk jacquard trimmed with black ribbon at the elbows and down the sides of a magnificent, flowing train. With its split skirt revealing a tucked and pleated under layer, the dress looked like an homage to the fashions of a century before. Surely Cinderella's gown could have been no finer than this!

Maria's bland familiarity with such luxury seemed almost rude. "You are expected at seven. I will escort you upstairs. In the meantime, we will practice your walk again and how to stand. The baron's assistant will be down shortly. Finish washing and the maids will dress you."

Still filled with the glow of the ride through the forest, and envisioning dinner with Josef while she wore this fairy-tale dress, for once Abigail didn't mind being ordered around by their "maid,"

Josef entered the castle's corner library with a bounce in his step. That American woman was so uncomplicated and genuine, and yet intelligent and more noble in spirit than any woman he'd ever met before. He strode past the desk and dropped into the leather chair as he pulled off his riding gloves.

Stretched out on the loveseat, Franz Antonius was reading a magazine from Paris. "You certainly seem refreshed from you little jaunt."

Josef knew better than to confide in Franz, who'd betrayed more than a few confidences when they were young, but he was feeling expansive. "I have never met anyone like her. Do you know—she is friends with the American author, Mark Twain! And she's a student at university. Can you imagine? A woman going to university!" He sighed.

Franz Antonius sat up and regarded his cousin with a frown. "You don't know what Rosamunde has in mind, do you?"

"What do you mean?" The darkness in Franz's face made Josef's stomach sink.

"You have no idea what the plan is. The real plan."

Dread washed over Josef. "No." He didn't want to hear the "real" plan, but he knew he must.

Franz leaned forward with intensity. "I need to tell you everything before you see that woman again."

CHAPTER SEVEN

A Rude Awakening

Dressed in their borrowed finery, Abigail and Daisy admitted in shared whispers that they felt like princesses going to the ball as Maria led the way to dinner. They passed a banquet hall, which could accommodate a hundred or more. Maria explained their destination was a private dining room where the monarch dined with family and favorites. Daisy let slip a giggle, but Abigail's friendly-but-stern gaze made her rein in her excitement. When they reached the dining room's door, Maria knocked, and at the order to enter, she opened the door and bid the two go inside.

Baron Mleist greeted them when they entered. The room had more of the hunting-lodge décor. Trophies hung on the wall, and a stuffed bear on its hind legs roared silently in the corner. The table could seat twelve, but six places were set. Franz Antonius sat at the head, Josef on his left, then a dark-haired younger man Abigail had not seen before. Three empty chairs awaited on Franz Antonius's right. The men were dressed in fine civilian clothing for the meal.

Abigail searched for Josef's admiring regard. But while he stood for their entry to the room, he gazed down at the table. Franz also stood for the women, even though the gesture seemed reluctant.

The baron escorted the two women to the table. Abigail glanced back at the door to see if Maria would follow and stand by in the room to serve as their chaperone, but she wasn't there and the closed door indicated she wouldn't be joining them, at least for now. Abigail sat in the place of honor on Franz's right, across from

Josef, and Daisy was given the chair next to her. The baron sat at Daisy's right.

The younger man was introduced as Baron Mleist's assistant, but as Abigail didn't catch his name. As she took her place, all her attention was on Josef. To her surprise, he kept his attention everywhere but on her. Perhaps he feared showing his interest in her among his peers. But didn't he even have the courage to look her in the eye? She lowered her head in fretful thought and admired the lovely dress she wore. When she was dressed in such splendor, how could he not look at her?

Franz glanced between the two, his usual smirk growing. He said to Abigail, "I understand you had a pleasant tour of the countryside this afternoon. I hope it met with your approval."

She said in even tones, "Yes, your countryside is quite lovely."

Franz pushed: "And the company?"

Josef occupied himself with taking a sip from his wine glass.

Abigail knew Franz was trying to provoke something, but she couldn't guess why. She might be annoyed, but she had been trained always to take the high road. "Excellent. Your cousin will make a fine ambassador for your land." She glanced at Josef to see if he reacted, but he was staring at nothing in particular on the table.

"Oh, pretty words!" Franz's eyes widened with exaggerated appreciation, and then he frowned at his cousin. "Josef, have you nothing to say in response to this fair compliment?"

Josef's eyes flitted towards Abigail for the briefest of moments. "Very generous. Thank you."

His face wore a pained expression, and Abigail's annoyance grew. Franz was enjoying their consternation, and she was afraid hers would boil over. For the betterment of all, she had to distract herself. She said to the man playing host for the evening, "Sir—I'm sorry, I'm not sure how to address you. 'My Lord'? 'Your Grace'?"

Franz chuckled. "Since you're playing Rosamunde, you should call me 'dear cousin.'"

Abigail heard the ruffle from the baron and his assistant at what had to be a breach of etiquette or possibly even an insult. She saw no need to go along with whatever game Franz Antonius was playing. "I believe 'My Lord' is appropriate for a count. If I am mistaken, I hope you'll please correct me."

"Well, whatever you called Josef would be appropriate for me as well. What did you call your charming host this afternoon?"

She'd play right into that. Any little regard she might have had for Franz Antonius disappeared. He'd missed a few spankings in his childhood, and he was the worse for it.

She said, "I called him 'sir.'"

Franz regarded her with a small smile. "Then 'sir' it is."

She nodded politely, not trusting him for a moment. In fact, she didn't trust either of them. Josef showed one face in private and another in public, while Franz enjoyed tormenting people who couldn't fight back. She indicated the animal trophies along the wall above the table. "Sir, can you please tell me what some of these creatures are? I'm not familiar with them."

Abigail didn't know if she had passed some sort of test, or if Franz Antonius knew he wouldn't get much more out of baiting her, but he allowed himself to be distracted. Until the soup arrived, he pointed out the different species and explained who had killed them and where. She wasn't interested in his stories, but it was a chance for her not to look at either man.

The meal continued with vapid, polite conversation. During the fish course, Daisy tried to ask Josef about Biedric, but before she could finish her question, it ended with an abrupt squeak as Abigail, without breaking her rhythm of slicing her salmon, delivered her friend a sharp kick at the ankle. Daisy's only response was a baffled glance at Abigail and a perplexed "Ow." The men—except for Josef— exchanged confused glances, but with no explanation forthcoming from the girls, they let the moment go and continued with the meal.

A different alcoholic beverage came with each course. In her annoyance, and at Franz's encouragement, Abigail sampled each and finished more than a few. Too late did she think better of it. Not used to so many strong spirits, she felt her head begin to swim. She asked the server to dilute her later portions with water, but it was too late.

By the time the servers had taken away dessert, Abigail could no longer focus her eyes. She had no idea how Daisy was faring—the world spun at alarming angles when she turned her head. She had been this bad off only once before, at a Christmas party at the Jacobsons' house when their oldest son—she couldn't think of that rat's name—it should be on the tip of her tongue. . . . Well, whatever his name was, he and his friend Erwin Lautenslauger had slipped hard liquor into the punch for the—Harry, Harry Jacobson, that was his name, the rat—anyway, those pests had put alcohol in the punch for the children and maiden aunts, and she was one of quite a few people who made fools of themselves. All was forgiven back in Cincinnati among friends and neighbors—except for the boys, who had to cut their own switches before they were taken out behind the woodshed—did they have royal woodsheds here?

Oh, dear, her brain was so muddled. She was about to become very silly. Her only hope was to sleap skowly—uh, speak slowly—and leave as quickly as possible. Without falling down.

She folded her napkin and set it on the table. "Gentlemen, I hope you will please forgive me, but I am a simple girl, from a simple family, in a simple country, and I'm afraid I may have. . . ." She couldn't think of a sophisticated way to say she'd had too much to drink.

Franz Antonius leaned on the table wearing a crooked grin she found oddly endearing. "Over imbibed?"

"Yes. Thank you. That is the word exactly. You are very kind. Sir. I fear I shall not be good company for the rest of the evening."

Franz Antonius got to his feet in a flash. "My dear *Fräulein*, of course. As a host, I would be most remiss if I did not escort you to your chamber myself."

Abigail wobbled as the other men at the table half-stood, muttering—were they objecting? Their words swirled around her, just out of reach.

"Now, now, gentlemen," the senior nobleman said, "I am quite capable of attending to her. Myself." He offered Abigail his arm to help her stand, which she found she needed.

Daisy rose to help her friend, but the suave Franz Antonius shooed her away. "No, please stay and continue to enjoy the evening and the company. I will be able to help Miss Smithfield myself." With a glancing apology to Baron Mleist, he corrected himself. "Oh, I'm sorry, 'the *fräulein.*'"

Abigail was aware the other men stood as she did, but she could only offer a vague thank-you and farewell before Franz helped her out of the room. In truth, she was grateful to have him as an escort because she had no idea how to get to her own room.

Franz held her arm in a firm grip as he guided her past the wavering walls and down a set of stumbling stairs. In a soft voice he said kind things, which was nice because her stomach did not feel well.

When they reached the bottom of the stairs—there seemed to be twice as many as they had climbed on their way up earlier—Franz put his arm around her waist and led the way down the hall. "We're almost there, *liebchen.* I will take good care of you."

Abigail hesitated. They had stopped in front of a door she didn't think was to her room. She didn't like this man calling her *liebchen.* Wait, she remembered now, he was a lout. And a bully. She didn't want him touching her. . . . They were alone, weren't they?

She tried to escape his arm locked around her waist. "No. You go back to your guests. I'll be fine now." She didn't feel fine, but she needed to get away from him.

Franz ignored her. "Now, now, my dear, enough with the pretense. You know how the game is played."

What game? What was he talking about? She tried to push him away, but she stumbled.

"See?" he cooed. "I help you, and you help me."

"I do *not* need your help." She pulled at his arm around her waist, but he tightened his grip. Fear choked her breath. "Let me go!"

With growing annoyance, Franz said, "We both know you don't mean that."

Abigail saw a heavy hand descend on his shoulder.

"I believe she does."

She turned her head, fighting the image of the swimming walls, and saw Josef standing behind them. A frightened Daisy watched from a few steps farther down the hall.

Josef's words had been polite, but the intensity in his eyes was not. "Cousin, I know you wish to help her, but we both know the best one to tend to her is *Fräulein* Daisy."

Franz glared at his cousin and the witness he had brought along, but after a few moments he relented. "My dear, sensible Josef, as always your judgment is excellent. We should avoid an occurrence that others might misinterpret."

He was slow to release his grip on Abigail, but she finally pulled free. After a moment's hesitation, Daisy hurried to her friend. "Come on, Abby," she said, "let's get you back to our room."

Daisy tried to lead her down the hall, but Abigail lingered, watching the cousins eye each other in bristling silence. Josef gestured back the way they had come, Franz nodded, and with a swagger he led the way. As they disappeared up the stairs, Josef gave a fleeting, concerned glance back at the women. Daisy finally got Abigail to move and guided her towards their quarters.

Abigail wasn't exactly sure what had happened, but she had black thoughts about what could have happened.

CHAPTER EIGHT

Regroup and Reconnoiter

Nursing a headache and a deep embarrassment, Abigail struggled the next morning to lift the fog from her brain and the darkness from her heart. Try though she might, she couldn't shake from her memory just how stupid she'd been—and how much it had nearly cost her. Yes, Josef had made her angry at dinner. But that was no excuse for allowing her fit of pique to channel into inattentive drinking and great personal risk.

Viewing the events from the safety of the next morning, she felt certain she hadn't encouraged Franz Antonius. He'd perpetrated an act of opportunity, and she meant no more to him than a mere diversion. Her memory wavered like the walls had the night before, but she thought he'd said something about pretenses, rules, and games, and he'd grown angry because she wasn't behaving the way he expected. Did he really assume she was a creature of the demimonde? What a selfish, despicable man!

Through her foolishness, she could have forfeited everything she held dear. She did not know these people. They were not her friends. She had no reason to trust them. In fact, by now she had many reasons not to trust them. This was no harmless Christmas party prank. She would never, *ever* let down her guard like that again.

And yet. . . . Sipping her morning coffee while the maids cleared away the breakfast dishes, she couldn't stop thinking about how Josef had come to her rescue. He wouldn't even look her in the eye during dinner . . . but when she so desperately needed him, he was there.

During breakfast, Abigail had quizzed Daisy about what happened in the dining room after she and Franz Antonius left. Hampered by her unfamiliarity with the language they used, Daisy could only say they had an "intense discussion" with Josef apparently disagreeing with the others. He ended it by getting up and asking her to go with him because they "had to find the others." He hadn't said anything on the way, and Daisy was so shocked by what she saw when they caught up with them that only afterwards did she wonder if they'd been discussing Franz's intentions.

Abigail knew Franz Antonius outranked Josef. What power could Franz wield over a person who challenged his right to do something? If her memory was correct, Josef stood up to him in a way that gave Franz a chance to retain some dignity. Abigail wondered if perhaps she wasn't the object of his rescue. As illogical as it seemed, maybe Josef intended to save Franz *from* her. She shook her foggy head. She couldn't believe that. But she didn't know what to think. Which man was Josef—the convivial companion from the horseback ride, or the spineless embarrassment from the dinner table?

Daisy returned from the toilette room and asked Abigail for the fourteenth time how she felt. "I am nearly perfect, and forever in debt to you for it."

"Oh, nonsense," Daisy protested with a blush. "You don't owe me a thing."

Abigail knew better, but she let the conversation drop when Maria entered. The woman said she was glad to see Abigail looking well this morning. "The baron and Count Ramsl will have a training session with you this morning when you are ready."

Despite her pounding head and rattled nerves, Abigail knew it was time to put her vow of strength to the test. "We can go as soon as I'm dressed."

Daisy had not been invited to Abigail's training session, but, as the maids helped Abigail into a simple gold-colored cotton morning dress, Daisy admitted she had no regrets. She had received a note during breakfast from Biedric, asking if she would be interested in a morning stroll through the castle's small gardens. Even though Abigail felt unqualified to give advice after making a fool of herself the night before, she told Daisy to "stay sensible and remember we'll be leaving here in a few days."

Steeled for her first lesson after her near-debacle, Abigail was delivered to her two tutors in the study. Baron Mleist rose behind the desk, and Josef stood before the large chair facing the desk. The baron seemed his usual businesslike self, and Josef's concern held no warmth. She looked for a sign of the charming man from yesterday's ride, but she saw nothing.

In a solicitous tone, the baron inquired about her health. She said in German, "I regret my misjudgment yesterday evening, and I thank you for your kind consideration. I shall be more circumspect in the future." That satisfied the baron, but Josef still regarded her with an aloof concern she found maddening. But she kept her promise that her emotions would not get the better of her again.

Baron Mleist explained, "The count thought you would find it useful to know something about the event you'll be attending. I agree. Her Highness has been to this on multiple occasions, and you'll need to demonstrate an appropriate familiarity."

She nodded. How nice of the count to think of that. Even if he wouldn't look her in the eye.

The baron continued, "I have not been to this particular celebration, but the count has, so he agreed to give you an introduction."

She glanced at Josef, who was studying a stack of blank papers on the desk with deep seriousness. At least, she thought, he was consistent.

The baron assured her, "I shall be here to help if I am able." He stepped away from the desk with a gesture for Josef to use it.

Josef pulled a smaller chair close to the desk and held it for

Abigail to sit. She did, without comment, and he sat in the chair vacated by the baron. Josef dipped a pen in the inkwell and began to draw lines on the top sheet of blank paper. In German he told her, "The ceremony will be held in the main square of Tirigovina. On three sides are shops and homes, while the fourth side is the cathedral. That is where Her Highness—you—will stand." He drew a long box on the plaza side of the church. "There will be a small reviewing stand built above the stairs leading up to the cathedral's door. It's level with the top step." He marked the door. "You will be inside the building before the event and come out through here."

She watched him as he explained that her attendants would be the few people who knew she was not the princess. His eyes were on the page, but hers were on him. He was so intense, as if telling her these simple details had a significance of life and death.

The baron had moved over to the seating area by the empty fireplace, where he picked up a book.

She wanted to ask Josef a question—any question—just to see what reaction she'd get, but she wasn't sure how to do it without embarrassing him or even possibly causing him trouble. She inquired in German, "What time is the ceremony?"

"Noon."

"What time will I arrive at the cathedral?"

"About a half hour before."

She nodded, then glanced at the baron, who continued to look at his book. She couldn't tell if he was really reading.

She whispered to Josef in English, "Thank you for last night."

He hesitated. He said in German, "Under normal circumstances, the ruler meets with the archbishop before the ceremony, but arrangements have been made for him to be out of the country. It's better if the archbishop doesn't know about the deception." He added in a barely audible whisper in English, "You're welcome. . . . I'm sorry about what happened."

What part was he sorry about? Her rashness with the liquor or his cousin's villainous behavior? Switching back to a normal speaking tone in German, she asked, "Are you not confident in the archbishop's discretion?"

"He's a cousin of one of the people we suspect is involved."

She nodded. That would be a problem. . . . Wait a minute. "Involved in what?"

Josef caught his breath.

Baron Mleist looked up and focused an intense gaze on Abigail.

She knew Josef had misspoken in some way, but she had no idea what to do.

The count said in even tones, "Her Highness is engaged in negotiations with certain people who wish . . . to take advantage of her youth and inexperience."

Abigail nodded as if that answered her question. With a nervous finger she tapped the paper. "So, what happens after I come out on the platform?"

Without looking at her, Josef said, "You will stand here. On your left will be either me or Franz, and on your right, off a few paces, will be Baron Mleist."

She turned to the baron. "So, you'll be able to attend the ceremony this time."

He nodded, then, after a glance at Josef, returned to his book.

Josef seemed to relax, just a little. He continued his explanation of the event. He gave her a brief history of the Sálacene and how in recent generations their relationship with the Swaviczens had become strained. His version of the Sálacene was more generous than Maria's, which didn't surprise Abigail. The ceremony would consist of a presentation by a representative of the Sálacene people, and she would be offered a few gifts of their delicacies, but she would only touch the items and the baron would accept them on her behalf. After songs and a dance or two by young people, with her escort she would go back into the cathedral and then return to the palace.

She asked, "Will anyone who knows the princess well be at the event?"

"No. Only those of us who are supporting you."

She nodded, then glanced at the baron, who had his eyes on his book. She whispered in English, "Thank you for doing this for me."

He regarded her, and then he looked down at the papers and replied in German in deliberate tones, "My loyalty is always to my monarch and my country."

His dark brown eyes had been so unreadable, but for a moment she had seen regret. She wished she understood it.

In abject misery, Josef sat alone on the study's sofa by the dark fireplace. He had just given Abigail a road map of the day that would most certainly be her last on Earth. This wonderful woman listened with such care to his instructions, as if any of it mattered. She even helped him get through his terrible slip of the tongue, although she could have no idea what it meant—and that he had given her a hint of her own doom.

If Franz was right, sweet, intelligent Abigail would be dead by the end of the ceremony. It was the most logical place for an assassin to strike. Out in the square, with a large crowd, the sound of gunfire would echo and no one would know where the shot had come from. The assassin would get away and the conspirators would have their victory, but their success would seal their fate.

Why did Franz have to tell him the truth about the plot against Rosamunde and Abigail's role in defeating it? Josef knew he could have been just as effective a Judas goat without knowing he was leading the lamb to slaughter. If only he could do something to help her. But he could not protect her without putting himself and his family in jeopardy.

Franz Antonius marched into the study and threw his gloves on the desk. "We have a problem, cousin."

Josef regarded him with a cool gaze. They had patched up their disagreement from the night before. Or, at least, Franz had forgiven him for his interference. "What is it? Will there be bad weather for the ceremony?"

"No. But there will be a storm of another kind. I just found out Gregorski, Medyev, and Guttmann are going to be there."

Josef launched to his feet. "*What?*" Those three men from the royal council of advisers were the primary suspects in the threat to kill Rosamunde. Why would they put themselves in jeopardy by being there? "They never come to this."

"I know," Franz fumed. "Gregorski sent Živo as his messenger. He said 'they were coming to show their support for their sovereign in her time of need.'" He coughed a mocking laugh. "More likely they're coming to make sure the job gets done right and they can be there to take control when it happens. The jackals!"

Josef's heart sank. Then he brightened, though he tried to hide it. He couldn't have dared to pray for this salvation. He hoped he sounded regretful as he said, "Then we must find a way to call off the ceremony. They'll recognize her as an impostor."

Franz grumbled, "You may be right." He scrutinized his cousin.

Josef hoped his true feelings were well hidden.

"However," Franz concluded, "how to proceed is not our decision. That's up to our dear sovereign."

Josef's hope faded when he read the note on royal letterhead that Franz Antonius handed him an hour later.

> *"Gentlemen, while this seems like a setback, it's a test to make sure you have the right person. Tell her that people who'll know her to be an impostor will be there. If she panics, she lacks the necessary mettle. Send her back with our thanks. If she accepts the challenge, she's what we need. Proceed."*

Franz took the note back. "What do you think your university girl will do?"

Josef gritted his teeth as he watched his cousin set a match to the note and toss it into the study's empty fireplace. It flared, blazed for a few moments, then gave up and crumbled into ash. Just like his hopes, he thought. "We'll find out soon enough."

CHAPTER NINE

A Useful Anger

In their room, after the maids had cleared away the afternoon tea dishes, Daisy dreamed aloud about Biedric while Frau Meyer used Abigail as a living dress form and fitted the collar of an outfit intended for Princess Rosamunde. To her surprise, Abigail realized the brusque woman had become fond of her.

With stiff red-and-black floral brocade pinned to the sleeves and bodice, the rich, smoky-red satin dress had a tall collar with more of the brocade and a small ruche of pleated lace around the top. Lavish gold buttons extended from the collar down to the waist. Standing before the full-length triple mirror that had been brought into the room, Abigail marveled at her reflection and the stunning ensemble.

"With your neck," the older woman explained, "you should either have a high collar such as this or wear something down across here." She held a swath of extra fabric across Abigail's chest just below her collarbones. "Something across here," she placed the fabric at the base of Abigail's neck," is not good for you. Up or down. But not in the middle."

Abigail had never thought about the shape of her face, or how the cut of a neckline could be so important, and she felt honored to have this talented woman's advice. "I'm so grateful you're teaching me this."

Frau Meyer nodded. "I'm happy to do this for you." She considered for a moment, then fiddled with the collar brocade as she leaned in next to Abigail's ear. In a barely audible whisper, she said, "You listen. You don't tell me my job."

Abigail looked at Frau Meyer and caught a knowing glimmer in her eye. The young American managed not to chuckle as she glanced in the mirror at the reflection of the reading Maria, who sat by the door. She said in a soft voice, "A wise woman always listens to a person who knows what she's talking about."

Frau Meyer nodded as she tried to suppress a smile. "Yes," she said in a resonant voice, "this style is very good for you." She turned Abigail to the side as she examined the dress's profile in the mirror. She signaled the maids to bring the ensemble's elegant and simple jacket and help Abigail put it on. As the dressmaker buttoned up the snug top, which had flourishes of lace at the collar and cuffs but no brocade, she said, "I wish you could wear this in Tirigovina. Fullness in the back, but no train. Perfect for moving on that wooden platform. You wouldn't want it to get snagged. Trains are good only when they don't get in the way." She spoke with a firmness that told Abigail she'd had that conversation before with someone else and lost.

Abigail faced the mirror again and admired her reflection. How regal she felt in this exquisite dress! She would never view clothes the same way. If she could find the money, a few things worthy of *Harper's Bazar* might find their way into her closet back home. She shivered. Frau Meyer smiled and patted Abigail's arms in encouragement.

The dressmaker said, "Now change out of that into a dressing gown. I have received a makeup kit. We need to work on your face."

A knock on the door stopped Abigail from undoing her top button. In the mirror's reflection she watched Maria open the door. When she saw Maria curtsy, she turned around.

Franz Antonius and Josef came into the room, and the maids turned to give respectful curtsies. This was the first time Abigail had seen Franz since the confrontation of the night before. Seeing him made her more angry that fearful. On the other hand, seeing Josef's grim sadness tightened her stomach into a knot.

The senior nobleman greeted the staff in German with a polished gesture of generosity. "My good women, you'll please excuse us. We must meet with the *fräulein* to discuss matters at hand."

The maids nodded and began to leave. As Frau Meyer followed

them, Daisy looked to Abigail for a translation, and, when she heard it, Daisy said, "I'm not leaving . . . am I?"

Abigail shook her head with a small smile of reassurance.

As the others took their leave, Franz Antonius approached Abigail with a solicitous nod. Still speaking in German, he said, "You appear to be feeling much better this morning. I'm glad."

She thought "No thanks to you," but instead she responded, "To what do we owe this visit?"

Franz said, "There's been . . . a complication."

Abigail frowned. "What kind of complication?"

Josef answered, "Three men who are well acquainted with Her Highness will be attending the ceremony. When they see you, they'll know you're an impostor."

Abigail tried to interpret how Josef had said this. He seemed troubled, almost as if he were trying to frighten her. And yet his words were neutral and matter-of-fact.

She looked at Franz Antonius. "So, what's your plan?"

He slid into a chair. "At the moment, we don't have one."

Franz seemed as unconcerned as Josef appeared worried. This did not bode well. Abigail grew annoyed, despite her vow to stay calm and in control of herself. She asked, "Can you prevent them from attending?"

Franz's attention drifted around the room, finally settling on the half-done trim of her dress. "Even if that were possible, it would be suspicious."

She didn't care for his lassitude. What a fine archduke he would make someday.

Daisy asked what was going on, and when Abigail told her, she shook with alarm. "Well, that's not going to work."

"I know."

Daisy asked Josef and Franz Antonius, "What'll happen if the men find out Abigail isn't the real princess?"

Franz replied with a languid, "There could be a bad reaction from the crowd, but the soldiers would be there to protect her."

Daisy's eyes flashed with fear. "You can't go, Abby."

At Daisy's words, Abigail thought she saw a flicker of hope in Josef's eyes. So, he didn't want her to go, did he?

Abigail asked the men, "Can you delay the ceremony until they go away?"

Franz shook his head. "No. They're coming to show their support. They'll wait."

"Shall the princess stay 'indisposed'?"

"No," Franz Antonius said.

"Perhaps one of you could preside over the ceremony in her place." She looked at one cousin, then the other. Neither was giving her something she could interpret.

Franz said, "That wouldn't solve the problem."

Tired of their shilly-shallying, she demanded, "Do you want me to attend the event or not?"

Josef said nothing, merely looking anxious. Franz said with an indolent shrug, "It would be better if you went, but. . . ."

Abigail felt disgusted. Someone had to solve this, and apparently that someone was her. She remembered the makeup kit Frau Meyer mentioned. "How close will they be to me? Less than ten feet?"

Josef nodded. "For at least a short time, they will stand directly in front of you."

That scuttled the makeup plan Frau Meyer had. Abigail knew there had to be a way out of this, even if these useless men couldn't help. Oh, they were making her angry all over again.

Abigail had minimized her high school acting history when she saw Lord Zaaf's horror back in Graz. Not only had she starred in *Twelfth Night* and *Much Ado About Nothing,* she'd also acted in several modern plays and helped backstage with even more. She knew a few makeup tricks, albeit ones painted with a broad brush for a theatre setting. She also recalled something her older brother Sam told her when he was teaching himself sleight-of-hand tricks. The best way to keep people from seeing something was to make them look at something else. He'd been referring to hiding coins, but the same principle applied here. An idea began to hatch. Could she do it? Her confidence grew. It was worth a try.

She glanced at the small table they used for their meals, then the largest window in the room. She said to the men, "Take the table and put it over in front of that window."

Josef took a step towards the table, but Franz Antonius only stared at her in bafflement.

She glared at the lazy fool. "Do you want me to help you or not?"

His only response was a blink of surprise.

"Then get off your hinder and help move that table."

With a look of astonishment he got to his feet and joined his cousin in shifting the table.

Abigail went to the room's door and opened it, startling the guard. "Send for Frau Meyer," she commanded. "And tell her to bring the makeup case and a table mirror."

She returned and asked Daisy to find a cloth that she could use to drape over her dress to keep the makeup from staining it. Daisy went to search the toilette room.

The men had moved the table to the spot in front of the window. Abigail pointed to a small chair and said to neither man in particular, "Move the chair over in front of the table." Franz hesitated, and Josef picked it up.

Frau Meyer came in, followed by Maria carrying the theatrical makeup case. The dressmaker asked, "Are we doing this in front of the gentlemen?"

Abigail took the case and walked towards the table. "Yes, if they want to watch. Where's the mirror?"

She answered, "I sent a maid for it. She should be—"

Beĺza bustled in with a pedestaled looking glass. "Where do you want it, miss?"

Abigail sat at the table, and Beĺza set down the mirror in front of her. Abigail moved it so she could see her reflection the full but indirect sunlight. She opened the case and found a combination of theatrical makeup and the subtle powders for women of society. Good, she would need both to make this work.

Daisy, Belza, and Frau Meyer gathered around as she pulled out the greasepaint sticks of red and white along with a small mixing plate. Even Josef came a little closer to watch the proceedings. She squeezed out dabs of greasepaint and mixed them into a dark pink. She asked the men, "Has the princess ever had the English measles?"

Franz Antonius said, "I don't believe so."

Josef nodded. "Your family was away. Yes, she did, when she turned eleven."

Abigail's heart fell as she looked at her reflection. Then she thought of something else and asked the cousins, "What about *windpoken?*"

They thought, then shook their heads. Josef's face lit up, and he regarded her with both admiration and dread.

Years ago, when Abigail had nursed her little brother through his bout, she never thought it would prove useful. She could also savor the small amount of revenge on the woman who'd put her in this mess.

Daisy didn't understand. "What's 'vind pokin'?"

Abigail mixed up a second lump of red and white greasepaint, this one three parts white to one part red. "I am giving Her Highness the chickenpox."

As Abigail concocted the greasepaint brews for her fake lesions, she asked questions: "My cheekbones and nose, correct?"

Frau Meyer nodded. "Yes. Her Highness's cheekbones are higher and her nose is narrower."

"Does the princess like these gentlemen who will be attending?"

Franz Antonius snorted a laugh. "Not at all."

Abigail had begun to know Rosamunde as vain, headstrong, and perhaps, like Franz Antonius, someone who enjoyed the discomfort of others. That would make this easier.

"Does the princess wear hats with veils?"

"Yes," answered Frau Meyer. "She has several."

"Please have a maid fetch one with a light, summer veil."

After a moment of hesitation, Frau Meyer gave the instruction to Maria to tell the royal wardrobe keeper that using something from Her Highness's current closet was absolutely necessary. Maria seemed reluctant, but she obeyed and went on her errand.

To the men, Abigail said, "Tell me about how these men will interact with the princess. Will they bow and greet her? Will we exchange words?"

Franz answered, "No, you don't have to speak to them. And the correct greeting to Her Highness is for them to kiss her hand."

Abigail tried not to smile. That would make this even easier still. "I assume the princess will wear gloves in public."

"Of course," Frau Meyer replied.

"Daisy," Abigail said, "I have a pair of cream gloves in my bag. Will you please find them for me?"

"Certainly." Daisy went in search of the items.

By the time Maria returned carrying a brown hat with a fine, lightweight veil, Abigail had created a collection of what looked like small blisters on her face. Even the unflappable Maria flinched at the sight. With some effort, Abigail managed to add one last faux lesion on the back of her right wrist between the hem of her glove and the cuff of her sleeve. With Frau Meyer's help, she donned the hat and pulled down the veil.

She studied her reflection in the light of the window. The spots on her face even frightened her a little. For all the world she appeared to be a woman who should be resting in bed with an ice pack on her forehead. "Gentlemen, what do you think? Will I pass for the princess, still somewhat indisposed?"

In the mirror she saw Franz Antonius smiling broadly, nodding his approval. Josef looked both amazed and pained. What did this man want from her?

But their opinions didn't matter. They wanted this to work. She needed a better test.

Abigail said, "Send for Baron Mleist."

When the baron entered the room, he greeted Franz Antonius with, "You sent for me, My Lord?" Then he did an embarrassed double-take when he noticed the woman in the fine red dress and veiled hat standing ramrod straight beside the two cousins. He immediately bowed and stuttered his apology: "Forgive me, Your Highness! I didn't expect you down here."

The woman held out her hand for him to kiss so he could make his amends, and he dutifully stepped forward and took her gloved hand. As he closed his eyes and placed his lips on the glove, Franz Antonius erupted with laughter.

The baron shot him a puzzled frown, and then he looked more closely at the woman. He recoiled in horror. "Your Highness—what has happened?" He squinted and examined her face, then swore roundly in Swaviczen at Franz Antonius, which made the nobleman laugh all the more.

Abigail lifted the veil and apologized to the fuming baron. "I hope you'll forgive me, sir. But surely you must agree this test was necessary."

The simmering nobleman gathered himself. "Yes, *Fräulein.* I have every confidence in the outcome." With Franz's permission, he took his leave.

In the flush of success, Abigail could share a bit of Franz's mirth.

But the pained expression on Josef's face drained her self-assurance. He seemed both proud of her and terribly sad at the same time. How could that be? Didn't he want her to succeed?

Abigail and Daisy dined that evening with Franz Antonius and Baron Mleist. Franz apologized on behalf of his cousin, saying he was away "attending to a matter of duty." Abigail wondered what duty could take him away at this time of day, but she was almost past the point of trying to decipher him.

The four dined in polite civility with the conversations spoken in English for Daisy's sake. Having learned her lesson, Abigail avoided most of the served alcoholic beverages and asked the staff to water down the ones she did have.

The only trouble during the meal came from without. From a distance, and an unknown direction, they heard a woman shouting in a burst of anger. The two men froze at the tirade, while Abigail and Daisy looked at each other. Abigail recognized the woman was speaking in German, but from so far away she couldn't understand the words.

Daisy said, "She sure is angry."

Franz Antonius addressed the baron in low-voiced German, "I told him not to tell her." He finished the thought, whatever it was, in Swaviczen. The baron nodded.

After another few moments the anger was spent, and silence followed. The men resumed eating.

Abigail said to the baron, "Sir, I assume no one behaves that way when the princess is in residence."

The men shared a long glance. The baron replied, "That is true. No one would dare behave that way in the presence of Her Highness."

Daisy smiled. "That would be a first-class ticket to getting fired." The men agreed. "Although," she continued, "my aunt and uncle have a cook who's a living terror. But she's the best cook in Connecticut, so they put thicker doors on the kitchen."

The baron considered her words, then chuckled. "That is very practical of them."

Franz Antonius gave the baron a sly smile. "Yes, Mleist, perhaps you should recommend thicker doors."

The baron's only reply was a frown. He changed the topic of conversation, and the meal continued in peace.

CHAPTER TEN

The Suspects

The next morning, as a warm rain tapped against the study window, Abigail had a last lesson with Josef and the baron before their scheduled departure for the capital. Josef was grim and circumspect, which she had decided must be his real self. The baron watched Josef as much as he watched her.

With his drawing of the plaza on the desk in the study, Josef reviewed the plan one more time. Using the royal coaches, they would leave Chetova in the late afternoon and arrive at the palace in Tirigovina, where Abigail and Daisy would be taken to the back entrance. With only servants from Chetova Castle attending the Americans, the regular palace staff would not know about the foreign guests. Late tomorrow morning, Abigail would travel by coach to a side door of the cathedral. If she encountered anyone, she should only nod to acknowledge their bows and keep going.

He said, "At noon you'll go out the cathedral door facing the town plaza onto the platform. There are steps that lead down to the ground so the Sálacene leader can make his way up to offer you the gifts and repeat the loyalty vow. Then a young boy and girl will bring food, followed by a girl with flowers. Then down on the plaza level a group will perform two dances. When the dances are over, the Sálacene leader will declare the festival started and you'll acknowledge the crowd and return to the cathedral, and then the coach will take you back to the palace."

"When will I meet the three men who'll know I'm not the princess?"

Josef took a deep breath as he stared at the drawing. "There is no precedent for this, so we believe they'll be waiting for you on the platform when we go out."

She brightened in spite of herself. "You'll be there with me, too?"

He nodded, not quite looking at her. "Yes, I will."

"Thank you," she said, thinking she saw a fleeting glimmer of kindness.

With the baron watching him, Josef seemed to be deciding exactly what to say. "You are welcome." He tapped the handmade map. "Franz will not be on the platform with us. I believe the plan is for him to be in the plaza with a detachment of soldiers. The council of advisers always likes to have soldiers visible on the roads leading in and out of the square in case of trouble."

"Has there been trouble in the past?"

"No. But we don't wish for this to be the first time."

She agreed with their caution. "So, do I need to know who these men are?"

Josef nodded and moved aside the map to reveal a formal photographic portrait of a thick-set man in his fifties with wild pepper-and-salt hair and a scowl that descended into deep jowls. He wore a civilian suit with a number of splendid medals pinned to the jacket. "This is Michael Gregorski. He's the head of the princess's council of advisers, which is similar to the Privy Council in England. His mother is from one of the important families of Swavicza, but she made a morganatic marriage to a commoner." He glanced at her as if to confirm she understood this disqualified him from the noble ranks. "Gregorski was appointed to the council because he's extremely wealthy and well-connected. Rosamunde had no choice. Her uncle, the late king, owed Gregorski a large sum of money, and when she ascended he offered to forgive the debt if she put him on the council. Then she suffered another humiliation when the other council members overruled her choice and made him their leader."

"It seems your cousin doesn't have as much authority as her male predecessors."

Josef's brows knit briefly, and then he looked at her. "I'm not her cousin. Franz is. His mother is from my family, and his father is from Rosamunde's. I'm not related to Her Highness."

Abigail felt an odd thrill at this revelation. Not only did this mean Josef wasn't part of this unpleasant woman's family, but also this was the first time he'd spoken to her in a natural tone—and looked her in the eye—since the horse ride. He withdrew back into formality as he glanced at the baron, who eyed him closely, and he returned his gaze to the photograph on the table. But for a moment she'd seen the other Josef.

Baron Mleist replied to her observation: "Women are not supposed to assume the Falcon Throne."

Abigail wasn't familiar with the turn of phrase, and she realized her confusion read on her face when Josef said, "The Falcon Throne is the symbol of the Swaviczen monarchy."

"Oh." The image of a jewel-encrusted seat topped with a glittering, gold falcon lit her imagination. "Will I have a chance to see it?"

The young count replied with mild chagrin, "No. It was stolen by a Hungarian prince during one of the last crusades."

"Haven't you tried to get it back?"

Baron Mleist ignored her sensible question and returned to the point. "The issue is things here are unsettled until she marries."

Aware of the baron's gaze, Abigail decided against responding to Josef's moment of openness. She said, "So, is that why she's 'indisposed'? She's searching for a husband before the council picks one for her?"

The baron nodded with a small smile. "You are an astute observer, *Fräulein.*"

She responded, "Men underestimate women at their peril."

She'd meant it as a witty retort, but his squint made her regret her attempt at humor between intellectual equals. In his eyes, she was not an equal. And perhaps it would be better if they did underestimate her. Hoping to deflect his scrutiny, she said, "But what do I know? I'm from a country that trades new leaders for old every four years."

Her statement had the desired effect. He gave a soft chuckle and returned his attention to the photograph on the desk.

She looked at Josef, and he quickly returned his gaze to the desktop. She realized he had been watching her through the exchange. Why couldn't he simply talk with her about . . . whatever it was that was eating away at him? Many things were happening below the surface here, but she couldn't figure it out. If nothing else, she wanted to respect their ways, even as her frustration grew. Small country, big rigmarole. Maybe the protocol and formality helped them feel important in the shadow of the large empires that ruled their part of the world.

Josef pulled the photographic portrait aside, revealing a second photograph of a man in his early fifties, balding, with graying sideburns that extended down into a beard below the line of his chin. "Vasily Medyev. His Russian grandfather purchased a small *Herrschaft*—similar to a baronetcy—that had become extinct. He bought the national bank a few years ago to keep the country solvent. I've heard he uses it to support Swaviczen business and drain money away from the Sálacene."

"Is that legal?" she asked.

"It shouldn't be, and it's stupid if it's true. But it's his bank."

She frowned. America had more than its share of business magnates who robbed the poor to line their pockets. Back home they even had a new term for people like Medyev—"robber baron." But here was a genuine robber baronet.

Josef continued, "Medyev is well connected with the financial leaders in the German Empire and in our neighboring country of Werenzland, which is not always an ally. The late king Rosamunde's father put Medyev on the council to help keep some control over his banking empire, and also to make sure he didn't manipulate the currency."

Abigail wondered why Josef was going into such detail about men she would only interact with for a few moments. It was almost as if he respected her thoughts and wanted her insights. She glanced at the baron, who had his eyes on Josef. She recalled the earlier incident when Josef had misspoken somehow and earned the baron's attention. She would not ask Josef about his motive.

He moved that photograph away to reveal an engraving of a man who had an unappealing lean-and-hungry look about him: late forties, with prominent cheekbones and sunken cheeks accentuated by his hooked nose and pose in profile. Unlike the others, this man was smiling, as if off in the distance he saw something he liked.

"Wolfgang Guttmann," Josef explained. "Fourth son of a landgrave. For six generations a member of his family has been either in personal attendance to a king or on the council. But in the recession five years ago, the main branch of the family lost most of its fortune. I'm told his oldest brother, the current landgrave, has given him the task of restoring the family's position or leave Swavicza. He himself lives simply, but the rumors say he's wealthy and trying to hide his money so his brother doesn't take it from him."

Abigail spread out the images of the three men. "A veritable viper's nest. Why do they want to show their public support now? Is one of them angling to become the princess's husband?"

The baron nodded with a quiet "Huh."

Josef stroked his chin. "I hadn't thought of that. One of them might be planning that in secret. These men are not friends, and it's not usual for them to be acting together." He and the baron exchanged a thoughtful glance. "Gregorski isn't married. Medyev was, but I don't know if he still is."

The baron added, "He is. But he has sons. And so does Guttmann."

Josef said to him, "It would be wise to watch them to ascertain possible motives. We might separate the wheat from the chaff."

Baron Mleist nodded to Josef, then to Abigail. He said, "I'm sorry you're not a man. You would have made a fine strategist."

She had backed off before, but she chose not to this time. "Sometimes the clearest perspective comes from the person who's the least obvious."

He pondered that, then gave her a polite nod.

She turned to Josef and asked, "And what happens after the ceremony in the plaza?"

Josef seemed caught off-guard by the question and looked away. "Well, that depends on Her Highness."

She wanted to know what he meant, but before she could ask, Josef nodded to the two of them and departed. How unrelentingly frustrating he had become! She knew if she could have two minutes alone with him she could make him tell her everything.

The Dress Rehearsal

The morning shower had passed, and as the sun peeped out between the pleasant afternoon's clouds, the caravan of three closed carriages exited Chetova Castle for the journey to the capital city of Tirigovina. At the lead rode a cadre of soldiers, then the coach with Abigail, Daisy, Baron Mleist, and Maria. Following on horseback came Franz Antonius and Josef, accompanied by Josef's soldiers including, to Daisy's delight, Biedric Halle. Then a carriage with Frau Meyer, Belza, and the other maids from the castle; a wagon of luggage; and, bringing up the rear, another coach with what appeared to be miscellaneous staff members.

As they descended from the dark mountains, the forest gave way to rolling hills and farmland interspersed with patches of trees. What a lovely place, Abigail thought, but for the first time on this summer's sojourn she missed Cincinnati. She longed to see the "seven hills" and the river rolling past on its endless journey to the sea. What she'd give to see a sternwheeler setting off for Louisville! More than that, she wanted her freedom back. She wanted to walk down a street without a guard. She wanted to talk with her mother and her friends. She wanted to go to a baseball game and hear a band concert after a picnic. She wanted to hear *Hail, Columbia!* She hadn't realized there were so many little things that meant so much to her.

Abigail said to Daisy, who was sitting next to Baron Mleist, "I'm sorry we won't be home in time for Independence Day." She sighed. "Missing that holiday didn't seem so important before we left."

Daisy perked up. "We can pretend."

They shared a smile. In a soft voice, Abigail began to sing, "'O, say can you see. . . .'"

Daisy shook her head with a giggle. "No, I can't sing that! It's too high!"

Abigail understood. "'My country, 'tis of thee. . . .'"

Daisy joined in quietly, "'Sweet land of liberty. . . .'"

In the tone of a sad lullaby, the two completed the song's first chorus under the bemused gaze of their Swaviczen hosts. When they finished, they shared a melancholy chuckle.

The baron asked, "What is this?"

"It's one of our country's patriotic songs."

He frowned. "I can't imagine singing a national song in a way that's not full and proud."

Abigail said, "We are full and proud."

Daisy added sweetly, "We just don't have to shout it."

Abigail smiled at her friend. The more she got to know Daisy, the more she appreciated the girl's deceptive strength and intelligence. Wherever the two of them ended up, she knew she and Daisy must always remain great friends.

Daisy's smile faded. "Oh, I'd just love some roasted chicken and corn on the cob." Abigail agreed. Daisy closed her eyes. "I'm going to pretend I'm at a picnic right now. Umm, what a spread!"

Maria quizzed Abigail about what Daisy had said, and after Abigail explained, the woman grimaced. "You eat maize? We feed that to our pigs!"

In a whisper Daisy asked for a translation, and when she got it she offered her friend a small smile. "More corn for us."

Abigail couldn't help but laugh, to Maria's deep displeasure.

A call came from outside, and the carriage rolled to a halt. Josef appeared on horseback next to the window. "We have to stop for a few minutes."

"Is there a problem?" the baron asked.

"No, they need to make some adjustments. It shouldn't be more than ten minutes." The baron nodded, apparently understanding what that meant. Josef turned his horse around and headed towards the end of the caravan.

Abigail asked, "How far are we?"

"About halfway to Tirigovina," the baron answered.

Tired of bouncing along the road, she stretched and yawned, then offered an apology. "I need to walk for a bit."

The baron didn't like the idea, but he nodded. He explained the plan to Maria and told her to accompany Abigail. Maria protested that she was comfortable and didn't want to go, but with a grumble she obeyed and got out of the carriage.

Abigail stepped out and looked back at the rest of the caravan. The problem seemed to be with the last coach. She couldn't see what was happening, but Josef and Franz Antonius were there, and the maids from the second carriage were also gathered around the door.

Maria said, "If you wish to walk, we will go this way." She indicated the opposite direction.

Heading away from the hubbub was fine with Abigail. She turned as Daisy stepped down from the carriage. "Want to come along?"

Before she even finished her question she saw Daisy searching for Biedric, who was with the soldiers still behind their carriage. She saw him, he saw her, they smiled at each other, and Abigail knew her friend would not be going for a stroll.

With Maria two steps behind, Abigail walked down the road. They reached a wooded patch between farm fields. Abigail could see well-kept farm buildings in the distance, and cattle in a nearby pasture looked plump and happy.

She tried to engage Maria in some chit-chat, but the woman had no taste for it. So Abigail concentrated on getting her legs stretched before she had to finish the ride in the cramped coach.

They were around a bend in the road when a soldier from the caravan caught up with them. He spoke to Maria in Swaviczen. She said to Abigail, "I'm needed back at the carriage. We must return."

Abigail replied, "They need you, but they don't need me. You go ahead."

Maria frowned. "You must come with me."

At the risk of being petty with her humorless keeper, Abigail gave a casual gesture around at the countryside. "Where am I going to go? I'll be fine."

"No," she demanded, "you must come with me."

The soldier spoke to her with urgency.

Abigail said, hoping there was no gloat in her voice, "You'd best hurry."

With a grumble of disgust, Maria followed the soldier.

Abigail savored the moment. What would she do with her few minutes of freedom? She looked around and noticed people in a field on the other side of a copse of trees. Even though they were doing fieldwork, they began singing. She couldn't resist the appeal of their music. She spotted a footpath and went through the small woods.

She emerged into a field where a family weeded along rows of grapevines. They sang in a language she didn't recognize, but even if she couldn't understand the words she knew it was a jovial song and even the children were singing along.

One of the children spotted her and with a gasp alerted the others. The singing stopped, and the family stared at the well-dressed stranger with alarm . . . and not a small amount of awe.

Abigail felt embarrassed at her intrusion. A man, who looked to be the father of the three children, took off his cap, and the boys and grandfather followed suit.

Interrupting them was not what Abigail had intended. She asked, "*Sprechen sie deutsch?*"

The man nodded with a stumbling, "*Ja.*"

"I'm sorry to intrude," she said in German. "I didn't mean to disturb you. Your music was enchanting. I just had to hear it more clearly."

The man nodded, and the two older children approached, tentatively. "Thank you for saying so. We are only singing a work song."

"With such a song, it must make work easier." She took a step towards the nearest vine. "I see you're growing grapes. What kind?"

Surprised and honored by her interest, the farmer began explaining the different grapes and what wines they were for. Some were for the noble family who owned the land, some for the village festival in the fall, and some for his family. Abigail noticed one of the children dash off, but she didn't think about it as the farmer continued his explanations. She'd grown up in a beer-drinking part of the world, so wine grapes were exotic indeed.

A short time later, with surprise she saw the little boy return with about twenty people. Some openly gawked at her, and others whispered and giggled excitedly amongst themselves. Abigail assumed they were from neighboring farms, but she couldn't understand why they were so interested in their unexpected visitor.

The farmer's talk was interrupted when the group saw someone beyond Abigail, and many of them nodded or gave unpolished curtsies. She turned to see Josef standing a short distance behind her, holding the reins of his horse. He regarded her with mild amazement. The farmer greeted him in Swaviczen, and Josef responded in kind. The man gushed to Josef about their visitor. From their familiarity, Abigail could tell he and Josef knew each other. Josef's reply to the farmer's comments made all of the people nod with deep respect.

He told Abigail in German, "The carriages are ready. We have to go back."

She thanked the farmer and his family, and the others said their goodbyes to her, some in German but most in Swaviczen. She returned with Josef towards the path through the wooded area. She patted the mannerly Hercules, who nickered in response, then walked ahead of man and horse on the narrow path. From behind her, she heard barely suppressed shouts of excitement from the group.

After they emerged from the trees onto the road, she thought about walking next to the horse, who might be better company, but she knew she shouldn't waste this brief time alone with Josef. She let him catch up with her and dropped in next to him. "You know that family?"

"Yes. This land belongs to my father."

"So you're 'the nice noble family' he talked about."

She watched for his reaction to the compliment, but he kept it to himself. "Pavi's a good farmer and a good man. Why did you go talk with them?"

"They were singing. I just wanted to hear them." Before they rounded the bend in the road, she glanced back at the group, which was still gathered in the field, buzzing with excitement. "Why were they so interested in me?"

Josef tried to contain a smile. "They thought you were Her Highness."

A short laugh of surprise escaped her. So they thought she was the princess? Well, perhaps that wasn't so odd, given that she was wearing the princess's hairstyle and one of her castoff dresses.

She chuckled again as they walked. In a moment of royal prerogative, she slipped her hand around Josef's arm. He stiffened with surprise, then awkwardly tucked his arm to provide a hand rest for her. Clearly he wasn't comfortable, but at least he had accepted her gesture.

Emboldened, she asked, "Are you ever going to tell me what's truly going on and why you're so different from the first day I met you?"

His face grew stony. "If the opportunity arises."

"The opportunity is not now?"

"No."

She waited for more, but none came. Still, she refused to let his gloom dampen her success at the opening act of her masquerade. "Well, I would say my first royal audience went well."

"Yes," he replied, his face still revealing no emotion.

"Then I shall consider it a good sign for tomorrow."

"I pray to God you're right."

She shuddered at the grim intensity in his words, but before she could reply he gently removed her hand from his arm and indicated for her to walk ahead of him. A moment later they rounded a curve and came within sight of the caravan. She stepped ahead and didn't speak to him the rest of the way back.

Despite her silence, her mind was churning. She understood now that he knew the reason for the strange, tight-lipped behavior around her. Yet his slip during her first lesson, along with the baron's reaction to it and subsequent eagle-eyed observation of him, told her he wasn't as much of an insider as the others. Should she trust him? She needed a friend. More than that, she *wanted* to trust him. For the time being, she would follow his lead until the situation compelled her to act on her own.

CHAPTER TWELVE

The Stage is Set

The caravan rolled into Tirigovina after the last hues of sunset faded from the western sky. By peering around the edge of the carriage's window curtains, Abigail could see the small country's modest capital, which was nestled in a valley between dark mountains. The town resembled an engraving of a fairytale city, only not so cheerful. Half-timbered houses leaned cheek by jowl with masonry buildings and old wooden structures. Just before they reached the incongruous and modern train station, the road became paved with a flat stone surface. She saw no signs of an urban night life, and despite the warm summer evening she saw only one open café. A detachment of soldiers saluted as the carriages passed through a wide gate in a medieval wall.

The town inside the wall was more of the same, only older. A few large homes indicated wealth and a short-lived building boom sometime in the last century. The caravan rattled through the large plaza ringed by buildings from various parts of the last three hundred years. Abigail recalled Josef's map when the cathedral appeared as a dark, looming shape at the far corner of the plaza. With no lights visible through the stained glass windows, it became an ominous shadow as they approached it. Along the opposite side of the plaza sat wagons and carts, with people gathered around them in the evening air. She guessed the Sálacene were already here in anticipation of the morrow. She noticed there were no gas streetlights, only lamps with sturdy candles. She could almost believe the coach had rolled into a different century.

The caravan traveled past the cathedral and down a narrow street lined with medieval and half-timbered buildings that overhung the thoroughfare, giving it a dark, cramped feel. The road of old shops and the occasional newer storefront eventually widened into a stately boulevard. After a block, on the right appeared a large and modern-looking metal fence. Soldiers with torches opened the fence's gate at their approach, and the lead carriage rolled through and up the drive to the palace. The royal residence, although small by the standards of other European countries, gleamed with eighteenth-century style and grandeur.

The first carriage moved past the building's main entrance. As arranged, the second carriage stopped in front of the steps that led up to the entrance. Looking back through the curtains, Abigail could see the maids emerge and, with a great fuss to attract any passing attention, headed up to the door. The first carriage traveled around the corner as soldiers followed the maids up the steps.

Their coach went to the back of the building and stopped before what appeared to be a service entrance. With their veils pulled down, Abigail and Daisy descended from the carriage with Maria and headed for the door. Carrying their light travel bags, including the all-important makeup kit, they passed two guards watching palace servants haul in boxes of produce. Maria said to the Americans in a voice loud enough for all to hear, "Her Highness has arranged for you to stay in the guest quarters. Please come with me, and I'll show you the way."

They followed Maria through a labyrinth of halls and back ways. The group climbed a steep and gloomy staircase to a room fronted by a modest door. Maria ushered the girls into what looked like the anteroom of a suite. Two small cots were made up on one side of the windowless chamber.

Maria said, "These are your sleeping quarters. Through the door on the left is a room for your toilette with a washstand and a close stool. This is the only suite in this section with such a washroom, so know you're honored guests in the best accommodations. Don't use the room on the right. The bedding hasn't been prepared, and we don't want you to suffer with stale sheets. Guards will be in the hall if you need something. The maids will come to help you in the morning. I will be back then. Have a good night's sleep." She went out through the door, which Abigail noticed she didn't lock behind her. Of course, with guards outside there would be no need.

Abigail explained to Daisy what Maria had said. The girl couldn't resist and went to open the door on the right, where she found a master suite on a par with their room in Chetova Castle. Daisy sighed at the nice décor, then closed the door and put her bag next to one of the cots. She sat with a small pout. "That was a long trip. I'm starving."

Despite Maria's assurance, Abigail didn't feel like an honored guest with no maids and apparently no arrangement for a light supper. Their early meal before they headed out from Chetova had been a long time ago. Fortunately, Abigail had planned ahead. She reached into her bag and pulled out a small parcel wrapped in a linen napkin. She unfolded it to reveal several bread rolls and a chunk of cheese secreted away from their castle meal.

Daisy brightened. "Oh, Abigail, you're a genius and I'll be your friend forever."

As they shared their modest repast, Daisy asked, "Do you know what's going to happen after tomorrow?"

"I suppose it depends on how well I do as the princess."

"Do you think you could get into trouble?"

"I don't think so. I'm impersonating the princess, but I'm doing it at her request."

"How do you know?" Daisy asked as she tore a corner off her roll. "How do you know these people really represent the princess?"

Abigail hadn't considered that. "Well, we are in the palace. I don't think they could've done that without permission."

"I suppose." Daisy munched in a moment of thought. "I want this to be over with. I want to go back to being just a tourist."

Abigail surprised herself with her own heavy sigh. "So do I. I hope everything goes as planned tomorrow."

Cleaned up after their journey, Franz Antonius of Heigenlizt and Josef of Ramsl and Tuharen, noble sons of illustrious fathers, moped like naughty schoolboys awaiting their punishment outside the private chambers of Her Serene Highness Princess Rosamunde. They could hear her stormy instructions to the maids unpacking her belongings. They understood her fit of pique. Once she decided to go to Chetova Castle so her substitute could return from there, she was forced to stay in hiding as a virtual prisoner in her own castle. Then, when her imprisonment was nearly over, Josef had the audacity to suggest another plan because Abigail's life shouldn't be sacrificed to reveal the conspirators. The entire castle had heard the tirade last night when Rosamunde made it clear his effrontery wouldn't be tolerated.

On top of every other inconvenience was Her Highness's decision to return with the caravan in the last carriage instead of with the maids in the second one. Despite the earlier rain near the castle, the road to Tirigovina had been dusty enough to trigger her sensitivities, and her sneezing and coughing fit halfway back to town cemented her foul mood. Now that she was back in her home, the men could hear her unleashing her frustrations on people who didn't deserve it, and the cousins weren't looking forward to taking their turn as whipping boys.

Franz kept pulling out his cigarette case and playing with it, but each time Josef shook his head and Franz put it back. If he went in there smelling of tobacco smoke, it would be worse for them.

Franz asked his cousin, "Are you really going out there tomorrow?"

Josef frowned. "One of us must be there. And you're not going to do it, are you?"

Franz spat out a scoffing laugh.

"And so I must."

"It's not going to be easy. I know you care for the girl. She is charming, in a certain rustic way. It would be easier if she were an adventuress after all. Why go through the torment? Not to mention putting yourself in danger."

"After all the preparations, we can't do anything to raise suspicions." He sighed. "Besides, maybe nothing will happen."

"You don't believe that, do you?"

"No." The public event would be irresistible for any assassin. As certainly as he stood here, tomorrow unknown persons would attempt to take Abigail's life, and they would most likely succeed.

"So, we both know what's going to happen. You could excuse yourself after the three vipers make their greeting."

No, Josef couldn't do that. Now that he knew he was the Judas goat, he had to play the role all the way to the slaughterhouse door. Besides, he might be able to help, somehow. He had no idea what he could do without tipping off the conspirators. But he had to hold onto hope, even a slim one. For Abigail's sake, he could not give up.

The door opened, and a haggard Maria appeared. It seemed her mistress had unleashed on her as well. "My Lords, Her Highness will see you now."

Each encouraged the other to go in first, but finally Franz Antonius had to accept as the senior cousin. With their helmets tucked under their arms, they went into the chambers to face whatever wrath Her Serene Highness had saved up for them and to receive final instructions for the morrow.

CHAPTER THIRTEEN

The Truth at Last

Abigail awoke before dawn. Her slumber had been disturbed by dreams of being exposed as a fraud and chased from the plaza by an angry crowd demanding their real ruler. Abigail slipped out of her cot and went into the bedroom of the master suite —it was the only room that had a window—and sat in a chair to look out at the palace grounds as the sky began to lighten. How had she gotten herself into this peculiar mess? Her intention had been to help, but she had a dark feeling that she was the one who needed help.

As the midsummer sun touched the tops of the trees, she returned to the anteroom to wait for the maids. She sat in a chair and watched Daisy sleeping in her cot. At least her friend had no place in the public charade. She would be kept away from whatever was going to happen.

About a half hour later, the maids Ada, Belza, and another girl Abigail didn't recognize arrived with breakfast. None looked well rested, and Belza tried to tell the Americans about their busy night, but Ada shushed her before she could spread her below-stairs gossip.

Thankfully, breakfast was light—just bread and sausages—and the two ate their fill in preparation for the long day. As they finished, a bleary-eyed Maria arrived with the schedule for the day's activities. By eleven Abigail must be ready to go. She would be led through the back halls of the palace to the upper floor, depart from Her Highness's bedroom wing in the guise of the princess, and then be taken to the carriage and driven to the cathedral. At noon she'd exit the building and take her place on the platform. The three men from the council would greet her, as well as the mayor of the city. The ceremony would begin with the Sálacene leader's speech, then the gifts and dances, and then she'd go back into the cathedral and return to the palace in the carriage. The whole outing should take no more than two hours.

Two hours seemed like a long time to Abigail, but she wasn't used to doing things on a royal scale. "And when I return, will I pretend to go to the quarters of the princess before coming back here?"

Maria scoffed at the question. "Yes, yes, of course. Frau Meyer will be here shortly to help you dress. It's time now for you to do your stage playing and make up your face. I shall return at eleven to escort you through the palace." She turned to leave.

"Will you be at the ceremony?"

Maria seemed taken aback by the question. Then she paused as if she hadn't realized something unpleasant. "Of course. My duty is to be with Her Highness. And you, in her place."

"Thank you. It'll be good to have you there." Abigail was surprised by her own gratitude.

Apparently unmoved by the kind words, Maria hurried off with preoccupied urgency.

As the maids bustled through the room getting the clothing and other details ready, Daisy asked Abigail in a quiet voice, "How did you sleep last night? I had a few bad dreams."

"So did I," Abigail confessed. When she saw Daisy's sadness, she added, "But in the theatre they always say 'bad dress rehearsal, good opening night,' so I'll take our dreams as a good sign."

This cheered Daisy a little. "I wish I could be as optimistic as you are."

Abigail wished she could be as optimistic as she sounded.

The maids had Abigail dressed to her outer petticoats by the time Frau Meyer arrived with the blue dress Abigail had so admired. The hat, veil, and matching dress shoes completed the ensemble. She didn't like the heeled satin slippers, which were too big. She would have preferred dyed kid boots, which seemed more sensible for an outdoor event, but she would have to make do.

The fashion expert muttered something in Swaviczen when the maids buttoned up the blouse portion of the outfit and it was too loose. The maids had forgotten the difference between Abigail's and Rosamunde's dress sizes, and they'd laced up her corset to the maximum compression. In her preoccupied state, Abigail hadn't noticed. Frau Meyer had the maids start over and add the padding under Abigail's breasts before they re-cinched the corset. This had to be repeated twice before Frau Meyer expressed satisfaction with the fit.

Abigail then went into the forbidden bedroom, to the mild concern of the maids, and set up her makeup on a table by the window. She began mixing her greasepaint chickenpox blisters, but this time she lacked the inspiring anger of showing the useless men that she could solve their problem. Now she doubted her plan. The first time had been a game; this was serious. She wondered what the consequences would be if she failed. She hoped the people behind the masquerade would protect her.

As she worked, she shifted a few times in her chair, trying to shore up her posture. What a disadvantage it was not having her corset laced tight. She would feel undressed when she went out in public. True, she'd have more freedom of movement, but a snug corset offered a feeling of security and reassurance she sorely lacked as she prepared for the great adventure of the day.

Maria glowered as she appeared at the bedroom door with the unfamiliar maid standing meekly behind her. "You're not allowed in here!"

For once Abigail was grateful for the high-handedness of "the maid" Maria. It gave her just the right amount of starch her backbone had been missing. Without a glance at her accuser or the meek little maid who'd tattled on her, she applied the first dark pink splotch on her cheek. "I'll be out in daylight, so I need to put this on in here to make sure it looks natural. You want this plan to work, don't you?"

Maria scowled, then said, "Don't touch anything," and stalked out in a cloud of frustration.

Abigail didn't consider herself a petty person, but after her earlier gratitude had been so thoroughly rebuked, she took delight in tormenting Maria, just a little.

Maria returned with the soldiers at eleven on the dot to collect the royal double. In her makeup and completed ensemble of dress, hat, veil, and gloves, Abigail was as ready as she would ever be. She recognized the soldiers as Josef's men, but to her friend's disappointment Biedric wasn't among them. They nodded their salutes and, with a last wish of good luck from Daisy, Abigail was on her way.

Through a labyrinthine back-hall route, the group arrived in a private corridor on the top floor of the palace. Before large double doors, Franz Antonius and Josef waited with more soldiers. They all wore splendid uniforms, Franz again in white and Josef in dark blue, and the soldiers in a rich green. The cousins greeted her with nods, and then they put on their helmets and flanked her as they began their walk out through the main hallways. Maria fell in behind Josef's men. Surrounded by her noble entourage, for once Abigail found it easy to walk in a manner befitting the princess she was imitating.

They came down the main stairs into a grand hallway. Abigail fought her desire to stop and look around at the ornate entrance with its profusion of decoration and architectural detail. No place in the entrance was unadorned, from the blue-flowered marble tile floor up to the ceiling three stories overhead with its magnificent mural of God and Jesus in the heavens. Across the entire hall, two score niches with statues crowned the filigreed walls just below the painted ceiling, and every alcove in the room held statues and *trompe l'oeil* murals of *putti* playing in golden landscapes. She hoped she would have the chance someday to give this place a proper study.

Too soon they were out through the front entrance into a glorious morning, perfect for a festival, with a clear sky and warm, light breezes. As they marched down the long steps to the awaiting carriage, servants and staff were lined up on both sides in low bows and curtsies. Their deference made Abigail both uncomfortable and invigorated. If the day's adventure started like this, whatever could be in store for her?

Abigail and the two cousins were soon in the closed carriage and rolling down the drive to the gate with soldiers on horseback in front and behind. Abigail was on the seat facing forward while the men shared the rear-facing seat across from her. While Josef sat in rigid silence, Franz Antonius smiled his friendliest smirk. "You did that very well. Are you sure there's no nobility in your family?"

With a glimpse at the approaching gate she said, "Only the noble professions of medicine and teaching."

He gave her an amused nod as the gate opened and the carriage rolled through. The soldiers in the lead turned to the left and headed towards the plaza. Abigail saw people on the sides of the road watching the carriage. Men doffed and flourished their hats while women waved handkerchiefs.

Franz Antonius said to her, "There are your people. You should acknowledge them."

Abigail's instinct was to wave back, but she caught herself. She gave a regal nod, and a cheer went up. She looked out the other side and repeated the gesture. "Huzzahs!" were the response.

Franz said to his cousin, "I think she will be quite convincing."

Josef nodded, a tight expression on his face.

The short trip to the cathedral continued in the same manner, with the substitute princess acknowledging the good wishes of someone else's people and Franz Antonius watching in amusement. When they passed the roadblock set up by the royal guard and arrived at the cathedral's side door, the party of three quitted the carriage and entered the church.

They walked into a side area of halls and rooms away from the main sanctuary. The deacon and the chief of the bell-ringers received the guests, along with a few choirboys and the bell-ringers who would peal the ceremonial arrival of the princess. As the two noblemen removed their helmets in the cathedral, the churchmen gushed at Abigail, not having met with the princess in a year. The deacon apologized for the absence of the archbishop, who certainly would know how to welcome her with more appropriate courtesy.

As instructed, Abigail didn't reply but nodded with a hint of a dignified smile under her veil. Josef assured the men their efforts were most suitable and the princess was pleased with their preparations. Four of Josef's soldiers joined the trio. Standing in the hall, the group listened to a brief serenade by the choirboys. Abigail found the boys sweet, but she doubted Rosamunde enjoyed this type of thing. When the choristers were done, she gave them a pleased nod of their own that bordered on a genuine smile. The boys grinned at her gesture, and the two cousins ushered her out of the entryway and into one of the rooms with a seating area and light refreshments.

Franz helped himself to one of the small meat pastries and a glass of champagne, but the others didn't touch the food. "It shouldn't be long now," he told her after draining his glass in one gulp. "Your signal to go out will be the bells." He nodded towards Josef. "I'm going to check the crowd. I'll see you afterwards." He set down his empty glass, then picked up a fresh glass. "Are you going to be all right?"

Abigail didn't understand Franz's concern for his cousin, and neither did she understand Josef's solemn nod.

"All right," Franz said and downed the drink. He put on his helmet, then took Abigail's gloved hand. "I wish you the best of luck. I have become rather fond of you." He kissed her hand. With a nod, he strode out the door.

Abigail looked at Josef, hoping for some sort of explanation, but the growing grimness on his face told her she wouldn't find an answer there. She regarded the pastries. She could lift her hat's veil and eat without disturbing her makeup, but she had no stomach for food. She looked at the soldiers, who seemed to share her concern for their commander. She gestured towards the food on the table. "I'm not hungry. Please help yourselves."

The soldiers glanced amongst themselves, then looked to Josef for instructions. He nodded, but with such sadness that even as the youngest soldier took a step towards the table, two others stopped him.

It was all grim and awkward and not what Abigail expected. Here she was, supposedly going out to a festival, and instead she felt as if she were going out to face a firing squad.

She examined Josef's men. They stood together in a sorry muddle. They had taken on their leader's gloom even though they didn't seem to know its cause.

Abigail had had enough of this. Josef had said that yesterday wasn't the right time for his explanation for all of this, but she decided now was the time.

"Would you please tell me what is happening here? You look like you're going to a funeral. We have every reason to believe this masquerade will work. What do you know that you're not telling me?"

A dreadful pain washed over Josef, but she forced herself not to feel bad for him. He lowered his head as if being pressed down by an enormous weight. The soldiers watched him, their eagerness to know the cause of his grief as strong as hers.

He lifted his head, then let go a massive sigh. "I . . . cannot."

She put a gentle hand on his arm. "Let us help you. You can trust us. Tell us what's troubling you so."

He gazed at her hand for a long moment, then looked at his men. Their loyalty was written across their faces. She could see him wrestling with a mighty foe. For a moment it looked as if he had the upper hand, but then he shook his head. "It is better for all of you if you don't know."

Abigail frowned. This was the last straw. "I'm not going out there until you tell me."

A flash of terror passed over his face. "You cannot say that."

She crossed her arms in defiance. "Tell me."

First one bell, then a cascade of ringing chimes from the bell tower filled the air with a merry announcement of the princess's arrival.

Josef said, "We have to go *now*."

"Then tell me quickly," she countered.

The clanging bells continued, and they were followed by a low roar of cheering.

Josef was the very picture of anguish. Seeing his pain, she nearly let go of her resolve, but then she rallied. She wouldn't let this go on a moment longer.

The cathedral deacon and his assistant knocked on the open door and entered the room. The deacon said in frantic tones, "Why are you still here, Your Highness? It's time. They're waiting for you."

Abigail said, not taking her eyes off Josef, "Not until he tells me what he's keeping from me."

The deacon looked at the nobleman, who seemed paralyzed. "Please, My Lord," he implored, "you must go. It's time." The deacon and his assistant hurried out.

Trapped, Josef made his grim decision. "If I tell you, do you promise to go out there, no matter what?"

"Yes."

The darkness that settled on his face told her perhaps she didn't want to know after all.

"All right. This 'masquerade,' as you call it, is because someone wants to take Rosamunde's life. She doesn't know who it is. And she decided the best way to draw him out was to put someone else in danger. That person is you."

The joyous peal of the cathedral's bells filled the void of the room's stunned silence. Abigail's mouth slipped open as she stared at him. Josef's soldiers, too, stood in speechless amazement. Abigail could not believe . . . and yet with his confession a dozen small oddities made sense, from the calculated arguments of the princess's representatives in Graz, to Josef's pained declaration that his first loyalty was to his monarch, to Franz Antonius's odd farewell.

And now she understood the ramifications of what he didn't want her to know. "There are people out there who will try to . . . kill me?"

His response was a stolid, "I have kept my promise. Now you must keep yours."

Did he expect her to go out there and be felled by an assassin? . . . No, he expected her to keep her promise. Heaven help her, she had given her word.

She looked at Josef's soldiers. She took a deep breath and straightened her shoulders. "Gentlemen, do you go before or after me?"

Two of the men regarded her with wonderment, one smiled with admiration, and one fought tears. The most senior of the men said, "The protocol is we will follow you."

The youngest, who saw only adventure in this, added, "Anywhere!"

Even though she had felt very old and tired in the moment before the young soldier spoke, his spirit lifted hers. Surely nothing could happen to her with so many protectors around . . . could it?

She turned to Josef. "Which way?"

He indicated the open door. She stepped out into the hallway and the deafening ringing of the bells. She looked to Josef for further guidance, but instead of giving her a gesture to show her which way to proceed, he took her hand and tucked it into his arm, escorting her down the hall in dignified silence. His soldiers fell in behind them.

Even if she had known what to say to Josef, they wouldn't be able to hear each other as the reverberations of the bells shook the hallway. Were they welcoming her or signaling her doom? As the group crossed the cathedral's sanctuary and approached the exit door where the deacon and his assistant waited, she said under her breath, "'Never send to know for whom the bells tolls . . . it tolls for thee.'"

CHAPTER FOURTEEN

The Incident in the Plaza

The churchmen opened the cathedral door, letting in the noonday glare. When Abigail's eyes adjusted, she could see hundreds of brightly dressed people waiting to greet their monarch and begin their festival. As she looked at the platform beyond the threshold, she wondered if Anne Boleyn saw the likes of this when she stepped out onto Tower Green to keep her appointment with the headsman. At least that tragic queen could find some comfort in knowing her sacrifice would protect her daughter. Abigail would only be protecting someone she didn't know or like and who didn't deserve the great gift she might be receiving this day.

They approached the doorway, where Maria and Baron Mleist waited. Josef gently removed Abigail's arm from his. He gestured for her to go first. She studied his face. Would he change his mind and send her out to her death alone? She saw something in his eyes she felt she could trust. She took a deep breath and went outside.

The crowd cheered her appearance, but the only cheer she felt was in seeing Josef come with her, half a step behind.

She stepped onto the platform, cursing her loose, slippery shoes. She needed to concentrate on her surroundings, not her unsteady footing! She scanned the crowd: a sea of faces and eyes and hands and smiles and colors and nothing to help her distinguish one person from another. She wanted to take it all in and dissect it to find whatever threat might be there, but the visual cacophony was more than her mind could parse.

Now that she'd kept her promise, what could she do to protect herself? She could run, make an announcement that she wasn't the princess, even just start talking in English. But while that might save her life in this moment, she was still a prisoner. If she stopped cooperating, not only would she be in danger, but Daisy would too. Oh, dreadful day! What was she to do?

As the peal of bells ebbed and ceased, a man appeared before her. He was thickset, with a wild shock of pepper-and-salt hair. His naturally downturned mouth struggled with his attempt at a smile. Several magnificent medals sparkled on the breast of his suit coat. With a fierce gaze, he looked as if he expected her to do something. Abigail stared at him, lost in the moment.

Josef leaned towards her. "Your Highness."

She came back to herself. Oh, yes. Michael Gregorski. Rosamunde didn't like him. By the possessiveness in his gaze, Abigail could understand her feelings.

Josef said to him, "Herr Gregorski, you'll please forgive Her Highness. She's still a bit indisposed."

He responded with a solid bow. "But of course. We are grateful you could attend the festivities at all."

A greediness in his manner didn't please Abigail one bit. She lifted her gloved right hand for him to kiss.

"Your Highness," he said in condescending tones. As he took her hand, he examined her veiled face with a squint.

She tilted her wrist down a little more to reveal the faux chickenpox blister between her glove and the cuff of her sleeve. As he leaned forward to kiss her glove, he caught sight of the blister and his eyes widened. He hesitated in his gesture, then with a quick and glancing move barely kissed her glove at her knuckle, bowed, and stepped away.

The second of the three men approached. With his lean-and-hungry look, the unmistakable Herr Guttmann bowed before Abigail and murmured a polite greeting. When he stood upright and saw her, his face fell open with surprise. "Your Highness! Are you well? You never mentioned—"

Josef interceded. "Her Highness is recovering from a mild inconvenience. She will be fine in a few days."

Guttmann expressed his gratitude at the news and wished her well before yielding to the third man, Vasily Medyev. The banker offered a polite greeting and well wishes while bent over her hand and backed away to join the others.

Even though her ordeal was far from over, Abigail breathed a sigh of relief. At least she had fooled these three men. She watched them form a small cluster at the end of the platform. Since they were not scheduled to attend the event, should they still be nearby? In a whisper she asked Josef, "Is it all right for them to be up here?"

He said, "Yes. They are on the council, so they have the status to stay."

Another man approached Abigail. He wore a fine suit, a red sash of office, two small medals on the breast of his jacket, and a tentative smile. She had no idea who he was.

Josef said to him, "Good day to you, Herr Mayor. What a splendid day for the festival."

Oh, yes, that's right, she was to be greeted by the mayor of Tirigovina. But was she supposed to acknowledge him? Offer her hand for a kiss? What was she supposed to do? Had they told her? Her heart began to pound.

The man's smile grew a little stiff as he gave her a deep bow with his hands at his sides. "Your Highness, it is always an honor to have you attend our events. I'm sorry to hear of your recent indisposition, and we are all glad to see you are feeling much better." He bowed again and stepped away.

Abigail didn't move, but she let out a deep breath. Josef was gazing out at the crowd when he said to her, "You're doing very well."

She also looked out at the crowd, which had quieted down. "Thank you. What happens next?"

"The presentation from the Sálacene elder. His name is Jovacź Chešqu. You don't need to worry about him."

"Only everyone else."

He did not respond.

A movement in the crowd below the platform caught Abigail's attention. She held her breath as a man moved through the throng, which parted for him. He was barrel-chested, graying, in his forties, and with a fine, full moustache that curled up at the ends. Dressed in what looked like a ceremonial costume that included an embroidered vest and magenta sash around his waist, he had determination written on his face, and he held a wrapped package. She couldn't take her eyes off him.

He came into the cathedral's shadow and stopped at the bottom of the steps that led up to her. In a booming voice he said something in a language she did not understand and that did not sound like Swaviczen. Her heart pounded, but Josef did nothing. The man said in an equally booming German, "Your Serene Highness, I, Jovacź Chešqu of the Sálacene, come here in all humility and appreciation. May I approach you?"

Josef whispered, "Nod."

She did.

The man climbed the steps. Abigail thought he'd prefer to take the stairs two at a time, but he walked up with modest respect. The package in his hands was wrapped in a brightly colored fabric with an unfamiliar woven pattern. He reached the platform and removed his wide-brimmed hat trimmed with a bright, floral garland. With a flourish he swept the hat down and offered Abigail a low bow. In German he said for all to hear, "Greetings to Your Royal Highness. I am here on behalf of your loyal Sálacene subjects to offer our allegiance and our gratitude for another year of serving your honored family."

Like the natural actor Abigail concluded he must be, Chešqu moved to face the audience without turning his back to her and began his oration in what she assumed to be the Sálacene language. She pretended to pay attention as if she knew what he was saying. Under the cover of her light veil, she cast her gaze over the crowd, searching for . . . she didn't know what . . . just something out of the ordinary. As if anything in this place could be called ordinary.

As Chešqu continued, she noticed Gregorski looking at her. His scowl, which she remembered well from his photograph, seemed even deeper as he examined her. Keeping her eyes on Chešqu, Abigail scratched her right arm, then her hand. Even from the corner of her eye she could see Gregorski shudder and wipe the hand he'd used to hold hers when he kissed her glove. In the heightened drama of the moment, it was all she could do not to laugh.

Chešqu began speaking to the crowd in German, giving a basic, if ornate, oath promising support, obedience, and eternal loyalty for every generation to come, and so forth. Abigail did not look at Gregorski, but for good measure she gave her wrist a quick scratch.

Without turning her head, she ran her eyes across the crowd. Nothing seemed amiss to her. Perhaps nothing would happen today after all.

The Sálacene representative finished his pledge on behalf of his people, and with a grand gesture he held out the wrapped package to her. "With our allegiance, we offer you the bread of peace."

A flash and the sound of a soft explosion from the ground level made Abigail gasp. Josef put a protective arm around her as she caught her balance and two of his soldiers jumped in front of her. Several soldiers on the plaza rushed to the cloud of acrid gray smoke at the base of the platform.

A startled photographer was yanked out from under the camera's black cloth by the soldiers. He dropped the flash bar as the heavy smoke from the flash powder was still dissipating. The soldiers searched him, but he produced his credentials from a newspaper in Vienna, and, after he received a few threats from the annoyed soldiers, nerves calmed and he returned to his camera.

Abigail gathered herself and apologized to Josef, who seemed to take no offense at her start. After making sure she was all right, he moved back to his place half a step behind her on the left. Chešqu was also solicitous, but with a nod Abigail reassured him she was all right and they could resume. With a less grandiose and more personal touch, he held out the wrapped package to her.

Thanks to the book seller in Graz, Abigail knew how to say one thing in Sálacene, and at this moment she took her chance to use it. As she accepted the wrapped bread, she thanked Chešqu in his own language. The man stared at her in astonishment. She even saw Josef react, but she didn't dare look directly at him as her stomach dropped. Had she said it correctly? She was afraid she'd done something horribly wrong. But her fear dissolved when she saw Chešqu's amazed smile.

Concentrating on everything else, Abigail had forgotten her instructions. She held on to the bread and, not knowing what else to do, tucked it into the crook of her arm. Then she remembered Baron Mleist was supposed to take it. Where was he? Hadn't he come out with them? She caught a glimpse of Maria next to her on her right. She wondered why the "maid" stood beside her. Abigail suspected interacting with a servant in the middle of this ceremony would be a slight to Mr. Chešqu, so she kept her eyes on the Sálacene leader.

For his part, Chešqu was clearly delighted by what Abigail had done and spoke to the crowd in Sálacene. His statement was received well and followed by exclamations of approval throughout the crowd.

Abigail noticed Maria getting irritated, and she didn't know why. After a grunt of exasperation, Maria stepped back and turned to move behind Abigail. She froze, thought hard for a few moments, and then chose to stand off to the side instead. Abigail returned her gaze to Chešqu as she listened to Maria's grumblings. She knew she would be on the receiving end of an angry lecture from the "maid" when they returned to the palace.

Chešqu signaled for someone to come up from the ground level, and two girls in brightly decorated dresses walked up the steps carrying small baskets bedecked with ribbons of every color. They offered the baskets to Abigail, who thanked them in Sálacene without thinking about it. The girls stared in amazement, then looked to Chešqu, who nodded.

Abigail saw the baskets had some sort of food in them, and then her instructions came back to her—Maria had been next to her to take the gifts. She turned and handed Maria the wrapped bread and indicated she should take the two small baskets. Maria stepped forward and accepted the gifts, but her annoyed glare told Abigail this sudden recollection would not prevent the lecture.

When Abigail turned back, she saw the two girls had gone down the steps. Coming up, one deliberate step at a time, was a tiny girl of no more than five clutching a bouquet of flowers. The little girl carrying the big responsibility was looking up at Abigail with fear, but she kept coming with her mighty burden.

At the sight of the solemn child, Abigail forgot all of her royal training and smiled. Such a terrible weight on those tiny shoulders!

The little girl reached the platform and gazed up at her dread lord and mistress ... and promptly froze. Chešqu gave her a gentle encouragement, but the girl couldn't move as tears filled her eyes. Flowers began slipping out of the bouquet, and the girl started to cry.

At the sad and touching sight, Abigail couldn't help herself. Whispering gentle words of reassurance to the girl, she got down on one knee to pick up the flowers.

A sharp, cracking sound echoed through the plaza. A shrill whistle passed over Abigail's head, and blood exploded from Maria's chest as she was thrown sideways across the platform.

Shrieks erupted from the crowd, and the people on the platform scattered. Still on one knee, Abigail tried to spin towards the cathedral door, but her feet slipped in the useless shoes and she fell sideways, landing on her left hip with a slap of her hand on the platform. Another crack, shrill whistle above her head, and the wood splintered a few yards past her. Chešqu scooped up the little girl as Abigail tried to scramble to her feet. She gasped as Josef's hands grabbed her shoulders, yanking her upright and pulling her away from the crowd. She saw splattered blood everywhere as the glassy-eyed Maria stared up at the brilliant blue sky.

Abigail tripped and lost a shoe as Josef's firm grip on her shoulders kept her from falling. By instinct she kicked off the other shoe as he guided her before him and they ran for the cathedral door. Another sharp sound was followed by a pinging echo before her. Josef stumbled but never lost his steadying grip on her shoulders. He regained his footing, and soon they were inside the building as the terrified deacon and his assistant swung the doors closed behind them.

Panicked people raced in all directions through the church. Abigail and Josef sprinted hand-in-hand across the sanctuary. The bells were clanging again, now in harsh rhythms of alarm. Abigail tried to fathom all of what had happened, but in her fright she could only concentrate on running.

They dashed into the far hallway they had passed through mere minutes earlier. They were alone for a moment, and Josef stopped and pulled Abigail into a crushing hug. He groaned "Thank God!" into the side of her neck. He was with her after all! She fought tears as she returned his embrace. He freed her and took her by the hand to run down the hallway.

Biedric Halle and two palace soldiers waited with a cluster of military and church people by the closed door that led out to the carriage. Even before they reached the group, Josef shouted to Biedric, "Use the phaeton!"

The loyal lieutenant put his hand on the door latch as the palace soldiers saluted and church people bowed to the approaching couple.

There was no time for Abigail to catch her breath as Biedric, with a courteous nod, took her hand and hurried her outside. She had not recovered from her dash, and her stockinged feet lacked traction on the stone steps, but Biedric's steady hand kept her upright. Through the open door behind them she heard Josef direct the church people to stay inside and then order the soldiers to follow him. She glanced back to see him turn into the building. His uniform's right epaulette was askew, but he disappeared before she could see more, and Biedric led her away down the steps.

The royal carriage stood directly in front of the door, and Biedric guided her into it. Before Abigail could question his apparent disobedience, he pulled her through the carriage and out the other side, where she saw a small, sleek phaeton facing the other way, its top up and two nervous horses pulling at the lead held by a shaking livery boy. Biedric lifted Abigail into the small buggy, then took the lead from the livery boy and ordered the carriage driver and coachmen to take the road to Chetova until they reached the next town. Biedric vaulted in the phaeton's seat next to Abigail and slapped the anxious horses with the reins. The phaeton jumped forward as the royal carriage with the full complement of soldiers lumbered off in the opposite direction.

The commotion in the plaza and the noisy departure of the royal carriage diverted all attention away from the smaller vehicle. Biedric directed the horses at a brisk trot through the chaos-filled streets. Abigail realized her hands were clenched, but when she forced them open she was surprised to see a smudge on the left glove's fingertips . . . blood. She checked her hand. Was she injured? The glove wasn't torn, and she couldn't see a wound.

When they arrived at the palace gate, the guards let the phaeton through and slammed the gate behind them. Biedric hurried the horses to the front steps, where frantic servants waited. He stopped the vehicle before them and jumped down.

Abigail tried to get out, but to her surprise she found she didn't have enough strength to pick up her legs. Biedric lifted her out and set her gently on her feet. She could walk, but she was unsteady and he kept an arm around her as he helped her up the long stairs. As they went, Abigail saw some of the servants were wringing their hands while others were crying. How surreal it all was. They weren't crying for her; they were crying for the princess who had put her into this peril. She heard someone exclaim "*Blut!*" as she was whisked past by Biedric, and she clenched her soiled hand shut.

They entered through the palace doors, and Biedric rushed her to the main stairs. He whispered to her, "I'm sorry. I must take you up to Her Highness's quarters and then we'll go back down to your room."

"That's all right," she said. "You just have to get me there."

Palace guards attempted to take charge of the princess, but Biedric waved them off. The two made it to the top floor and down to the end of the hall and the princess's private chambers. Belza and another of Abigail's maids waiting there. Both were dazed by the general alarum, but they went into action and helped their mistress down the back stairs with Biedric at their flank.

They rushed through the doors into Abigail's modest sanctuary, where a frantic Daisy cried out in relief. Biedric and Belza helped the exhausted Abigail to a chair.

Abigail fought her torpor as she listened to Daisy go on about how she knew something was wrong but no one would tell her what was happening.

Abigail yanked away her hat and veil, then peeled off her gloves and threw them on the floor. Despite her fall, her left hand wasn't injured. Where had the smudge come from? She gestured towards the makeup table, which she would never be able to reach on her own. "Take me over there. I need to get this greasepaint off."

Belza and Biedric pulled her to her feet, but as Abigail turned towards the table, Daisy shrieked and dropped into a faint. Biedric rushed to her aid while Belza kept her mistress upright. Daisy groaned as Biedric tried to awaken her, so Abigail knew her friend would be all right. She took another step towards the table, but then she caught a glimpse of her reflection in the triple mirror.

Blood was splattered across the back of the beautiful, modern, stunning, ruined blue silk dress. Maria's blood.

Abigail made it to the chair at the makeup table, but as she reached for a cloth to wipe away the makeup, in the mirror she saw her own haggard reflection. It was more ghastly than any illusion greasepaint could create. She buried her face in her hands and sobbed.

CHAPTER FIFTEEN

A Desperate Plan

"No one is more shocked by today's events than I am."

Baron Mleist spoke as he paced back and forth in Abigail's room. The royal decoy sat, elbows on the table, holding a cold compress to her forehead with both hands. Her freshly washed hair spilled down across her dressing gown. Daisy and a meek maid from the palace sat off to the side.

"But, *Fräulein,* I am pleased to report that the situation is well in hand, and I am certain everything will be fine now."

Abigail listened as the baron continued his protestations. She didn't need the cold compress, even though she had asked for one with the claim that her head was aching. She'd asked for it so she could listen to the baron with her face obscured. She wanted to concentrate on his words, and not on looking as if she believed him.

She had been doing a great deal of thinking in the hour since she'd returned from the plaza. Many things were clear to her now: The baron was a part of the conspiracy to make the would-be assassins reveal themselves; the baron was not a gentleman, since he'd allowed Maria to go out onto the platform when he himself had stayed behind in the safety of the cathedral; the Swaviczens she'd met in Graz lied to the banker Mr. Ignatius Porter, who relayed the lies to the U.S. ambassador in Vienna; she and Daisy had to get out of this country as soon as possible; and since everyone in Swavicza owed loyalty to the princess and, therefore, could not be trusted, she would have to be the person who got the two of them out of this mess.

The conundrum in all of this, however, was Josef. He'd told her the terrible truth that she wasn't supposed to know, and he'd stood by her side in harm's way. By being honest with her, he must have now put himself in a precarious position regarding his monarch and her plans. And . . . that embrace. She had no doubt there was more to it than mere relief. She wanted to believe he was indeed the warm and gracious man she'd met on the first day. But as a subject of Swavicza, he owed his loyalty to his sovereign. How could she continue to trust him, when helping her meant treason?

While Abigail had been in her bath to soak her bruised hip, she asked Daisy to have Belza bring paper and pencil so she could write up two quick telegraph messages. The first was to the U.S. ambassador in Vienna, explaining the developments and asking for assistance. The second was to Mr. Samuel Clemens in Heidelberg, begging him to help in any way he could, up to and including renting a cavalry unit and riding in to rescue her. She decided against trying to reach her cousins outside Nuremberg because she would have to write in German, which would increase the odds that the telegraph operator would understand the message and report it. In her haste, she hoped the telegrapher on duty would find the messages in English unreadable so he would merely tap out the letters without understanding the words. Belza assured Abigail she would take the messages to the office and make sure they were sent. But the maid hadn't yet returned with the tickets confirming her calls for help had gone through. Until Abigail's rescuers were in the same room with her, she would have to go along with this game being played by her hosts—no, her captors.

Now, after the pacing baron had finished his apologies and assurances, Abigail removed the compress and hoped she had a trusting look on her face. "Thank you. I'm glad you have the situation well in hand. Has the person who killed poor Maria been identified and arrested?"

The baron winced at the mention of Maria's name. "Every effort is being made to locate the man and bring him to justice."

Abigail considered her next statement. She wouldn't get the reply she wanted, but she had to say it anyway. "Baron, in light of what's happened, I'm sure you don't want Daisy and me here anymore. We're an unnecessary complication in this complex time. We can be ready to go on the next train to Vienna, or Graz, or even Budapest. And, of course, you can rely on our complete discretion in the matter." She had trouble saying the next part, but she felt she needed to include it. "We owe you a debt of gratitude for your kindness and hospitality."

The baron waved his hands in a dismissive gesture. "No, no, it's much better for you to stay here for another day or two. Things are still unsettled. And because of your resemblance to Her Highness, I could never forgive myself if something happened to you in a case of mistaken identity."

With that last statement, which lacked irony or any indication of discomfort on his part, Abigail knew her goose was truly cooked.

In response to a knock on the door, Baron Mleist gave the order for the person to enter. Beĺza came in with a meek look when she saw the baron. She had a wrapped box in her hands.

The baron frowned at her, and for a terrible moment Abigail feared Beĺza would blurt out something about the telegrams. Abigail said, "Baron, thank you, I would like to rest for a while."

He nodded. "Perhaps would you like a light supper brought to you later?"

Abigail wondered if the box Beĺza had could have something to do with the telegrams. She said to the baron, "Yes, thank you, that would be nice. I'll let you know when we're ready." The baron nodded and departed.

Beĺza came to the table with a smile and held out the box to Abigail. "This is for you, miss," she said in English.

The wrapping paper was from a store whose name she didn't recognize. Abigail peeled back the paper to reveal the cover of a box of chocolates from a shop in Vienna. "Where did you get this?"

Beĺza answered, "A man from the mayor's office gave it to me when I was at the tel—"

"While you were in town," Abigail cut her off. The new maid

seemed sweet and good-natured, but Abigail didn't know if she could be trusted, and she didn't want to find out the hard way.

"Oh," Beĺza said, correcting herself, "yes, well, anyway, a man from the mayor's office gave this to me. He said he was very sorry about what happened and he knew this was your favorite chocolatier—well, Her Highness's favorite—and he hoped it would help brighten your day a little."

Abigail was in no mood for sweets, and she set the box aside. But she needed to get rid of the other maid for a few minutes so she could quiz Beĺza. She said to the maid in German, "What's your name?"

In a soft voice, the girl said, "Griechen, *Fräulein*."

"Griechen, can you please fetch us a pot of tea? I promise we won't leave." The girl nodded and left on her mission.

The moment the door closed, Abigail asked Beĺza, "You delivered the messages?"

"Yes, miss."

"And there were no problems?"

"No, miss."

"And you waited for the telegrapher to send the messages?"

"Yes, miss."

"And you got the confirmation ticket from him?"

Beĺza's confidence lost some of its shine. "Well, no. . . ."

Abigail couldn't believe what she was hearing. "I told you to get the confirmation ticket so we would know the messages went through."

"Well, I gave him the notes, and I paid, and he said he would send them, and then the man from the mayor's office came in, and he said he was hoping to find someone from the palace, and he said I should take you these right away. And I asked the telegraph operator if he sent the messages and he said yes, and so I came here."

Abigail's stomach rolled over. Telegraph messages didn't always go through right away. Especially in this country, a confirmation was worth a thousand promises.

"Miss," Belza said, "I'm sure it will be fine."

Abigail couldn't rely on Belza's optimism. She had to find another way out. "I want you to locate Count Ramsl and ask him if he would please come here for a few minutes." She had to risk trusting Josef with her plan. If she couldn't trust him, then all was lost.

She saw Belza's gaze fixed on the box of chocolates. Abigail knew the maid had meant well, even though she hadn't completed her task, and she would need Belza's help in the future. Besides, she liked the lively girl who was the most honest and open person she'd met in this country. "Would you like the chocolates?"

Belza's eyes sparkled with delight. "I would love to have one!"

"Take the whole box. Go and enjoy them."

The maid could barely contain her glee as she scooped up the package, gushed her thanks, curtsied and practically skipped out of the room.

Daisy pouted. "I like chocolate."

"I'll buy you a box—two boxes—when we get to Vienna."

This appeased her friend, who promised to hold Abigail to her word.

Abigail told Daisy her plan: Since they couldn't count on outside rescuers, one of Josef's soldiers would buy them train tickets to Vienna, and then—somehow—with help they would escape the palace. With luck, they would be out of the country before they were missed.

The maid Griechen came in with tea and cookies, and Abigail told her it had been a stressful day, she should take a little time off, but would she please return in half an hour with Frau Meyer and whatever evening clothing they had for her to wear? The fresh-faced girl curtsied and opened the door just as Biedric was raising his hand to knock. Abigail asked him to enter.

As the maid exited, Josef came in with Biedric and the four soldiers who had been on the platform. Biedric sat down next to Daisy, while Josef sat at Abigail's table and the other soldiers stood by. To Abigail's eyes, they all looked beaten and exhausted. Josef was tired, sad, and . . . something she couldn't interpret. She noticed he had changed into civilian clothes. Biedric and two of the others were also in civilian clothes, while the last two were still in uniform. She suspected the clothing of the men who'd changed had been splattered with Maria's blood just as her dress had been. The stain on her glove must have come from Maria as well. She didn't want to think about how far the poor woman's gore had been scattered in that terrible moment. She hoped the little flower girl had been shielded from all of the suffering.

Abigail thought to have this conversation in English so she wouldn't leave out Daisy, but when she looked at her friend and saw all her attention was on Biedric, she decided German would be a better choice to include Josef's men. She asked Josef to tell her what had happened after they'd parted ways.

He told her that the soldiers and police spent the afternoon combing the town for anyone who knew anything, but no one had useful information. "The town police determined the shot had been fired from the top floor of a building on the left side of the plaza. They found the rifle still in the window. A British Whitworth, very accurate. But no one saw who fired the rifle."

"Was anyone else . . . hurt?" She noticed all of Josef's men look at him.

He said, "No significant wounds." He concluded his narrative of their activities, explaining how the soldiers and policemen had no suspects and everyone in town was agitated and afraid.

While he spoke, Abigail watched the four stalwart soldiers at the back of the room. The youngest, the one who'd been so enthusiastic for the adventure before it began, now looked bedraggled and downcast. His uniform had been replaced with rough peasant garments. If she remembered correctly, he had been the one standing closest to Maria. It had been a hard day for him, and his optimism was one of its casualties.

She asked the young soldier, "What is your name?"

He was surprised by her question and looked to his leader for permission to reply. Josef nodded. The young man said, "Jowan Halle, *Fräulein.*"

She asked Biedric, "You're related?"

Daisy's beau said, "He is my youngest brother."

Abigail said to Jowan, "I think you could use some of the refreshments. It's only tea and cookies, but if it's all right," she said with a glance at Josef, "I would like you gentlemen to have them."

Josef nodded his approval with a small smile.

The men's spirits lifted as Abigail asked Daisy if there were extra cups or glasses, and she found several drinking glasses for the soldiers. The men gathered around the table and set to polishing off the treats.

Abigail said to Josef and Biedric, "I never thanked you properly for saving my life. Both of you. You were quite heroic." Josef gave a humble nod, and Biedric flashed a smile, earning a question from Daisy and then after his explanation an arm-squeeze of appreciation.

Abigail asked Josef quietly in English, "Who was Maria?"

Josef said, "Rosemunde's chief lady in waiting. She was from an important family in Prussia."

Abigail thought about the last minutes on the platform. From Maria's actions, Abigail surmised she knew what was likely to happen, and still she was brave enough to go out there. And yet that knowledge, and second-guessing the probable direction of the attack, had been her undoing. Abigail felt guilty for being an indirect participant in the woman's death. She admitted, "I'm embarrassed now about not liking her."

"I didn't like her, either. But it wasn't her role to be liked. It was to get things done. Rosamunde is very distressed."

Abigail was surprised. "She knows already?"

Josef considered his response, then said, "Yes. She's here."

"She's in the palace?"

"Yes, in her chambers. She was in Chetova, too, when you were there. She knows about everything. Except the chickenpox," he said with a shake of his head, which triggered another flinch.

She hadn't considered the necessity of Rosamunde staying in close proximity. She also realized these people were well organized and had plans for all contingencies. Not only that, but she had made another innocent mistake. "She doesn't know about something else. A little while ago I gave away a box of chocolates brought here for her."

Josef glanced at his men enjoying their refreshments. "Was it from Gerstner's?"

"I believe that was the name on the box."

Josef shook his head slightly. "That's too bad. It's her favorite."

Well, she thought, another black mark in her book. But what was one more with such a long list?

As Abigail looked at Josef, she reveled in the company of the friendly man she'd met on the first day. He wasn't as cheerful and flirtatious as he had been on their ride, but it was unrealistic to expect that after everything that had happened. Now instead he exuded calm, support, and compassion—all traits she admired in a man. As she saw a small flinch of pain cross his face, she recalled their running exit from the plaza. Josef had been between her and the assassin, and when she heard a noise he'd stumbled. His tired face, several flinches, the damaged epaulette of his now-missing uniform, and the glances of his men at her earlier question added up to a deep suspicion that the blood on her glove might have come from someone other than Maria. She asked him in German, "May I ask, who received the 'not significant' injury?"

The soldiers gazed at him. He glanced away from her as he said, "One of the men guarding you."

She understood now. Not only had he put himself between her and danger, he had paid for his heroism in blood. His wound must be minor, since she could see no sling or external bandages, but of course he would not discuss it. How could he tell her without sounding as if he were trumpeting his own gallantry? Gentlemen do not brag.

She said to Josef, "I hope you will extend to him my deepest, personal gratitude for his courage and heroism. I owe him my life."

He looked at her. As they gazed at each other, she had her final confirmation of his true nature in those honest brown eyes. He was a man of honor. He'd been willing to die for her. He had betrayed the princess's plan to her. He was now trusting her with his reputation and perhaps his own life. She smiled in spite of herself. With his small smile in return, all the logic and reasoning that had protected her heart from him crumbled. She sighed. This could not possibly end well.

Abigail regarded the refreshed soldiers. The vanished tea and cookies had done their work. She hadn't intended to bring Josef's men into her cabal, but since they were privy to the other intrigue now, and they were his men, she dared to draft them into her cause.

Before she started, however, she realized she had never gotten past a particular formality. She looked at the Count of Ramsl and Tuharen. "May I call you Josef?"

He smiled. "Of course."

She said in German, ". . . Since your men know what's going on—and I assume Biedric does—I would like to speak openly." She told Josef that she and Daisy hoped to leave as soon as someone could obtain train tickets for them.

He listened in circumspect silence. When she finished, he said, "This will not be easy. You'll be watched much more closely now. When we were coming in, we heard a messenger telling Mleist that someone had attempted to send telegrams in English out of the country. It will only be a matter of time before they're delivered to him."

Abigail's heart sank. This was a disaster. Her messages hadn't gone through, and now they would be used against her. Curse her haste! She should have taken the time to use hog Latin or double Dutch that an American would figure out but that would be nonsensical to the telegrapher. Was there a way to salvage this? "I used my name, so I can't deny I wrote them." Thinking her way through as she spoke, she said, "I suggest you go to Mleist and say I asked if you would take a message for me to the telegraph office. You can say of course you refused." Josef nodded thoughtfully. "That way you will tell him something he'll already find out, but you can stay in their good graces."

"Yes," he said with some reluctance. "That's a good idea. Although I am sorry to be . . . how do you say it in English . . . a rat?"

She nodded. "Yes, but at least you can gain something from my mistake." She rubbed her head, trying to think. She hadn't anticipated this setback. Since she couldn't escape now, they had to get a message to the ambassador in Vienna. He had to be told the plan he'd agreed to was a lie and he must pull some diplomatic strings to get her out of there. But how. . . .

She looked at Daisy, who was cozied up next to Biedric, her face a mixture of worry about their situation and comfort at being close to her beau. A plan came to Abigail in an instant.

She said to Josef, "They'll be watching me, but they won't be paying much attention to Daisy."

Abigail hesitated. This plan was her only hope, and it would be better for Josef if he didn't know about it.

He frowned. "What are you thinking?"

She didn't have a good poker face, at least not without preparation. "I believe it's time for you to talk to Mleist."

He glanced from her to Daisy and back again. "What is your plan?"

Abigail knew she was doing the right thing by keeping him out of this. In a firm tone she said, "The longer you wait, the less convincing your story to Mleist will be."

His frown told her she'd pushed too far. As understanding as he might be, he also lived under the yoke of a demanding and manipulative woman. Being coerced by another woman had to gall, especially after everything he'd done for her.

Her fears were confirmed when he stood and gave her a curt bow. "Whatever 'Your Highness' wishes."

As she watched him leave, she took cold comfort in knowing that antagonizing him would make his "betrayal" seem more authentic. She could apologize to him later. For now, she had to hurry.

Not knowing which of the other soldiers understood English, she spoke to Daisy in a hushed voice. "You're going to have to escape, and go to Vienna, and talk with the U.S. ambassador and tell him what's going on." Daisy's eyes grew wider as the set of instructions continued. "And after you talk with him, you need to send me a telegram to let me know what he says and when I can expect help. But you can't send it to me, because they'll intercept it. Send it to Josef. And you have to use some sort of code, so no one else will know what you're talking about."

Daisy fought being overwhelmed. Biedric could see her dismay, but without being able to understand the conversation, he could only help by taking her hand.

Daisy said, "But how . . . I . . . I mean, how am I going to escape—and get to Vienna?"

Abigail studied the love-struck man beside her friend. She knew she could trust him with Daisy's life and honor, but this presented a terrible gamble. Desperation emboldened her. "Daisy, I have no right to ask this of Biedric, and I fear it may come back to haunt both of you later. . . . I want you to ask Biedric to go with you, and if he says yes, and if you manage to escape, when they ask me where you've gone, I'll tell them that you've eloped."

Daisy's eyes lit up, and when Biedric pressed her in French for details, she happily told him. He betrayed more than a bit of concern.

Abigail explained, "You won't really marry him, Daisy. . . . But you'll be traveling alone together."

The terrible risks weighed on Abigail. Even if the couple made it to Vienna in complete propriety, Daisy's reputation could be ruined by malicious talk . . . and their tour group contained just the gossip-monger to start it.

Daisy considered the situation. "What if some of the other soldiers went as chaperones, like Biedric's brother?"

Abigail shook her head. "If Biedric goes with you, he's deserting his post. I feel bad enough asking him to do this. We can't ask others to do the same. Besides, that would be a red flag to our captors. It has to look like it's just a couple running away together. Otherwise they'll know something's afoot, and they'll hunt you down." Surely Josef would understand and forgive them all . . . eventually.

Daisy thought more, and her frown grew. They both knew life back home could be ruined if her noble and courageous mission was sullied by rumors that painted a far different picture.

The door opened wide with a thud. Baron Mleist, red-faced but trying to contain his anger, marched into the room. Josef appeared behind him, not enjoying the proceedings but playing his part. Josef's men rose at the baron's entrance.

"So," the baron glowered at Abigail, "you have decided to take matters into your own hands. That was very unwise. You agreed to help us. Now you must do as you are told."

As the baron continued to vent his spleen, Abigail caught a glimpse of Daisy nodding to her. Her gaze was serious, intense. God bless Daisy, Abigail thought, willing to hazard her good name on a terrible gamble. As she concentrated on Mleist, she acknowledged her friend's message with the slightest of nods.

Daisy tugged on the cuff of Biedric's sleeve, and he sat down next to her. She began to whisper to him, and his concentration grew as he listened.

Mleist did not stop his lecture to Abigail, but Josef saw the entire exchange. Abigail saw him frown as he turned his gaze of growing concern from Abigail to Daisy to Biedric. In spite of the hurt feelings she caused, Abigail was glad she hadn't told him the plan. This had to be on her shoulders when it all came to fruition.

Abigail did her best to appear chastened for Mleist's benefit, and when she tried to interrupt him—to keep his attention on her and away from her friend's conversation—he would have none of it. "*Fräulein*, you have no idea of the scope of the situation. You should be very grateful that we are taking such good care of you." In her mind's eye, Abigail saw herself stooping to help the little flower girl and a moment later the assassin's bullet finding Maria. His "good care" could leave her six feet under.

An urgent knock on the frame of the open door ended the baron's lecture. After another glower at Abigail, Baron Mleist bid the person to enter. A maid Abigail didn't recognize came in and addressed the baron in breathless Swaviczen, but he cut her off. He commanded, "Only German when the princess is in residence!"

The maid gathered herself and said, "My Lord, please come downstairs. There's a problem. Two of the women are sick."

The baron rolled his eyes with a mighty sigh. "This is not important now. Have Frau Hellig take care of it."

The maid insisted, "But she sent me to get you!"

The baron groaned with frustration. "I will come down later, when I am done—"

Shrieks echoed through the halls, followed by racing footfalls. A woman screamed, "She's dead!"

The baron dashed out into the hall, and the others clustered by the door. Several panicked women ran past them.

"Who's dead?" demanded the white-faced baron.

A woman slowed. "Griechen!" She dashed down the hall with the others.

Abigail knew the quiet maid who had brought in the tea and cookies was named Griechen. She had just been here a few minutes ago. They couldn't mean her. There had to be another woman with the same name.

The baron pulled Josef along with him and headed towards the emergency. Before Mleist disappeared, he stopped and pointed at the four members of Josef's household cavalry, then pointed at Abigail. "Watch her. Do not let her leave your sight." As he headed off at a trot, the four looked to Josef for instructions, and he gave a slow, reluctant gesture of agreement. He glowered at Abigail with an inscrutable scowl, then followed the baron.

Abigail dipped her head at the four soldiers to show her obedience. She gazed at Daisy. She nodded the other way, down the hall . . . to the exit.

Daisy frowned, then her face fell open as she understood the message. She took Biedric by the hand and kept him from joining the others in escorting Abigail.

Biedric realized the opportunity had presented itself without warning. He glanced in the direction Josef had left. He thought for only a moment, then he gave Abigail a serious nod. Her heart swelled with gratitude as she mouthed *"Danke schön"* and turned back to the room.

In a last glance over her shoulder, Abigail saw Biedric and her friend—her last hope—hurrying away towards freedom.

CHAPTER SIXTEEN

A Changing of the Guard

Once the extent of the day's crises was realized, palace guards replaced Josef's soldiers outside Abigail's room. The leader of the guards told her everything that had happened, and then he went out into the hall and locked the door, leaving her alone with the news.

Maria's death in the plaza had been horrible enough. Now Abigail had to dwell on the deaths of two of her maids. The box of chocolates intended for Her Serene Highness, which Abigail so casually gave to Belza, had been laced with poison. The bubbly maid had taken the special treat to a quiet corner of the palace pantry to enjoy with her friend, the sweet-natured Griechen. Both were now dead.

Abigail's brain knew she hadn't killed any of the three women, and yet guilt lay heavy on her heart. Her simple, thoughtless gestures of helping a child and being nice to a maid had spelled doom for them. She had no stake in the outcome of this country's power struggle, but with growing anger she wanted these heedless killers to pay for what they'd done.

She worried about Daisy and Biedric. It had been nearly an hour since they'd slipped away. In the commotion, no one had mentioned Abigail's friend was missing. Had the couple been intercepted? Were they out of Tirigovina yet? Since Daisy lacked the horse riding skills to make a dash across the countryside, had they rented a buggy? Would they be caught on the road by pursuing riders? Or had they chosen the train? Even if they succeeded in reaching Vienna, she worried about their lack of opportunity to sort out the details. What code might they use in the telegram? How would she know what they meant? Hog Latin in an outgoing telegram would have worked, but in an incoming message to Josef it would raise too many suspicions.

She already missed Daisy's sweetness and giddy humor. Now that she had no one to share her troubles, she appreciated Daisy's hidden strength and surprising good sense all the more. It would be a lonely time until the diplomatic cavalry came to her rescue . . . assuming it would come at all.

Then there was Josef. Her mind kept returning to Josef pulling her off the platform and then embracing her in the cathedral hallway. He had brought her to safety and revealed he was not in league with the others. But just as they had seemed to reach an understanding, she'd undercut him. How would he react when he heard the story that his soldier had eloped with her friend? Josef would know it was a fabrication, but in this interrelated society it would probably cause trouble for him that his lieutenant had acted in such a reckless way. If she'd had more time, she could have concocted something feasible that didn't cause so much damage. But she didn't have time, and she would have to live with what she'd done. All of it. She sat with her face in her hands. What a miserable, confusing, terrible day.

Almost two hours later, after Abigail concluded she would be in solitary confinement for the night, there was a short knock on the door and it opened. In came one of the palace guards, followed by Josef and then a stout matron of about fifty wearing a formal dirndl. Josef's serious expression made Abigail's heart sink.

He said in English, "*Fräulein*, I would like to introduce you to Frau Witj. She will be in charge of your care while you are a guest in the palace."

Abigail sized up her new guardian. Behind the woman's firm smile, she looked stern and unyielding. Abigail guessed there would be no room for negotiation with her.

Frau Witj spoke in English, but with an accent so thick that if Abigail hadn't known German she wouldn't have understood her.

"*Fräulein*, I am pleazed to meet you. I am zure ve vill get along very vell togezzer, you and I."

Abigail didn't know what to make of this. Why were they speaking English instead of German? This must be intentional on Josef's part, but it didn't make sense. Before she laid any of her cards on the table, she needed to have a better idea of what new game she was playing. She nodded politely.

Frau Witj continued, "I vill overzee your new maids. I pick zem myzelf. First iz Elga. She iz my niece. She speaks ze Englesh almost as vell as I do. You vill be most pleazed. Ven I am not here, she iz alvays here."

Abigail said in English, "Thank you. I appreciate your kindness."

"Zank you," the matron responded.

Josef went over to the washroom and looked inside, and then he crossed to the door of the forbidden bedroom. He looked inside, then turned back to Abigail. "I see your friend is not here. Can you please tell me where she is?"

She should have practiced saying this, but she had not. She'd been hoping he would hear it from someone else. At least she could give him an honest answer. "I do not know."

He didn't approve of her honesty. "When was the last time you saw her?"

"Several hours ago."

He also did not seem to appreciate having to draw out every detail. "Was she alone? What was she doing?"

"Walking with Biedric."

"Yes, my lieutenant is also missing. Do you know where they were going?"

"She didn't say."

He frowned. "But do you know?"

"I could be mistaken . . . but I believe they intended to elope."

Josef's frown turned to a scowl.

Frau Witj had followed most of the conversation, but she asked Josef what "elope" meant. When he told her, she glared at Abigail and puffed up with indignation. "Shame on zem! And you did not stop zem?"

Abigail ignored her and kept her chagrined gaze on Josef. The young nobleman took in a deep breath and let it out slowly. "It has been a day of many surprises." He looked through the bedroom door to the window and the approaching sunset. His words spoken more to Frau Witj than Abigail, he said, "It would be unlike Biedric to marry without getting the blessing of his parents. His home village is a few miles south of here. We'll look for them there."

Abigail understood his message. Vienna lay to the north. He was sending soldiers in the wrong direction. He might be angry, but he was still on her side. She wanted to talk with him. "Sir, would it be possible for me to go for a walk? I've been locked up in this room all afternoon, and I need some fresh air."

"No." His tone was not congenial. "It is not safe, and we have work to do. Frau Witj will attend to your needs here." He gave her a quick nod, then departed.

Frau Witj went into the bedroom and opened the window, letting in the fresh evening air. She checked the bed linens, and they must have passed inspection because she fluffed the pillows and made the room ready. Abigail guessed the bedroom was no longer forbidden. She wondered why her status had improved.

Abigail did not see Josef again that evening. Her new maids settled into the anteroom and her things were moved into the bedroom proper. However, despite the improvement in her accommodations, with no friend to share her troubled thoughts, she spent a long and lonely night.

In the gray morning light, Abigail breakfasted alone, observed by her three new maids. Elga, solid and a bit of a snob, enjoyed a higher status because of her aunt's position. The other girls were quiet, polite, and otherwise subdued. Perhaps they were thinking about their dead colleagues. They even seemed reluctant to tell Abigail their names.

What was noteworthy, however, was that none of them seemed to think Abigail spoke German. Elga, with her broken English, served as the spokeswoman for the maids and was quick to interpret between Abigail and the others. She also heard the buxom Elga disparage to the others the way Abigail fit into Her Highness's clothing—"she is much too skinny through the bosom, she is not an ample woman." Abigail could not imagine Elga would say that in front of her if she thought she could understand it. This misunderstanding had to be deliberate, but she couldn't figure out its purpose or who was behind it.

After the morning dishes had been cleared, Abigail was summoned to a "meeting for future events." More training, she thought with a sigh. Escorted by two palace guards, she followed Frau Witj through the halls.

In a back section of the building, they were passed twice by groups of maids. They regarded her with curiosity but no surprise. Perhaps the truth about her had made its way through the palace rumor mill. Poor, sweet Beĺza, she would have been such a good source of all the below-stairs information.

Abigail was delivered to a long, open room that held almost no furniture. A bank of windows ran the length of the room, letting in the dull light from the rainy day. Near the door was a small seating area of chairs clustered on a beautiful Persian carpet, and at the distant end of the room, on the rich wood floor, sat a table for six. The chair backs looked as if they were crafted from antlers. The white walls were covered with more antler trophies and storage racks for swords and other weapons.

Standing at the table and going over papers were Franz Antonius, Josef, and three men Abigail had never seen before. Baron Mleist was absent.

The men looked up at her arrival, and Josef came across the room to join her. "I hope you had a restful night," he said in English.

She had not, so instead of answering his question she said, "I hope you were able to find your lieutenant."

Josef dismissed Frau Witj, but the soldiers stayed behind. He indicated for Abigail to move to the carpeted sitting area, and they both sat. The soldiers stood at a close distance, so they could not speak freely.

"We were not. I must assume he and your friend have left the country."

She did her best not to react.

"When Swaviczens are impatient to marry, most travel to a town just across the Werenzland frontier to the east. I have sent people there to look for them."

Again, he had sent people in the wrong direction. But he gave her no clear sign that he cared about her plight—or her. "I hope any indiscretion on his part will be rectified someday."

"Not easily. And in the meantime, I had to dismiss his brother from my service."

"Oh, no! Jowan!"

She saw the people at the table look up at her exclamation. They watched her for a moment, then returned to their papers. At that moment she noticed a white triangular cloth draped over the back of one of the chairs at the table. It looked like a sling. So, Josef did use a sling, except when she was around.

"Yes," he said, "but at least this gave Jowan the chance to talk with his parents and explain what's happening." He regarded her. "I wish his brother had taken the time to consider other options." She knew Josef really meant her.

She said with well chosen words, "On some occasions, there isn't time to be careful."

"There was time."

She hoped he wouldn't mind if she disagreed, especially if she let William Shakespeare speak for her. "'There is a tide in the affairs of men, which, taken at the flood, leads on to fortune. . . . We must take the current when it serves.'"

"Some currents create dangerous waves."

"But if you steer well, they can speed you on your way."

He studied her, but he did not reply. He cast his gaze around the room, then looked at the closest rack of swords on the wall. He stood and retrieved two of the weapons from the rack. "On our ride, you asked about the difference between using a sword in battle and using it in a match."

They had discussed no such thing, but when he gestured for her to stand, she did without hesitation. He approached her with the lightweight swords. "These are for fencing school. They teach you technique." He tucked them under his arm and stood next to her, taking her right hand in his and holding it palm up.

Abigail shivered at the tenderness of his grip. His smile was genuine and a little shy, and nothing like his studied circumspection of the last days. With that, she knew he was her ally in spite of everything. She smiled and fought to keep in a laugh.

He said, "Hold your first finger and thumb together, very gently."

She mimicked the gesture he demonstrated.

"This is how you control the foil." He placed the weapon in her hand, then showed her how to hold it with her palm up.

They were standing side by side, shoulders together. She whispered, "Why am I here?"

"To keep you distracted."

"It's working."

He smiled at her admission but kept his eyes on the sword.

"I thought I was being brought to a meeting."

"It was easier to call it that. I thought you'd like to get out of your rooms."

She suspected he was the reason why she was now allowed to sleep in the bedroom instead of on a cot. How sweet and thoughtful he was.

"You see?" With slight adjustments of his fingers, he moved his own foil. He stepped away and faced her. He held his sword pointed in her direction but with the tip angled down. "Now, try to hit me." He tapped his chest over his heart.

As she pointed her sword at him, she heard Franz Antonius's laugh from across the room. "Cousin, what are you doing? You're taking your life in your hands!" He laughed again.

Josef ignored him and urged Abigail to strike. She looked at the narrow blade's blunted tip, then took a deep breath and thrust the weapon's point at his chest.

Even though he didn't alter the position of his hand, with a simple change in the angle of the weapon his blade flashed up and caught hers from the inside, directing it just past his arm. "Try it again."

Was he actually trying to teach her how to fence? She repeated the gesture, and the result was the same off to the other side, her blade redirected just enough to avoid harm.

"You see," he said with intensity. "It is about being subtle." Using his whole arm, he pushed her blade far to the side. "Not this." He pushed it high in the air, for a moment yielding to a wince. "Not this. That is for the stage. When you are fighting in real life, only do just enough to deflect attacks and attention away. That is how you succeed."

She understood. At the risk of a silly joke, this was about making a point, not about fencing. "But are there not times when a grand gesture is more effective?"

He took the sword from her with a glance at the table across the room. "Not in this game."

He placed the swords back on the rack and indicated for her to sit. As they returned to the chairs, she looked at the group around the table. "Where is Baron Mleist? I would expect him to be at what appears to be an important meeting."

Josef glanced at the group, then said in even tones, "He has returned to Chetova Castle."

She knew it had to be a demotion, even though he didn't say it.

"It was the baron who suggested Maria pretend to be a maid to watch you, and he let her go out onto the platform in his place. Not only that, your friend escaped while he was in charge, and he allowed poison into the palace. We have talked with the people in the mayor's office. Of course they know nothing about a box of chocolates."

"So, if the baron is gone, who's in charge now?"

"The palace has its own major domo. Baron Austerlanden will be in charge of the day-to-day operations. Franz is in charge of security."

That didn't make Abigail happy. "Did he volunteer to be in charge of my care?"

"He's in charge of the security of the palace, but he is not in charge of your care."

"Then who is?" She couldn't imagine these men would give that kind of authority to Frau Witj.

"I am."

Abigail blinked with surprise. Did they not suspect they were putting the fox in charge of the henhouse?

But even as she brightened, he grew serious. "There's something you must do this afternoon for Her Highness. You must attend the mass for Lady Maria at the cathedral."

She hadn't considered that possibility. She didn't want to go out again so soon after . . . yesterday. "What do I have to do?"

"Nothing. It will be a mass."

That presented another problem. "I'm not Catholic. I won't know what to do."

He assured her that it would be a private ceremony, so she wouldn't interact with the public, and he and Franz Antonius would be there to guide her. He looked at the men around the table. "They hoped to avoid this by saying Her Highness was too distraught to attend, but no one would believe it, and it would only make her look afraid."

Abigail understood about being afraid. She gazed out at the steady rain. But she had no choice. Besides, she felt she owed a gesture of respect for the woman who had more courage than most of the men.

Dressed in another borrowed gown, this one of heavy black, and with a loose weeping veil draped over an equally somber bonnet, Abigail was taken in the closed royal carriage through solemn and rainy streets to the cathedral. As promised, Josef and Franz Antonius accompanied her. They were both in civilian mourning suits. Franz Antonius complained about the weather, but otherwise no one spoke on the short trip.

Abigail saw a rain canopy set up next to the cathedral door ... the same door she'd entered and fled through yesterday. By instinct she peered out through the coach's curtains looking for danger, but soldiers were in place to keep the peace. As the three exited the carriage, Franz Antonius went on ahead to make sure everything was ready. Josef helped Abigail step down. With no discernible emotion on his face, he held onto her hand after she reached the ground, then gave it an encouraging squeeze before he placed it on his forearm as a royal support.

As Josef predicted, Abigail's duties during the service were minimal. The cousins, under the guise of supporting their afflicted sovereign, sat on either side of her and guided her through the times to stand, sit, and kneel. The sacrament was brought to her, and she apologized to God for any impropriety as she accepted the bread and wine under the cover of her loose veil.

Through most of the service she gazed at the body in the open casket. Maria's face was stern and disapproving, even in death. Abigail no longer blamed Maria for her aloof behavior. If she knew about the plan from the beginning, and her loyalty lay with Rosamunde alone, then to her Abigail was little more than a veal calf destined for an early demise. And Maria had the courage to go out onto the platform. Abigail knew the woman's death wasn't her fault, but in an odd way she felt guilty for surviving. In the small purse that was part of her mourning ensemble she found a handkerchief. Its glaring white—despite being trimmed in black—would draw attention to her action. But she began to sniffle and needed it. Franz Antonius watched her with a dubious frown as she reached under the heavy veil and dabbed her eyes.

At the end of the service, the cousins escorted Abigail up to the coffin so she could say Rosamunde's farewells to her faithful lady in waiting. Abigail looked down at the silent face. What an unnecessary loss. "I'm sorry, Maria," she whispered. "Please forgive me." She wiped her eyes and turned away.

On the way back to the palace, she noticed some men standing on the sidewalk. They saw her and removed their hats. They seemed sad for the woman they thought was their grieving monarch. Touched by their kindness, she gave them a small nod of thanks. Moved by her attention, they lowered their heads and one man wiped his nose.

When the carriage returned to the palace, the cousins proceeded to the royal chambers while Abigail was escorted by several soldiers back to her empty room. She removed the veil and hat before dropping in exhaustion across her bed.

To Abigail's surprise, that evening Franz Antonius invited her to join him for dinner in a small dining room. Two of the men from the morning enclave were there, but Josef was not. As Franz told her, "He's attending to other matters," she had the impression he didn't know what those matters were. She wondered if what Josef was doing had something to do with her.

The men were introduced to Abigail as Baron Austerlanden, the major domo of Schoenberg Palace, and his assistant, Pol Schmidt. Abigail was happy to have the others present in the room so she wouldn't have to dine alone with Franz. Baron Austerlanden was urbane and politic, while his assistant, a quiet fellow cursed with large ears and sallow hair, was obedient and utilitarian.

Franz Antonius behaved himself, aside from drinking two glasses of wine too many. He complimented her performance during the service. He said word had gotten out to the public about the "courageous but brokenhearted" princess saying her tender farewells to her faithful servant. She knew he was making fun of her, but she chose not to rise to the bait. He then said Her Highness expressed her delight with the goodwill Abigail's tears had earned for her.

Playing the good listener, Abigail asked the relaxed Franz Antonius about the reasons for this impostor charade and let him talk. He obliged her by going on at length about the clever plan of having Abigail be Rosamunde's double, even though he omitted the part about knowingly placing her in mortal danger. He portrayed the whole thing as a chess match between rivals. Of course, he didn't know what she knew about their willingness to sacrifice her, so while he talked in terms of an intellectual board game, she knew he was talking about a battle to the death, including her own. On several occasions she watched Baron Austerlanden take in a breath as if to interrupt his speech, but then it seemed the baron thought better of correcting his superior and clenched his jaw. To dispel the baron's well-founded concerns that Franz Antonius was saying too much, she did her best to look merely fascinated and impressed.

Franz Antonius talked until he grew sleepy from the wine and the good company. He dismissed his male guests and thanked them for an excellent evening. Of course, it had been entirely about him, so how could it not be excellent? Abigail steeled herself in fear he would insist on escorting her to her room but, instead, the yawning nobleman bid her a good evening and sent her off with two palace guards to guide her.

Back in her room, listening to the snoring maids, Abigail lay awake for a long time. If Josef was in charge of her care, then it had to be his doing that her new servants thought she didn't speak German. Josef had used the departure of those who knew the truth to give her a tactical advantage, and she hoped she'd be able to exploit it. The only one who might accidentally spoil things would be Frau Meyer. Since Abigail knew she would certainly encounter the royal dressmaker again, she would have to find a way to talk with her when the others weren't present.

Until long past midnight, she thought about Josef's smile, her life as a clay pigeon, and when a coded telegram might be arriving from Vienna.

CHAPTER SEVENTEEN

A Princess Among the People

"Have you seen this, Your Highness?"

Rosamunde glanced up from her cold beet soup as Franz Antonius put the newspaper on the anteroom table before her. The front page of a Vienna paper from this morning had a headline declaring another bank crisis somewhere. What did this have to do with her? She said, "My glasses are on the desk." He went to retrieve them.

Rosamunde resented being confined to her chambers on the top floor of her palace. Franz Antonius had locked it down as if it were a prison. While she did appreciate his concern for her safety, she wanted to eat her lunch on the back veranda. She wanted to go out. She wanted this silly farce to be over so she could get on with choosing a husband and running her country.

Franz presented her glasses to her. Now she could see what had caught his attention. On the right half of the page was a story about yesterday's events in Tirigovina's Cathedral Plaza: *Monarch Survives Assassination Attempt.* The engraved illustration, a melodramatic envisioning of the event, showed the intended target kneeling to talk with a child while the victim, a shocked look on her face and her hands in the air, was falling back into the arms of the startled soldiers behind her. The figure bore no resemblance to Maria, so Rosamunde felt no discomfort with the representation. The story told by the illustration didn't match the way Mleist had reported it, but it certainly made for a dramatic and memorable image. This was so sympathetic and heart-touching that, aside from the loss of Maria, the turn of events was almost as good as having the whole episode over. This was how she'd always be remembered—an act of kindness had saved her life.

She read through the article, which gave a thorough account of the event—most of the details matched the reports from the police and her spies—and even made some rather complimentary remarks about her bravery. The article included a statement from the police chief saying they suspected anarchists. Good. That's what he was instructed to say. All in all, she liked the article, and the artist had omitted her double's veil and had made her look pretty. Since the image bore no resemblance to her or her decoy, the fact that it was her decoy and not her looking attractive didn't bother Rosamunde, either.

However, studying the illustration did make her miss Maria again. Such a good servant, and so efficient. Rosamunde knew her life would never be so well run again. And here she was, stuck in this prison, unable to accompany Maria's body to Berlin and condole with the family. She wanted to visit Berlin and talk with two of the important Prussian families about a possible marriage alliance, not to mention get some new dresses. This would have been the perfect opportunity to leave without being accused of abandoning her country. But until her enemies revealed themselves, she was stuck here.

"Well, Your Highness?" Franz Antonius said.

"The article says what it's supposed to. I'm alive, and I'm brave. And the villains have no reason to suspect we know about them."

"Cousin, have you not considered how you should capitalize on this?"

She stirred her beet soup. "How?"

"Your Highness should be out in town, being seen by your people as unafraid and scoffing at danger."

She gazed out the window. Going outside would be very nice indeed. But as much as she fancied Franz Antonius—and she did even more ever since this dangerous game began—she didn't trust him. Was he trying to put her in danger, just so he could rescue her? She knew him well enough to suspect it. He wanted to be king, but to what lengths would he go?

"What do you intend, my dear Heigenlizt? Parade me before another loaded rifle?"

He sat in the other chair at her table and leaned forward in a beseeching pose. "Not you, fair cousin. Your double. Let her ride through the streets—in your landau, with the top down, to show you're not afraid. She takes the risks, and you take the credit."

She marveled at the idea. "Zaaf wouldn't like it."

"Don't tell him."

They shared a smile. Doing something behind her stodgy councilor's back was tempting.

Franz Antonius said, "He's old and plays by old rules. You and I are not bound by outmoded restrictions. 'Honor and duty' only serve a purpose if they aid us. We understand that. He does not."

Yes, she did understand that. Zaaf had not approved of her decoy plan, and recently he'd begun dragging his feet in the matter. Moving the archaic councilor to the periphery appealed to her. But did Franz Antonius have something else in mind? "And if you send out my double, will you go with her?"

"Not I. I'm responsible for watching over the security here." A smirk touched his lips. "Send her keeper with her."

So, she thought, Franz Antonius was willing to send Josef into harm's way, too! She knew they weren't close, but what a cold heart he had. And a calculating mind. She could use that mind. Of course, if she did decide to marry him, he represented extra work, since they were cousins and the archbishop said she would need a dispensation from the Pope to marry him. Then again, the archbishop didn't like her, and she'd heard of second cousins marrying, so perhaps the annoying churchman had fabricated the problem. Franz Antonius was worth the time to investigate.

Then again, Josef had demonstrated tremendous loyalty by being wounded in her service while protecting a mere decoy. If he was willing to go out into danger again with her double, his character would be redoubtable indeed. He'd also lobbied on behalf of the foreigner when they were in Chetova, even though he'd only met the girl a day or two earlier. Courage, intelligence, compassion and a protective spirit were all great attributes for a consort. Josef was also sweet-natured, and he would be good company at the end of a long day. It might work out well if she married Josef and made Franz Antonius the equivalent of a prime minister. One for his heart, and the other for his brain. She liked the idea, but she wanted to know the motivations of this cousin.

"My fair Heigenlizt," she said, "I am reluctant to put my good-hearted Ramsl into such danger."

"We have no knowledge that your enemies will be out there today. And if they do try something, they won't be shooting at him."

"They weren't shooting at Maria, either."

He acknowledged the truth of her statement. "That was an unfortunate fluke not likely to be repeated. Oh, and don't send them with your palace guards. Have him use his household cavalry instead."

His thoroughness made her smile. "So I don't lose any of my people if something happens?"

"Of course. And it serves them right for the ridiculous behavior of his lieutenant. Eloping with that silly girl, and in the middle of all this, too. All of his soldiers should have to pay for that."

Rosamunde took another sip of her soup. She'd heard Franz's stories about her decoy's empty-brained little friend. "Do you really think that was merely an elopement?"

He sat back in his chair. "Oh, it's genuine. I witnessed their unseemly displays of affection from the beginning. Besides, Josef was quite unhappy when he heard the news. The boy is much too transparent. I'd know if he lied about that."

"True."

Franz Antonius chuckled. "Besides, if my life were in danger, and I were trying to send for help, the *last* person on this earth I would rely on would be that bubble-head." He laughed at the thought of such a rescuer.

Not sure what to expect, Abigail left her room accompanied by Frau Witj, Elga and another of the new maids. All she knew was she would be going for a drive through town on the order of the Count of Heigenlizt himself.

For the occasion she had on an outdoor dress and matching jacket in dove gray with black trimming, indicating it as a dress of "half-mourning." Presumably full mourning for a lady in waiting only lasted a day or two. The matching hat had a fine veil in light gray. The veil would be enough to soften the details of her face, so a makeup disguise would not be necessary. Frau Witj cooed over the dress, saying Abigail should be honored to wear this because the princess herself had worn it after the death of her uncle the late king.

Abigail followed her escort down the hallway towards the front of the palace. She wondered why they weren't doing the charade of going up to the door of the princess's chambers first. They reached the stairway and encountered a manservant and two maids. The servants stopped to watch Abigail's small entourage, and as she passed one of the maids gave her a slight curtsy. Surely the servants hadn't mistaken her for the real princess, because their gestures of respect would be much more pronounced.

Her attendants led the way down the stairs towards the ground level, and they encountered two other manservants carrying baskets up the stairs. The men halted, and as Abigail passed she heard one of them murmur in German, "God bless you." It wasn't in the form of a benediction or a eulogy. It was a statement of gratitude.

Abigail's group reached the ground level and walked through the grand foyer to the front door. Three butlers and several female servants watched her go past. Abigail wondered if she was seeing things— were they looking at her with admiration? One young maid approached her and took her gloved hand. To Abigail's astonishment, she kissed Abigail's glove and said in German, "Thank you for going into trouble so our lady is safe."

Abigail patted the young woman's hand with a smile. Word about her must have spread through the palace staff. No wonder her keepers no longer felt the need to disguise her, at least indoors.

The other servants gathered around her, expressing their appreciation in German and Swaviczen. Such heartfelt concern touched Abigail, and for a moment her resentment over the ordeal faded away. Elga seemed a little impatient, while Frau Witj translated all their gratitude and basked in the borrowed glow of the moment. But they had to go, so Frau Witj broke up the enclave and sent the gathered people off to their appointed tasks.

The group reached the front entrance, where two smiling manservants opened the doors at their approach. Four palace guardsmen stood outside the entrance, two on each side. Abigail didn't remember seeing soldiers posted there before. She had to assume Franz Antonius had tightened security after the attacks. The guards saluted her—she was now officially standing in for the princess—and she descended the front stairs with Frau Witj and the maids.

The afternoon was glorious, with fresh breezes, fleecy clouds, and a chorus of birds singing from the treetops. She hoped it wasn't ironic that she felt good to be alive. At the base of the stairs waited an open carriage. The small landau had plush benches in front and back, each large enough for two people, but it lacked the usual bench on the back for additional coachmen. Only a driver and one coachman sat on the front driving bench. The convertible roof was all the way down. Even though there were two mounted soldiers in front and two behind, she was being offered up as a tempting target for whoever might wish to take another shot at her. But when she saw the person standing next to the landau's step and open door, all her worries eased.

Josef bowed as she descended from the last step. She couldn't keep her smile hidden. He was not bowing to his princess, or even to his princess's dress. He was bowing to her. With only the slightest smile in his eyes, he held out his left hand, which she accepted, and he guided her to the rear seat. He followed her into the carriage, then closed the landau's door. To her slight disappointment he sat opposite her in the rear-facing front seat. But she savored the silver lining that it would be just the two of them on this ride. She looked at the women watching from the bottom of the stairs. The maids seemed glad to be rid of her for a while, but Frau Witj waved farewell with a broad smile.

Josef gave the driver and coachman the instruction to proceed, and the landau with its escort began to move. Only then did Abigail notice that the soldiers were Josef's, and the driver and coachman were in the indigo and white of Josef's livery. "I see I'm among friends," she said in German.

"Yes." His face remained calm and collected, but she saw an unmistakable warmth in his eyes.

"I don't suppose we can leave town and simply keep going."

He smiled at that, even as he shook his head. "No."

"Why not? Rosamunde has proof now that someone wants to kill her. She doesn't need me anymore."

"I've learned she intends to keep you as a guest until she finds out who's behind the plot. Then you may leave."

He made it all sound so very polite. Of course, and unfortunately, Rosamunde's plan was well-reasoned. Abigail knew she'd be in this to the bitter end. "It was worth asking."

The group slowed as the front gate opened for them. Again she noticed additional soldiers at the entrance. The carriage passed through, and the gate closed after the trailing pair of horsemen. They turned right, heading in the direction away from the plaza.

She said, "I want to thank you for the improvement in my sleeping quarters. I assume you're behind that decision."

He nodded. "You're welcome."

"And also please accept my belated thanks for sending searchers in the wrong directions."

"Of course." The landau bounced over a rock in the road, and his soft smile disappeared into a wince.

"How's your shoulder?" she asked.

He frowned at her question in feigned ignorance, then relented. "It hurts."

"It's all right to wear a sling. There's no need to suffer just to put on a brave show."

He nodded. "I'll remember that."

"Where were you hit?" She hoped her question didn't sound indelicate.

With his left hand he gestured halfway between the base of his neck and the tip of his right shoulder. "Just across the top. The doctor said it missed all the important things, which is good."

She agreed. "I'm sorry you were hurt on my account."

He gave her a steady gaze. "I was not hurt on your account. I was hurt on the account of Her Highness. And a mere nick is a small price to pay for keeping the truth from you."

Abigail reflected on the vast difference between how he had acted on the first day during their afternoon ride and then at dinner that evening. "Did you know the plan when we met?"

"No. I found out later that day."

A wave of relief flowed over her. Now his abrupt change in temperament made complete sense. Her trust in him was vindicated. She looked at the buildings going by. "What exactly are we doing?"

"We are driving around for an hour or so, enjoying the beautiful day, and showing the people of Tirigovina that Her Highness is not afraid."

Abigail could not resist. "Or that she's overstuffed with bravado."

He snorted as he tried to suppress a laugh. "You should be careful. This is not America. We do not have 'freedom of speech.'"

She looked at the small shops as the carriage rolled past. A few people recognized the royal landau and waved salutes. She offered her most dignified nod in response.

"Sam Clemens is right," she said. "Travel changes you. I never really thought about what it meant to be an American. The longer I'm here, the prouder I am of a place I took for granted."

He nodded as she acknowledged a handful of citizens and their smiling calls to her in Swaviczen. He explained, "They are telling you how proud they are of you." She smiled at them, which prompted exclamations and waved hats as the landau rolled on past.

Josef continued, "When I was a child, I wanted to be Austrian and be from an important country. But when I moved to Vienna, I found even though they rule over many peoples, they have little regard for anyone who is not one of them."

Abigail nodded to a man who waved to her.

Josef said, "Their arrogance and jokes chafed. The high and mighty forget that not everyone admires them or wants to be like them. The more they denigrated us, the more I loved Swavicza."

She nodded, then responded to greetings shouted in German by a green grocer in front of his shop.

Josef asked, "When you are back in America, if I am able, may I come and visit you?"

She tried to keep her smile regal and dignified. "Of course. But I have to warn you. Americans are a very simple people. We are peasants, one and all. At least the ones I know."

"Including your Mark Twain?"

"Yes, including my Mark Twain. Not only will they have never heard of Swavicza, but your rank will mean nothing there." They acknowledged well wishes from people along the street. "You'll get none of the reverence you enjoy here."

He considered that, then scanned the second stories of the buildings on either side of the road. "It will be a good challenge for me to earn respect instead of assume it will be rendered."

She felt a twinge near her heart. Before this flirtation continued, however, she needed to make her amends. "I'm sorry about the elopement ruse."

He frowned, but not with disapproval. "Yes, that was very difficult. There were ramifications here that you did not understand. You put Biedric and his family in an awkward position." Something caught his eye, and he focused his attention behind her, but apparently it turned out to be unimportant because, before she could turn around, he looked at her again and continued his thought. "For me, the biggest problem is my lieutenant is gone. Everything is in disorder without him."

She read a more personal element to his words. "And I took your friend away from you. I'm sorry."

"I understand you did not have a lot of choices, but I wish you could have waited and come up with something else." They responded to more well wishes from people on the sidewalk.

Abigail could see the cathedral steeple several blocks ahead. She realized the driver had made a large loop, and they were heading into the center of town. Josef seemed more on guard.

Abigail said, "I wonder if Daisy has met up with her aunts and talked with the ambassador in Vienna." She wondered what the girls in the Escorted Tour for Young Ladies of Quality had made of Daisy's far-fetched tale. If Abigail weren't living it, even she might not believe it.

Josef regarded her as she acknowledged another greeting from some citizens. "You are so calm. Why aren't you afraid?"

To her surprise, she realized her fears before the ride had dissipated. "Nothing is going to happen."

He scowled. "How can you be so certain?"

"The shooting and chocolates were well thought out. They knew where and when the ceremony would happen, so they could prepare. The box of chocolates was an excellent secondary plan. If Rosamunde survived, she would be agitated and inclined to find solace in her favorite treat. But they couldn't plan for this. There's no advantage for them in acting in haste. It's more important for them not to get caught, because once they are, the game is well and truly up. No, I'll be fine today."

She hadn't thought it through before she said it, but she was favorably impressed as her calm logic unfolded. Of course, now she knew the terrible danger in anything planned and publicized. She needed to get out of this country before the next event could be arranged.

Wonder filled his eyes. "As Baron Mleist said, you are a fine strategist."

"Just don't tell 'em that. I like being underestimated."

He smiled with undiluted admiration.

Her heart melted at that smile. As much as she needed to get out of Swavicza, and as much as she wanted to believe he really did want to visit her in America, she knew once she left she would never see Josef again. How dreadfully unfair.

As they approached the block next to the plaza, she saw children playing in front of some shops. They looked between the ages of eight and twelve. They were running, chasing, laughing. How she envied them their youth. Then she saw a boy pull a girl's braid, and the girl spun around and took a swing at him. He laughed at her anger, but then another girl kicked him in the shins and it was the girls' turn to laugh. Abigail didn't miss that part of childhood.

A gathering of adults chatted a short distance away. From the group Abigail heard a familiar voice bellow a greeting. She saw Jovacź Chešqu, the Sálacene representative, with wide-stretched arms smiling at her and calling out something in a language she assumed was Sálacene. Abigail wanted to find out how he had fared and how the little flower girl was doing. She asked Josef to signal the driver to stop. After a quick assessment of the group, he relayed her command. The landau came to a halt before the adults, to their astonishment.

Chešqu, the natural showman, called out to her with full throat despite her proximity. "Your Highness!" he said in German. "So good to see you well!"

She replied in German, "The same to you, Herr Chešqu. You are well? And the little flower girl is all right?"

Tenderness lit his eyes. "She is fine, Your Highness. She was so frightened by you that she didn't understand any of the rest of what happened. She did not see your poor lady at all."

"Thanks to your protection of her, Herr Chešqu."

He bowed with dramatic flair.

The other adults gawked at their friend exchanging comfortable pleasantries with their monarch. He, of course, was enjoying every moment of it.

The tussle of playing children came over to see the excitement, and parents corralled their youngsters with firm grasps and nods of apology to the noble visitors.

As the rascally boy was drawn in by his father, Abigail caught sight of a movement behind a woman in the group. When the boy tugged at his father's grasp, Abigail saw the half-hidden movement again. It was a fair-haired little girl who could not have been more than eight. As the slight child slipped around her mother to stay out of the boy's sight, Abigail saw a homemade crutch, then two. The girl had a good leg, but the other was short and withered. When the girl saw Abigail looking at her, she tried to duck behind her mother. She couldn't hide from both Abigail and the boy, and when he caught sight of her he shouted a taunt. The girl tried to disappear into the fabric of her mother's skirt.

Abigail guessed the lame girl spent most of her life at the mercy of the other children. For the first time in this masquerade, she realized she had some power at her disposal. Now would be a good time to use it.

"Little girl," she said to the hiding child, "little girl, what is your name?"

Large eyes peered out from a fold in her mother's skirt. The mother was staring open-mouthed at the American college girl she believed to be her monarch.

Abigail tried again. She asked the mother, "How did she come to have this problem with her leg?"

The woman gathered herself enough to say, "A difficult birth."

Abigail nodded in sympathy. "I never get to talk with children. May I have your permission for your daughter to ride with us for a while?"

The rascally boy made a protesting whine, but his father silenced him with an apologetic smile to the nobles and a rough pat on the boy's cheek.

Abigail looked at the little girl, who had emerged from the folds of her mother's dress. "Would that be all right with you?"

The mother shook her head with embarrassment. "She cannot climb up there."

Josef opened the low door of the landau and stepped out. He knelt next to the little girl. "Would you like to ride with us? I can help you up."

Abigail felt a pang in her heart at his simple act of compassion. The fondness she felt for him turned into something richer. She had to glance away.

The girl warmed to Josef's offer, but she looked to her mother for permission.

Abigail regained her composure. "We promise to take good care of her."

How could the woman say no to her sovereign? Overwhelmed, she offered a deep curtsy, then knelt by her daughter, giving her dress an unnecessary straightening. She whispered her soft instructions, then nodded.

Josef stood as the girl kept a grip on her crutches and raised her hands in delight so he could pick her up. With an easy gesture and only a small wince, he lifted her up and set her on the floor of the landau. Abigail shifted over so she could sit beside her. Josef resumed his place on the front bench.

The girl looked up at the woman beside her. Abigail asked her, "What's your name?"

"Rosamunde," the girl answered.

Abigail replied with delight, "That's my name, too."

Josef signaled the coachman, and they were off, leaving behind a crowd of amazed adults and bewildered children.

Little Rosamunde savored the sights of the plaza as they rolled through. In excellent German she said, "I've never ridden in such a fine coach, not in my entire life!"

Abigail acknowledged smiles from the people they passed, then said to her, "You speak German very well."

The girl stated with a child's pride, "My grandfather says 'you have to speak German to get ahead.'" Abigail nodded. Encouraged, the girl continued, "He works in the palace. He's very important." The girl scrutinized her for a long moment. "You're important, aren't you?"

Delighted at the girl's boldness, Abigail glanced at Josef, then gave the girl a small shrug. "Some people think so, but not really." Josef chuckled.

Abigail and the young Rosamunde chatted as the landau and its escort made a circuit around the plaza. All signs of the interrupted festival were gone, including the platform outside the cathedral.

The landau exited the square and headed towards the palace. The girl pointed out the opera house, the government offices, the Austrian embassy, the police station, and the palace. She asked Abigail, "May we go to the train station? There might be a train!"

Abigail looked at Josef, who nodded and relayed the command to the driver. They continued down the street and out through the majestic medieval gate.

At the station, a waiting train sat, a steady hiss of steam venting from the engine's boiler, as the last passengers hurried to get on board. Abigail glanced at the clock on the depot building: 2:30. She might need that information someday. At little Rosamunde's pleading request, they waited until the train pulled away. The horses jigged nervously at the locomotive's whistle and the startup blasts of steam from the cylinders, but the landau's driver kept the animals in place. The little girl—and in turn the adults with her—waved at the passengers on the departing train. Several waved back, some with astonishment. Abigail made mental notes of the ticket window's location and where the station crew stood as the train pulled away. The depot was small and open. Slipping through it unnoticed would be difficult. She noticed Josef watching her as she studied the building's layout. She gave him an innocent and opaque smile. His response was a cocked eyebrow. She decided it was time to leave.

At Josef's command, the driver took the landau on a loop back through town. Abigail chatted with the girl, delighting in her curiosity and intelligence. She hoped the child would have a chance to get a real education. They returned to the waiting assemblage of adults and children in front of the shops. The group had doubled in size during the short time the carriage had been away.

As the landau rolled to a stop, little Rosamunde gave a large man next to her mother an excited "Papa!" She stood and reached out for him, and he easily hoisted her out of the carriage as the mother accepted the crutches from Josef. The father held the slender girl tucked in his arm as she excitedly described the route and how much they'd seen and how much fun they'd had. She concluded with, "And Papa, she liked the way you made my crutches fit just right for me." The mother began to cry, and with tears in his own eyes the man nodded to the couple in the landau, unable to speak.

At first hesitant, the group warmed to this strange, friendly woman dressed as their princess, and people soon gathered next to the carriage to admire and gawk. Abigail felt a ripple of fear with the closeness of so many people she didn't know. She looked to Josef for guidance, but he seemed at ease, so she relaxed, a little.

She said to Rosamunde's parents, "Thank you for letting me get to know my young namesake." She turned her attention to the girl. "My friend, I hope you continue to grow big and strong and listen to your parents and work hard on your studies." A murmur passed through the gathering as little Rosamunde beamed and nodded.

Before Josef could give the coachman the signal to leave, from the corner of her eye Abigail saw a quick movement towards her. She shuddered as a large hand reached out and grasped her gloved hand. Jovacź Chešqu gave her glove a heartfelt kiss, to expressions of approval from some of the others.

With a quiet sigh of relief, she had to smile. "You are a charmer, my dear Chešqu." He laughed. He didn't let her hand slip from his grasp until the landau pulled away.

Some in the group waved and some applauded as the carriage and soldiers headed back towards the palace. Chešqu held a hand aloft and called after her: "Long live Princess Rosamunde!" Shouts echoing the sentiment followed.

Abigail laughed as she stopped herself from turning and waving. They were cheering someone else, not her. But she realized this was the first good laugh she'd had in days, and it felt exhilarating. She looked at Josef, who gazed at her with such admiration and fondness that it made her chest hurt. She had to close her eyes. He must stop looking at her like that. It was not fair.

As they approached the palace, Abigail saw a handful of people talking with the guards at the gate. The people weren't happy, but the guards were adamant. The conversation broke up as the landau and its escort neared the gate. The people stepped aside with bows as the gate opened and the group rolled through. The gate closed swiftly, and the argument resumed behind them. "What's that all about?" Abigail asked Josef.

"They say they are employed at the palace and they're not being let in to report for work."

"Why not?"

"After what happened, the place is locked up. If you are in, you stay in, and if you are out you must stay out. Only a few of us can come and go."

"Who are the lucky few?"

"You—under guard, of course—me, Franz, our personal soldiers, Baron Austerlanden, some senior palace guards, and Rosamunde's secretary, Varni. He is the only one she trusts. He is her true eyes and ears of the outside world."

"No one else can leave?"

"No one." He glanced back at the gate. "If those people persist, they might be thrown in jail."

Abigail wondered what would happen when the people from the American embassy in Vienna arrived for her. She prayed they would be let in. They had to be.

Back in her room, Abigail had barely finished changing into her usual borrowed afternoon dress when two of Josef's soldiers came to see her, Mikal Schwarze and Phillip Zujaken, a cousin of Biedric and Jowan Halle. The men were all-business, which raised her concern.

Phillip told the maids in German that their mistress was required for a short time in the old library, but she would be returning soon so they should not interrupt their duties here. The maids nodded, then shared a mischievous glance. Phillip said the same thing to Abigail in excellent English, and she exited with the two men as her escort.

They headed down the rear stairs and then out through the back halls to a small library where Josef stood waiting. She noticed the men stayed in the room by the closed door.

Josef wore a sling, which she was glad to see, but the troubled look on his face alarmed her. He nodded to Abigail with a gesture for her to sit at the library's table. As she did, he said to her in English, "I hope you're not fatigued after the tour this afternoon." He sat in the chair next to her.

"Thank you," she said, "not at all. I could have gone for hours—in a straight line."

When he didn't respond to her flippant remark, she became more worried.

From his pocket he produced a piece of paper. "I have received a telegram. I assume it is for you."

She held out her hand, yielding to her impatience. He gave the paper to her.

After the routing information and salutation it read in German: "Regarding your inquiry. Met with representative. Store never received order. No knowledge of book. No authorization given to proceed. No business ties with S. Can offer no help. So very sorry." The signature read "D. Millansohn" of a bookstore in Vienna.

Abigail stared at the message. She knew "D. Millansohn" had to be Daisy MacMillan, and "so very sorry" sounded just like her. Even though they hadn't established what their code would be, clearly this was not good news.

Josef asked, "What's the matter?"

Abigail wasn't sure how diplomatic relations worked. "Is there an American embassy in Swavicza?"

He shook his head. "There used to be one a while ago, but after an incident, it was closed. And then your civil war happened, and it never reopened."

"Is there is an American . . . anything here?"

"No."

Trying to work through this, she asked, "If there's no diplomatic relationship between two countries, can an ambassador from one country have official contact with representatives from another?"

His frown deepened. "What does this message say?"

Abigail explained the visit in Graz with Mr. Ignatius Porter and how he said the ambassador in Vienna would help ensure her safety. "But the way I'm reading this, not only did the American ambassador know nothing about this plan, but even if he did, there's nothing he could do to help me and. . . ." She glanced at Josef, his two men, and then stared at the paper as tears filled her eyes. "Oh, no." Josef put a consoling hand on her arm.

Details of her conversation with Mr. Porter came back to her: his discomfort at some of her questions, his statement that Swavicza was an ally and her actions would be supported by the U.S. government. She tried to blink away her tears. "So Swavicza and America aren't allies?"

Josef shook his head. "I'm afraid the king at the time, Rosamunde's father, poisoned the waters."

She crumpled the paper in a tight grip as she wept openly. Mr. Porter had lied. He must have been paid by the margrave and the colonel to win her cooperation at any cost. He probably didn't even ask why they wanted her. He was a blackguard of the lowest order.

Josef said in a soft voice, "You were counting on the American ambassador to help you?"

Abigail nodded. She needed to gather herself and think clearly. She had no handkerchief to dry her eyes, but Josef gave her one from his pocket. She accepted it with gratitude. "I'm sorry. I'm such a ninny."

"No," he said. "You are very brave. And we will find a way to get someone here to help you escape." He took her hand in his reassuring grasp.

Abigail could not let herself savor his comfort. She had to get out of this place, but she had no idea how.

CHAPTER EIGHTEEN

Plans Set in Motion

The next morning's edition of the Tirigovina newspaper had a long article about the princess's carriage tour of the town. It praised her courage and efforts to cheer her subjects even while she dealt with her own personal loss, and it concluded her presence had instilled confidence in the populace.

Rosamunde was delighted. So delighted, in fact, that she decided to demonstrate her bravery to the upper echelons of society—and celebrate her quick return to complete health—by scheduling a palace ball in three days. She invited everyone who mattered. She was especially keen to have in attendance her primary suspects in the assassination attempt. It would be a splendid affair, albeit subdued in honor of the mourning period. With that as an excuse, all weapons brought by the guests, no matter how small or ceremonial, would be held at the entrance to the palace and returned to the owners at their departure.

The palace managers were beside themselves with frustration, especially Baron Austerlanden. The erudite and harried major domo of Schoenberg Palace had had enough of a headache when the palace rumor circuit learned of Abigail's presence. The only way he could keep word from spreading into town was to lock the facility down. After much work he figured out a sophisticated way to keep the necessary goods coming in and the refuse going out while making sure no information changed hands in this gossip-addled society. But how could he keep the staff from intermingling with the ball guests? He concocted a plan to have palace guards take the place of the servants and keep the regular staff below stairs. Training soldiers to work as servants posed a challenge, but the baron's managers would have to make it work. They had no other choice.

The person who should have been the guest of honor at the princess's party hadn't been invited. But Abigail was in no mood for festivities anyway. After her meeting with Josef about the telegram, he had dropped out of sight. Even his soldiers were absent. There seemed to be no reason for alarm, but she felt the absence of her last remaining friend.

Tired of being cooped up in her room, she talked the palace guards into letting her take morning and afternoon walks in the hallway outside her room. They insisted on escorting her "for her safety and protection." The maids had no interest in walking with her, so with her guards in tow she walked and thought.

She spent most of the days trying in vain to come up with a plan for escaping the country and trying not to listen to the incessant gossip of the maids. Sometimes they spoke in Swaviczen, but most of the time they obeyed the palace directive of speaking German when Her Highness was in residence. The girls talked endlessly about the other servants, their off-target theories about why someone would want to murder Beĺza and Griechen, and their annoyance at being stuck in the palace. Abigail disliked gossip, but while most of it turned out to be useless, at least she could glean a few details that might come in handy. The hard part was acting as if she couldn't understand what they were saying. She pretended to read the few books in English from the palace library.

If only she could talk with Josef, even for a few minutes, or write him a note. Surely he must be doing something to help her.

Surrounded by the lush, well-tended splendor of the family estate's garden, the Duke of Zeltatlandia listened in silence as his youngest son explained his plan. When Josef had asked to speak with him in private, Fernand knew the discussion would be serious and chose this setting to keep the conversation away from the rest of the household. They stood by a trellis covered with pink climbing roses. He and his wife had received the rose bushes as a wedding present from his wife's mother. Everywhere in the garden were memories of the past and hopes for the future.

As the duke regarded his son, he was taken with two things. The boy's scheme was well-planned and subtle enough to work without being detected. He also noted how much Josef had matured during his two years in Vienna. Unlike his sturdy and sensible older brothers, Josef always had something of the dreamer about him. He took after his mother that way. They both believed in trying to make the world what it could be and not settling for how life was.

However, Josef's proposal had a great risk. Even if he did not intend to harm Princess Rosamunde, he was working against Her Highness's stated intentions. She could interpret that as treason. If the unknown conspirators behind the assassination attempt found out about his plan, they could fuel that suspicion to draw attention away from their schemes. Traitors brought down dreadful retribution on their families as well as themselves. This was a dangerous game and no place for beginners.

As Josef concluded and asked his father for his opinion, Fernand had a test for him. "So, you wish for me to speak with my friend?"

Josef shook his head. "No, father, you misunderstand. I would be the one to talk with him. I wish only for your guidance and your secret blessing."

Fernand countered, "But wouldn't it be more persuasive if I had the conversation instead of you?"

"Perhaps. But no one else must be involved. If it goes badly, all of it must fall on me. The family must be protected. I believe before I do anything you should complain to a few select gossips about how

I've become difficult and how if it continues you may have to disown me. That way I'll already be grist for the mill. It should direct suspicion away from you. And you must promise not to rescue me or admit you knew anything about this."

The older man smiled, his confidence in Josef confirmed. "I shall place a few thoughts in several well-chosen ears."

Josef's eyes lit up. "So you approve my plan?"

"If it works, not only might it help the young woman, it might also help the country." Fernand regarded his beaming son. At first he had suspected Josef's stories about the young American woman were enhanced by infatuation. But now he understood this was no mere youthful fancy. He hoped he would have a chance to meet this remarkable woman someday. One last test: "I hope she's worth the danger."

"She is." Josef's smile grew wistful. "Even if I never see her again."

On the day of the grand fete, Abigail's isolation came to an end with a knock on the door at the regular time of her morning walk. Instead of the usual anonymous palace guards, the new arrivals were Phillip Zujaken and Mikal Schwarze. She managed to keep her excitement hidden as Phillip, in his splendid English, invited her to take her morning walk in the hallway. To her relief, the maids had their usual lack of interest in accompanying her. She would be able to talk with Josef's men in private.

They followed her in the usual formation of two steps behind and waited until they were fully a third of the way down the hall before Phillip stepped up next to her. In a quiet voice he said, "Our lord wishes to convey to you his greetings and apologies for not being present. He has been working on a plan to bring important Americans here, and he's just learned the plan will come to fruition."

Abigail gasped at the good news, but Phillip hushed her with, "You must not tell anyone. The plan was presented to Her Highness by someone else. If others find out our lord is behind it, it will arouse suspicion."

Laughter echoed down the hall, and Phillip dropped back to walk behind Abigail as two chambermaids appeared at the end of the corridor. They walked towards the group, gave Abigail a quick curtsy, and then hurried on, continuing their hushed conversation. Abigail caught a few words before the women disappeared around the corner. They were discussing one of the palace handymen.

The three reached the end of the hall and as they turned back to complete their lap, Phillip joined Abigail again. "Our lord must attend the ball this evening, but he will see you when he can. He thinks there will be one more event you must attend, but he doesn't know the details. He urges you to stay strong and do nothing to bring attention to what is unfolding."

She nodded in agreement. Hope at last!

Phillip shared one last request. "Our lord values your judgment. He would like you to observe the people as they enter the ball to see if anyone arouses your suspicion. If you can ascertain who is behind the attacks, the sooner this will be over and the sooner you will be free. He hopes you are able to find a way to leave your maids this evening. I will come for you before the guests arrive."

"How will I get past the guards outside my door?"

"The soldiers will be busy tonight. It's unlikely guards will be outside your room."

Abigail was no mentalist, and she had no idea how she would be able to see anyone when they kept her locked in her room, but she was willing to give Josef's plan a try. She promised to do what she could to give her maids the evening off.

Phillip nodded, then hesitated. "My lord said if you were agreeable to help . . . please have the maids undress you before they leave."

Startled, she stubbed her toe on the carpet and had to catch her balance. She eyed him askance, but he shrugged, as ignorant of the reason for the odd request as she. Abigail agreed with more curiosity than trepidation.

CHAPTER NINETEEN

The Disciples of Saint Joshua

As the evening and the start of the grand ball approached, the palace hummed with anticipation. The maids buzzed about all the important people who would be under the same roof. Even Frau Witj enjoyed the excitement, joining in the discussion of what Her Highness and all the great ladies would be wearing. According to the below-stairs fashion experts, Her Highness's gown of soft Celadon green would certainly cause a sensation. The rumor mill also said the dress had kept Frau Meyer and a platoon of seamstresses in a commotion ever since the ball had been announced. With luck the other servants would get a glimpse of some of the leftover fabric.

Abigail asked Frau Witj about all the excitement, and the woman relayed the news. Abigail asked if the servants would be allowed to participate, and the woman laughed. "Not only are ve not zelebrating, ve are not even zere to help. All ze soldiers are taking our place. Ve are locked avay!"

Abigail had come up with an idea she hoped would solve her problem, and perhaps this perfect opportunity would make her maids a bit happier. "If you're not needed for the entire ball, then you of the palace staff should have your own party."

Frau Witj scowled as if to dismiss the idea out of hand, but then her scowl lightened as she began to think of the possibilities. "Zat would be most goot. People are not being happy kept here all percent of ze time. I vunder. . . ."

Before several minutes had passed, the woman had worked out

the entire affair and was instructing the maids in how and where to marshal the forces. Only after the gleeful girls had scampered off did the matron remember the person who had started things in motion. "Bot vot about you? It is not proper vor you to be zere."

Abigail said, "I'll be fine on my own. I've already had my dinner, and I have a book. I'll probably go to bed early." Frau Witj wasn't convinced, so Abigail added, "You'll break some poor girl's heart if you force her to stay in here and stare at me all night. I promise to make do on my own. I will be fine." She patted the skirt of her dress. "In fact, why don't you help me into my dressing gown now? Then you can stay at the party as long as you want."

Frau Witj clapped her hands with delight. "Is most goot! I vill come back und check on you—"

"No, no—no need to do that," Abigail said as she stood. "I'll be safe and secure the whole time. You go and enjoy yourself."

The last of Frau Witj's reservations faded away. "*Jah*, iz goot. You are zo goot."

Within minutes Frau Witj had Abigail undressed down to her chemise and pantaloons and wrapped in her dressing gown. Abigail went to the door to open it for the excited matron—and to confirm Phillip's statement that there were no guards outside her room. "I'm certain I'll go to bed early. I hope all of you have a wonderful night."

The woman paused in the open doorway. "To you ve vill raise ze first glass!"

"And the last," Abigail added, to the woman's laugh. Abigail stood in the doorway and returned Frau Witj's wave as she disappeared around the corner. Abigail waited in the doorway for a full minute, praying the woman wouldn't think to come back and lock the door. The minute came and went without Frau Witj's return, and Abigail let out a sigh. She closed the door and returned to her chair. As she straightened her dressing gown, Abigail wondered if there were any confidence artists in her family.

A knock on her door half an hour later brought Phillip and Mikal. When she ushered them into the room, she was surprised to see them in servants' clothing and carrying three baskets of linens. "This will make us invisible," Mikal explained.

A cloth-wrapped bundle sat on top of Phillip's basket. He gave it to her, and when she undid it she saw yet another uniform . . . a man's, complete with shoes. Phillip explained, "That will make *you* invisible."

She smiled. Now the dressing gown request made sense. "What about my hair?"

Phillip pulled back the cloth across the top of his basket and produced a small military-style cloth cap. "A cadet cap."

In the toilette room Abigail began her transformation. Little did she know when she played Viola in *Twelfth Night* just how handy her experience in wearing men's clothing would be. After snugging the chemise close around her chest and securing it with a tie from her dressing gown, she put on the uniform. She donned the cadet cap and tucked her hair up inside. She regarded her reflection in the tiny mirror. She stood tall and straightened her shoulders, grateful for the uniform's loose jacket. She tried to look as serious and self-important as a new cadet, then opened the door and marched out. She offered a sharp salute to Phillip and Mikal. "Cadet Schmidtfeld, reporting for duty."

The soldiers gave her dubious frowns. Mikal said, "It's better if you don't draw attention to yourself."

So much for her acting career. The three gathered up the baskets and set forth on their mission.

Mikal led the way through the back halls. They passed a group of palace soldiers chatting at an intersection. Abigail stiffened when she saw them, but the soldiers only gave them nods as they went by. When they moved out of sight, Abigail let out a breath and Mikal gave her an encouraging nod.

By another set of stairs they stopped before a panel in the wall. Mikal pressed something on the molding that Abigail couldn't see and swung the panel open like a door. They went through into a small entryway at the bottom of a narrow flight of steps. Mikal closed the panel behind them, and soft light filtered down from the top of the secret passageway. They set down their baskets and climbed the steps.

The three came out into a narrow corridor just below the ceiling level that ran the length of the ballroom. As they walked, they passed intermittent window panels covered with sheer fabric that let them see down into the room without being noticed. The musicians were already playing waltzes to a small audience. No one was dancing yet; Mikal explained the dancing would not begin until after Her Highness made her entrance.

This hidden corridor reminded Abigail of the upper reaches of her high school theatre's backstage, where stagehands could tend to the curtains and the rigging for anything that needed to "fly." In school, only the boys were allowed up there. Now, in a much grander theatre, she was one of the boys and she herself was aloft.

They continued down the dim corridor to the end, where they found a short door no more than three feet tall. Phillip knelt and unlatched the door, letting in a warm light and the rush of sounds from people below. Before them hung a sheer curtain of soft green, and on the other side stood a statue facing away. They were behind one of the niches above the grand entrance hall. The statue was about three feet tall, and the niche itself no more than four feet high. She understood the other reason she was dressed as a boy—they would have to crawl through the door and sit on the niche's floor behind the statue.

She knelt at the door and gazed out at the entrance hall's ceiling with its magnificent mural, which was only a foot above the top of the niche. The ceiling's proximity made Abigail's head spin for a moment, and she looked away as Phillip edged through the small doorway. Staying behind the sheer curtain, he turned and helped Abigail crawl through, and they settled into their vantage point. Mikal gave them a nod and stayed outside, closing the door behind them.

The curtain behind the statue was secured to the niche floor to keep it from billowing. With the light of the main hall shining on the front, the curtain acted as a theatre scrim, and even though they had an excellent view of the entrance hall she knew they were invisible to the people below. She examined the other niches she could see from their angle. All appeared to have solid walls behind their statues.

"How did you know about this?" Abigail whispered.

"Mikal worked in the palace when he was a youth. All the servant boys know the secret of Saint Joshua," Phillip answered with a nod towards the statue. "Mikal will stay outside and make sure we are the only ones who use it tonight."

She found a comfortable pose to watch the people coming through the entrance. She wondered how someone from the Old Testament could become a saint, but once again her background as a Protestant proved a disadvantage.

She concentrated on the people who mingled in the entrance hall. The first thing Abigail noticed was that all the servants were men, and they moved with polite but singular confidence. This was especially noticeable when arriving male guests were required to surrender swords and other weapons, even those that appeared to be merely ceremonial. Some guests balked, but all eventually complied. Phillip confirmed her suspicion that this was not normal when he explained, "All the servants are palace guards. Her Highness is taking no chances this evening."

That explained why no one was outside her room. "If the princess is so careful, I'm surprised she doesn't have someone using this."

Phillip gave her a knowing smile, then pointed at the niche at the end of the top row on the opposite side of the great hallway. "They're using the one over there. It has a better view of the ballroom."

Abigail looked again. She had thought all the niches had solid backs . . . but now that she examined that last one, she could see the shade of pale green was just a bit lighter than the others.

"They don't know you're here?"

"No."

"But you know they're there."

He smiled. "Yes."

She nodded with appreciation. In this life-and-death palace intrigue, she was grateful Josef and his men were so thorough.

The stream of guests increased. Sophisticated gentlemen, beautifully dressed women, and old soldiers with chests full of medals made their way inside. Abigail recalled her first holiday season away from home when her family visited her mother's oldest brother in Chicago. The children watched from the head of the stairs as the guests arrived for the Christmas party. Abigail and her cousin Sophie thought the professors and their wives were so splendid in their suits and fine crinoline dresses. What a far cry that modest Midwestern celebration was from this!

Her reminiscence ceased when she saw Josef enter. Dressed in stylish evening attire, he wore a sling of black fabric that matched his suit. With him was a fine-looking older gentleman, whom she thought Josef resembled, and two handsome women who must be mother and daughter.

"That is our lord's father," Phillip said, "the Duke of Zeltatlandia. He's second in rank only to the Count of Heigenlizt's father. He's a very fine gentleman. The women are our lord's mother and his sister, Phoebe." With a glance back at the niche door he added, "Mikal and Phoebe are fond of one another, but it is hopeless, of course."

Abigail found herself annoyed at the resignation these people had about their society, but this was not the time to begin that conversation. She offered a neutral inquiry instead. "Josef has two brothers, correct?"

Phillip nodded.

"Why aren't they here?"

"The oldest is at the court in Berlin, and the other is now in Vienna. They go where Her Highness wants them to be."

As Abigail watched the activity below, she thought about her own family. Did they know about her predicament yet? Now that the people at the American embassy in Vienna knew, someone must have told them by now. How worried they must be! If only she could get word to them that she had friends and a fighting chance. But there was nothing she could do, so she distracted herself by watching Josef and his family. They seemed close, and the respect Josef showed his parents made Abigail sigh. She caught a glimpse of Phillip smiling at her, and she blushed. She returned her attention to Josef's family as they were greeted by others, and the group eventually made its way to the ballroom.

Soon Phillip started pointing out people as they entered. A flurry of attention accompanied Michael Gregorski, who arrived without a woman at his side. Remembering the way he had stared at her before the plaza ceremony, Abigail had the feeling he intended to marry Rosamunde himself. Showing up with a woman would not improve his chances. A cluster of attendants came after him. At the lead was a slender, bookish man who looked out of place in the grand setting. Phillip said, "That is Julius Živo. He's Gregorski's right-hand man. The rest are servants." He added in a disapproving tone, "They won't be allowed in the ballroom. He only brought them here to show off how many people he can afford to employ."

As Gregorski stepped forward to greet others in the room, the next group to enter was led by Vasily Medyev. His brilliant scarlet tunic reminded Abigail of clothing she'd seen in portraits of Russian nobles. With him was a tiny, sweet-looking woman with a thin face and squinting gaze. A son and two daughters followed. One of the girls also squinted. Abigail assumed nearsightedness ran in the family, along with a vanity about wearing glasses.

She saw Gregorski and Medyev notice each other. They offered polite nods but no true greetings. She said, "They're not friends, are they?"

"No. They're unfriendly rivals."

Three more couples came in, and then a small group caught Phillip's attention. A tall man in his fifties had a paunch tucked into a splendid uniform. On his arm was a dignified and aloof woman of the same age. Behind them followed an eager and wide-eyed man who looked to be their son. "That's the Landgrave of Tratano. He is the oldest brother of Wolfgang Guttmann." She nodded with recognition of the name. "Rumor says the landgrave wants to marry off his son there, Siegmund, to Her Highness, but he is known to be a nincompoop." Abigail had to smile. He did not have a visage that promised intelligence. "If the landgrave has arrived, his brother should be. . . ."

Before he could finish his statement, through the door came Herr Guttmann and his family. His brown-haired wife was as plump as he was slender. Two of his three sons favored his Jack Sprat shape, while one took after their mother. The first son had a woman on his arm, but the other two walked together. Bringing up the rear came two younger girls, one slight and one plump, who were trying to be ever so serious and dignified.

More guests followed through the door. Most stopped to exchange pleasantries and went on to the ballroom. The notable exceptions were Gregorski and Medyev, who, like politicians during election time, continued to work the room and greet everyone possible. She recognized three familiar if unwelcome faces with the entrance of the aristocratic Lord Zaaf and the formidable Lady Zaaf, who was still wearing black and, not surprisingly, did not look happy to be here. They were followed by Colonel Lutz of the splendid muttonchop whiskers. He had a handsome woman on his arm. Phillip identified them as Rosamunde's chief counselor and the head of her household cavalry—her most trusted men. Abigail thought she should feel honored that the princess had sent her top people to snare her, but being an ungrateful commoner she felt no such thing.

No one else prompted a comment from Phillip until two dashing figures in uniform came in. "Baron Adolf von Redki and Major Gustav Schilz. They are the two who forced Her Highness to sign a document selecting a boy from another part of the family as her heir. Keep an eye on them."

But Abigail's attention was distracted by someone else. Moving along behind the line of soldier-servants was a young blond man trying hard to seem as if he belonged there. He kept a sharp lookout as he sidled along the wall, glancing at all the others as he reached into his trousers pocket. "Who is that?" she asked.

Phillip saw him. "His name is Kaspar. He is Her Highness's valet. He should not be here."

They watched him as he made his way along the wall. Von Redki noticed him. The baron turned away from the valet and focused on the rest of the room—yet, at the same time, he took small, unobtrusive steps backwards in Kaspar's direction. Von Redki stopped and pretended to straighten the gold braid on his uniform jacket. He took another step back as if he were getting out of the way of passersby, and with another step backwards he kept drawing closer to the wall along which Kaspar was moving.

Kaspar had pulled something from his pocket, but at this distance Abigail couldn't identify what it was. He kept up his slow, inconspicuous progress in the direction of von Redki. She glanced up at the false niche across the hall. It was directly above the valet who was not supposed to be there. She doubted observers in the other false niche could see him. Kaspar inched and stopped, inched and stopped, always looking around like an attentive servant waiting to play his part. Abigail didn't know if she should hope Kaspar succeeded or not.

The out-of-place valet was mere feet away from the baron when a soldier-servant clamped a heavy hand on Kaspar's shoulder. The young blond man let a small, folded piece of paper slip from his hand as he turned to speak to the soldier. She could not hear his words above the noise of many conversations in the great hallway, but from his gestures she surmised he was making excuses. She could also tell he was trying to keep the soldier from noticing the folded paper on the floor.

As the conversation continued between Kaspar and the soldier, Abigail glanced around the hallway to see if anyone might be reacting. Von Redki ignored the conversation but continued to drift towards the piece of paper on the floor. Almost everyone else seemed unaware of what was going on. One person was watching, however. Julius Živo, Gregorski's right-hand man. He observed the scene with concern. Then she saw two other persons with their heads turned towards the conversation—Gregorski and Medyev. Both had their backs to Abigail, so she couldn't see their faces to know what they might be thinking.

Von Redki drew within reaching distance of the note. He bent down as if to wipe away a scuff on his boot with the back of his glove. He moved his hand back towards the folded piece of paper.

Kaspar lost his disagreement with the soldier, who pulled him away. With the valet now out of the line of sight, another soldier-servant spotted the paper on the floor. Like an osprey he launched forward and scooped it up before von Redki could touch it. With a smooth pivot, von Redki turned and stood tall, holding out his hand to the soldier as if he'd dropped the paper and was thanking him for retrieving it. The soldier had the note open and read in moments. He eyed the baron, who realized he had lost and made a small gesture imitating a woman's flowing hair as he spoke. Perhaps he was telling the soldier he thought it was a love note. When whatever he said didn't convince the soldier, von Redki shrugged as if to say "my mistake" and ambled back to talk with his friend Schilz.

Abigail glanced around the entrance hall to see if anyone reacted. Medyev was no longer watching and was talking with someone. However, she saw Živo turn away from the scene with a concerned question on his face and glance at . . . not his employer Gregorski, but Medyev. He didn't stop to speak to him, but instead continued his turn away from the quiet confrontation and went to talk to Gregorski, who watched the denouement as the two soldier-servants escorted Kaspar out of the room. Gregorski said something to Živo. The right-hand man replied, but nothing about their gestures gave Abigail an indication of what they might be discussing.

What little concern had rippled through the room settled down as the entrances and conversations continued. Gregorski went to the ballroom, and Živo quit the palace with the rest of his employer's servants. Medyev greeted an arriving dignitary. Von Redki and his companion Schilz strolled through the room, stopping to chat with no one, and went into the ballroom.

Phillip said, "I think Kaspar is in deep trouble."

Abigail nodded, trying to understand the dynamics of what she had just seen. It didn't make sense. She could understand Kaspar trying to secrete information out of the palace to a conspirator, but the small details of the rest of it did not create a clear picture. She pondered the scene as she and Phillip watched the continuing entrances. She didn't want to contemplate what was in store for Kaspar.

Resplendent in her soft green ball gown, a lightweight tiara, her favorite diamond earrings, and a modest diamond necklace suitable for dancing, Her Serene Highness Princess Rosamunde removed her reading glasses. She sat at her dressing table and looked into the mirror at the reflection of her trembling valet.

"'Beware—R using a double.'" She set down the refolded piece of paper, and watched Kaspar stand, head lowered, hands together, awaiting her judgment. "We assume you were paid, or coerced. By whom, Kaspar?"

He didn't answer, which annoyed her but did not surprise her. Deaths for treason were rare in Swavicza, but they were notoriously messy and not something one volunteered for.

"Perhaps staying in the oubliette will help you remember." She smiled at her clever joke, but, alas, she was the only one who appreciated it. She nodded to the guards, who took hold of her valet and began to pull him away.

Kaspar slipped free and threw himself on his knees before her. "Mercy, Your Highness!"

She regarded him without emotion. "Who?"

He struggled to answer, then said with defeat, "Von Redki."

"Yes, we all know that. Who's behind him?"

"I . . . I don't know."

"Who is it?" she insisted.

He whimpered, "I don't know, Your Highness."

She looked at the guards, who gathered up the young man and hauled him away as he wailed and begged for mercy.

She regarded her annoyed reflection as Frau Meyer hesitated, then stepped forward from the back of the room. The dressmaker made final adjustments to the black trim on the gown's elegant short sleeves that accentuated the princess's soft, white arms. "There. Your Highness is ready." Rosamunde admired her dress again as Frau Meyer paused, then said in a hushed voice, "Will Your Highness really have him . . . executed?"

Rosamunde responded with a heavy sigh. "I'll probably spare him. *After* everyone else is rounded up." She straightened a pucker in her sleeve. "Generous in victory. That will be well received."

She stood and stepped away from the dressing stool. Several maids came forward to fluff out the billows of her gown. She turned to go to her waiting subjects, then stopped by the door. She studied the newly finished red dress and matching jacket on the dress form. She liked the red and black floral brocade on the dress's sleeves and bodice. The jacket was quite smart, but the satin's highlights were a little too orange . . . too paprika. And the bodice looked a touch too snug.

She told Frau Meyer, "I've decided. Your craftsmanship, as always, is wonderful. And I know you say it's a good color for me, but I just don't care for the shade." She sized up her petite dressmaker. "Can you wear it?"

The woman shook her head and then gave a low nod of gratitude. "Thank you, Your Highness, but I am too short."

Her Highness swept out of the room on the way to her ball. "Dispose of it."

Up in the niche of Saint Joshua overlooking the grand hallway, Phillip and Abigail heard the orchestra stop mid-waltz and strike up a royal salute. The few remaining guests who lingered in the entrance hall hurried to the ballroom, where an ovation of applause and calls wishing the princess a long and happy life echoed off the gilded walls. Phillip said, "Her Highness has arrived. And all of the important people have come through. We can go."

After Phillip and Abigail crawled back out through the short door, Mikal reported to Phillip, "No problems." The three went back down the dim corridor above the ballroom.

As they passed the window panels with the sheer fabric, Abigail paused to look at the party below. She could not see Josef, which was just as well, since with his injury he shouldn't be dancing. In the sea of dancing couples, it was easy to spot Rosamunde in her stunning dress and brilliant jewelry. She was sharing a waltz with Franz Antonius, and they smiled as if they enjoyed each other's company as much as they did being the center of attention. How remarkably unconcerned they appeared, despite all the mischief they had created for others. Abigail had to admit the princess was pretty, in a vain sort of way. She caught herself sighing. Oh, to be dancing down there on such a night. But she had no time to dawdle and dream. She followed Phillip and Mikal down the corridor.

Alone in her room and back in her dressing gown, Abigail tried to read, but the lively galop drifting in through the open window on the warm evening air lured her attention away from the pages. She gave up and set the book aside. She was soon on her feet and stepping to the music. She laughed to think she could tell her friends, "I enjoyed dancing on the night of the royal ball," while leaving out the part that she wasn't actually in attendance.

A knock on the door brought her to a stumbling stop. After a moment of uncertainty, she went to open the door. She exclaimed at the sight of a friend: "Frau Meyer!" She invited in the woman, who had a large fabric-wrapped bundle draped over her arm.

"I am pleased to see you looking so well," Frau Meyer said. "I am sorry you cannot be at the ball. But this is how it must be."

Abigail explained to Frau Meyer that when others were around they would not be able to talk in German. The woman listened to her explanation, then said, "I see you have learned how to get by here. I understand. But if I forget, you will please forgive me, and I will forgive you for pretending to ignore me." The older woman gave her a sly smile. "I have a present for you from Her Highness."

Abigail found that hard to believe. "She gave me a present?"

Frau Meyer replied with care, "Well, it is a present, and it is from the princess, and perhaps that is enough." She held out the bundle for Abigail to unwrap.

Abigail pulled back the cover, then laughed with joy. The beautiful red dress! She cast aside the wrapping as Frau Meyer delighted in her happiness. Abigail hesitated. "Is it really for me? To keep?"

"Yes."

Abigail gazed at the work of art. She didn't understand how it could be hers. But she wouldn't question it again. "Would you please help me put it on?"

A half hour ago Abigail had been a lowly cadet, but now, to the distant strains of a royal orchestra playing music written for kings and emperors, she put on the ensemble made for a princess. But perhaps it was not made for Her Highness after all. The waist and bust fit her perfectly, which made them too small for Rosamunde. As she buttoned the jacket and admired the ensemble in the mirror, she had to believe the expert seamstress had made an "intentional mistake."

Before she could comment, another knock on the door interrupted her. After Abigail's nod, and Frau Meyer's call to enter, in came two of Josef's other soldiers whom Abigail did not know well, Stephan Pulkrabe and Jóri Petka. The uniformed men nodded their respects to the women. Stephan said to Abigail, "*Fräulein*, we have been told that since the palace guards are making sure everyone at the ball stays inside the palace, you may enjoy an escorted walk outside for a short time."

Abigail thought she saw a twinkle in his eye as he spoke, but he seemed quite serious. Being outside meant she might get closer to the music and the party. "All right." She slipped into her shoes, then took Frau Meyer by the hands. "Thank you. I may not be at the ball, but I know I'm the belle." The woman smiled, and Abigail departed with her escort.

After a walk through the labyrinth of the back halls and stairs, the three went outside into the rich, warm night. The sky was overcast with no moon. Only the candlelight spilling out from the open windows of the ballroom one story above lit the path on the pavement alongside the building. No music played, and the ballroom buzzed with a hundred conversations. The orchestra and dancers were taking a break. Alas, she thought, she would not be able to walk to the music.

Abigail and her escort continued on their way until she noticed a shadow ahead near the corner of the building. She slowed, but her guards were not concerned. Then the shadow turned and smiled. Oh, she would know that smile anywhere. Forgetting decorum completely, she hurried up the path and took Josef's outstretched hands. Momentarily embarrassed by being out-of-doors without gloves, she was glad to see he wore his from the ball. His sling was missing, but she was in no mood to scold him.

Josef whispered, "I expected a cadet, not a beauty."

She was grateful that the darkness would hide her blush.

He said, "I have only a few minutes. I must go back. But I wanted to tell you what will be happening on Friday."

"Yes?" It felt so good holding his hands. She did not want to think how it couldn't last.

"There will be here at the palace several people from the American embassy in Vienna. They will talk with Her Highness about reestablishing diplomatic relations."

"Wonderful!" she whispered.

"They are arriving with representatives from an American bank to talk about opening a branch here."

She took a deep breath and savored that wonderful scent again of dark, rich spices from the Chetova forest. There was no forest here; she wondered if it could be his after-shave astringent. She forced herself to concentrate on the conversation. "How did you arrange it?"

He paused as the orchestra upstairs signaled the dancers to return to the floor and the buzz of conversations above them eased. He said just above a whisper, "A friend of my father's has been trying to bring in a foreign bank. When you asked about an embassy, I remembered my father once said the former American ambassador was working to get an American bank here. Her Highness worries about Medyev's monopoly. So I suggested to my father's friend it might be time to try again. He doesn't know about you. As you know, sometimes the most convincing messengers only know part of the story." His frown had no anger behind it, and she smiled.

The orchestra began to play an enchanting, unfamiliar waltz, slow and stately, but she could ignore it to hear the rest of Josef's story.

He continued, "My father's friend suggested the idea to Franz. My cousin liked it, especially since he could present it as his own. I sent Jowan Halle to your embassy in Vienna to explain all of this and ask them to have some of their people accompany the bank officials. This afternoon Jowan sent back a message saying the bank has received an invitation to meet with Her Highness on Friday afternoon, and the people from the embassy will be with them. They will ask about you."

Good news on top of good news! Rescue would soon be at the doorstep, and Jowan wasn't being punished after all. "Does Jowan have news from Biedric or Daisy?"

"He only said he saw Biedric and all is well. I am sure we will know more at the end of the week."

Such a magical night, with the music, the soft breeze, and so much good news. And Josef here, helping her. All she had to do was stay out of trouble for four more days.

She began to sway from side to side with the music, and he smiled. He let go of her hands, then held out his left hand, palm up, in a silent invitation to dance. She accepted, but when she reached for his shoulder she thought better of it and put her left hand above his elbow. In a moment, he had a gentle grip under her left elbow and they were dancing in small, contained steps, staying out of sight from the windows above.

The waltz changed into a longer, sweeping melody, and in a tentative gesture Josef slipped his hand from her elbow to her waist. She caught her breath. Grateful for the dark night, she feared she was blushing. After some hesitation, she put her hand on the edge of his shoulder, avoiding his injury.

He smiled. "If I come to America, will you show me a buffalo?"

She laughed, then hushed herself. "They look very much like wisent."

"It's not the same. I want to see buffalo filling the prairie."

She nodded. "There aren't nearly as many as there used to be, but yes, I'll find some for you."

As they twirled, Abigail tried to memorize every detail, every sound, the aromas, the feel of Josef's hand on her waist. She wanted to recall this moment for the rest of her life.

She caught a glimpse of Stephan Pulkrabe and Jóri Petka smiling at them. Four days until freedom would drag on forever, and yet those same four days with Josef would fly by.

Too soon the waltz ended. After a brief moment of awkward delight, they released their dance pose. He bowed his thanks, and she gave him a proper curtsy in reply. He said with regret, "I must get back before I'm missed. I don't know why Rosamunde wants me near her now." He glanced down, then gave her a shy smile. "I would rather be here."

He regarded her with such softness in his eyes. After a glance at his men, who were still standing by and watching with grins on their faces, he seemed to change his mind about what he wanted to do and instead took her hand. His lips on her bare skin made her shiver. "I will see you in the morning."

Her voice betrayed none of the trembling in her heart. "Thank you for everything, Josef. I . . . I can't thank you enough."

He took a step towards the door. "Find me a herd of buffalo." With a smile, he disappeared inside.

Abigail let go a mighty sigh. She had to go back to her room, didn't she? She walked towards her guards, who were still smiling. A rustling sound behind her made her turn with hope that Josef had returned. She saw no one, just some branches in nearby bushes moving in the evening breeze.

As she resumed her path back to captivity, another waltz began up in the ballroom. She wanted to dance all the way, but instead she let her thoughts float her back to her quarters.

CHAPTER TWENTY

The Trap Door Opens Wide

Abigail was in her night clothes but wide awake in bed when the maids returned from their below-stairs party. She pretended to be asleep as the maids gossiped and giggled through most of the night, even after they extinguished the last candle. Abigail didn't mind. The girls were happy, and it wasn't as if she would be sleeping much herself as her thoughts kept returning to Josef, the dance, and the plans for Friday.

But she did sleep at last, and in the morning she awoke refreshed and happy for the first time since she'd arrived in Swavicza. Even though she would have to hide her feelings, she couldn't wait to see Josef. She asked the maids about their party, and they went on and on about the music, food, and dancing. It had been a roaring success, even though they had to break up earlier than they wanted to clean up after the ball.

Frau Witj arrived at the usual time and announced that today Abigail would have a new visitor. The Count of Heigenlizt had hired a makeup artist—from Italy, no less—from a touring opera company recently arrived in town. She would be helping Abigail look more like Princess Rosamunde for those times when she would not be able to rely on veils. Concerned about what that might mean, Abigail said nothing but decided she would ask Josef about it later.

Breakfast ended with a knock on the door. Abigail stood and tried to control the flutter in her stomach as the door opened. With a touch of disappointment she watched Franz Antonius come in and give the women a courteous greeting in German. "I hope all of you

had a pleasant evening. I understand you had quite a grand time."
The maids giggled.

He said to Abigail in German, "We shall be working together closely over the next several days, you and I."

His use of German startled her. Frau Witj and the maids looked at Franz Antonius with surprise.

She also didn't care for the sound of what he was saying. In English, she asked, "What do you mean?"

He replied in German: "We must polish your appearance and your skills until you are the exact mirror of Her Highness. You have an important event in your future."

The consternation of Frau Witj and the maids grew. Despite Abigail's efforts to return the conversation to English, he expected her to understand German . . . and she could not deny that she did. She hoped she was giving nothing away, even as her stomach tightened. Still in English, she said, "Why are you doing this? Where is your cousin?"

"Josef?" he asked.

Why was he playing with her? What other cousin did he think she would know? She nodded.

He said with sly regret, "He is on his way to our consulate in Budapest."

She couldn't keep the surprise out of her voice. "Budapest?"

"Yes. He has been reassigned there by Her Highness. He set out early this morning."

"Why?"

He gave her a stern, patronizing gaze. "The two of you were quite indiscreet last night, and it was reported to Her Highness. Rosamunde wisely does not have faith in divided loyalties. Now that the truth of the situation has been revealed, he's been sent away until your services are no longer required."

Abigail turned away from him. Josef gone! What a disastrous turn of events! She slumped into a chair at the table, but before she could sink into dismay she needed to do a quick assessment of what the others knew and what resources she had available. Josef's soldiers were probably sent away with him. If Franz Antonius thought the visit from the American bank officials was unrelated, it would still go on . . . she hoped. Oh, Josef. She never meant to get him into trouble.

Franz Antonius stepped up next to her and said in oily tones, "I know, it must be a disappointment for you to lose your lover, and with no chance to say your tearful farewells. I know I will be a pale substitute, but I shall endeavor to fill his shoes as best I can." He lingered long enough to make his closeness uncomfortable. In a low voice he added, "I must thank you for helping me. One less rival to worry about. I'd be happy to show you my gratitude, if you're so inclined." He waited a long moment. In her mental jumble, she could not fabricate a civil response. When she didn't reply, he took a step back and said with gusto, "In the meantime, you have work to do. And a new adventure ahead. You are going to the opera!" He quit the room with a swagger of victory.

Before Abigail could contemplate that disturbing news, Frau Witj approached her. She spoke in German with high indignation. "You told us you did not speak German. But we see now you have been lying to us from the very first. We have been honest with you. I have become fond of you. But now I see you are not worth our kind regard. You have behaved shamefully. I am deeply disappointed. We will continue to serve you, but expect no further goodwill from us."

Abigail tried to sort through her muddle of conflicting thoughts. She wanted their kind regard; she had no friends left. And she *was* sorry she had misled them. In truth, she'd never told them she didn't understand German, but to point that out now would only throw fuel on the matron's fire. More than anything, she needed to regain her footing. Whether she escaped this, whether she lived or died, was now up to her.

"I'm sorry, Frau Witj," she said in English. "I have tried always to follow instructions given to me by others. In the future, I hope to show more discretion and courtesy."

A tinge of confusion passed over the matron's face. Whatever she had expected from Abigail, that didn't seem to be it. "Well, since you understand German, we shall speak it so there's no room for misunderstanding."

Abigail nodded. She wished to be left alone so she could sort things out. But another knock on the door dashed that hope. Into the room swept a grand woman of the theatre. Her dark hair and eyes spoke of a sunnier climate, as did her animated gestures and flashing smile. When she saw Abigail, she declared in Italian-accented German, "Ah, *signorina*, I see you are the one. I am here to help you." She turned back to the hall and signaled for someone to come in; a palace guard entered, carrying several small suitcases. She gestured for him to put them down, then returned her attention to Abigail. "I am Anna Victoria Madelina Rosetti. I am here to make you the perfect image of the princess."

Anna Victoria transformed Abigail's cloister into a backstage dressing room. The charismatic woman had the maids hopping to move the furniture and clear the space. Abigail sat in disheartened silence as the woman compared her face with a photograph of Rosamunde. As she studied the two faces, she explained that she had been a coloratura soprano in her prime and now she was with a traveling opera company that had arrived in Tirigovina this very morning.

After her makeup cases were set up, she went to work turning Abigail into the perfect image of the woman who wanted Abigail to die in her place. Anna Victoria talked as she worked, explaining what she was doing and chatting about life with a touring opera company based out of Milan that, on one day's notice, could perform any of fifty-two operas in four different languages—including the brand-new English sensation, *H.M.S. Pinafore*, which they had per-formed to many ovations in Rome and Munich and would surely do the same in Berlin when they arrived in a few weeks.

The Escorted Tour for Young Ladies of Quality had seen *H.M.S. Pinafore* in London, and as Anna Victoria worked on her Abigail roused slightly to wonder if their performances were authorized since the opera had only debuted a month or so ago. She decided it was better not to ask. Besides, she hoped they'd perform it here, as it would be interesting to see how the German-speaking audience would respond to Italians doing a light opera that relied heavily on English wordplay.

Abigail wanted to take this time to think, but the charming woman's monologue, with every fourth or fifth word in Italian, kept her in perpetual distraction. As Anna Victoria searched for a misplaced jar of makeup, Abigail had a chance to ask her what they would be performing on Thursday.

"Berlioz. Not my favorite composer. And we need extra time to set up the *complicato* stage business for the *finale*. The *teatro dell'opera* here is not so big as we are used to. But we will be ready by Thursday."

"Which opera is it?"

"*Benvenuto Cellini.* As I said, not my favorite."

The woman continued with her list of favorite operas, but Abigail did not hear her. She knew that opera. She knew that complicated stage business in the finale, where the artist Cellini pours molten metal into a mold for a statue. The resulting explosion of music and pyrotechnics made for a fiery piece of great theatre.

Abigail shuddered. The explosion would be a perfect way to disguise the sound of a gunshot.

She asked, "Do you know who arranged for your company to be here? And who chose the opera?"

"I do not know. I assume it was Her Highness *la principessa.*"

Abigail's last hope faded. Rosamunde was setting her up and inviting the killers to take an easy shot at her.

Anna Victoria said, "I'm finished." She turned Abigail towards the mirror. "What do you think? Good, eh?"

Abigail recognized the person in the reflection. She had seen her dancing in a green gown last night. A tremor passed down Abigail's spine. Her brother Sam used to say that deep shiver came from someone walking on your grave. She was not ready to die. But wearing Rosamunde's face was her invitation to assassination.

CHAPTER TWENTY-ONE

A Roll of the Dice

Wearing the makeup Anna Victoria had applied, Abigail was helped into another of Princess Rosamunde's old dresses and brought out of the palace for a carriage ride around the town. With the makeup on, she had no need for a veil. In fact, as she passed with palace guards in attendance, a few of the servants gave her confused looks. Anna Victoria had done stellar work.

The gray day held no threat of rain, so once again the landau's cover was down. She would be in full view of one and all, friend and foe alike. She also saw the driver and coachman were not in Josef's livery colors but in the green and burgundy of the royal household.

As she came down the main steps of the palace, she saw a glimmer of good news. On horseback at the rear of the landau, in their uniforms of Josef's household cavalry, were Phillip Zujaken and Mikal Schwarze. Why were they here and not in Budapest? Their grim expressions told of their dark mood, but they were blessedly good omens. All was not lost if she still had friends.

They gave her no sign of recognition as she walked towards the landau. The coachman came forward to open the low door. She glanced at Josef's men. They sat at attention and did not look at her. They had mistaken her for the real princess. She needed to clear the confusion right away.

The coachman held out his hand to help her step into the carriage, but she shook her head. She commanded, "Have one of them get down and help me," and nodded towards Phillip and Mikal. The coachman seemed surprised for only a moment and then did as she bade. Perhaps Rosamunde was given to unexpected gestures, or she liked to remind others that she was more powerful than they. The coachman spoke to Phillip, who frowned but dismounted. As the coachman returned to the front of the landau, Phillip stopped before her, his head bowed and his hand held out for her to steady herself and ascend into the carriage. "Your Highness."

She put her hand on his and said in a low voice, "Saint Joshua, I need your help."

He froze, then glanced up in astonishment. She gave him a slight nod as he recognized her, and then she stepped into the landau. She sat on the back bench. When Phillip had quickly remounted, she gave the signal, and the coach moved forward.

They were through the gate and on the street before she decided how she could talk with Josef's men. The group moved down the quiet street in the direction of the medieval gate and the train station. In a gesture of regal self-assurance, she signaled Mikal on the left and Phillip on the right to come forward and ride beside her. They obeyed, and soon they were trotting on either side of her.

Without looking at them, she asked in German, "Phillip, what happened?"

In a morose voice he answered, "One of the sentries saw you and our lord outside the palace. We were told he was called in to see Her Highness even before the ball ended. Jóri and Stephan were there, too. When Her Highness and the Count of Heigenlizt challenged him, he didn't deny it. The rumor is she was furious and he remained quite dignified, which made her even angrier. Her Highness decided he should leave immediately. He and all the other soldiers were gone in an hour. The only reason I know is Jóri left me a note."

"But why are you two still here?"

"We were on an errand in town. When we returned, everyone else had already gone. Apparently they decided it was easier to keep us here than to send us after the others."

Mikal added with a growl, "They want us to be the ones to go out with you—or Her Highness—so we're the ones in harm's way, not their own precious men."

Abigail saw a man on the street remove his hat for her, and she nodded to him. "I hope I haven't put Josef in trouble."

"It's not your doing," Phillip said. "He just prefers you to her."

Mikal added, "And the fact that you were seen is his fault, not yours."

Abigail wondered if Josef would tolerate such criticism from a servant; she suspected he might when it was true. She asked, "I don't suppose we could get rid of the driver and coachman and make a dash for the border?"

"No," Phillip answered. "I heard Colonel Lutz send out the command to all the frontier posts to be on guard in case you tried to escape."

Her last, faint hope was dashed. She could not have felt more forlorn. Then again, she could. She looked at the front of the opera house as the landau rolled by. She did not want to keep her appointment there.

Phillip saw her gaze and regarded her with curiosity. "Is there a problem?"

"They plan to kill me there on Thursday night."

He recoiled with surprise. "How can you know that?"

She explained about the thunderous explosion at the end of the opera and how that would be a perfect cover for gunfire. The soldier considered her logic and nodded. "That is excellent reasoning. But why would you even think of that?"

She gave a glum nod to two men on the street who bowed to what they mistook for their passing princess. "Any American over the age of five would." He didn't understand. "When I was a little girl, a man killed our president in that exact same circumstance, taking advantage of a large noise in a theatre."

Phillip nodded, deep in thought. "This knowledge is good, then. You know when they're coming. So you can plan."

"I suppose." Her thoughts darkened. What could she plan? All was lost. Josef was banished, and she would never see him again. She couldn't escape this country. Her American friends couldn't help her. The only hope of rescue would arrive the day after she'd be shot in the theatre.

The clatter of the wheels and the horses' shoes on the stone-paved road tapped out a melancholy tattoo. She couldn't have felt farther from home if she were on the far side of the moon. She began to hum along to the rhythm of the wheels, and then in a soft voice she sang in English.

> *From this valley they say you are going.*
> *I shall miss your bright eyes and sweet smile,*
> *For you take with you all of the sunshine*
> *That has brightened my pathway a while.*
>
> *It's a short time, my dear, I've been waiting*
> *For the words that you never did say,*
> *Now, alas, all my fond hopes have vanished,*
> *For they say you've been sent far away.*
>
> *So consider a while ere you leave me,*
> *Do not hasten to bid me adieu,*
> *But remember the Red River Valley*
> *And the girl who has loved you so true.*

Her changed lyrics were a mere pastiche, but they made her feel better.

Phillip nodded. "That's a pretty song, but it's sad."

"Yes."

"Can you teach it to me?"

In her dolor she'd forgotten he was the one who sang so well during the ride through the woods outside Chetova, that wonderful day that seemed a hundred years ago. Maybe he would sing it for Josef someday after she was dead. "Sure."

From the corner of her eye she saw Mikal nodding to Phillip as if urging him to do something. Phillip acknowledged him. "There was another message in Jóri's note. Our lord asked him to write it down so we could relay it to you."

She was well-settled into her gloom, and this news did not rouse her.

"He said for us to tell you he was sorry for doing what he was expected to do. Instead of obeying the rules of honor, he should have done the truly honorable thing and helped you escape when he had the chance. His punishment now would have been easy if he had a clear conscience. He says he doesn't have that now."

She sulked in the landau as it rattled down the road. Yes, he should have done more to get her out of the country. After she learned Rosamunde arranged for the opera performance, Abigail had begun to suspect that, even if she somehow survived, the princess might dispose of her to tie up all the loose threads. Now it was too late to do something. He was banished and she faced certain death alone.

Alas, she had to forgive him. Of course he would do what was expected of him. He'd been trained from birth to do as he was told. He was almost as much a prisoner of this society as she was. The only difference between them was she knew she was a prisoner and she was fighting against it.

She began to hum *Red River Valley* again. Then, in the middle of the chorus, she stopped.

Doing what he was expected to do.

. . . And what had she been doing this entire time? That very thing.

Her funk burned away like fog before a blazing sun of anger. She deserved every ounce of bad luck these Machiavels had dropped on her, and more. From the very beginning she had done what everyone wanted her to do. Perhaps her reasons had been sound: She'd stayed in line to protect Daisy and not to discredit Josef. But with Daisy safe and Josef in disgrace, even the excuse that she was protecting herself no longer held water. These people wanted her to die.

Abigail intended to disappoint them. She had no plan . . . yet. All she knew was the time had come to turn the tables and take some control of her destiny.

"Thank you, Mikal. Thank you, Phillip. I needed to hear that. If we have a chance to talk about it, I'd like to discuss Thursday night with you."

The two nodded and, from the lightening of their expressions, she thought they'd taken heart with her change in attitude.

The landau and its escort continued down the street as Abigail ruminated. What could she do?

A call in German from the street pulled her from her thoughts: "Good health to Your Highness!"

She looked up and saw the mayor of Tirigovina on the sidewalk. He had his hat in his hand and concern on his face. She ordered the driver to stop the landau, and it halted just beyond the mayor. Phillip and Mikal stopped their horses behind the carriage so the man could approach her.

"Good day to you, Your Highness," he said. "You looked so troubled. I hope I didn't disturb you."

She was about to reply when she realized she had never spoken to him. How well did he know Rosamunde's voice? She made a vague gesture towards her throat. With a bit of a rasp, she said, "Forgive me, sir, if my voice is a little off. . . . I'm still not quite myself."

He said, "It's good to see you so much better, Your Highness."

Her ruse seemed to be working. "I hope the people are recovering from the shock of what happened in the plaza."

He nodded and offered a smile. "Thanks to you, Your Highness. Your bravery has been an inspiration."

Abigail suddenly remembered the royal "we." Royalty really talked that way, didn't they? The mayor hadn't seemed to notice. Was it too late to switch? There were too many things to remember! She abandoned that worry and hoped for the best. She concentrated instead on studying him. The mayor seemed like an honest man. She recalled the box of poisoned chocolates that hadn't been from the mayor's office. Could he actually have been involved? His concern seemed genuine. If he had been privy to the scheme, he might have avoided her instead of hailing her. She decided he had no part in it . . . and she wondered if he might be able to help her. Could she trust him? She wanted to talk further and sound him out. What would they discuss? For the moment, she was a princess. What did good rulers do? They helped their people.

Abigail said, "How are things in town? Are there problems where I can help?"

He seemed surprised by her questions, and glanced at the coachman, then Mikal. He said to her with hesitation, "Everything is the same as always, Your Highness. I'm grateful for your inquiry."

Nothing about his statement sounded heartfelt. She gestured across to the landau's rear-facing bench. "Please, would you join me? If you are available, of course. I would like to hear how things are."

The mayor's mouth had fallen open.

By now Abigail was used to this response, and her time was limited so she didn't hesitate. "Are you available?"

The man stammered, then looked around at the people who had stopped to watch the conversation. He nodded to her. "Yes, Your Highness, of course, I am always at your disposal." He opened the low door of the landau and, after a moment of hesitation, he crept into the carriage on uncertain legs and sat opposite her. She signaled the driver, and they were off.

Abigail had begun formulating a vague idea of finding someone who would be able—and courageous enough—to help her escape. In the guise of the princess, she would tell this trustworthy person that assassins were after her and she needed to escape the country without her councilors knowing about it. It would be an unfortunate, cruel trick to take advantage of a citizen and make him think he was helping his monarch when, in fact, he would be working against her, but Abigail thought she could find a way around that when the time came.

As they proceeded down the street, she watched the mayor shift uneasily on the seat even as he attempted to put on a brave face. Abigail hoped his discomfort was not from knowing an assassin waited ahead. It seemed reasonable to assume Rosamunde had never shown much interest in him as a person. Being vague would serve her well. "How are things going? Everyone is well?"

He nodded. "Yes, Your Highness. My wife is much better. Thank you." He seemed surprised she knew about his wife.

"Good. So tell me about Tirigovina."

The mayor seemed a bit flummoxed. "Things are good."

She waited for more, but none came. "So, everything is perfect? There's nothing that can be improved?"

He hesitated, then said as if he were apologizing, "Well, there is the traffic problem."

She glanced around. There was no traffic. In fact, now that he mentioned it, she had seen nothing in the way of carts or drays at all during her trips out. "Please explain."

He hesitated a little less this time. "Ever since the late king your uncle banned commercial traffic during the daytime, it's meant everyone has to do their hauling at night, and people complain about the noise. They can't sleep."

She could understand that. The ancient Romans did the same thing, and it wreaked havoc at night. "Have you brought this to the attention of the pr—" She caught herself. "To the council of advisers?"

"They say it's a town problem, not theirs. But because it was put in place by a king, it can only be undone by you." With meek courage, he leaned forward and said in an urgent tone, "So the council never told you about our requests?"

She gave Rosamunde the benefit of the doubt. "This is the first I've heard of it." The mayor shook his head in dismay. She asked, "What else should I know?"

Emboldened by her interest, he began to discuss issues with getting cooperation from the Sálacene population in town, especially regarding some of their customs that were annoying their Swaviczen neighbors.

As she listened to the mayor's polite whinging, she paid more attention to how he spoke than to what he said. After several minutes, she had to accept that he couldn't help her. He was sincere, and she was thoroughly convinced he had nothing to do with the poisoned chocolates, but she sensed weakness in him. She concluded he was someone who meant well but lacked the initiative to find solutions on his own. If she asked him to help her, she felt he would hesitate or, even worse, consult with others on what he should do. With some disappointment, she let go of the idea of asking him for help.

After he finished complaining about the Sálacene, she asked, "Have you tried talking with them?"

"They don't want to talk." He started to hem and haw about how they were never available to talk about what they didn't consider a problem.

However, as she listened to his excuses, she realized he was helping her—by pointing her in the right direction. She knew a man of courage who wasn't afraid to take action. Even Josef trusted him.

She shifted over to the right on the plush landau bench and signaled for Phillip to come forward. He nudged his horse and was soon next to her. She saw no reason for the mayor to know what she had in mind, and for all she knew he might bolt when he found out her intentions. She leaned over and quietly asked Phillip, "Do you know where Jovacź Chešqu lives?"

The soldier shook his head, then nodded back towards his comrade. "Mikal should know. He's from Tirigovina."

As the mayor observed the proceedings with puzzled concern, she repeated the process with Mikal on the other side of the carriage. He nodded his answer to her question.

"Good," she said in a low voice. "Tell the driver to take us there." Mikal glanced at the mayor with a half-hidden smile. He went forward and spoke to the coachman. Abigail watched the brief conversation. Both the coachman and driver questioned the order, but when Mikal insisted they complied. At the next corner they turned back towards the other side of town.

The mayor frowned and asked her what was happening. She gave him a nonchalant smile. "My dear mayor, I'm helping you."

She distracted him with questions about his concerns as they crossed town and entered a neighborhood that had seen better days. The landau stopped in front of a house with a small vegetable garden in front. The mayor glanced around, ill-at-ease. "Your Highness, this is a Sálacene area. It's better if we leave."

As she watched Mikal dismount and go to the house's door, she said to the mayor, "We will, in just a moment."

The door opened, and there stood the man himself. Jovacź Chešqu looked at Mikal, then saw the royal carriage at his doorstep. He held up his hand in a grand gesture. "Your Highness! It is indeed a great honor you are paying my humble home!"

She called to him, "Herr Chešqu, are you available for a chat?" Out of the corner of her eye she saw the mayor's horror-stricken face.

Chešqu came forward with an eager step. "I am always happy to talk with you, Your Highness!" He stopped when he saw the mayor, and his smile faded. It was clear he shared the mayor's distrust.

She told Chešqu, "Excellent. Please join us."

Chešqu seemed uncertain. He didn't take his eyes off the mayor, and he made no effort to enter the carriage.

Abigail was enjoying this moment of absolute authority more than she wanted to admit. "Herr Chešqu, we're waiting."

The Sálacene elder had no choice. He reached for the low door and opened it, then looked at the mayor, who was still sitting in the center of the rear-facing bench. Abigail gestured for the mayor to move over, which he did with reluctance. Chešqu sat next to him and latched the door shut. Mikal was back on his horse, so she gave the order to the driver and they were away.

She beheld the sulking men across from her. In a cheerful voice, she said, "I understand you've been having a difficult time getting together to talk about your concerns. So, let's talk."

They eyed each other, but no one made the first gesture.

What little boys they are, she thought. She needed to get a conversation started, and then she wanted the mayor to leave so she could talk with Chešqu about escaping. She had to offer them something irresistible. "Gentlemen, I need your help. The job of every leader is to make things better. But rulers can't do that if all the advice they are given comes from people who represent less than one-half of one percent of the population. A leader needs to hear from everyone. This is your chance. I am here to listen. Talk with each other. Work together. Please—talk."

The two stared at her. For all Abigail knew, she had just spoken treason. But when they looked at each other, she saw the mayor's hardness subside.

As the two men began a tentative discussion of the neutral topic of sewage, Abigail noticed Phillip and Mikal ride forward until they were even with the driver and coachman. She stopped paying attention to the sewage chat to listen to what the soldiers were saying, but Phillip was talking to them in a confidential manner and she couldn't hear his words. She wondered if they were distracting the men from listening in on this highly irregular, and perhaps dangerous, conversation.

She had been hoping the mayor would want to leave or she could find an excuse to send him on his way, but instead she realized she had started the first real conversation between these rival leaders . . . perhaps ever. Each seemed surprised the other shared his concerns. They wanted the same thing, but they had spent all their energy on distrusting each other and making excuses instead of working towards a solution.

As the rivals talked, Abigail's thoughts drifted to her college dilemma. When this trip began, the squabble between the Amos College president and the leader of the trustees had weighed so heavily on her, yet it was petty in comparison to all of this. But as she listened to the mayor and Sálacene leader, she knew this was a lesson for her. If she made it back to Connecticut, she needed to find a common ground between Professor Penwright and Miss Amos.

Was it possible for them to work together? She would have to find a way.

But first things first—she had to escape. Phillip and Mikal had dropped back to their expected place behind the carriage. She signaled for Mikal to come forward. She told him to have the driver return the carriage to where they had picked up the mayor. Mikal relayed the message, and the carriage made a wide turn in the quiet street.

As the landau approached its destination, she interrupted the men. In a quiet voice so her words wouldn't carry to the driver and coachman, she said, "Gentlemen, it's clear that what unites you is far greater than what separates you. But this will require more than one conversation. I suggest you go to your communities and talk with them about their needs and concerns. Herr Mayor, this is your stop. Please go and talk with the others. Herr Chešqu, I will take you back to your home. If you all work together, perhaps someday there will be room in the council chamber for both a council of advisers and a council of the people."

The men looked at each other as if they couldn't believe what they were hearing. The mayor stammered, "Your Highness!"

Not one to be at a loss for words, Jovacź Chešqu announced, "Your Highness, you are the greatest Marespi of them all!"

Even as she shushed him, Abigail wondered what a Marespi was, but she took his statement as a compliment.

The landau pulled to a stop. The mayor descended to the pavement and turned back to bid them farewell. Chešqu said with a bit of hesitation, "Your Highness, and Herr Mayor, if I may, I would like to get out here and continue our talk."

"Yes!" the mayor responded with delight. "That's an excellent idea. My wife was baking *pogacha* when I left. I'm sure it's still warm."

Chešqu started to descend from the carriage.

Abigail's heart sank. She couldn't let her only opportunity to confer with Chešqu slip away. "Herr Chešqu, there is something I wish to discuss with you. Can your conversation with the mayor wait?"

The Sálacene leader turned back to her with an apology in his eyes. In a quiet voice he said, "Your Highness, forgive me, but the mayor has never wanted to talk before. Would you not agree it's bad luck for us to turn our back on this miracle you have created?"

The pleading in his eyes withered her resolve. She couldn't take this away from him. In a sad voice, she said, "I would never turn down a miracle."

Beaming with gratitude, he stepped down from the carriage. He joined the mayor and then turned back to her with a reverent nod. "Of course, Your Highness, I would be pleased to meet with you at your *very* next convenience."

She blinked away tears of disappointment. She had been right about Chešqu. A man willing to say no to his monarch could have been her means of escape. But she couldn't force him back into the carriage without losing his support.

Chešqu reached up to take Abigail's hand and kiss it. With misty eyes he said, "I thought I would never live to see this day."

Looking at the men with their bright-eyed smiles, she was embarrassed that her goal had been so self-serving. She also wondered what she had started. There had to be a reason why someone would want to keep a wedge between these two peoples, and the person might not be happy to see them working together. Rosamunde also might not appreciate the ideas Abigail had put into their heads. She needed to temper their enthusiasm. "You may never see it again, Herr Chešqu." At their puzzled expressions, she said, "Whatever comes of this, my friends, remember, be patient. Be respectful. If it does not work out now, don't be angry. No matter what happens, stay loyal to the true, good heart of Swavicza and your long and peaceful history together."

She signaled the driver to go, and the landau pulled away. Phillip reined his horse forward next to her. He asked with half a laugh, "Do you have any idea what you've done?"

Truly, she did not. But she told him, "I may have opened the door for your country to enter the 19th Century."

Phillip chuckled, then said, "The driver and coachman work for Her Highness. I told them they should tell their superiors about this 'silly' chat of yours trying to get to know the people. They would report it anyway, but I hope this way they'll make less of it." He shook his head at her with disbelief, then with half a smile he fell back to his place behind the carriage next to Mikal.

Before they turned the corner, Jovacź Chešqu's voice called after them and echoed down the street: "You were sent by God, Your Highness!"

As the carriage carried her away, Abigail wondered if in a few days she might be sent back to Him.

CHAPTER TWENTY-TWO

The World in a Chessboard

As expected, after the driver and coachman reported to their supervisors about Abigail's "silly chat" with the mayor of Tirigovina and Jovacź Chešqu, her carriage rides through town were canceled. That evening Baron Austerlanden gave her a lecture about leaving government matters to officials. Fortunately, there was no fire in his words, only condescension. Phillip's intervention to misdirect how they interpreted the carriage conversation had paid off.

Abigail sat alone in her room and wondered *why* she was alone. The maids had been with her on a less frequent rotation. On Tuesday she had been left on her own twice, and now on Wednesday she had been left by herself for at least an hour before each meal. She knew a palace guard stood outside the door, but the absence of people in the same room presented a new and unsettling pattern. She concluded the palace managers knew things would be resolved tomorrow evening, so as long as they kept her contained there was no harm in leaving her unattended. Besides, since Frau Witj and the maids had taken offense at the deliberate misunderstanding about her not speaking German, they were glad to be out of her company. In truth, she didn't miss them, either.

A knock on the door interrupted her reverie. Wary, she said, "Come in."

Phillip entered, carrying a chessboard and a wooden box under his arm. He left the door open as he said in German, "*Fräulein,* here is the game you requested."

She knew better than to refute his statement as he set the board on the small table in front of her and produced a box of pieces. She looked at him, then at the guard just outside the door, who had turned away from the hall to watch the proceedings in the room. She asked Phillip, "Have you been provided as my opponent?"

He gave her a polite nod. "If you wish it."

She looked at the guard. "Is that permissible?"

The palace soldier, a sturdy fellow nearly as tall as the doorway, did not appear to be gifted with much imagination. He gave her a nod and returned to looking out at the hall.

Phillip began removing the pieces from the box. "I am not well versed in chess," he said to Abigail, "but I hope I will provide some diversion for you." He was speaking for the benefit of the guard.

She watched Phillip set the pieces on the board. She glanced at him, but he was concentrating on his task and not giving away why he was there. He finished and pulled over a chair to sit opposite her. She noticed he now had his back to the open door. She could just see the guard over his shoulder. Phillip had placed the white pieces in front of her, but he asked her, "Would you like to be white, or black?"

"White," she said, still waiting for an explanation.

He nodded. "Excellent choice." He then turned the chess board ninety degrees, so the white pieces were on her right and the black were on her left. He quickly rearranged a few of the pieces, including moving the white queen to the far corner and moving the black queen off the board in front of her. He said in a low voice, "This is the opera house."

She sat up straight and studied the board.

"My Lord Ramsl in Budapest heard about the opera performance. He knows the story of your president, and he agrees with you about the night's purpose. He sent me a note with a plan."

She took comfort in knowing Josef was still helping her, even from so far away.

Phillip tapped the board in front of him. "This is the stage." He nodded towards the edge in front of her. "That is the entrance." He touched the white queen, which was next to the stage. "You will be here, in the royal box." He pointed to other important pieces on each side of the board towards the edge representing the stage. "There are six boxes on each side, three above, three below. The ones on your side you won't be able to see, and they won't be able to see you."

Abigail noticed the guard watching them. She picked up a pawn and slapped it on the board. "Aha!" she crowed. "I take your bishop."

Phillip realized what she was doing and looked at her for a signal if he needed to do more for the benefit of the guard.

The man outside the door had no interest in their game, so he went back to gazing down the hall.

Abigail gave Phillip a nod and, returning her attention to the board, said, "Your move."

Reassured, he sketched out the rest of the hall. Directly across from the royal box was the box owned by the wealthiest man in the country, Vasily Medyev. Next to it was Gregorski's, and then a box for the Duke and Duchess of Zeltatlandia, Josef's parents. The boxes below those, starting from the stage and going towards the rear of the house, belonged to the Landgrave of Tratano, Wolfgang Guttmann, and the Archbishop of Swavicza, who was still out of town.

He explained, "All the boxes are accessed by the hallways behind them. When the monarch is present, guards are in the hall outside the door of her box. I believe you and my lord are correct about what they intend. Mikal and I have been told we won't be needed tomorrow. So, unlike your carriage rides, we will not be the ones protecting you. Palace guards will be on duty. If Her Highness wishes for an assassin to gain access to you, the guards will most likely leave at some point."

This brought to Abigail's mind the terrible story of President Lincoln's bodyguard at Ford's Theatre wandering away from his post to watch the play, leaving the President defenseless on that fateful night. She shivered but tried to concentrate on being grateful that at least she would know what was unfolding.

She also thought of something that might be helpful to have with her. She stood and said, "Think about your move. I'll be right back." She went to the dressing table with its hairbrushes and combs. She saw a large hand mirror, but it was too big. She went to her own satchel and found what she wanted—a small, enamel-covered compact containing a mirror that fit in the palm of her hand. She glanced around for a hiding place so the maids couldn't remove it if they cleaned out her belongings before she went to the opera. The room had a shelf with a vase and meager silk flowers. She tucked the compact behind the vase. With a glance at the guard, who was facing away, she picked up a glass and poured herself a drink of water before returning to the table. As she sat, she looked the board and pronounced, "Oh, dear, I didn't see that move coming. I'm in trouble now."

Phillip whispered, "What did you take out of your bag?"

"A mirror. I'll be able to watch the door without turning around."

Surprised, he asked, "How did you think of that?"

For the guard's benefit, she studied the chessboard as if puzzling over a move. "A few years ago when I was back home in Cincinnati, I saw a performance by a woman sharpshooter. She hit targets behind her back by putting the shotgun on her shoulder and aiming with a mirror. After the show, I tried it in the orchard behind the house. It was fun and easier than I expected."

He marveled. "I think America is full of amazing things."

She continued to look at the board. "I suppose it is."

He returned to his instructions. "Mikal and I will not be able to get into the opera house. But we'll wait for you out front with horses. My lord asked me to provide you with a drawing of the theatre's hallways, but I can't get one. So I can't tell you how to get out the back of the theatre. And since we don't know where that door is to meet you, you'll have to come out the front."

He laughed as if he'd made a good move in the game, and she reacted as if she had just lost a major piece.

"So," she said, "all I have to do is foil the assassin, escape him and any cohorts *and* the palace guards, and make it all the way through the theatre and out the front door. By myself."

He nodded with a sigh. "Yes."

As orders went, that was a tall one. Either Josef thought of her as a heroine from a dime novel, or he'd run out of ideas at a most inopportune time. She asked, "So, assuming I'm able to meet you outside the theatre, then what?"

"There's an evening train for Vienna. We will have a change of clothes for you and money for a ticket." He stopped, then turned his head slightly towards the door. She glanced at the guard, who was yawning. She nodded for Phillip to proceed. "My lord also provided this." He removed from his jacket a folded, official-looking document with a wax seal on the back. He put it on the center of the chessboard and slid it to her. The front was printed in German on the left side and Swaviczen on the right with the royal seal of Swavicza in the center. Across the top was printed *Travel Permit*.

She hadn't thought of that—of course she would need papers to cross the frontier. Heaven only knew where her American passport was. It had mysteriously disappeared from her satchel somewhere between Chetova Castle and Tirigovina. She sent Josef a silent thanks for using his position at the consulate in Budapest to her advantage. But if her escape failed and this was found, he would be in jeopardy.

Phillip continued, "The paper says you're a Swaviczen subject of Sálacene descent. Your name is Ana Chešqu."

She smiled. Herr Chešqu was coming to her aid after all, if only by lending her his name. She slipped the paper into the deep pocket in the side seam of her skirt. "Why Sálacene?"

"Many of them don't speak Swaviczen. If you're stopped by a soldier, you won't raise suspicion if you only understand German."

Yes, she thought, that would have been difficult to explain. She sent Josef another silent thanks for his thoroughness.

Phillip said in a voice the guard could hear, "Look out, your knight is in danger."

She most certainly hoped not.

In a low voice Phillip continued, "The evening train—the Mountain Star Local—is supposed to leave about ten p.m. It is often late, sometimes as late as midnight. Because it's so often delayed, it won't be safe for you to use the station here. We'll leave town on horseback and meet the Star Local at its next stop. They'll be looking for you in whatever you'll be wearing to the opera, so I hope we have enough time for you to change into your disguise before you board the train. If not, you'll have to board in your opera clothes and then change."

She glanced at the guard, who was still not paying attention to them. "How far away is the next stop?"

"We can reach the town of Saint Florian in about half an hour. The train takes longer because of the grade. If we miss it there, it makes one more stop during the summer, in the resort town of Senzarowa. The road is good, but it's a long ride at night."

She liked the plan to leave town on horseback and catch the train in Saint Florian. That way any pursuers would have to search both the roads and the train. Dividing their forces increased her odds of success. She would need to choose her opera clothing carefully for as much freedom of movement as possible.

However, she couldn't remember how long *Benvenuto Cellini* ran. Three hours? A little more? How long would the intermission here last? So much depended on the timing, it worried her. "Does the Star Local make other stops?" What was the name of that town near Chetova Castle? "What about Mytiwa?"

Phillip shook his head. "The only northbound train that stops in Mytiwa is the Mountain Cloud Local, the morning one. And even if the Star Local did stop there, the town is nearly to the border and too high in the mountains. The horses would never make it in time."

"All right. Saint Florian is the first choice with Senzarowa as the last resort." She smirked at her pun, which didn't translate into German. "If we arrive early, we can hide until a few minutes before the train leaves. And then you can find your way back to Tirigovina and profess your ignorance of the entire affair." She tapped a pawn on the chessboard. "I hope they believe you."

He nodded. "I will see you tomorrow evening outside the theatre. Remember: be strong. You have friends."

She smiled at his kind words. He looked at the board and then gave a theatrical gesture and exclamation of loss. "You win, *Fräulein*. I am no match for your skill." He gathered the pieces and put them in the box. He picked up the chess set and went to the door. He gave her a polite bow. "I do not hasten to bid you adieu."

It was all she could do not to smile. She would never sing *Red River Valley* again without thinking of him. "I hope we shall have a rematch later."

He bowed again and turned to go. As Phillip passed through the doorway, Abigail heard the guard say to him, "Did you let her win?"

Phillip replied, "I am a gentleman."

The guard guffawed as Phillip winked and departed. The guard gave Abigail and the room a quick look, then closed the door.

CHAPTER TWENTY-THREE

The Rescue Party

As sisters Mrs. Deborah Caruthers and Mrs. Esther Weatherwax walked from the Tirigovina train station with their burly escort, they were beginning to regret their plan to retrieve Abigail. It had all made complete sense when the detective suggested it. But now it seemed impetuous and terribly unwise.

In Vienna, after Daisy had arrived with her surprise escort and rejoined the Escorted Tour of Young Ladies of Quality, the sisters took their niece to the American embassy. When they learned the dreadful truth that the ambassador knew nothing of Abigail's predicament and couldn't help her, they were all at sea. After bemoaning their error and heaping blame on themselves for being taken in by those deceitful foreigners, they made Daisy promise to keep every bit of this information to herself while they worked on a solution. The other girls were curious and frustrated about not knowing what had happened, of course, but that was better than having them know about their guardians' shameful blunder. When the sisters came up with no solution by the end of their prearranged time in Vienna, with terrible reluctance they continued with the tour schedule, all the while hoping for Providence to lend a hand.

Everything changed when they arrived in Berlin. On the building next door to their hotel, they saw a sign for an office of the Binterman Detection and Investigation Agency of the United States of America. How reassuring to see the familiar name from back home and its slogan of "We Never Rest." Without a word of discussion, the sisters rushed into the building in search of help.

In the office they found the man who was now striding down the Tirigovina street ahead of them like the king of the world. Mr. J. D. Briscoe, late of Chicago, was a sandy-haired mountain of a man with a walrus mustache and walrus physique and a taste for good beer and cheap cigars. In Berlin, he'd reassured the MacMillan sisters he knew all about the little countries in this part of the world and he would not rest until he had Abigail Smithfield safe from those scoundrels and back in their care. Despite the fact that they could not quite disabuse him of the idea that Abigail had run away, the sisters agreed he was their only hope.

Mr. Briscoe insisted they stage their rescue out of the closest major foreign capital, which meant going back to Vienna. At Daisy's surprisingly wise suggestion that they not split up the Escorted Tour, the entire group returned. While many of the girls found the detour an exciting adventure, a few girls from one faction offered bitter complaints, especially when their leader realized the trip back gave Daisy the opportunity to reunite with the gallant soldier from her "escapade." Deborah and Esther wondered the same thing, since Daisy had been moping for him after they left him behind in the Austrian capital, but Ruth observed how much Daisy had grown up in the last two weeks, and she suggested the girl be given more respect. For his part, her beau was pleased to see Daisy again when they checked in at the American embassy, where he seemed to be lingering as if awaiting instructions. So many mysteries, and none they could solve!

Mr. Briscoe charged the sisters for his services while he sampled the luxuries Vienna had to offer and "studied the situation." When he announced he had a plan that would begin that evening, the sisters drew lots for who would go with him and who would shepherd the restive girls. Ruth lost yet again and stayed in Vienna.

However, now that they'd reached their destination, both Deborah and Esther were reconsidering who had won and who had lost. The languages they'd heard on the train were incomprehensible. The architecture here had hints of eastern lands, and the local dress was just too different from what they had seen before—the bright colors and billowing costumes on some of the women were downright exotic. Between the uncertainty, the unfamiliarity, and the threat of danger, it was all too upsetting. The American women were relying on Mr. Briscoe to get the matter settled as soon as possible so they could return to the safe and familiar.

Using a small map from the train station, Mr. Briscoe led the sisters up to the front gate of the royal residence. It wasn't on a par with the continent's great palaces, but the stout fence around the place certainly commanded their respect. They were even more impressed by the number of guards at the gate.

Briscoe stopped square in front of the guards and swelled up to his full, impressive height. In not-very-good German, he announced, "My name is Mr. John Donovan Briscoe." He handed a business card to the man who seemed to be the head guard. "I'm with the Berlin office of the Binterman Detection and Investigation Agency. We are here to see Her Serene Highness Princess Rosamunde. Please announce us."

The gray-haired guard read the business card, then eyed Mr. Briscoe with undisguised suspicion. "What is the purpose of your visit, Herr Briscoe?" he said in languid English.

"I am here to escort Miss Abigail Smithfield back to Vienna." He parked his hands on his hips with absolute confidence.

The guard looked at the sisters. "And who are these women?"

A hint of indignation passed over Mr. Briscoe's face. "They are her chaperones."

The gray-haired man regarded the sisters, then gave Mr. Briscoe another onceover. "Please stay here." He strode up the drive to the palace and went inside.

Deborah Caruthers was not favorably impressed with the way Mr. Briscoe had conducted the conversation. Perhaps that kind of abrupt and domineering tone worked in Chicago, but she thought the circumstances here called for a bit more diplomacy. She was beginning to wonder just how long Mr. Briscoe had been in Europe.

She didn't dare disclose her concerns to Esther, who had been worrying even before they crossed the frontier. She could only hope for the best and pray they would all be laughing about this tomorrow—with Abigail—back in Vienna.

While they waited, Mr. Briscoe recounted a few of the adventures he had not treated the women to on the train trip down here. If he was to be believed, he was the most important detective in the agency and deserved a medal or two from several governments. However, as they shared dismayed glances, the sisters were no longer inclined to believe his stories. They were relieved when, ten minutes later, the head guard returned and instructed the sentries to open the gate.

Briscoe rubbed his hands together as he chortled at the sisters. "What did I tell you? Now we're going to get somewhere."

The gray-haired guard commanded the gathered soldiers, "Arrest them."

Briscoe bellowed his outrage, and the sisters wilted into a frightened hug as the soldiers gathered them up and started across the street with them. Briscoe shouted at the head guard, "You can't throw us in jail! We're Americans! We haven't done anything! Why are you arresting us?"

The head guard gave no answer as he ordered the palace gate closed again.

The sisters wept as they trudged off to their fate. Oh, the humiliation! Jail! How could this be happening?

Briscoe struggled in vain against his escort. People on the street stared at the commotion. He shouted, "I'm a Binterman detective! You can't do this to me! I demand a lawyer! An American one!"

The small parade of shame reached the front door of the city jail and disappeared inside.

♔

Before her maids came back, Abigail stretched out on the bed and pulled out the travel permit Phillip had just given her. She read it over and over. Not only did she need to know all of the details, but it was also her last communication from Josef. He had risked his reputation and possibly his life with this. She would hold it dear forever. But if something happened, and she knew all was truly lost, even if she were taking in her last breath, she would make sure to destroy this to protect him.

The paper contained all the standard formalities. It gave permission to leave the country and return at will for the next three months to one Ana Chešqu, occupation teacher, born in Tirigovina to Peti and Nava Chešqu. Abigail looked at Josef's signature and ran her fingers across the official wax seal of the embassy. She read the physical description and smiled at the thought of him writing her characteristics with such precision. *Age 21. Height 1.62 meters. Forehead medium. Eye color blue. Nose small and straight. Mouth petite. Chin round. Face oval. Hair light brown. Complexion healthy. Countenance modest and honest.* She wasn't sure how petite her mouth was. Could that be a coded message that she should keep it closed until safely across the border?

Abigail heard a conversation approaching in the hallway and then Elga's raucous laugh. With no time to hide her travel paper with her mirror in the toilette room, she slipped it under the edge of her dress and closed her eyes to pretend she was asleep.

The hall door opened, and the laughter of the maids ended in abrupt shushes. They came into the anteroom and closed the door. It sounded as if they were putting down clothes or towels or something else soft, but Abigail didn't dare open her eyes to see.

One maid whispered in German, "She's asleep."

Elga said, "Good. Less to do."

She could hear the women moving around—it sounded like the usual complement of three—and they were trying to be quiet until one began to chuckle. Another one tried to hush her, but she whispered, "I keep imagining how Johani described his face. 'I'm a detective,'" she said, imitating a gruff man's indignant voice. "'You can't throw me in jail!'"

Another one chimed in, her whisper a little louder. "'You have no right! We are Americans!'" She erupted in a giggle, and the other two quieted her.

Abigail's eyes flashed open, but she quickly shut them. Americans? In jail? And if the maids had heard about it, this must have happened at or near the palace perimeter. But what Americans would be trying to reach the palace? Her heart sank. Oh, no, not the ambassadors or the bankers! This was terrible. Had her interlude in the carriage scotched their mission and put them in jeopardy? She emitted a melancholy sigh, and then when the maids stopped moving around she realized she'd been loud enough to be heard. She had to find out what had happened. She let out another sigh as if waking, then stretched. Making sure her travel permit was still hidden under her dress, she sat up and blinked at them. She said, "Oh, I'm sorry, I must have fallen asleep."

One of the junior maids rolled her eyes as Elga said, "I hope we didn't disturb you."

"No, and I'm sorry if I disrupted your work. Did I hear you say someone went to jail?"

The other junior maid explained, "Some people at the front gate insisted on seeing Her Highness." Elga cut her off before she could continue.

Abigail said, "They couldn't have been townspeople. They wouldn't be so rude."

The two junior maids looked to Elga, who was thinking over her response. She replied, "No. They were foreigners. They do not know our ways."

Abigail was afraid of giving away what she knew, but she had to find out if the people were the diplomats and bankers. "Who could they be? What would they want? Were they soldiers?"

Again the two maids looked to Elga. The senior maid answered, "No, not soldiers."

Abigail waited, but as Elga seemed intent on keeping the information to herself she would have to try something else. "I hope they weren't important. That would reflect badly on where they came from." Keeping her hand on the edge of her dress over her travel permit, she pivoted and swung her legs off the bed. She stood, sliding the permit into the seam pocket of her skirt. She passed through the anteroom and went through the open door of the toilette room. She stopped before the wash stand and poured water from the pitcher into the basin to splash on her face.

The first young maid murmured in German in a mocking voice, "Yes, 'important *women.*'" Elga shooed her off to take care of what they had brought into the room.

As Abigail washed her face, she tried to put together what they had said. It couldn't be people from the American embassy. Women—plural—here with a detective, at least some of them American, at the palace gate. . . .

Her mind reeled. She stood over the wash basin and covered her face. Even as she tried to deny it, she knew they couldn't be anyone else—two or more of the MacMillan sisters had come to Tirigovina with hired help, trying to rescue her. And now they were in jail. What a disaster. She could not escape and leave them here.

Elga asked her, "*Fräulein*, are you feeling well?"

Abigail straightened, keeping her back to the others as she tried to make her face as neutral as possible. "I must have stood up too fast from my nap. I'm fine now."

Elga said, "This is good. We have your dress for the opera tomorrow evening. You must try it on so Frau Meyer can make any necessary adjustments."

Abigail dried the water from her face, then put down the cloth as she finished collecting herself. She turned and stepped out of the toilette room to see a junior maid smiling and holding up the dress for Abigail to admire. It was the same one she had worn to the dinner in Chetova Castle when she'd had too much to drink and nearly gotten herself into terrible trouble. Not only did the dress bring back bitter memories, it was the exact opposite of what she needed: creamy white, tight sleeves, a constricted bodice, and a narrow skirt with a long train of flowing ruffles. It would be unwieldy and restrict her movements, especially riding. And it would be easy to see even in the darkness of the opera box or shadows of the street. It was the perfect garment to bind the sacrificial lamb and deliver it to slaughter.

The maid's smile faded. "Does it not please you, *Fräulein?*"

All of Abigail's frustration welled up over the multitude of stupid things she'd done and how sick she was of feeling helpless. "No! I will not wear that! Take it away!"

The maid blanched, but Elga had no interest in humoring her. "You must wear it. It has been chosen for you."

Abigail fumed. Perhaps she'd taken her royalty lessons too much to heart, but she had no interest in being told what to do by this smug, disrespectful heifer of a woman. With a fire that surprised even her, she excoriated the dress, Elga, and the entire despicable country. The maids fled with the dress.

When a preoccupied Baron Austerlanden came in to settle the kerfuffle, Abigail was still in a fine temper.

"What is wrong with the dress?" he asked.

"It's a dinner dress. It's completely inappropriate to wear to the opera. The princess would be a laughingstock if she—or I—wore something like that in such a public setting. Ridiculous!"

From the erudite baron's jaded response, she could tell he was used to such outbursts. "And what would be appropriate?"

Her pique was easing, but she could see it was getting results so she decided to continue with it. "Well, first of all, she's still supposed to be in mourning, so it should be dark. Elegant but without frills, and a full skirt."

He frowned at the last requirement. "Why a full skirt?"

She needed a quick lie. "I've been at the theatre and the opera in London, Munich, and Graz, and this year no woman of quality is wearing a narrow skirt to the theatre. For someone of the princess's standing, a full, voluminous skirt is required. Anything else would make her look unimportant. And I'm sure she doesn't want that." What she'd told him about the latest fashions was the opposite of the truth, but she counted on the baron caring only about appeasing her to accomplish his mistress's aims.

The baron considered what she had said, then heaved a weary sigh. "We will find something." He gave her a polite nod, then withdrew from the room.

Abigail was invigorated by her success. It might end up being a small victory, but it was a victory nonetheless. She was regaining her confidence that she could succeed. But how could she get the MacMillan sisters out of jail before she escaped? She couldn't leave them here in Swavicza, especially since they would face any unspent wrath from her captors.

The baron returned some minutes later, followed by the three maids each carrying a dress. Abigail noticed the young women were a little nervous to be back in the room with her, but she was still playing the indignant mistress and ignored them. The dresses met her specifications, but one was a standout: a rich, dark blue silk ball gown with a wide neckline, loose, pleated cap sleeves, and a billowing skirt too wide to be fashionable anywhere outside a ballroom. But it would give her the freedom of movement she wanted.

She sent the baron away and had the maids help her put on the chosen outfit, and when the baron returned to inspect it he declared it a handsome success. She knew he'd say anything to bring this contretemps to a close, but Abigail agreed. It was everything she needed, and it was quite lovely. Something was missing, however. She asked the baron, "What jewelry shall I be wearing tomorrow?"

The baron frowned. "Jewelry?"

"You can't expect Her Highness to go out in a formal setting without jewelry."

While that might be true for Her Highness, the baron's scowl made it clear he was prepared to send her double out that way.

She asked, "What did she wear at the ball? That should be appropriate at the opera."

The baron didn't seem to like her sensible suggestions, but he answered, "I shall see what accommodations can be made." He nodded and turned to leave.

"Oh, and a small bouquet of flowers. It's the latest thing."

Without looking back at her, he nodded again.

She couldn't help herself. "Thank you, baron. You're very kind."

He hesitated, then exited.

As the maids helped her out of the gown and back into her day dress, Abigail pondered what had just happened. Perhaps she was learning to play their game, and maybe she could use that to find a way to release the MacMillan sisters.

Abigail had started dinner in her room when the baron's assistant Pol Schmidt came in with news that jewelry would be provided. Hoping he would have more information about the detained Americans, she asked the young man to stay for a little while because she was tired of eating alone and she would enjoy the company. The dutiful fellow was not a disagreeable chap, so he sat with her. She offered him some of her meal of seasoned beef and brown bread, but he declined politely.

She tried to engage him in small talk. "Will I ever have a chance to meet Her Highness?"

"I don't know."

Silence followed, so she tried another approach. "What's Her Highness's schedule tomorrow? I'd like to know if I need to reflect her day's activities, such as being tired after hunting."

"She'll be attending meetings most of the afternoon at the Austrian embassy, so you don't need to concern yourself about anything like that."

Abigail skipped to the real reason for the conversation. As she cut off a slice of the beef, she asked, "Did anything interesting happen at the palace today?"

"Not that I know."

Abigail took advantage of the maids' absence. "I heard the staff talking earlier about some people at the front gate being arrested."

"I heard that."

She'd taken a bite in anticipation of a longer response, so she had to chew quickly for her own reply. "What had they done?"

"I heard they were demanding to see Her Highness." With a smirk and a shake of his head, he revealed his low opinion of them and their efforts.

"Why would Swaviczens do something like that?" she asked as she buttered a piece of bread.

"They were foreigners. I think they were British or something."

"You'd think British people would be better behaved regarding royalty," she said.

"You never know what people are going to do when they're away from home."

"True." She quizzed him about his own travels, but they were few. Then, with a casual wave of her piece of bread, she asked, "What will happen to those British people in jail?"

"Since the incident happened on palace grounds, Tirigovinian laws don't apply. It's up to Her Highness, because she was the one who gave the order that sent them to jail. So I guess it depends on how she's feeling on the day she's reminded they're in there."

None of this boded well for her friends. All she said was, "I hope she's in a good mood that day." But Abigail knew Rosamunde would not be.

CHAPTER TWENTY-FOUR

Into the Lair of Her Highness

Abigail spent a restless night. In addition to all her worries, the weather had turned hot and humid overnight and the room was stifling, even with the window open. She spent most of the dark hours trying to guess how the attack at the opera would unfold and devising a way to have the MacMillan sisters released from the town jail. When at last she did find sleep, it was drenched in nightmares.

She crawled out of bed with the dawn. One thing was for certain: The only way her friends could leave jail today would be if she impersonated the princess yet another time. Since she wouldn't have the chance to go to the jail, she would have to do it in writing. That meant finding Her Highness's office, locating stationery and samples of her writing, and trying to come up with a note to the jailors that would sound authentic. How she would do it, she had no idea.

She had a few advantages: She knew how to get to the princess's chambers, and from Baron Austerlanden's assistant she knew Rosamunde would be at the Austrian embassy during the afternoon. So Abigail knew where to go and when. She'd also noticed no guard posted outside her door. The rest of her thin and desperate plan consisted of seeing what opportunity presented itself.

The plan could not begin until the maids were absent. As inattentive as usual after breakfast, they presented Abigail with a bad omen by keeping a new and frustrating pattern of one girl staying with her while the other two would be gone for an hour or more.

This continued all morning. Not only were they ever-present, they were ill-tempered from the hot weather.

By the time a junior maid brought her a late lunch of sausages and potatoes swimming in gravy, Abigail was beside herself. Through the open window of her bedroom she heard the familiar sound of the landau passing by. They were preparing to take Rosamunde over to the Austrian embassy. Abigail had to get her plan started, but she was stuck here with the maid. If she'd been told the young woman's name, she didn't recall it now. The bored woman sat at the table near Abigail's full plate, yawning and in a sour mood.

Unable to bear the idea of eating the heavy lunch in this heat, Abigail began to pace around the room. Now she knew how wild animals in the zoo felt.

The maid grumbled, "Why are you walking around? Isn't it hot enough?"

Abigail saw no reason to antagonize the young woman, so she ignored her insolent attitude. When Abigail saw her yawn again, she got an idea. She sat down at the table and indicated her untouched meal. "Have you eaten yet? I'm not hungry. Please help yourself."

The girl's eyes grew wide as she looked at the feast. For a moment, Abigail thought of Belza and the box of chocolates. She pushed the thought from her mind.

The maid glanced at Abigail. "Are you certain?"

"Yes. Eat all you want."

The woman scooped up the fork and dove into the meal. As Abigail watched her gobble down the mouthfuls of potatoes, she said, "I'm sorry for the inconvenience I've caused you."

The young woman nodded, too busy to talk.

"I hope it's over soon."

Despite her mouth full of food, the maid managed to say, "Rumors say we can finally leave tomorrow."

Yes, Abigail thought, the palace officials would no longer have a secret to keep after they expected her to be dead. "That must be why the guard is gone. They're getting ready to return to normal."

The maid shook her head as she stabbed a whole sausage with her fork. "I don't know. I just know it'll be a relief to get out of here. Everyone's been so disagreeable the past few days. They're blaming you."

Abigail's sympathy for her ended when she seemed to agree with that sentiment.

She watched the maid gorge herself, almost surprised when she didn't lick the plate. As the young woman sat back in her chair with a contented sigh and small burp, Abigail stood with vigor. "I know what I need. I need to have a good walk session up and down the hall. Then maybe a nap. Come on, let's go."

The maid's face fell as she put her hand on her full stomach. "Now?"

"Yes. It'll do me a world of good."

The young woman looked at the closed hallway door. "But, it's so hot."

Abigail protested, "It's not that warm. Oh, but you just ate, didn't you? I have an idea. You stay here and digest your food, and I'll walk the hall, and I'll leave the door open so you can watch me from here. How does that sound?"

The expression on the maid's face said anything other than getting up was a good idea.

"It'll be fine. You stay here, and I'll go and come back." Abigail went to the door and opened it. She looked down the empty hall. She pushed the door all the way open. "You'll be able to see me and hear me from where you are right now." With a reassuring nod, she stepped through the door.

The hallway was only slightly less sweltering than the room, but Abigail kept a quick pace as she walked to the end and then back. She nodded to the maid, who hadn't moved from the table and who gave her a drowsy nod. When Abigail returned from her second lap, the heavy meal and warm air had done their work. Still sitting in the chair, the maid snored lightly.

Abigail went to her bed and arranged the pillows under the

bedspread so it looked as if someone were napping. If the maid woke up, with luck she would only glance into the bedroom and be satisfied with that. Taking a last glance down the empty corridor, Abigail made sure the door was unlocked, then closed it behind her as she left.

She saw no one along the way to the princess's chambers, although as she passed one room she heard two people shouting at each other in Swaviczen. Apparently the day's heat was taking its toll. When she reached the hall and saw no guards posted outside the wide door, she hoped that meant the princess was not present. She put her hand on the doorknob, and she said a silent prayer. She turned the knob, and the door opened. She slipped into the chambers.

Abigail had no time to appreciate the elegant rococo décor of the drawing room. She went over to a writing table with a small stack of papers and envelopes. There were letters, a fine gold dip pen on a stand, and a crystal inkwell, but no sign of official stationery. The desk had two small drawers. She opened one and saw a pair of glasses and a notebook but no stationery. In the second drawer she found what she was looking for. She pulled out several small sheets of paper with the princess's name in gold leaf across the top. She sat at the desk and dipped the pen's nib in the ink. Now, what to write?

"What are you doing?"

Abigail shuddered at the sound of an indignant male voice. She turned to see a stooped, gray-haired man scowling at her from a side doorway.

"Who are you?" he asked. "What are you doing?"

"I'm sorry. . . . I needed a pen and paper." She stood and moved away from the desk.

The old man's frown softened. "Oh. You're the double."

"Yes. I'm sorry. I know I shouldn't be in here."

"Why did you come here? It's very dangerous."

"I know. But I wanted to write a note. Friends of mine are in the jail. They came to rescue me. I wanted to write a note as Her Highness so they would be released and sent away."

Abigail couldn't believe she'd blurted out the truth. She'd had a half-formed lie prepared just in case, saying she wanted to write a letter to her parents. Oh, Dear Lord, she'd just undone everything.

The old man eyed her, then the paper on the desk. "That's her personal stationery. You need official parchment." He went back out through the door.

Abigail stared at the empty doorway, her heart pounding. What had she just heard?

The old man came back with several large sheets of paper and tottered over to the writing table. He put the small sheets and envelopes in the drawer and set the large pages on the cleared desktop. "And you need to use specific language or else the jailor will question the document." He removed glasses from his vest pocket and put them on. He dipped the pen in the ink and, in official lettering, started to write the beginning of a royal order.

Abigail had to gather her wits as she stared at him. "Why are you helping me?"

He continued to write. "What do you want the order to say?"

She hadn't thought of wording to write an official order. "Um, I want them removed from the jail, and taken to the train station, and put on the next train to Vienna."

He nodded as he wrote. "I suggest you add a statement that they stay under guard at the station until the train leaves. I understand the man has been very boastful at the jail that they can't stop him."

How would this man know what was going on outside the palace? Wait, Josef said a few people were allowed to come and go. One of them was Rosamunde's "true eyes and ears." She said, "You must be Varni."

He nodded as he continued to write.

Varni had been described to Abigail as Rosamunde's trusted secretary. "I don't understand why you're helping me."

He paused but did not take his eyes from the document as he scanned what he had written so far. "Why are you doing this for your friends?"

"I'm the only one who can help them."

He resumed his writing. "Why not write a note for yourself?"

"Well, first of all, no one would believe she'd change her mind and release me. Second, I have to make sure they're safe before tonight."

He stopped and studied her over his glasses. "Why tonight?"

Under the circumstances, she felt she should be honest with him. "Because they're going to try to kill me at the theatre."

He set the pen on its stand. "You know that, and you're trying to save the others?"

"Yes. They don't deserve to be punished for trying to help me. And I don't want to be worrying about them and myself at the same time."

He nodded and picked up the pen, and dipped it in the ink before resuming his writing. "If I may have the effrontery to be plain-spoken, I know why the young count fell in love with you."

She watched Varni as he continued to create the document. Of course Rosamunde's secretary would know everything, both good and bad. "The count isn't in a great deal of trouble . . . is he?"

The old man thought about his answer. "That depends on how everything ends." He resumed writing.

A great many things hung in the balance, she thought. "I still don't understand why you're helping me. I haven't done anything for you."

He blinked a few times, then stopped and set down the pen. He pulled a handkerchief from his pocket as he removed his glasses and dabbed his glistening eyes. "You are mistaken. I owe you a debt I cannot repay." He tried to resume his work, but he stopped and wiped his eyes again. He said as he composed himself, "I will add a note to the order saying this should be destroyed after the task is completed. She sometimes gives that instruction, especially if the order is distasteful to her."

Abigail couldn't figure out what debt he could possibly owe her. She watched him finish the order. It was written in German, so she could read that it contained exactly what he said. This didn't seem to be a trick.

He finished but didn't sign the document. "I will not forge her signature." From under the new order he produced another legal document. Rosamunde's splendid official signature graced the bottom. "Are you able to copy this?"

At that moment, she felt she could do anything. "Let me practice." On a blank sheet she tried it a few times, then took a deep breath and put a careful "Rosamunde RF" on the counterfeit order.

Varni nodded his approval, then crumpled her practice sheet and put it in his pocket. "This won't require the official seal, which is good. I have pledged my life to protect that. I would not use it, even for you." When the ink on the document had dried, he folded the paper in thirds and on the outside flap wrote a name she assumed was that of the jailor. "I will have this delivered after Her Highness returns from her meeting. I believe she'll be in good spirits, so her generosity will not seem out of place."

Abigail still couldn't believe what had just happened. With a futile gesture, she said, "Sir, I cannot thank you enough. This is. . . ." She had no words for her gratitude.

He tucked his glasses into his vest pocket. His careworn face softened as he looked at her with brimming eyes. "No. It is I and my family who are forever in your debt. With an act of kindness, you have changed the life of a little girl who means more to me. . . ." He could not finish.

Now she understood. "*You're* little Rosamunde's grandfather!"

He nodded as he wiped his eyes and tried to collect himself. "My daughter and son-in-law love Roszi so much, but they cannot protect her from the cruelty of the world. How the other children treated her broke their hearts. But when I saw my daughter yesterday, she said ever since you showed Roszi such generosity and called her your friend, the other children. . . ." He had to wipe his eyes again. "She was invited to a party. That has *never* happened. You've changed her life."

Abigail had to blink away her own tears. "What's the point of having power if you can't use it to make things better?"

He nodded, then clasped her hand. "Please do not judge Her Highness severely. She has a great burden. She has to be both king and queen. And these are perilous times. She has to make decisions for the entire country . . . sometimes at the expense of individuals who do not deserve it. I hope you can find it in your heart to forgive her."

Abigail had never thought of Rosamunde in those terms. She could tell Varni cared for his sovereign as a person. He had probably watched her grow up from a child. Abigail would try to be generous . . . depending on how things turned out, of course. She patted his hand. "Thank you."

They shared a smile, and then he went to the door to the hallway and looked outside. "It's empty. Go. I will take care of this for you."

She thanked him one more time and went out into the corridor and down the stairs. She ducked into a side passage as two valets went past, and then she hurried down to her door. She listened for a moment—no voices—and opened the door. The maid was still asleep in the chair. Abigail slipped past her into the bedroom and threw back the covers on her bed. She scattered the pillows and stretched out. Then she began breathing again.

CHAPTER TWENTY-FIVE

Preparations for Battle

Supper was served early. Last meal of the condemned, Abigail thought. How silly for it to be something as ordinary as hasenpfeffer. Perhaps this would be an able substitute for a lucky rabbit's foot. She forced herself to eat. She'd need her strength for the long night ahead.

Then it was time to get dressed. As she stood before a triple mirror set up in the anteroom, Elga and the maid Abigail had tricked into taking a nap began with her hair. They drew heated rods through her curly mane to straighten the top six inches as best they could, leaving the bangs in their naturally curly condition. Then they arranged her hair in the princess's favorite evening style, with the front and sides pulled up towards the crown and secured in a large knot. They added a lush accumulation of false curls to create long, manageable ringlets.

The maids helped her into her chemise, stockings, and shin-length drawers. Elga mocked her choice of such long undergarments on a warm summer evening, but she stuck to her guns. Riding sidesaddle without a riding habit would be risky, but the long drawers would give her the coverage and freedom of movement she'd need on a long night ride. Next came the corset and the many petticoats. Those extra layers would be warm and make things awkward in the restrictions of a sidesaddle, but they were required for the dress and would be less awkward than fighting with the sturdy hoops of a large crinoline. She had also insisted on light boots instead of the more usual flimsy shoes. She pretended with convincing embarrassment that she had twisted her ankle on her hallway walk and needed the snug laced support of the boots to prevent her from limping. The maids laughed at her clumsiness but found a pair of kid boots dyed dark gray that would not be noticeable under the gown.

After her underpinnings were in place, Abigail excused herself to use the close stool in the toilette room. Leaving the small mirror in its hiding place until after she was dressed and ready to go, she removed her travel permit from behind the vase. She tucked it into the corset's décolletage so she would have access to it when the time came. She was glad the chemise fabric was heavy enough to hide the permit from the maids, even if hiding it there meant the corners of the thick paper dug into her skin.

She pulled out of the vase the last items she'd hidden. Everything else of hers she could leave behind, even the lovely red dress Frau Meyer had made, but she would never leave without *Oma* Siebold's pearl drop earrings, which she'd wrapped in the handkerchief Josef gave her when she cried after reading Daisy's telegram. Having the gifts from her grandmother and this special man made her feel for a moment as if she were putting on armor. She tucked the handkerchief into her corset between the front laces. With a gaze in the small wall mirror, she took a deep breath to steel herself.

When she emerged into the anteroom, the makeup artist Anna Victoria stood by the table, waiting to work her magic. The retired coloratura watched as Elga and the other maid helped Abigail into the separate skirt of the ball gown and then assembled the bodice in place.

Being in the dress made vivid the reality of what was to come and undid her resolve. Abigail had to concentrate on the details and not think about why she was being dressed up. She knew she wasn't prepared. She fussed with her ensemble to hide the trembling of her hands.

Once the lovely blue gown was on, the maids helped Abigail put on elegant dark blue opera gloves that reached nearly to the hem of her sleeves. Anna Victoria had her sit down in front of the dressing table and mirror as the maids draped a protective cloth across Abigail's shoulders. As she worked at applying Abigail's disguise, Anna Victoria talked about how fine the performance would be, how handsome the tenor was, and how exciting the dramatic effects at the finale would be. Abigail could only think about how the final pyrotechnics would be more exciting than anyone could imagine.

As the makeup artist was finishing her magic, Frau Meyer came in with a small bouquet. She nodded her approval of Abigail's transformation. Anna Victoria removed the protective cloth and packed up her implements. In a cheery voice she wished Abigail a happy evening at the show and swept out of the room.

Abigail stood as Frau Meyer stepped up to give the gown a final primp. The royal dressmaker put the bouquet on the table. "I have never heard of this bouquet 'fashion,' but I suppose. . . ."

Abigail flashed her a look that pleaded for her to stop. Frau Meyer hesitated as Abigail glanced at the maids. They were sitting at the dining table, bored and anxious to leave. Frau Meyer's eyes asked for an explanation. Abigail turned to face away from the maids and said in the faintest of whispers, "Can you get them out of here for a few minutes?"

Frau Meyer turned to the listless women. "I have forgotten my dust brush. It is in my closet. Go fetch it."

The two looked at each other. Neither wanted to volunteer.

Frau Meyer snapped, "Both of you lazy things."

The maids hauled themselves out of the chairs and left in grudging steps.

Once they were out of the room, Abigail went into the toilette room and retrieved her hand mirror from behind the vase. "Thank you. I didn't want them to tell anyone about this." She found a secure spot to lodge it between the flower stems and the wrapped handle of the bouquet. A quick check proved the palm-size compact disappeared behind the floral camouflage.

The older woman frowned. "What is happening? Everyone is behaving so strangely. The staff is restless, and the superiors are acting as if they are preparing for a battle and not the opera."

Yes, Abigail thought, the battle at the opera. Relieved that Frau

Meyer wasn't part of the conspiracy, she set the bouquet back on the dressing table and looked around the room to make sure there was nothing else she needed. She said to this woman she now considered a friend, "You've been so kind to me, when all I represent is extra work for you. I want to thank you for everything . . . because chances are we will not meet again."

Frau Meyer took her hands with concern. "What's happening?"

Abigail couldn't burden her with all of the truth. "I tell you this in confidence: Tonight is my final performance as Her Highness. If all goes well, by this time tomorrow I will be released from my service and out of the country."

Frau Meyer was not fooled by the optimistic words. She gave Abigail's hands a concerned squeeze. "I am worried for you, my dear. I will ask God to watch over you."

They heard Elga's complaining voice approaching the door, so Abigail only had time to give her friend a grateful squeeze of her hands before the door opened.

Abigail turned to the triple mirror as Elga and the other maid lumbered in. Frau Meyer began fluffing out the fabric on the ball gown's small sleeves. She gestured for Elga to give her the soft whisk brush. "Good. You found it." She brushed out the billows of the gown as the maids tried to resume their resting spots in the chairs. Frau Meyer tucked the brush under her arm and clapped her hands. "Get up, you worthless girls! This woman is more important than you will ever be. Show your respect." Groaning, the maids stepped up and helped smooth the fabric.

As they finished, a knock on the door announced the arrival of Baron Austerlanden and two valets bearing the royal jewelry on small cushions: a brilliant tiara with a teardrop diamond dangling from the crest, a diamond necklace with a solitaire the size of a pigeon egg descending from a framework that held hundreds of smaller diamonds, and sapphire and diamond earrings that at first glance seemed nearly as large as the eyes Abigail was afraid were popping out of her head.

The baron said, "From Her Highness's private collection."

As the valets laid down their splendid burdens, Abigail could only marvel at the wealth available to the princess. Rosamunde knew these pieces were going into danger, and yet she was willing to risk them. If these were her less important pieces, Abigail could not imagine what her favorites were like.

First on was the necklace. It was old and heavy, and it didn't have a clasp so both maids lifted it over her head and onto her shoulders. The cold of the metal on her bare neck and chest made her shiver. Too late she realized its weight would restrict her movements. Why had she asked for this?

Next came the earrings. They were an old style that didn't hang down like the drop earrings she knew. An odd, unfamiliar ring clasp held the precious stones over the earlobes. She didn't know how to work the clasps, so the annoyed maids had to put the earrings on her. The jewels were lighter than they appeared and glittered with an astonishing fire.

Last came the tiara. It wasn't a complete circle like a diadem; the jeweled section across the front wrapped around into two sturdy side bands that tucked into her hair above and behind her ears. The piece was heavier than she expected, but once the maids secured it in place, the well-balanced adornment settled perfectly on her head. She regarded her reflection in the mirror. Who was this bejeweled creature with someone else's face? She didn't know anymore.

A quick knock on the door announced the entrance of Franz Antonius in his finest white uniform. Abigail turned to face the smug blackguard, and his condescending smile withered under her fierce gaze. He caught himself and shook his head. "My dear," he said, "for a moment I thought you were my royal cousin."

"Are you accompanying us this evening?" she asked.

His brows knitted as he looked at her. "Yes." He studied her more closely, then, apparently reassured that she was not the real princess, he said, "I say, you are positively regal."

She intoned, "We have taken our lessons to heart."

He frowned. "You're beginning to frighten me, a little. Shall we depart for the theatre?"

A shiver raced down her spine. Death or freedom. One awaited her at the opera. "Yes, let us go."

She started for the door, but then she heard Frau Meyer's exclamation of surprise. "My Lady—uh, I mean, *Fräulein.*"

Abigail saw the royal dressmaker reaching out with the small bouquet of flowers.

Frau Meyer's eyes were beginning to fill with tears. "Please don't forget this."

Abigail went back to accept the precious item she had forgotten. In a quiet voice, she said to Frau Meyer, "Thank you, my dear friend. For everything. Most of all, for your friendship."

The woman nodded, a tear dropping from her lashes. "God be with you."

Franz Antonius came up to them and took Abigail by the hand. "Why is she crying?"

Abigail turned back towards the door with him and replied, "Doesn't every fairy godmother cry when her charge leaves for the ball?"

Franz Antonius was unsure of her answer, but with a last glance over his shoulder at Frau Meyer he escorted Abigail out of the room and down to the waiting carriage.

CHAPTER TWENTY-SIX

Taking the Field

The carriage ride was full of the usual ceremony, plus many extra soldiers in escort, even though the pre-sunset journey was all of two blocks from the palace to the opera house. Cheers from the common folk on the street greeted Abigail and Franz Antonius as they traveled in the landau, which for once had its top up. Despite the fact that the people were looking at her as they applauded, she chose a diplomatic deflection and said to him, "You appear to be popular."

He shook his head. "They're cheering for Her Highness."

She wondered. She detected a joy and light in their eyes she hadn't seen before on her carriage rides. Had something happened during her days under house arrest? Perhaps there was a festival in progress, or they responded this way to hot weather. Whatever had inspired their good spirits, it seemed genuine.

She looked up the road that led to the grand medieval gate and on to the train station. She wondered if the afternoon train had been on time. Were the MacMillan sisters and their detective gone, or were they still in the station, under guard, waiting to leave? She prayed the train had left with the group on it. She wanted them out of reach before the evening was over.

When the landau approached the front entrance of the opera house, a gauntlet of soldiers awaited to keep the bystanders back and offer the two a clear path to the door. Abigail was surprised to see so many people gathered by the entrance. There had to be a crowd of a hundred or more on the walkway in front of the building. Was watching the country's important personages a popular pastime? All of her other carriage excursions were spontaneous, but everyone would have known about this trip. She'd been in the country long enough to begin to distinguish between the bright Sálacene costumes and the more subdued Swaviczen clothing, and the people represented a mix of the population.

A chorus of cheers greeted the arrival of the landau, and Franz Antonius got out first to help Abigail descend the carriage's step. As she emerged, the chorus rose to a roar of shouts and applause. She stepped to the ground and acknowledged the gathering with a wave and a smile too broad to be regal. Above the commotion she heard several calls of "God bless Your Highness!" and a "God watch over you, kind monarch!" Franz Antonius seemed surprised by the ovation as they went through the tunnel of soldiers to the front door.

Holding her elbow, he whisked her through the opera house's busy foyer towards a quiet passageway on the right. The crowd inside was welcoming, but not on a par with the excitement outside. Baron Austerlanden and his assistant waited in the hallway. Abigail and Franz Antonius stopped as several of the soldiers from the escort caught up with the group. "That was certainly rousing," Franz Antonius said as he looked back at the front entrance.

The baron asked him, "What was all that cheering for?"

"Her Highness," came the count's answer with a shrug.

Shaking his head, the baron led the way down the corridor.

Abigail now realized the crowd's greeting wasn't normal. As she walked with her escort, she wondered if this had something to do with her getting the mayor of Tirigovina and Jovacź Chešqu to talk to each other. Perhaps she was humoring herself, but she wondered if they were cheering for her instead of Rosamunde.

The group continued to follow the baron down the hall. Abigail looked around for other passageways that might provide a way to a side exit, but she saw nothing. They approached a flight of stairs. The baron and his assistant went first, followed by Abigail and Franz Antonius, and the soldiers at the rear. Clutching her small bouquet, she grasped the skirt just below her waist to lift the hem out of the way of her ascending steps.

As they climbed, Franz Antonius kept his hand on her elbow. She didn't know if he was assisting her or controlling her. Through the wall on the left Abigail could hear the buzz of many conversations and the orchestra warming up. She recognized a thumping heartbeat rhythm by the timpani from the crescendo before the climax's explosion—the cue for the assassin—and she shuddered.

Franz Antonius said, "Are you all right, my dear?"

She was neither all right nor his "dear," but she answered, "Sorry, I almost tripped."

"Watch your step," he warned. "We don't want anything to happen to you."

She was certain those sentiments were more hers than his.

At the top of the stairs, a narrow corridor ran along the length of the opera house. Behind them was an interior hall with doors, but the group headed in the direction of the stage. Abigail could hear the sounds from the audience below and to their left. The passageway's walls were solid on both sides, so at no point was the group visible to the people in the house. Abigail hoped that wouldn't work to her disadvantage.

As Abigail visualized the chessboard and Phillip's description of the house's layout, they passed the door to the first box. A small engraved sign on the door said *Olernica*. Abigail didn't know the name and wasn't sure if this was a friend or foe. The next door had *Zaaf* on it. The margrave and Lady Zaaf were not her friends. A sniff of disdain from Franz Antonius revealed his opinion of the occupants. The last door at the terminus of the corridor had no name. The two guards stationed in front spoke more eloquently than any sign as to whose box this was.

The urbane baron stopped in the light of the gas lamp opposite the royal box's door to address a down-to-earth matter. He didn't look her in the eye as he said, "If you need to use a chamber pot, one will be brought to you and you can use it here. Once you're in the box, you must stay there until the intermission. It is disruptive for you to come and go because protocol demands everyone stop and stand for Her Highness when she enters and leaves. Even if you think you are not visible, people are watching you."

Abigail was certain of that last statement. She reassured the baron she had no needs at this time.

He continued with only the briefest moment of looking at her: "At the intermission, you will be escorted to a small reception in a room on the other end of this floor. It will be attended only by people who know who you are. You will not interact with the public. Then you'll return here for the second act."

To test his reaction, she looked him straight in the eye and asked him, "Will I meet with members of the opera company after the performance?"

As she expected, the baron seemed surprised by the question. With a flitting glance at her he said, "Oh, yes. I will arrange that."

Yes, she thought, of course he would.

Baron Austerlanden said to her, "If you are ready. . . ."

She nodded.

The guards opened the door, and Franz Antonius stepped out of her way.

Through the doorway she saw a light curtain pulled back to reveal the box and two sumptuous, high-backed chairs with the opera hall beyond the box's railing. Franz Antonius indicated for her to take the chair on the right. Of course, that was the one closer to the stage. Sitting there she would have her back to the door as she watched the opera and have no angle to see the door in her peripheral vision. Indeed, these men were the very devil about the details. Taking a deep breath, she stepped through the door.

Abigail moved to the box's railing in order to take her place in the chair, and the orchestra ceased its tuning and the murmur of conversation stopped. The orchestra played a royal salute—the same one Abigail had heard at the ball—and the audience members rose to cheer her arrival. The nobles and important people in the boxes and the front of the house applauded her, but the commoners in the back of the hall offered her a resounding ovation. She responded with a dignified wave to all. As the cheers from the commoners continued with enthusiasm, she saw some of their social superiors exchange curious glances. Abigail had her final confirmation that Rosamunde was never greeted this way. Abigail wasn't sure what she had done, but it had earned the gratitude of the masses. She gave another wave of acknowledgment and sat in her chair. The ovation subsided, and the orchestra resumed its final preparations.

Baron Austerlanden released the light curtain from its hook and let it hang between the chairs and the door. "I'll see you at the intermission," he said in a quiet voice before retreating and closing the door.

As Franz Antonius settled into the chair next to her, she felt she needed to diffuse the public's response to her appearance. "It's good to know your cousin is so well loved."

He regarded her with suspicion. "Yes, and that love seems to have blossomed recently."

For the first time in days she could respond with a look of honest innocence. But changing the topic still seemed like a good idea. "Is the reception at intermission a customary event?"

He allowed himself to be distracted. "Yes. It's usually hosted by one of the nobles or someone from the moneyed class. But we've told everyone you need to rest after overextending yourself at the ball. You're recuperating from the chickenpox, after all."

She looked out at the hall. Being in a box did not give one a good view of the performance, but it did offer an excellent perspective to take in everything else.

She saw Franz Antonius smirk. "Your first time in a box," he observed.

"Yes. When I go to the theatre, I go to see the performance, not to be seen."

He chuckled. "A princess does not have such a luxury. You will be as much the center of attention as the singers."

How well she knew that. "I hope I don't disappoint them."

The orchestra's tuning and warming-up quieted, and a hush of anticipation fell over the hall as the house lights began to dim. He said, "I'm sure you will not."

For once, she agreed with Franz Antonius.

The traveling opera company gave a spirited performance of *Benvenuto Cellini*, but Abigail did not watch it. She sat as if she were looking at the stage, but instead she surveyed the interior of the house. She knew the only logical direction for the attack would be from behind, but she needed to observe every detail just in case she could glean something useful.

The boxes across the way matched Phillip's description. Directly opposite the royal box sat Vasily Medyev, who was alone. She wondered where his near-sighted family was this evening. He held some papers and seemed more interested in them than the opera. In the next box was Michael Gregorski, who sat forward in his chair and leaned on the railing as he watched the performance with a rapt gaze. There was that possessiveness she recalled from their meeting in the plaza. Perhaps he felt that way about everything, that it was his for the taking if he could figure out how to get it. In the next box sat Josef's father, mother, and younger sister. In the row below, the first box was occupied by Wolfgang Guttmann's older brother, the Landgrave of Tratano, and his wife and their son, the "nincompoop." In the next sat Herr and Frau Guttmann. The archbishop's box on the end was empty.

Abigail noticed Josef's father conferring with the women. He had his head lowered, and they leaned towards him in a pose of confidentiality. When he finished, the women looked across at Abigail. All three nodded to her with deep respect. Josef must have confided in his family, and they all knew who she really was. She nodded back in acknowledgment, and the young woman smiled at her. The three returned their attention to the opera and seeing who else was attending the performance. How she wished she could talk with them, for only a moment, to express her gratitude for what Josef had done for her.

"That's my uncle," Franz Antonius said.

Abigail snapped out of her reverie. "Who is?"

"The family in the box over there that just nodded to you."

"Is the princess friendly with them?"

"Yes."

"Then it's all right I nodded back?"

"Yes."

She waited for more from him, but her professed ignorance seemed to smooth over any suspicion. Even a glance or simple gesture spelled danger tonight.

She regretted the long gloves on such a warm evening, as they were now clinging to her hands and forearms. Keeping her movements small, she undid the pearl buttons at the wrist openings to vent the damp warmth. It offered meager relief.

Abigail took her mind off the discomfort and scanned the hall over and over again. Something here had to be useful. She did see two familiar faces in the ground floor seating towards the back. Sitting with women who were presumably their wives were the mayor of Tirigovina and Jovacź Chešqu. The mayor leaned over and said something to Chešqu, who nodded and smiled. Their new friendship seemed to be flourishing.

Franz Antonius shifted in his chair. "Would you care for a snack?"

She glanced around the box. She saw nothing to eat. "What snack?"

"They have the most exquisite almond tortes in the lobby. Would you like one?"

A shot of panic rolled through her. It wasn't time yet. She wasn't ready! ". . . You're leaving?"

"Just down to the lobby. They always run out. I want to get one before intermission. Would you like one?"

She saw nothing hidden in his face and tried to calm down. "No, thank you."

He frowned at her as he slipped out of his chair. "My dear, you were positively frantic. Being on display up here appears to be wearing on you. Try to hold yourself together until intermission." He moved behind his chair and passed through the opening in the light curtain. He opened the door only enough to slip through. The glare of light from the hall's lamp illuminated the narrow gap in the curtain for just a moment, and then the door closed and he was gone.

Her heart pounded as she sat alone in the box. What if he wasn't coming back? Were Phillip and Mikal outside already? Where was the train at this hour? A hundred confused thoughts flooded her brain. She looked out at the house. Had anything changed? The boxes across from her seemed the same . . . except was someone missing from the Landgrave of Tratano's box? She couldn't remember. She fumbled with her bouquet, trying to remove the mirror. Nerves and perspiration took the steadiness from her grip, and she couldn't extract it. Now what? Panic began to rise.

The door unlatched.

She shuddered.

She turned and looked as the door opened a few inches. Light poured in through the curtain's gap, casting against the wall the shadow of a hand . . . holding a plate with a small pastry. She began to breathe as Franz Antonius slipped into the box and closed the door behind him. He sat in his chair and carved out a bite of the pastry with his fork.

Abigail gathered herself. If she reacted this badly when the assassin appeared, she would be dead.

CHAPTER TWENTY-SEVEN

The Battle of the Opera

Intermission arrived, and Abigail was whisked away to the other end of the hall and the small reception hosted by Franz Antonius. Despite his levity and the trays of champagne cocktails offered by swarms of waiters, the air crackled with intensity in the grim gathering of royal minions. Lord Zaaf and his dour wife were there, as well as Colonel Lutz of the muttonchops—unaccompanied by the well-dressed woman from the ball—and Baron Austerlanden with his assistant. A few other men and women she didn't recognize were also in attendance. She assumed they were miscellaneous assistants and the princess's ladies in waiting. They talked amongst themselves, but no one talked to her.

She noticed Lutz and Austerlanden stealing glances at her. She wanted to flatter herself that they were feeling regrets over sacrificing her, but Lutz's casual laugh over a comment by the baron forced her to face the truth. In their eyes, she was already dead.

Surrounded by the aloof crowd, Abigail contemplated her only friend in the room, the bouquet clutched in her hands. She became aware of mocking glances from two of the ladies in waiting, and she realized she had left her gloves' wrist openings unbuttoned to vent the heat. Yes, ladies, she thought, you have a bumpkin in your midst—a bumpkin who intends to outsmart you . . . somehow. She ignored them and studied the splendid necklace resting across her shoulders. It had seemed so heavy when it first went on, and yet now she'd all but forgotten it and the other jewelry. She wondered if they would impede her escape from the theatre in whatever form it would take. She regretted not having a pastry when she had the chance. It had been a long time since supper, and she needed something to sustain her through what was to come. She watched a waiter go by with a tray, but it contained only champagne, no food.

Franz Antonius appeared next to her with a champagne glass in his hand. "How are you feeling now? You looked ghastly earlier."

The ladies' disdain had rekindled Abigail's spirit enough for her to make a small joke. "I was ghastly, I'm afraid."

He managed to peel one of her hands from the bouquet and put the glass in it. "Here, you need this. A light champagne cocktail. It will make you feel much better."

She didn't like the idea of alcohol with no food in her stomach, but maybe just a little would help. He waited for her to take a sip, and she lifted the glass to her lips.

Then she remembered the dinner at Chetova, and how he had been so solicitous with the liquor served during each course. She looked at him. The concentration in his gaze was anything but casual.

She lowered the glass and inquired sweetly, "Any chance of a bite to eat?"

"Let me see what I can do."

As he turned his back to talk with Baron Austerlanden, one of the waiters passed with a tray of drinks, and she switched her glass for another. When Franz turned back to her, she took a sip from the new glass. He smiled. "The baron will find something for you."

"Thank you." She took another sip for his benefit. It was indeed a light cocktail, more fruit juice than alcohol. It seemed Franz Antonius wanted no one impaired when the evening turned dangerous. No one, perhaps, except her.

A waiter brought her a bit of sweet bread from the lobby, which she ate after only a moment of hesitant examination. At the insistence of Franz Antonius, she finished her drink, and then it was time to return to the box. As the party dispersed, Abigail could not shake the feeling of everyone watching her as she left.

Abigail settled into her chair in the royal box and wondered what had been in that drink. She assumed it was knockout drops, or at least something to dull her reflexes. A stationary target is easier to hit. Was that their plan? To let the assassin think he had succeeded so he would reveal himself, and then they would descend on him? She hoped she would not still be in town when all that came to fruition. As Franz Antonius sat next to her, only then did she wonder if someone else had taken that glass off the tray.

As the second and final act of the opera began, Abigail steeled herself. Soon it would unfold, and she'd have to be ready for death or freedom, whichever she met at the end of the evening. Despite the stifling heat that filled the opera house, she felt a chill settle over her. She shivered.

Franz Antonius responded with a solicitous hand on the arm of her chair. "Are you well?"

"Just a little tired. I'll be fine."

He nodded. "Relax and listen to the music."

She settled into her chair and rested her head against the cushioned high back. He was expecting her to fall asleep. But when?

She had her answer sometime later when an intermittent low roar started emanating from their left. What was that sound, like pushing a dull saw across a log and then drawing it back? She saw annoyed audience members looking in the direction of the Zaafs' box as the jarring sound continued. Then she realized someone was indeed sawing logs—thunderous snoring echoed from next door.

She heard a commotion through the wall and what sounded like a chair being moved. The snoring ceased, but she could hear a man's low, anxious voice asking his "dear" to wake up. Abigail realized Lady Zaaf must have ended up with her champagne cocktail and was now being rewarded with a deep and uninterruptible slumber.

With some urgency, Franz Antonius excused himself to go to the rescue. Abigail heard the men discussing this strange development. Franz Antonius called in the guards from out in the hall, and she could hear a great deal of quiet, but strenuous, shuffling and lifting, and then they lugged their burden out of the box and down the hall. Poor Lady Zaaf, she would never live this down.

The door to the royal box opened again. With a firm grip on the flower bouquet in her lap, Abigail put her head against the back of the chair and shut her eyes. Franz Antonius returned to his chair and said in a hushed voice, "I'm afraid our dear Lady Zaaf has had too much. . . ."

He stopped.

She could feel him lean in close to her. He touched her forearm.

She forced herself not to respond.

He gave her arm a gentle jostle. "Are you well?" he whispered.

She did not move.

She heard a small chuckle. He whispered to himself, "We couldn't have planned that better."

Abigail knew what he meant. They now had an excuse for the guards not being outside the box. For good or ill, she had aided the would-be assassin.

For an unsettling length of time Franz Antonius sat next to her, even though his work was done. By her reckoning, there were maybe twenty minutes left before the explosion. To her surprise, she wanted him to leave. While he sat there she was safe, but she had more reconnaissance work to do. From the angle of her head on the back rest, she could see the boxes on the other side of the hall . . . if she could open her eyes. But he had to leave for that. Was this some strange form of chivalry, keeping watch over the woman he was setting up to be killed?

Finally—and she almost sighed when she heard it—he shifted out of his chair. He put a hand on her arm. "I wish you luck. I hope he's a bad shot." A movement, the spill of light from the hall, and he was gone.

She opened her eyes. After a deep breath to settle her nerves, she slipped the small mirror out of the bouquet. She held it in her hand on her leg so she could see the door behind her. Surprisingly, the light curtain was pulled back, leaving a gap wide enough for someone to slip through. Had it caught on something, or had Franz Antonius made it that much easier for her killer? Not that it mattered.

Now what? She glanced at the stage. She had about five minutes. Should she announce to the audience that she was an impostor? No, that would only divert the assassin. She'd still be in the hands of her captors and she could very well disappear forever. Without knowing to flee, Phillip and Mikal would be taken into custody, and they—and Josef—would be punished. And if the MacMillan sisters were still in town, they would pay as well. No, she had to play the role of princess to the end. But what would she do?

Three minutes to the explosion. The opera was in its crisis. Benvenuto Cellini was trying to cast his magnificent bronze statue. Pulling off this masterstroke meant life for the artist, and failure guaranteed his death. Cellini's workers were rushing around, gathering up all the other statues so they could be thrown into the mold and sacrificed for the sake of the all-important project.

Two minutes. She scanned the boxes across the hall. If the ringleader was on this side of the house, she would have no warning, no telltale clue. But that seemed unlikely now. The three suspects—Gregorki, Medyev, and Guttmann—were sitting on the other side. How had they distinguished themselves from one another? They had all attended the princess's ball in the palace, but when they entered only Guttmann went straight in to the ballroom while Gregorski and Medyev stayed behind. Her exchange with Guttmann during the Sálacene ceremony on the plaza came back to her. When he saw her phony chickenpox blisters, he reacted with surprise and said something to the effect that she hadn't mentioned she was ill. Abigail guessed they had been in contact after she went into seclusion. She crossed Guttmann off the list.

So, it had to be Gregorski or Medyev. She looked over at Gregorski. In his familiar pose of leaning on the railing, his gaze was focused on the frantic activity on the stage. She glanced across the way to Medyev's box. It was empty! She scanned the other boxes—no, there he was, down in the last box on the second level. Why had he moved? Perhaps he was late returning from the intermission and slipped into the closer box. He held papers in his hands, as he had during the first act, but he wasn't reading them. He was glancing around the hall, at the stage, and up at her. She half-closed her eyes in hopes he would not see her observing him. He was fidgeting and having trouble sitting still. Gregorski, on the other hand, was intent on the opera.

Now she knew why Medyev had moved down to the archbishop's empty box on the end. He knew if he stayed in his regular place, he would be in the line of fire. He was the one.

The door latch clicked behind Abigail.

She forced her hand to stay still as she looked at the image in the mirror.

The door inched open. No light came in from the hall. Someone had turned off the lamp. The mirror held only shadows. She couldn't see who it was.

The shadow came through the door, leaving it open. Abigail could see a pistol, but not the face.

The shadow took a step to the left. She was no longer protected by the back of the chair.

The man now stood in the reflected light from the stage. He raised the small gun with a trembling hand and watched the stage, waiting.

Julius Živo.

That made no sense. He was Gregorski's right-hand man. Then again, perhaps he wasn't. Živo's glance in the palace's grand hallway during the ball told a different story. When both Gregorski and Medyev watched the soldiers detain Rosamunde's valet, Živo had looked at Medyev first, then Gregorski.

But something was missing. She had been here long enough to suspect Živo was a Sálacene name. Hadn't Josef said Medyev was in favor of forcing the Sálacene out of the country?

As the connection eluded her, for a moment she thought to turn him over to the audience and escape in the furor. No, she could not do to him what her captors intended for her.

Then Abigail put it all together. It was a triple cross. With an apology to Josef, she knew nothing short of a grand gesture would save her now.

She launched out of her chair and turned to face the astonished Živo.

The crowd began to murmur in confusion and stand according to protocol.

The orchestra hesitated, then the crescendo in the string section sputtered and stopped as the conductor shut down the performance. The singers, who were waiting for the make-believe mold to blow its top, looked at each other and then the conductor.

"Herr Živo," Abigail said in arched German, projecting her voice so it carried throughout the theatre. "What are you doing here? And with a pistol?"

Stunned, the bookish man stammered as a wave of surprise rolled through the opera house. He finally blurted out, "I—I'm here to protect you!"

"From whom? You're the only one here with a gun."

He stared at her in frozen silence.

If he had been a step closer, she would have snatched the gun away from him. But she hoped she had another way to disarm him.

"Herr Živo, were you promised money? Or were you promised safety for your people?"

The man sputtered.

"You think you were sent here to kill me. But no one told you that you are supposed to die, too, killed by my guards so everyone would blame the Sálacene *and* Gregorski—and no one would know who was really behind this." She spun to point an accusing finger across the house. "Medyev!"

The banker stood with a stumble, his papers scattering at his feet. "No! Your Highness! You don't know what you're saying! If anything, this is Gregorski's evil handiwork! He's the Sálacene sympathizer!"

Gregorski erupted with professions of his own innocence.

Abigail saw Živo's astonishment and growing betrayal. She said to him with quiet urgency, "Medyev used you. Do *not* let him triumph." She turned back to the hall and pulled the shaking Živo to the railing. She glanced down to snatch the gun from him, but—*curse it!*—he held it in his left hand, beyond her reach. "Listen to him—he knows the truth!"

Before Živo could speak, Medyev shouted, "This is Gregorski's man! Of course he will accuse me!" Medyev turned to the confused crowd. "My fellow Swaviczens, she does not know what she is saying. She sees enemies where there are none. She is intimidated by men of the people, men of business who know more than she of how the world really works. Do not listen to the hysterics and rantings of a woman I have heard talk of you as cattle!"

A harsh murmur from the audience rose at his words. Abigail's stomach knotted. With such insults for his sovereign, he had thrown down the gauntlet of treason in a fight to the death. She also knew she was fighting another enemy as dangerous as Medyev—the public's opinion of Rosamunde. The people did not love her. If Medyev turned them against her now, Abigail knew she might be killed by a mob instead of the conspirators. She said to the house, "Good people—save Swavicza from the evil manipulators who would tear it asunder and take it for their own personal gain!"

Medyev's mocking laugh echoed in the hall. "Who is the taker? Look at those jewels! Your labor and your taxes bought those adornments for her! She knows nothing of hard work and sacrifice!"

Abigail had no words for a rebuttal. She was certain he had spoken the truth.

She scanned the uneasy crowd. All she could do was speak for herself, not the woman they thought she was. "I have always tried to help you. Always."

Rumbles of low dissent began to rise in the hall.

Abigail gazed at the people. She saw anger and resentment. She glanced at Medyev. His sneer of satisfaction made her sick.

Medyev pounced on her silence. "Do you hear? She had nothing to say. She can't speak to you. She doesn't even speak Swaviczen!"

The rumbles grew louder.

Abigail didn't know Swaviczen, but she had learned something more powerful.

"Rulers are the leaders of all, not just one group," she told the hall. "If you will not learn the other's language, how can I speak to everyone if not through our common, neutral language?"

The murmurs subsided.

She looked at Jovacź Chešqu and the mayor of Tirigovina. "My good friends, you most of all understand what we have been up against, and you *know* it can be overcome. Will you support the people who wish to bring you together, or will your silence support the ones. . . ." She glared at Medyev. "The one—who wants to tear you apart?"

Chešqu held out his arms in a dramatic gesture. "My friends and countrymen! The princess is for us! And I am for the princess!"

The mayor put a hand of support on his friend's shoulder. "We know this! And you know us! Believe what Her Highness says. Do not listen to her 'advisers' who kept her away from us. Do not listen to the men who buy and sell us for their own profit!"

The low voices churned again as the people looked at one another, and then up at Medyev. The support he expected had ebbed, and he blanched at the anger coming from the people on the ground floor. "It is a trick! She doesn't mean what she's saying! You *know* her!"

Abigail looked at her would-be assassin. Živo's tear-streaked face was white with rage as he faced the man who had betrayed him. She said to him, "Go on. Tell them his plan. Tell them his false promises."

After a sputtering start, the bookish clerk began a breathless, bitter recitation of the names of the conspirators and how he had been promised peace for all the commoners if he killed Rosamunde, but he knew now it was a lie and no one was safe from Medyev.

A riot erupted. Medyev tripped over his chair as people from the ground floor rushed for his theatre box.

Abigail headed for the royal box's door. She shuddered when a pistol shot rang out behind her. She turned to see a sobbing Živo pointing the gun across the opera house towards Medyev, who was scrambling on the floor of the theatre box to get out of sight. Živo squeezed off three more shots before two palace guards dashed into the royal box.

Abigail pointed at Živo: "Arrest him!"

The soldiers descended on the man as she fled through the door.

Halfway down the stairs to the main lobby, Abigail ran into the crush of people trying to get up to the first balcony level. The ones who realized who she was—or who they thought she was—tried to make way for her, but the push from below kept her stuck on the last flight of stairs. Then two more gunshots rang out on the floor above them. The crowd on the stairs scattered both up and down. Abigail saw an opening and rushed the rest of the way down the steps.

She reached the ground floor just as an explosion rocked the building and sent people screaming in panic. It came from the direction of the stage. In the chaos someone backstage must have set off the opera's final pyrotechnics.

Abigail was almost to the front door when she was blocked by a woman and two men. The men were soldiers; the woman was Her Most Serene Highness Princess Rosamunde.

The monarch wore a magnificent burgundy and gold dress with an extravagant train, but as she faced her double, her rage was anything but regal. "You . . . *doppelgänger*! What have you done? *Give me my jewels!*"

The young woman from Cincinnati had no time for a showdown. She pulled the tiara from her hair and peeled off the heavy necklace. At first she held them out as if to give them to the soldiers, but as a fleeing couple dashed by, Abigail suddenly thrust the treasures into their hands. "Take these to safety!" she commanded. The startled pair held them tight and hustled out the door.

Rosamunde screamed and ordered her soldiers to go after her jewelry. The men rushed away through the swarming crowd as the princess lunged at her foe. Abigail ducked, and the princess only ended up with a handful of fake hair. She flung it to the ground and grabbed Abigail around the neck.

The wrestling match lasted a mere three seconds. The girl who had grown up with three lively brothers slipped free with a twist that spun the royal only child off-balance. Rosamunde tripped over her dress's train and bounced hard on the lobby's carpet. Abigail dashed out the door into the night.

The street roiled with shouting and people hurrying in all directions. Where were Phillip and Mikal in this chaos? A whistle of *Red River Valley* sent her bumping through the crowd to the left, where she found the men at the mouth of the alley next to the opera house. They were in civilian clothes and holding the reins of three horses.

"Hurry!" Mikal extended to Abigail the reins for the sturdy mare with a sidesaddle.

As she reached for the reins, a gloved hand thrust in and pushed her away, snatching the reins from her. The hunted animal that was once the suave Baron von Redki cursed when he saw the sidesaddle, but in a flash he was up astride the horse and galloped away in the direction of the center of town. Rifle shots followed him.

Four soldiers appeared at the mouth of the alley, rifles trained on the three. The head soldier laughed. "You thought you could. . . ." He hesitated when he saw Abigail.

She seized the moment. "Excellent work, soldiers. But don't let von Redki get away!"

They wavered in the face of this unexpected development.

Abigail pointed at one of the soldiers: "And you—find this man a horse." She gestured over her shoulder at Mikal.

No one moved.

"Now!" she snapped in a perfect fit of royal temper.

The cluster of soldiers broke up as three followed von Redki and one returned with a fine cavalry charger.

"Excellent, soldier," she said. "Now aid your fellows!" He saluted and took off at a run after the others.

Phillip and Mikal were distressed as she made quick work of shortening the stirrups on the charger's saddle. "Your Highness—I mean. . . ." Phillip stammered for a moment. "*Fräulein*—the evening train left on time. By now it's past Saint Florian, so we must ride to Senzarowa. But there's no sidesaddle for you. You cannot make it so far in time."

With a hop to catch the stirrup and a swing of her billowing gown, she was astride the cavalry charger. Flush with excitement, she forgot her manners. "Pardon my French, but like hell I can't!" At a touch of her heels, the horse sprang towards the medieval gate and freedom.

The men shared a baffled glance as they mounted their horses. "How can she think that is French?" Mikal said as they took off after her.

Abigail had never ridden such a magnificent horse, and she had to hold him back from his top gait as they sped through the last of the scattering crowd and then ran into the night traffic of carts and wagons. Before she was down another block Phillip and Mikal were behind her, and soon the daunting medieval gate loomed ahead.

To the surprise of her companions, she slowed her horse and stopped before the gate's sentries, who had responded in force to the alarm of their sudden arrival. She called out to them, "Who here is in charge?"

A barrel of a man emerged from the group with a grumpy, "I am." When he got a better look at her in the pale light, he straightened and saluted. "Your Highness!" The rest were quick with their own salutes.

"Good soldiers," she said, "at the theatre this evening a coup was foiled." Anxiety washed across their faces. "Some of the rogues are still on the loose. Don't let anyone escape! Close the gate!"

As the men scrambled to their task, she eased her horse through the group. Phillip and Mikal followed her.

With a grinding screech the giant doors began to move. She looked back and saw distant horsemen galloping towards them from the center of town. Whether they were conspirators or loyal soldiers, they were no friends of hers. "Quickly, men! Seal up the town!"

The soldiers redoubled their efforts.

The charging riders sent the scattering crowd into a panic, but the wagons could not get out of the way fast enough. Just as the lead rider began to shout to the sentries, his horse bolted to miss a wagon and threw him onto the stone pavement.

The mighty gate swung closed, shutting off the chaotic scene.

Abigail gave the soldiers a gallant wave as her impatient horse snorted and reared back on his haunches. "Well done, men! Protect Swavicza!"

The soldiers cheered as she sped off into the darkness with her escort close behind.

CHAPTER TWENTY-EIGHT

Death or Freedom

Two minutes before the train's scheduled departure from the station in the sleeping resort town of Senzarowa, Abigail presented her travel papers as she purchased her third-class ticket to Vienna on the Mountain Star Local. Having hastily changed her clothes in a dark alley and washed off all traces of her makeup disguise while standing over a rain barrel, she wore peasant Sálacene garb of a large headscarf tied under her chin, a bright shawl over a plain white blouse, and a simple, black skirt. She carried a small satchel, which Phillip assured her contained a token amount of items to help her look like any other traveler. As they hurried from the shadows to the station, Mikal made a remark about how she would find "additional help in the book," but she didn't have time to ask for an explanation before the men dropped back and she arrived alone at the ticket booth.

The Mountain Star Local had modern cars, and even the third class car was a corridor coach, with an interior hallway on the left side and small compartments on the right. She found an empty cabin and settled in next to the window. According to the schedule, it would be less than an hour until they crossed the border and left Swavicza. Her plan was to sit, show her papers, answer questions with polite deference, and draw no attention to herself whatsoever.

When the train began to move, she let out a sigh of relief. She gazed out the window at the blackness. The starlight cast a gray mantle over the dark mountains. One last ascent through the forbidding landscape, and she would be free.

Spilled light from the train car caught something next to the tracks ahead. Men on horseback! Her heart raced as the train continued forward, but when she saw the familiar faces, she smiled. Phillip and Mikal. They saw her and in a single gesture offered her a salute. As she passed in her last royal review, her smile was broad and genuine and not at all regal. She turned on the bench to watch them as they disappeared into the night. How steadfast and resourceful—she owed them her life. She prayed they would find a way to blend back into the chaos in Tirigovina and avoid suspicion.

She shifted in her seat to face forward again, but she caught her breath at a dark movement ahead of her car. From the shadows another large form bounded up the slope to the edge of the tracks. As the light from the first class coach spilled out onto the figure, it took shape as a dusty man on a sweating horse.

Josef.

He had ridden all the way from exile in Budapest with the hope of one last glimpse of her. What confidence he had in her ability to escape!

As he looked at the windows of the second class coach ahead of her, she found the latch and slid open her window. He spotted her, and as her car caught up with him he eased his tired horse to walk alongside her window. The train was slowly accelerating up the grade, so they would only have a few moments.

Even as she reached out to him, the train began outpacing Josef's winded horse. Their fingertips brushed, then he slipped out of reach. She leaned out onto the window ledge as she gazed back at him. "How's your shoulder?"

"I think it fell off south of Zamárdi."

Finally, he could make a joke, bringing out a wistful smile from her. "I wish you could come with me." Of course he couldn't jump aboard the train and escape with her. Shame and retribution would fall on his family. This last, reckless, romantic gesture was the most he could do.

"I wish I could, too." Despite the rumble of the distant engine, his voice was soft, intimate. "Write to me. In care of the embassy in Budapest. Tell me everything that happened. I won't believe what anyone else says."

"Yes. As soon as I reach Vienna."

He was falling behind as the train pushed onward, upward, towards the frontier and freedom. She felt the tug of the rail pulling the car to the left. The line of cars behind hers began to bend with the turn away from him. In a moment or two Josef would disappear.

She put to her lips the tips of the fingers that had brushed against his. With a sad smile he did the same. They gazed at each other, and then he was gone.

She continued to stare back at the darkness and the rattling train car that blocked her view. Tears were waiting to overwhelm her, when she caught sight of the face of an older man in the next car back. He was leaning out his window, smiling at her with the look of "oh, to be young again and in love." What memories in his heart had been stirred by their parting, she could only guess. With a smile of chagrin, she slipped back into her seat, then closed the window.

She gathered herself. This was not over yet. It was time to focus. She concentrated on looking like any other passenger. She switched back to the forward-facing seat and removed the book from her satchel, a stiff volume of German devotional poetry. She turned to the first page and pretended to read.

As her eyes passed over the words without seeing them, she heard people talking together while they came up the corridor. She tried to fix her eyes on the text, but something was amiss, or at least out of place. Women's voices . . . chatting . . . in English!

She glanced up to see Deborah Caruthers and Esther Weatherwax pass by her compartment on their way forward to the second class car. They were talking about those nice-looking young men on horseback outside the train and what their salute could have meant. As Abigail stared at the women in disbelief, Mrs. Weatherwax caught sight of her and stopped in stunned silence while Mrs. Caruthers continued on. Abigail flung open the door. Exclamations of delight poured out, but Abigail hushed the sisters and ushered them into her compartment.

Tears and hugs and excited questions tumbled out. Abigail simply told them that she had managed to escape. Worried about their enthusiasm, she promised to tell them more once they were safely across the border.

Mrs. Caruthers cast a sad glance at her younger sister. "Yes, my dear Abigail, I'm afraid we're not safe yet. The detective we hired to bring you back—"

"Yes," Mrs. Weatherwax interrupted, "we were in the capital and tried to rescue you, and for our efforts we were arrested!"

Mrs. Caruthers shot her a glare. "Esther, let me finish, this is important *now.*"

The young sister frowned but kept her silence.

The older continued, "We hired a detective to help us bring you back, but I'm afraid he was rash and boastful when we were . . . in jail. . . ." She shook her head to distance herself from that thought. "And when they released us, Mr. Briscoe vowed he would come back and get you, so they sent along someone from the jail to make sure we crossed the border."

Abigail ran the details through her mind. "Someone from Tirigovina is with you?"

Mrs. Weatherwax replied, "Yes, dear. And he's not very nice."

If he was from the jail, Abigail knew he would not have seen her, except possibly when she was disguised as the princess. And because the train had already left when the battle of the opera began, he would know nothing of her escape. Even better. "Is the detective cooperating with him?"

Mrs. Caruthers answered, "He's complaining, but he's being mostly compliant."

"Good." If they all behaved themselves, they would get across the border, the jailor would leave the train, and they would be all right.

Mrs. Caruthers said, "You must come forward and join us in our compartment."

Mrs. Weatherwax added, "Yes, it's not safe for you here by yourself. A woman traveling alone in this country. My word!"

Abigail knew she would be fine on her own, but it seemed she should be concerned about the detective. "Does he know what I look like?"

The sisters exchanged a glance. Mrs. Caruthers answered, "He never asked."

She nodded. "All right. Here's what we have to do. . . ."

The two sisters, followed by their young guest in Sálacene clothing, entered their second class compartment just as Mr. J.D. Briscoe was promising the blasé jailor that once they got back to Vienna "this little country would see some real trouble." Mrs. Weatherwax interrupted him by telling the men about their guest, who had been sitting all alone, and since they were concerned about a woman traveling by herself and she spoke a little English, they had invited her to join them. The sisters sat next to Mr. Briscoe while Abigail gave a polite nod and sat next to their escort from the jail and across from Mr. Briscoe.

The jailor, a man in his forties who did not seem to be enjoying his assignment, took no particular interest in Abigail. However, the detective eyed her as she removed the book from her satchel. He watched her read for a while. She grew nervous that he was going to realize who she was and spoil everything.

Briscoe finally spoke. "You know English?" he said in stilted German.

With a thick accent that she hoped sounded Sálacene, she said, "A little."

Briscoe nodded and continued to ponder her.

The jailor muttered to her in German, "Don't pay attention to him. He's a blowhard."

She resisted the urge to smile as she gave the jailor a simple nod. She went back to her book. The pages at the back felt oddly stiff. She flipped through the pages, only to discover the back half was stuck together. She tilted the book spine up enough so the others couldn't see what she was doing and went to the spot where the sheets were stuck. She saw a small latch on the first unyielding page, and she realized there was a cutout edge in the paper. The book had a hidden compartment. Trying to look as if she were reading and tracing her finger along the text, she undid the latch and opened the paper door. Snugly wedged into the hidden compartment lay a small pistol. She caught her breath, then redid the latch and turned the pages back to the front of the book. A last gift from the disciples of Saint Joshua. She hoped she would not need it, but what a comfort to know it was available.

In English, the detective asked, "Are you studying to become a nun?"

Abigail was confused by Mr. Briscoe's question. "Sorry?"

"With your head all covered up like that." He looked at the book. "Or are you a teacher?" he asked.

She brightened her eyes. "Teacher, yes. Very good."

He nodded with satisfaction. "I thought so." He glanced at the sisters as if inviting them to share in his triumph. They were busy distracting themselves with their handbags and not looking at the others.

The jailor glanced out the window. He stood and told Briscoe in choppy English, "We are going fast enough now if you jump out you will break your neck. Maybe you should try it."

Briscoe shot him a sour frown.

The jailor turned to Abigail and said in German, "I'm getting a bite to eat. Would you like something?"

In truth, she was famished. She nodded at his kind offer. "Yes, bread and cheese, or a little something warm. Whatever they have. Thank you." She searched in her satchel for money, but he shook his head.

"No, they gave me money when I left. My treat for a young teacher." He winked and left.

Mrs. Weatherwax tried to launch into questioning Abigail but her sister cut her off, and they fussed in half-words while Mr. Briscoe stared at them. Abigail was now sorry she had joined their party.

Time to distract their companion. She said to Mr. Briscoe in accented English, "You are important, yes?"

His already big chest swelled. "That's right, miss. I'm with the Binterman Detection and Investigation Agency of the United States of America. Perhaps you've heard of us."

She let her eyes sparkle with recognition. "You are BDI man!"

Abigail didn't need to say another word for the next twenty minutes. Mr. J.D. Briscoe regaled her with stories of his most thrilling and lurid investigations, not even stopping when the guard returned. The jailor had warm beef pastries and gave one to her. She ate with gusto. She couldn't remember the last time food had tasted this good. Even Mr. Briscoe's tall tales couldn't spoil her appetite.

The train slowed to a crawl as they passed through a small, unlit station. Abigail recognized it as Mytiwa. They were almost to the border. Then, just as the station was disappearing from sight, she saw through the window two mounted soldiers each leading away a pair of riderless horses. Oh, no, the train must have picked up soldiers.

Ten minutes later, a group of four Swaviczen soldiers came up the corridor from the back of the train. Abigail picked up her book and pretended to read as if she was now bored with Mr. Briscoe's endless stories. She did not dare look at the sisters.

A dark-haired captain opened the compartment door. "Good evening," he said in smooth German. "It is a pleasant evening, is it not?"

Abigail glanced at the sisters, who looked baffled and frightened.

The jailor reached into his pocket and produced several sets of papers. Abigail pulled her travel document out of her satchel.

The captain read the jailor's papers, then studied the sisters and

Mr. Briscoe before handing the papers back. He took Abigail's document. There was something about him that reminded her of Baron von Redki, smooth and not trustworthy. He read over her forged papers twice. "Teacher?" he said in German.

"Yes. I will be tutoring a merchant's children in Vienna."

"What are you doing in second class? Your ticket is for third."

She nodded towards the sisters. "They saw me alone in my compartment and thought it would be safer for me here. The conductor has not yet been by to collect my extra fee."

He continued to regard her and her papers. "Have you been to Vienna before?"

"No."

"They don't like Sálacene there. You'll need to dress Austrian." Then he said something to her in what did not sound like Swaviczen.

Her heart raced. It sounded like Sálacene. He was trying to trick her.

She nodded and lowered her head. She said the only words she knew in Sálacene. "*Thank you.*"

His brow knitted in disappointment, and he handed back her paper. The captain turned to the sisters. He said in English, "Your papers?"

The women fumbled with their handbags as Mr. Briscoe announced in his awkward German, "That ruffian over there has mine."

The dark-haired captain took the offered papers from the sisters. He said in English, "And why is that, Herr Briscoe?"

Mr. Briscoe wound up to begin what surely would be an epic piece of bombast, but Mrs. Weatherwax put a hand on his arm and shook her head. He thought, then unwound. "Due to a misunderstanding, my presence was no longer welcome."

The captain nodded. "I see. I am glad you are cooperating."

The jailor harrumphed, and the soldier smirked. He then turned to the sisters as he read their papers. He drew the moment out longer than necessary. "And how was your stay in our country?" he asked in English.

The two looked at each other, then at Abigail, then at the soldier, then the jailor, and then at Abigail again. Mrs. Weatherwax began to tremble.

The smooth captain asked, "Have I said something wrong?"

Abigail stared at her book. In three seconds she could have the pistol out. . . . But then what?

Mrs. Weatherwax began to stammer.

"Yes?" the captain said.

Abigail tapped her book, then thought better of it. She'd only used her marksmanship skills against targets, not living things. And a true disciple of Saint Joshua could find a better way. Time for one of Josef's small gestures.

With only a glance up from her book, she said in German with a confidential tone, "They were complaining earlier about doing something stupid and being detained by the police. I think they're embarrassed."

The soldier looked at Abigail, then the trembling women. He spat out a laugh. "Foreigners," he said in German.

The jailor chuckled, and Abigail smiled as the captain gave the papers back to the sisters. In English he said to them, "I hope your next visit to our country will be more pleasant." He gave them a polite nod, then stepped into the hallway and closed the compartment door before moving up the corridor.

The sisters sat in a quaking lump with their hands locked together. Mr. Briscoe complained about the lack of chivalry and a few other things, but it seemed more habit than heartfelt. Abigail returned to reading her book and found a suitable prayer of thanks for divine deliverance.

Ten minutes later, the train slowed to a stop. They were at the frontier. Soldiers of the Austro-Hungarian Empire passed through and checked papers. After they left, the jailor stood and said his good-byes to Mrs. Caruthers and Mrs. Weatherwax but only gave Mr. Briscoe a grunt of disgust. As he wished Abigail good luck in Vienna, she thanked him again for his kindness, and he departed. A minute later, the train began to roll. Out the window beyond the corridor on the left, she could see the cluster of Swaviczen soldiers and the jailor chatting with the Austrian frontier guards as the train pulled away.

They were free.

Abigail waited another minute for safety's sake, then with a sigh of triumph she peeled off her headscarf and shook out her hair. She beamed at the perplexed detective. "Mr. Briscoe, let me introduce myself. I am Abigail Smithfield of Cincinnati, Ohio—the reason for your trip to Swavicza."

The dumbfounded man stared at her, then tried to put on a good face as if he weren't at all surprised.

Abigail smiled at the sisters, but her smile faded at their looks of astonishment.

"My dear!" Mrs. Caruthers exclaimed.

Abigail touched her bangs. "Oh, yes. They cut my hair."

"No," Mrs. Weatherwax said. "What magnificent earrings!"

Abigail gasped as she put her hands over the princess's sapphire and diamond treasures. In the rush to escape, she'd completely forgotten them. She never could have explained such finery to the soldiers. Her humble Sálacene headscarf had saved her life.

She smiled. For once Abigail didn't mind that Rosamunde was undoubtedly cursing her name.

CHAPTER TWENTY-NINE

The Prodigal Returns

City of Vienna
Austro-Hungarian Empire

In the bright early-morning light, the four Americans formed a dilapidated procession as they departed the Mountain Star Local at the main Vienna train station and trundled towards the exit. For safekeeping, Abigail had tucked the royal earrings into her book's hidden compartment, but the combination of her loose hair, bright Sálacene clothing, and regal stride turned more than a few heads. Behind her the sisters limped with exhaustion, and Mr. Briscoe brought up the rear in an uncharacteristic silence.

It seemed a year had passed since Abigail left here with Daisy and the Swaviczen delegation. How different she was from the girl who'd started that journey less than two short weeks ago!

Despite only an hour's nap on the trip, Abigail was trying to figure out what she should do first. Finding the American embassy seemed her first priority so the staff could send a reassuring telegram to her family. Getting to the embassy would mean hiring a cab, but she was sure among the four of them they had the fare in the currency of an acceptable country.

Even at such an early hour, the station bustled with a cosmopolitan crowd of people leaving, arriving, and waiting. Austrians, Bohemians, Magyars, Serbs, and Slovenes brushed shoulders on their way to and from the corners of the empire. Abigail even recognized a couple in Swaviczen clothing, but when she gave them a nod of recognition they gazed down their noses at her and turned away. Apparently they hadn't heard yet about how yesterday the Sálacene and Swaviczens had worked together to save their country.

As the group moved towards an exit, two men caught Abigail's eye. Dressed in nondescript suits, they loitered near a newspaper stand, studying the departing people . . . and when they spotted her they exchanged a few words and stood at the ready. Leave it to Rosamunde to plan this far ahead and have agents at the station just in case she made it to Vienna. If she'd been by herself, she would have tried to escape. But while she was confident Mr. Briscoe could take care of himself, she couldn't abandon the sisters. She would have to brave her way through this.

Energy surged up and down her spine as the two men stepped out to greet them. "Miss Smithfield?" asked the older one with dark hair and a curled mustache.

She hesitated, aware that the sisters had stopped behind her. "Yes?"

The men beamed and took off their hats. The younger one, who had red hair and a splash of freckles across his face, said in an accent that could only come from Kentucky, "Miss Smithfield, we're mighty glad to make your acquaintance. I'm Jedidiah Jones from the American embassy."

Surprised by her tears of relief, Abigail brushed them away with a laugh. "Mr. Jones, you have no idea how grateful I am to hear a voice from home."

The other man nodded and departed as Mr. Jones introduced himself to the others. When Abigail asked him how they knew she was arriving, he said they didn't. "Dr. Van Abel—he's the ambassador, you'll be meetin' him soon—has had men at all the depot exits to meet every train comin' in from the south ever since he heard about you. Pete and I just happened to be the lucky ones. He's gone to fetch the others."

Within minutes Abigail and her entourage were surrounded by a jubilant collection of men eager to escort her and the sisters to the embassy. Mr. Briscoe tagged along, trying to make it known that he had rescued her, but by the time the group reached the embassy the others had discerned the truth of the matter and he was kept apart to be interviewed by others. As she was being whisked in to meet the ambassador, Abigail spotted her would-be rescuer, left behind and crestfallen. She stepped away from her escort and returned to the BDI man. "Mr. Briscoe, thank you for doing your best to help me. I wish you every success."

The big man gushed with pride. "You're welcome, miss. I hope the same for you."

As she went into the embassy's conference room, she heard a rejuvenated Mr. Briscoe extolling his adventure to all those unlucky enough to be in earshot.

Abigail spent the rest of the morning with the ambassador and his immediate staff giving a detailed report of the events of the previous week and a half. Despite her lack of sleep, her presentation to the diplomatic staff was calm and complete with the types of details she thought they would find useful. As she spoke, a clerk transcribed her information so a coded telegram could be sent to the assistant ambassador, who was already in Tirigovina with the bank officials and preparing to meet that afternoon with Her Highness.

Mrs. Deborah Caruthers and Mrs. Esther Weatherwax were present during the interview until Abigail got to the incident in the plaza, at which point Mrs. Caruthers shrieked in horror. Two embassy clerks escorted the sisters to a private room where they could collect themselves—and not interrupt the rest of the interview.

Only once did someone scoff. When Abigail answered the ambassador's question about how she knew Živo was coming into the royal box, she told him about her hand mirror. A young man, who had been alternating between a scowl and a smirk through most of her interview, coughed out a derisive laugh. The ambassador, the venerable Dr. Josiah Van Abel, turned on the young upstart and pronounced, "Miss Smithfield is more intrepid than you will ever be. Get out." Flummoxed, the young man stammered and scuttled out of the room.

Dr. Van Abel quizzed her on her impression of the country, everything from its stability to the prospects for business involvement. Regarding the idea of reestablishing diplomatic relations, he seemed to know the story behind the previous embassy being shut down, but he didn't disclose it. She answered these questions and three score more as best she could from her perspective as a prisoner of the realm. What she noticed most about his questions was his genuine interest in her answers and an unmistakable air of respect.

After four hours of giving her narrative and answering their questions, she was exhausted and Dr. Van Abel concluded the interview. As the group broke up, some thanked her for her efforts, and one or two congratulated her. They dispersed to their tasks, including trying to figure out how to code all this information for the assistant ambassador.

Dr. Van Abel and two of his assistants stayed behind. He asked, "Is there anything I can do for you in return?"

She'd been thinking about the vile conduit that led to her adventure. "Yes. There's an American businessman in Graz who deserves your attention." She told him about Mr. Ignatius Porter of the Connecticut Premier Bank and Life Assurance Corporation.

A dark smile spread across the venerable man's face. "I will deal with Mr. Porter personally."

"I'm sorry I won't be able to witness that."

"I can assure you, by the time that conversation finishes, it won't be suitable for a young lady's ears."

She chuckled, then remembered her need for new travel papers since hers had disappeared. He promised to have a new passport delivered to her hotel as soon as possible. He gave the task to one of the remaining men, who departed with all urgency.

She thought about the matter that had piqued her curiosity. "If it's not indelicate, can you please tell me what happened when the American embassy in Tirigovina closed? I've heard intimations of a scandal, but no one would tell me."

The ambassador thought for a moment, then smiled. "It is indelicate, but since you're no ordinary girl, I'll tell you. The king had a liaison with the ambassador's wife. The story goes he even bragged to the ambassador about leaving a cuckoo in the nest."

To her surprise, Abigail was neither shocked nor discomfited by this revelation. "What happened?"

"The ambassador and his wife returned to the United States, and I believe he divorced her, but I don't know the entire story, so it's not appropriate for me to dwell on gossip."

No wonder the gentlemanly Josef would not tell her the story of seduction and a misbegotten child. She thought of the margrave asking her about the year of her birth during their first interview. Based on what she had learned of Swaviczen history, the king at the time would have been Rosamunde's father. A child born before 1854 would be older than the princess. If Rosamunde ever found her half-sibling . . . it was an apt if impolite choice of words, but heaven help the poor bastard.

Dr. Van Abel asked, "Is there anything else I can do for you?"

She thought for a moment. After everything she had been through, nothing about the challenge awaiting her back at school had changed. "I don't suppose you know Professor Dardanel Penwright of Amos College and could put in a good word for me so he won't flunk me." In response to Dr. Van Abel's inquiry, she told him the tale of deception and hurt pride.

He chuckled. "My dear Miss Smithfield, you'll please forgive me for this, but I'm rather amused that someone who faced down two assassination attempts is now worried about flunking out of school."

Abigail had to smile. It did seem rather ridiculous. And yet, that still lay in wait for her. "Some challenges may be larger than others, but all are challenges nonetheless."

Dr. Van Abel gave her a kind smile. "I'm afraid I don't know him, and a letter from me would be from a stranger and probably not well regarded. But if you would consider a career working for the State Department, I am an old college friend of Secretary Evarts, and I would give you the highest possible recommendation. Regardless of your sex, Miss Smithfield, you will be an asset wherever you go."

She thanked him for his generosity, but his words reminded her of a concern that had troubled her for most of the overnight train trip. "May I ask your opinion of another matter of some importance?" He nodded. "I'm unsure if I should share what happened with anyone not already involved."

"Why wouldn't you?" Dr. Van Abel asked. "Surely your resourcefulness is a fine feather in your cap. Especially when you're concerned about proving your worth to your college president."

"Well, there are two reasons. First—who would believe me? It's so remarkable, the tale would sound like braggadocio. Second, Rosamunde has been very happy to take credit for what I did. I can't imagine she'll want my participation known. And if a different version of the events surfaces, I'm afraid others within her reach would suffer for it. So, as much as I might like to crow, I think I need to keep my mouth shut."

He smiled at her turn of phrase. "Miss Smithfield, your insight into human nature does you credit. Are you certain you don't want to forego that last year of college and work for us?"

She chuckled. "After all the money they spent on my tuition, I believe my parents would object to my leaving without a degree."

Dr. Van Abel laughed. She suppressed another yawn, and he sent her on her way with final words of thanks and admiration. She was at the door when he called her back because she had left her satchel on the floor. She was so tired, she hadn't noticed. Fearing she'd lose the two valuables within it if she lost track of the satchel again, she begged his pardon and opened the bag. She tucked her forged travel papers from Josef into the waistband of her skirt, and then she opened the prayer book's secret compartment and removed the earrings. She didn't know if Dr. Van Abel was more astounded by her pistol or the jewelry, which she managed to put back on without assistance.

She found the MacMillan sisters waiting for her in the main lobby, anxious to hear the rest of her story as soon as she was ready to share it. Abigail wasn't looking forward to telling them that once again they would be sworn to secrecy. With a combination of exhaustion and relief, the three got into a cab one of the embassy staff members had hailed for them and departed for their hotel.

Harabeth Pritchard seethed with frustration. Ever since breakfast she and the other Young Ladies of Quality had been cooped up in one of their dreary hotel's small private dining rooms. They were supposed to be out having a guided tour of something or other—as if they hadn't already seen everything of importance the first time they were in town—but instead they had been instructed to sit here and wait. And wait.

Even Daisy MacMillan's questionable young soldier was back and waiting with them. He didn't speak English, so how clever of Daisy to be able to talk with him. Miss Ruth MacMillan, who spoke German, claimed he had been assigned to guard Daisy, and he wasn't a mere hanger-on, but Harabeth wasn't convinced. She'd sent Cecily Markham to eavesdrop on the two since she knew some French, but her spy could only report they spoke about polite and acceptable topics, much of it centered on concern for their friends. Their situation was too strange to be right. Daisy and her soldier had traveled together—alone—all the way from some little country Harabeth had never heard of. And then while they were in Vienna he had lingered at the fringe of the group, "protecting" her. Harabeth didn't like him. He was too . . . foreign. After being stood up by that handsome stranger in the Graz market, she knew "foreign" was untrustworthy. And now she was stuck in the same room with this man. She was glad she couldn't be expected to exchange pleasantries. She had no pleasantries for him or anyone else like him.

Not only that, but because the tour had returned to Vienna, she was sure they were missing places she might have actually liked. If they lost even one day of Italy, she was going to demand a refund of her father's money.

After much complaining, Harabeth had gotten Miss MacMillan to admit they were stuck here waiting because her sisters had just this morning returned with that irritant, Abigail Smithfield. Oh, Great Pie for Breakfast, her again! That Ohio so-and-so had spoiled this entire trip from beginning to end. And now here she was again after Harabeth thought they'd seen the last of her.

Too many farfetched stories surrounded the entire affair. Did the sisters really think the girls would believe the tale that Daisy's fellow had helped her escape mortal danger? And how utterly convenient that he was waiting in Vienna when they were "forced" to return. Daisy and her aunt gave them the unlikely story that her fellow's boss had told him to wait here until he was sent for, but Harabeth suspected that somehow Daisy had arranged the whole thing.

Finally, when it was almost time for lunch and the day all but ruined, Her Royal Highness Miss Smithfield made her grand entrance. That Midwestern clodhopper's wild peasant costume was beyond preposterous—she resembled some sort of itinerant fortune teller. The other two MacMillan sisters looked like they'd been through the mill. It must have been quite a struggle to get Smithfield out of the jam she'd gotten herself into. And then to add to the deplorable lack of decorum, Daisy's young foreign man greeted her like a long-lost princess, and in turn she could not have been happier to see him. How unseemly! The others in the tour obviously didn't grasp the big picture as she did, since many of them squealed like children when they saw their gaudy prodigal. Ridiculous. Harabeth kept her own followers in line with stern looks.

Harabeth could laugh at Abigail's absurd costume, but her amusement ended when she saw those earrings. Never in her life had she seen anything so astounding. No good American woman outside the highest levels of society had any right to wear such ostentation—and with that outfit!

That's when the pieces fell into place and the nature of Abigail's misadventure became apparent to Miss Harabeth Pritchard. Oh, the shame. First Daisy had returned unchaperoned with that young soldier. Now this! How could Mrs. Caruthers think of bringing a fallen woman back and sullying their own reputations with her presence? And to see so many of the girls eagerly gathered around her made Harabeth sick. She would complain to the sisters in the strongest possible terms. But first she would make sure to tell her girls exactly what she thought of Abigail. Of course, she wasn't sure about the details, but mere suspicions were good enough for the stories she would tell.

By the time Harabeth had reduced her followers to scandalized giggles with her comments and aspersions, a knock on the dining room door was followed by the appearance of a nice-looking man of forty or so who greeted Abigail like a friend. Was there no end to this woman's casual infamy? Harabeth stopped her gossip to listen to the conversation in hopes of gleaning more dirt.

"Miss Smithfield," the dignified man said, "I'm sorry, I just missed you at the embassy. Here's your new passport."

The Midwestern troublemaker smiled as if she hadn't caused a world of misfortune for everyone. "Thank you, Mr. Johnston. I'm sorry you had to come all this way."

"Oh, it's no problem at all. I wanted to repeat our thanks for all the information you provided about Swavicza. It will be very helpful as we establish diplomatic relations. And again, our apologies for being unable to help you. I can't imagine what it must have been like having to face that danger all alone."

With no shame whatsoever, Abigail smiled at Daisy's young man. "I was never alone." How brazen! Harabeth was making mental notes left and right.

Mr. Johnston nodded with appreciation. "I'll let you return to your reunion. I just want to say that I hope you'll take up Dr. Van

Abel's offer of a position with the State Department. He is very sparing with his compliments. He's certainly never called any of us 'intrepid.' It would be an honor to work with you."

Harabeth needed a few moments to understand what she had just heard. This man, who was clearly someone of importance, had actually spoken to that jezebel . . . with respect. Harabeth knew her ears had to be deceiving her somehow.

Mr. Johnston told the young ladies in the room, "Although I can't tell you why because of diplomatic reasons, you should feel honored to know Miss Smithfield. She's a remarkable young woman." He bid his farewells and left.

Harabeth watched in dismay as the others gathered around her most unworthy rival. She knew some important information had to be missing here. Abigail Smithfield was an object of contempt. She should be shunned. How could Harabeth be the only one who saw this? The final humiliation came when even her most loyal companion, Emily Lockett, turned her back on her and went over to wish Abigail well.

At that moment Harabeth knew she hated Europe. Everything was upside down here. She wanted to go home, and when she got there she would never be tricked into leaving again.

CHAPTER THIRTY

Reluctant Farewells

Once Abigail was safely in the Austrian capital, Daisy Mac-Millan had to bid a sad farewell to her gallant beau, Biedric Halle. His duty required him to return to Swavicza and face whatever punishment might be dealt out by the authorities. His story would be that her aunts had forbidden their marriage and he was returning with a broken heart. The last part was true. As for Daisy's aunts, they were smitten with the honorable young man. In particular, Ruth MacMillan had become his champion. When her sisters departed for the rescue mission to Swavicza, she left the girls with the local chaperones and spent most of her time hoping for news at the American embassy, where she befriended Biedric as he awaited instructions from home. Miss MacMillan stoutly defended him against the rumors spreading among the girls about the reason for his presence. She wasn't the only one who wept when he left for his uncertain fate.

Abigail also wrote to Josef with her promised description of what had happened at the opera. In case it was intercepted at the embassy, she wrote in the guise of a fictitious acquaintance of his who had been at the opera performance. Then she wrote a second letter, detailing everything that had happened after he had been sent to Budapest . . . including her heartfelt gratitude and sorrow over not being able to continue their friendship. She mailed the first letter; the second one would have to wait until she knew he was no longer under suspicion. That might be years. She would keep it close to her heart until then.

For the remainder of the Escorted Tour's European sojourn, Abigail picked up a copy of every newspaper and journal she could find with the latest information about Swavicza. Even though the attempted coup happened in a tiny and unimportant country, the events garnered a lot of reportage.

As Abigail expected, Rosamunde received credit for the victory, and no mention was made of another woman being involved. Through the news stories, Abigail learned several prominent people had died as a result of the uprising. In the skirmishes after the opera, the losses included conspirators Baron von Redki and Major Schilz and the "valiant leader" of Her Highness's household cavalry, Colonel Lutz.

Medyev and his surviving coconspirators were rounded up and forced to forfeit their estates to the crown. Rosamunde allowed Medyev to commit suicide to spare his family from sharing in his punishment. Abigail still knew little about the Catholic religion, but she was fairly certain suicide was a mortal sin. Surely Rosamunde's advisers had tried to dissuade her from an act of personal vengeance that must carry terrible consequences for her as well as his family. Two other conspirators were executed—an Italian newspaper gave especially detailed accounts of the grisly affairs—and the rest were exiled. Looking at the rainy Rome street outside their restaurant, Abigail recalled Medyev's near-sighted wife and children. How quickly their fortunes had reversed after their grand entrance at the princess's ball.

An English paper she found in Florence included an observation that answered some of Abigail's lingering questions. According to the newspaper, the citizenry had corralled most of the surviving conspirators. The article included an unlikely observation: "The popular uprising that thwarted the usurpers represents the first time in living memory that the commoners rioted in support of a monarchy instead of against it." Abigail had to believe somehow she was responsible for inspiring that. She hoped Rosamunde would appreciate what the people had done for her and respond with gratitude.

After they returned to their hotel after a lovely Parisian day at the *Exposition Universelle*, Abigail received a wonderful and cheering letter from Samuel Clemens, in which he lamented not being able to ride to her rescue like the cavalry officer he always was "in his own high self-opinion," and if she wrote her story, either as a novel or a memoir, he guaranteed his publishing firm would accept it. He did ask one indulgence of her, as he wanted to borrow some details from her adventure and include them in a novel that he was "just now" thinking of writing about what could happen if a commoner and a prince exchanged places. He said they would discuss it further when they were both back home in Hartford.

Four days later, as the Escorted Tour was about to depart from Le Havre, Abigail found an edition of a Paris newspaper with a long article about the recently ratified Treaty of Berlin, which had realigned the political loyalties of many countries in central Europe. It even contained a brief mention of tiny Swavicza, saying the Austro-Hungarian officials had championed its independence, and as a result it had escaped becoming a fiefdom of one of the major powers. Large cash payments from Swavicza to the Austrians were rumored but not confirmed. Abigail added that newspaper to her collection. At least Swavicza was still independent. Rosamunde could be happy with that.

As their steamship churned out of the harbor, the only people not looking forward to returning home were Abigail and Daisy. The others had gone to their rooms to unpack for the crossing, but the two survivors of the Swaviczen adventure stayed on deck. As they watched the French harbor town drift away, Abigail's thoughts returned to her last moments with Josef, and the soft touch of his fingers brushing against hers as the train pulled her away.

Daisy said, "You know, what we went through was so horrible and so frightening. . . ." Tears began to drop onto her jacket, and she sniffed a small laugh. "And yet all I want to do is go back."

Abigail smiled through her own tears and took her friend's hand. "I know."

Daisy dabbed a handkerchief to her eyes. "Do you think we'll ever see them again?"

She didn't think that was possible, but she gave Daisy's hand a squeeze. "Let us be hopeful and see what happens."

Daisy agreed, and they looked at the shore.

Abigail thought of her letter to Josef. She wondered when he would ever be able to read it.

CHAPTER THIRTY-ONE

A Complicated Agreement

Town of Amos Falls, Connecticut
United States of America
Early August 1878

Sitting in the dark-paneled and academically luxurious office of the president of Amos College, Abigail regretted asking for this meeting. Ignoring her completely, the dour, sphinxlike Miss Yael Amos and the stern Professor Dardanel Penwright, whose bald pate and high collar gave him an uncanny resemblance to a buzzard, were dragging each other through the same arguments they'd had for years: women should attend the same classes as men versus women had no place in higher education. With words as their weapons, the old opponents were slugging away at each other like exhausted gladiators, too spent to strike the *coup de mort* but too proud to admit defeat.

Abigail sympathized with both. Like so many women from the Civil War generation, the granddaughter of the school's founder did not have the chance to marry and chose to be an educator, one of the few paths open to unmarried women. The school with her grandfather's name, and with her lengthy purse strings wrapped around it, gave her the opportunity to effect educational equality for women.

Penwright, a man in love with tradition and continuity, had fought Miss Amos tooth-and-nail from the moment she'd started her efforts. If women attending a men's college was the future of education, he would defy it to his dying breath.

As the two traded personal insults of being a fool . . . an enemy of education . . . in league with the devil, Abigail sighed. When she had arrived at the president's office, she knew what she wanted to say. But before she could begin, they had launched into each other. To interrupt them would serve her purpose but also offend people from whom she needed respect and cooperation. She had outsmarted an assassin and convinced rival ethnic leaders to work together. How could she be stymied by these two ill-tempered academicians? The answer was that *there* she had been a princess, but *here* she was just another student—and a girl to boot.

But that was not true—she wasn't just another student. She wasn't even the same Abigail Smithfield who had left for Europe two months ago. She *had* outsmarted an assassin. She *had* brought rivals together. Perhaps someday history professors would be giving lectures about her. . . .

Her smile halted Professor Penwright's tirade about women's incapacity for complex thought.

"Yes, Mr. Smithfield?" He had called her "Mister" from her first day. If he'd intended it as an insult or intimidation, it had never worked.

Her smile deepened. She had her entry into the melee.

With hard-won confidence, she said, "While it's clear that both of you are passionate about your beliefs, so far I haven't heard a single piece of evidence to back up your suppositions."

The combatants glared at her.

She ignored their stares. "A logical argument demands that you provide substance to back up your claims. So far it's all been 'if P, then Q.' Your statements can be neither proved nor disproved. Therefore, they have no value. You need data to back them up. So, if I may, I would like to propose that you work together on a research project."

The two had a shared moment of dumbfounded silence.

Professor Penwright finally spluttered, "Work *together*?"

Miss Amos asked a suspicious, "What kind of research project? What would be the object?"

"The object would be to determine if women can withstand the rigors of a full four years of the men's college curriculum. . . . And the subject would be me."

With succinct clarity, she outlined her plan: She would be a test case for them to analyze. She'd complete her senior year in the men's curriculum and take her required classes from Professor Penwright. Since he had already admitted he was not impartial, she proposed her classwork be judged by a committee of five teachers. Two would be chosen by Penwright, two by Amos, and a fifth instructor, agreed upon by both of them, who would be from another school and who would know nothing about Abigail. If she succeeded, it would be a victory for Miss Amos. If she failed, it would be vindication for Professor Penwright.

They peppered Abigail with questions about how this would work. In the end, they justified her belief that neither would be able to resist the chance to prove the other wrong.

They set to work creating a protocol and making a list of names for her committee. She tried to hide her smile as they hammered out the details. There was nothing quite as effective as a shared concern for bringing rivals together. Abigail wondered how the sewage plans in Tirigovina were progressing.

When the two had reached a feisty accord, Professor Penwright turned his attention to his unwanted student. "You may regret this. I'll give you the most rigorous assignments. Graduate level work. You will have no time for friends or socials. Or trips to see the opera," he promised with more than a hint of a sneer.

"No noble thing can be done without risks. Or sacrifices," she said, paraphrasing de Montaigne.

"And I suppose you expect to receive a diploma if you succeed."

She nodded. "If I earn it." A twinge in her chest reminded her of something she had earned but he had withheld. "And if I succeed . . . I would like you to give me my freshman award."

Professor Penwright frowned. "The pocket watch?"

"Yes."

He glanced at his desk, giving her hope that he still had it and hadn't disposed of it in his anger. He asked her, "What value would that be to you?"

"What value has a trophy on a shelf? At least a watch will tell me the time."

She was afraid he would consider her response insouciant, but his frown turned to a taunting smirk. "Mr. Smithfield, if you survive what I will be throwing at you—which no *natural* woman would be able—I will give you that watch."

She smiled. Yes, she would survive.

CHAPTER THIRTY-TWO

A Simple Trade

Nook Farm Neighborhood
City of Hartford, Connecticut
United States of America

Abigail walked back to the Stowes' home with the household's letters. The maid usually ran the daily errand to the post office, but since it was her birthday Abigail hoped to receive a card or two and volunteered to retrieve the mail. She wanted to enjoy the bright and sunny August day, and she wanted time to ponder the strange dream she'd had that morning.

In the dream, she found herself in Chetova Castle, but the self-contained community in the Swaviczen mountains was empty of all its residents. She stood in the courtyard near the smithy, and when she realized no one was there—even Daisy was gone—she followed her instinct to escape. The drawbridge was down and she hurried through the portal and across the bridge. She emerged and found herself on the path in the woods. She walked down the horse trail under the trees and stopped in the spot where she'd thought to challenge Josef to a race. She stood alone on the trail, not knowing where it led, or which way was forward or backward. Should she go or should she stay? She awoke with that question lingering in her mind.

Abigail decided the dream was about whether she should stay in Hartford until classes started in September or return home to Cincinnati. A birthday card in the morning mail from her sister-in-law

305

restated her family's wish to see her but their understanding if she wanted to stay in Connecticut to prepare for her senior year. Before the dream, she'd concluded it was better for her to remain here with her godmother's family, but now, after this chance to walk and reflect, she decided it was worth the distraction to see everyone again before facing Professor Penwright's challenge. She had more than enough time for the trip by train. She would consult with Mrs. Stowe when her godmother returned from her morning visit to her sister Mary.

As Abigail came around the corner, she stopped at the unusual sight of five horses tied up in front of the Stowes' house. Her first thought was something had happened to their neighbor Senator Gillette, who had not been well. But the Gillette house was practically next door, so the horses being tied up in front of the wrong house offered an unlikely explanation. Perhaps they were soldiers here to visit retired General Hawley, but she discounted that notion because all five riders would not dismount and go into the Stowes' house to ask directions. She studied the animals as she walked past. The saddles had the name of a local livery company on them, indicating the horses were rented.

When she walked past the home's fragrant garden to the front door, she heard voices coming through the front parlor's window. From the step she could only see Eliza Stowe talking with the people who were just out of sight.

Abigail entered the front hall as the maid headed upstairs with bed linens. She asked the girl about the visitors. "They're here to see you, Miss Abigail. A Mr. Herron or something like that. It was about a business proposition. Miss Eliza and Miss Hattie are entertaining them until you got back from the post office." The maid continued with her errand.

With trepidation Abigail approached the parlor's open double doors. She knew no one named Herron, and she had no prospects for a business proposition. She could hear the dignified, quiet voices of her godmother's oldest daughters as they were giving directions on how to get to New York. Then she heard Hattie's sparkling laugh. Despite being fifty, the twin sisters maintained the vitality of youth, and Hattie's laughter felt reassuring. Perhaps Abigail's concerns were misplaced.

Then she heard an unfamiliar male voice . . . speaking Swaviczen. She froze. Had Rosamunde sent soldiers to kill her? Should she run? No, if they had trailed her to this place, they would find her wherever else she might hide. It was better to face them here, among friends. She hoped no one else was in danger.

She stiffened her spine and put on a strong face before walking into the parlor. The sisters greeted her warmly. But Abigail did not hear their words when she saw who rose to greet her.

Lord Josef, Count of Ramsl and Tuharen, smiled and gave her a low nod of greeting. Also standing at her entrance were Biedric Halle, Jowan Halle, Phillip Zujaken, and Jóri Petka. It was Jóri's voice she hadn't recognized. The men were in civilian clothes.

She beheld them with delight and exclaimed in German, "My dear friends!" The four soldiers gathered around her with enthusiastic greetings as Josef and the Stowe sisters looked on. She told them, "I thought I would never see you again," but finished the sentence gazing at Josef. His smile brought out a knowing glance between the sisters, which was not lost on their mother's goddaughter. Abigail asked Josef in English, "How did you find me?"

"You said you lived next door to Mr. Mark Twain in Hartford, Connecticut. His wife sent us over here."

Thank goodness for her chattiness that day! "Why are you in America? Have you run away?"

"No," he said. "I have been sent by Her Highness."

She couldn't imagine why.

"She wants her earrings back."

That she could believe. "She sent you all this way for a pair of earrings?"

"You don't understand. They gave you the wrong jewelry to wear. You were supposed to receive minor things. Those were her best items. The earrings were a gift to her great-grandmother from the Empress Maria Theresa. She wants them back."

Abigail had suspected she might have to return them someday. When the Escorted Tour arrived in Boston, she'd had the earrings appraised, and the jeweler was speechless when he saw the gems. She'd even gone to a photographer here in town and had a portrait of herself made wearing the earrings as a souvenir of her adventure.

She asked, "Why did she send you? Are you rehabilitated in her eyes?"

He chose his words carefully. "She sent me because she thinks I am the only one who can get them from you."

She tried to hide her smile. "She's right."

Hattie Stowe laughed, but otherwise the sisters offered no opinion as they relished this exchange.

He added, "And I will be rehabilitated if I can get the earrings."

"And if I give them to you. . . ?"

"I'll take them back to her."

Oh, she thought, that would never do. But first things first. She found a pencil and paper in the drawer of the parlor table and wrote down an address and directions in German. "Before we settle our affairs, I must render aid to a poor, sad young woman who has been pining ever since we left Vienna." She handed the note to Biedric, and told him in German, "There's only one person in the world who can cheer my dear, sad Daisy."

Biedric beamed. He looked to his master for permission to go. Josef took in a deep breath, then nodded. Jowan looked to Josef, and then Phillip and Jóri followed suit. Josef gave up and gestured for them to go. The soldiers departed after courteous farewells to the women.

The count regarded the college girl with an expression that tried to be stern, but hints of a smile kept undercutting him. "I have a present for you, if that will help you make up your mind." He glanced at the corner of the room, where she saw a large, flat box on a side table.

She couldn't quite believe it, and yet she knew what it must be. "Is it from Frau Meyer?"

"Yes."

She laughed. "My dress!"

"Yes. Now will you give me the earrings?"

She looked at Josef, then the smiling sisters. Abigail's adopted aunts had never married but, far from stern spinsters, they were enjoying this almost as much as she was. She regarded the royal messenger again. She had one last move in this chess match.

Abigail called the maid as she started to write another note. When the maid arrived, Abigail told her she had a note for her to take to the telegraph office. She wrote a simple message in German with the delivery information in English. Josef tried to read it, but she kept him at bay. She held out the paper to the girl along with a few coins from her pocket. "Take this right away. Stay for the confirmation." As she spoke the words, she saw not the prim and collected Connecticut girl waiting to run an errand, but the flashing eyes and insouciant smile of Belza. Blinking moist eyes, she gave the maid the paper and sent her on her way, then pulled a handkerchief from her pocket. No one understood her tears as she dabbed them away, but at their concerned looks she reassured them with a shake of her head.

Even as she was saddened by the memory of Belza, she found a secret cheer with the handkerchief. It was the one Josef had given her when she wept after receiving Daisy's telegram.

Josef saw his embroidered initial on the handkerchief and seemed to take heart at the sight. He asked, "What was the message?"

Collected again, Abigail answered, "I asked Rosamunde a simple question. 'Which do you want more: your earrings or your messenger?'"

To Abigail's dismay, Josef's face became stern and surprisingly unreadable. What had she done? She had overplayed this. Why would a nobleman choose her over his family and country and everything he knew? She regretted her foolish confidence.

The Count of Ramsl and Tuharen said to the sisters, "Ladies, if I may ask your kind indulgence, there is something I must say to Miss Smithfield in private."

Abigail glanced at the women. What would they do? She had shared with them all of her adventure, including her feelings for this man. At this moment, she wasn't exactly sure what she wanted.

Eliza declared, "Sir, this is a proper New England household."

Hattie added, "We have rules of decorum here."

The sisters stood as Eliza stated, "What you are asking is out of the question." She turned to leave.

As she followed her sister, Hattie said, "My word, leaving a young couple alone together. What will the neighbors think?"

Eliza was through the doorway as Hattie turned with her hands on the doors. She could not quite keep the smile off her face. "I'm ashamed you even asked." She closed the doors.

Abigail knew she had missed something, but she was still concerned when Josef stepped up to her and took a firm grasp of her shoulders. Then she saw the soft light in his honest brown eyes. He drew her into his strong embrace.

In that moment she knew all was well and smiled into his kiss. Not only was he freshly shaven, he smelled of bay rum, something he never had before. He must have gone to an American barber. He wanted to stay. She would insist he return to using that dark, spice-rich elixir from his home. But, oh, the confidence he had that she could make this happen!

The office for the Kingdom of Swavicza, Washington, D.C.'s newest and smallest embassy, received expected yet surprising visitors. Surrounded by boxes waiting to be unpacked, the front desk clerk watched in wonder at the entrance of a well-dressed nobleman and, on his arm, a handsome woman in a striking red dress that reminded him of home. They were followed by a smiling blond woman, who had to be a maid or attendant, and four soldiers in the livery of, if he wasn't mistaken, the Duke of Zeltatlandia. He had been told to expect visitors from the duke's family, but why did the woman look familiar. . . ? He gasped. How could *She* be here? He rose in a hasty pose of attention. "Your Highness!"

The couple approached the clerk's desk. The woman said in exquisite German, "I'm afraid you've mistaken me for someone else."

The clerk began breathing again. "I'm sorry."

She gave him a gracious nod. "That's all right. It's happened before."

The young nobleman said, "You are expecting a package for Her Highness." From his coat pocket he produced a small jewelry box.

The clerk nodded. "Thank you, sir. I will call the ambassador." He rang a bell on his desk, which sent another man to a back office.

The dignified ambassador emerged and approached the young nobleman. The two greeted each other warmly as friends of long standing. The ambassador said, "How good to see a familiar face so far from home. I understand your mission was a success."

The younger man smiled at the woman. "Yes, very much so." He introduced to the ambassador the young woman in the red dress, and then introduced the blond woman as well. They both had American names. The ambassador gave them a kind greeting.

The older man accepted a small box from the nobleman and opened it, dazzled for a moment by the magnificent sapphire and diamond earrings. He closed the box with due reverence. "These shall be sent to Her Highness by the next available courier. Have you heard the news?"

The couple had not.

"Her Highness is to be married next month."

Both of the noble visitors asked, "To whom?"

"Ludovic Guttmann, a nephew of the Landgrave of Tratano."

The nobleman reacted with surprise while the woman said to him, "I told you Guttmann was angling to marry off a son." She sighed, "Poor Franz."

The man shook his head. "It's just as well. He never would have been happy being just a consort."

The woman added, "That also explains where she got all that money to pay off the Austrians."

He smiled and kissed her hand. "As always, my dear, you are right."

The ambassador asked the man, "Are you returning to Swavicza, My Lord?"

"Someday." He looked at the woman on his arm. "But now I am going to Cincinnati."

The woman added, "And then I am going to show him a herd of buffalo."

This did not make much sense to either the clerk or the ambassador, but both wished them a safe journey as they bid their farewells.

The couple and their escort turned to leave, and the clerk thought he had never seen such a happy couple as they went through the door and disappeared into the glittering morning light.

Foreword

(WHICH, IN THE MODERN FASHION, IS AT THE END)

The hallmark of a fine work of fiction is it seems so real you think it must be true on some deep level. By the same token, the mark of good non-fiction is it hangs together so well you suspect significant parts of it were invented for the convenience of the author. The same can be suspected of some forewords, but I stray from my subject.

Miss Young has written a work so exquisite on every level, so unmatched in quality, that I encourage her never to write again. And when I say she should never write again, I mean she should not write to excess. Writing two novels a month is plenty for any sober-minded author. Anything more is a sign of an immodest upbringing.

Instead, I advise her to trade in the art of writing for the artifice of being a *grand old writer* so she can poke fun at the world for the remainder of her natural life and beyond. The expectations of the public are lower, and the pay is better. I say this with some knowledge of the subject.

However, I understand writers and cats share a singular independence, and I expect her to ignore my advice to the detriment of her sanity and the betterment of a world of unrepentant sinners. Such is the curse of the truly gifted.

-- *Mark Twain (retired)*

ABOUT THE AUTHOR

Melinda Young has a bachelor's degree in English and advanced degrees in film and journalism. A third-generation journalist, she has lived in North America and Polynesia. Her peripatetic career outside the newsroom has included public broadcasting, construction, and the unexpectedly exciting world of government service.

Ms. Young reads books old and new, but her favorite authors are from other centuries: Gustave Flaubert, Molière, Rafael Sabatini, William Shakespeare, Harriet Beecher Stowe, and Mark Twain.

She loves books, music, travel, Thanksgiving, research, geography, photography, art, eating with chopsticks, and the cricket chorus on warm summer nights. She once ate Christmas dinner with chopsticks. She keeps threatening to move to Alaska—or maybe London—and one of these days she just might do it.